'Three little words,' she repeated. 'What does that mean to you?'

He stared at her, then a soft smile curled his lips upwards. 'I love you?'

She broke away from him. 'I thought you might say that. In fact it's a Yankee dance-step, a new one we're going to try out. I found it in a book I've been reading.'

'Three little words,' he mused. Very Yankee.

'I love you – that's exactly what I thought when I first came across it,' she said, and went over to the gramophone to put a record on.

'Norma?'

She glanced at him over her shoulder.

His voice was suddenly husky, and far steelier than usual. 'I do, you know . . .'

*Also by Emma Blair in Sphere Books*

STREET SONG

PRINCESS OF POOR STREET

*Emma Blair*

# WHEN DREAMS COME TRUE

SPHERE BOOKS LIMITED

This book is dedicated to Mr John Towle, formerly of West Division High School, Milwaukee, Wisconsin, USA, and all *good* teachers everywhere who must often wonder what became of the many pupils who passed through their hands, and what effect their particular teaching had, if any, on those pupils.

Herewith, one individual answer.

SPHERE BOOKS LTD

Published by the Penguin Group
27 Wrights Lane, London W8 5TZ, England
Viking Penguin Inc., 40 West 23rd Street, New York, New York 10010, USA
Penguin Books Australia Ltd, Ringwood, Victoria, Australia
Penguin Books Canada Ltd, 2801 John Street, Markham, Ontario, Canada L3R 1B4
Penguin Books (NZ) Ltd, 182–190 Wairau Road, Auckland 10, New Zealand

Penguin Books Ltd, Registered Offices: Harmondsworth, Middlesex, England

First published in Great Britain by Michael Joseph Ltd, 1987
Published by Sphere Books 1988



Made and printed in Great Britain by
Richard Clay Ltd, Bungay, Suffolk

# *Contents*

*Part 1*

# THREE LITTLE WORDS 1932–36

## *Chapter One*

March had been a rotten month filled with rain, wind, cold and sleet. But with the arrival of April the weather had changed, with the sun appearing and the grey skies turning to blue.

Norma McKenzie hummed happily to herself as she walked along the path which would take her home. She'd just been to the wee town of Kirn about a mile away on the Argyllshire coast to get some messages for her ma, and while there had had a good crack with Marion Cockburn, a school pal of hers in the same class. During the school holidays - and it was now the Easter ones - Marion helped in the family shop, a licensed grocers.

Norma stopped to stare out over the Firth of Clyde, and watched the paddle-steamer *Maid of Lorne* head for Kirn pier, *en route* from Gourock. She knew all the steamers on the Clyde, having been able to recognise and name them before she could read or write.

Then something on the road running parallel to the seashore caught her eye. It was the big swanky car that belonged to the new owner of Kilmichael House, her da's new boss.

As the car turned in at the drive gate she caught a glimpse of Mr Hodgart, and beside him his wife. The Hodgarts had a son called Rodney and a daughter Caroline who was just a little older than herself.

Norma didn't like the Hodgarts very much. There was an aura about them - Mr Hodgart in particular - which made her uneasy. The one time she'd bumped into Mr Hodgart he'd smiled at her, but it had been a smile she hadn't believed. There was a bully at school who smiled in exactly the same way as he was nipping you or giving you Chinese Burn.

Despite their wealth, the Hodgarts weren't real toffs in the way the previous owner, the Earl of Arran and Clydesdale, had been. They might be stinking rich but they didn't have class. Their money was new – and it showed.

The Earl's family had owned Kilmichael House, and the ten acres of grounds belonging to the house, for over three hundred years, but the Earl had fallen on hard times financially and, after a long struggle, had been forced to put the property on the market where it had soon been snapped up by Mr Hodgart.

Mr Hodgart was a general importer and exporter who also owned a big factory in Greenock. A factory, according to her da, that made pipe fittings and ball bearings.

'Norma!'

She turned at the sound of her da's voice, and there he was striding towards her, coming round from behind a stand of rhododendron bushes.

Not for the first time it struck her what a fine upstanding-looking man her da was. There was a dignity and purpose about him which suited his position as head gardener to Kilmichael House. He had three other gardeners working under him.

'I've just been to Kirn to get some messages for Ma,' Norma explained.

Brian McKenzie glanced at the basket she was carrying and nodded. Effie had mentioned earlier she was going to send Norma in for a few things, adding tobacco to the list when he'd told her he was about to run out.

'Did you get my 'baccy?' he asked, accepting the tin when Norma handed it over.

'McLean from the House came searching me out to say that the master himself wants a word when he gets back. As that was his car I spied I'd better away up and see him.' McLean was a footman.

Gardening business, Norma presumed, as had Brian.

'Tell your ma where I've gone and that I may be late for dinner as a result. I'll try and get home as soon as I can.'

'I'll tell her da.'

Brian smiled softly at his eldest daughter, the eldest of three. Norma was fourteen, Lyn a year younger, and Eileen, the baby, eleven. He loved them all but – maybe because she was his firstborn – he loved Norma the most, something he'd never confided to a living soul, not even to Effie.

Brian slipped the tobacco tin into his jacket pocket. 'Away with you then and I'll see you by and by,' he said.

Norma waved to her father, then he was gone, hidden from view by another stand of rhododendron bushes.

When she arrived at the cottage Norma found Lyn laying the table while Eileen was cutting bread into slices and buttering them. Her ma was at the range stirring a pot of stew. The smell from the stew and from the potatoes baking in the range oven filled the kitchen, and was delicious.

'I saw Da,' Norma said, then proceeded to give her ma his message.

Effie wiped her hands on her pinny, then pushed back a stray wisp of hair which had tumbled down onto her high forehead. She was wearing her hair in her usual way, swept up and held in place by a great many pins and a brace of tortoiseshell combs. It was only when going to bed, or washing her hair, that she let it down.

'Well I'm glad we don't have to wait. I'm starving,' Lyn said hopefully.

'Who said we don't have to wait?' Effie queried, the corners of her mouth twitching upwards.

Lyn dropped her gaze. 'I just thought that's what Da's message implied,' she mumbled.

'Trust you to think that Podge,' whispered Eileen.

Lyn glared at her younger sister. She hated her nickname, positively loathed it. If Ma hadn't been there she'd have skited Eileen round the ear for using it. And she might still, later, if she could get the wee so-and-so alone.

'I don't see how you can be that hungry after the breakfast you've eaten,' teased Norma. Lyn had eaten a whopping breakfast – but then she always did. She ate as much as Norma, Ma and Eileen put together.

'We'll wait for Da. Not that he'd mind if we went ahead, but I would,' Effie said.

Lyn sniffed, and listened to her belly rumble. It rumbled a lot; she was known for it.

When she thought Effie wasn't looking Lyn swiped a bit of breadcrust from the table and quickly popped it into her mouth.

It wasn't her fault she had a healthy appetite, she told herself. Ma and the others were just pickers anyway. Why, a bird ate more than they did!

'I saw Caroline Hodgart while you were out, she was riding that horse of hers,' Eileen said to Norma.

'It's a smasher, that chestnut mare,' Norma replied, her voice tinged with jealousy.

Eileen sighed. 'I'd give anything to own a beastie like yon.'

Me too, Norma thought, as daft on horses as Eileen was. The pair of them did get the chance to ride from time to time, but only on the old broken-down hack over at Boyd's Farm. There was no comparison between Tom-Tom and Caroline Hodgart's chestnut mare.

It must be great to be rolling in it, Norma thought, to be able to afford anything you want. Just a snap of the fingers and there it was – a horse, a dress, whatever.

She fell to day-dreaming about being rich, and in that day-dreaming did an awful lot of finger snapping.

They all looked up when the door opened and Brian came in. It was over an hour since he'd met Norma returning from Kirn.

Brian's face was tight and drawn. His expression was strange, sort of bemused. Going to his favourite chair he plonked himself down.

'I'll get the dinner out now you're back,' Effie said with a smile.

Brian didn't answer, just stared straight ahead.

'Lyn's been fair champing at the bit, you'd think she hadn't eaten for a month,' Eileen said to her da.

Brian produced his pipe and a new tin of tobacco. Still staring ahead he opened the tin and began filling his pipe.

'Da, dinner's going on the table,' Norma admonished.

'I've had the sack,' Brian said.

Effie went stock still, ladle filled with stew poised in mid-air.

Lyn laughed. 'He's at it again!'

Effie's face cracked into a grin that became a large smile. 'Och see you, you're terrible so you are!' she said to Brian, filling the plate she was holding.

Norma stared at her da. He was an awful joker, mickey-taker, forever saying the most outrageous things. Why only the previous week he'd told them that moonmen had landed in

London and were even then in private consultations with the Prime Minister Mr MacDonald.

Brian put his pipe to his mouth and lit up, then blew out a long thin stream of blue smoke.

'I'm afraid it's true,' he said, his voice leaden.

'Da, will you stop it! We know you're only trying to get us going,' said Lyn, pulling out a chair and sitting at the table.

'I'll have two of those jacket potatoes Ma,' she said to Effie.

Eileen scrambled into her place and reached for a slice of bread and butter. 'Is there anything you want me to do this afternoon Ma? If not I thought I'd go and play with Helen Millar,' she said. Helen was the daughter of one of the gardeners under Brian, and lived in another cottage close by.

'Mr Hodgart said he's nothing against me personally but wants to put his own chap in as head gardener, the chap he had at his last place. He's promised to give me a good reference,' Brian went on.

Norma suddenly saw there was a sheen of sweat on her father's brow. Sweat that glinted as it was caught by the light streaming in from the window by the sink.

Fear clutched her insides. 'Da?' she whispered.

Brian looked at her. There was none of the humour in his eyes that there usually was when he was having them on. On the contrary, there was a deadness about them that she'd never seen before.

'Come on you pair, will you get in at the table. And put that pipe out Brian. Honestly!' Effie grumbled, sitting down at her customary place.

'Pass the butter please,' Eileen asked Lyn.

Lyn helped herself first, putting two huge dollops on her plate.

'If you're not careful you'll be the size of a barn door before you're much older,' Eileen said to Lyn.

'Don't be cheeky,' Effie told Eileen. Then turning to Lyn she went on, 'but she's right, you are eating far too much. Put half that butter back, and no arguments either.'

'Ma, I think it's true,' Norma said softly to Effie.

'What dear?'

'About Da being sacked.'

Effie opened her mouth to laugh, but what she saw written on Brian's face stopped her.

'Dear God!' she muttered in a strangled voice.

'We've to be out of here by the first day of June, whether I've got another job or not. In the meantime I'm to take as much time off as I need to find one.'

'It *is* true then,' said Effie, a hand going to her heart.

'Wants his own chap as head gardener,' Brian repeated.

Eileen put down the bread she'd been munching on. A film covered her eyes, then she burst into tears.

'But you've worked for the House man and boy. Didn't he take that into consideration?' Effie asked, desperation in her voice.

'There's no question about the standard of my work, or of my loyalty. It's just that he wants his own chap,' Brian replied.

'It would seem the loyalty's all one-sided,' muttered Norma.

'Nor did Mr Hodgart think I should stay on under the new fellow. He didn't think that would be right for either of us,' Brian added.

Effie pushed back her chair and stood up. Going to Eileen she cuddled her youngest daughter to her.

Norma was not only stunned – she was devastated. Leave the cottage where she'd been born and brought up. Why the idea was inconceivable! And yet, that was what she was going to have to do. What they were all going to have to do.

'I just couldn't believe it when he told me. I thought I was hearing things,' Brian whispered.

'Damn him!' Effie exploded in a sudden burst of anger.

Brian ran a hand through his hair. The hand was trembling slightly, he noted. Then realised that the other one was as well.

'This doesn't need to be as bad as it sounds. I heard there was a head gardener's job going in Innellan, I'll bicycle down there after breakfast tomorrow and apply. With a bit of luck I'll be fixed up again before we know where we are,' he said. Innellan was south on the coast road, about ten miles away.

'Does a cottage go with the job?' Effie asked quickly.

'I don't know, but I'd imagine it would. Anyway, I'll find out the details when I go there tomorrow.'

'When did you hear about this job Da?' asked Norma.

'Last Friday down the pub. It had only come available, so news of it can hardly have spread very far yet.'

'Let's keep our fingers crossed then,' said Effie.

'Aye,' Brian agreed.

Eileen stopped crying, and wiped her cheeks with her sleeve. There was a lump in her throat that felt the size of a turnip.

Effie took a deep breath, then another. 'Well, that was a bombshell and no mistake,' she declared.

'I couldn't face any dinner love. I've no appetite at all,' Brian told her, and took a lengthy drag on his pipe.

'Me neither Ma,' said Norma.

In the end only Lyn ate. She looked guilty as she did, but she ate nonetheless.

Norma was the first to hear the squeak of her da's bike approaching the cottage. The chain needed oiling, a task Brian had been meaning to get round to for some time.

She glanced up from her darning and over to where Effie was bent over the ironing board. She saw her ma stiffen – she too must have heard her da's approach.

Effie bit her lip, then, consciously trying to relax, went back to her ironing. She wanted to appear casual and not betray the inner turmoil she was feeling.

She was whacked, having been awake worrying most of the night. Brian hadn't had much sleep either. And what sleep he had managed to get had been filled with restless tossings and turnings.

'It's Da!' exclaimed Eileen excitedly. She and Lyn were sitting together mending a sheet that Lyn had put a big toe through and ripped. The sheet might be gey thin but it still had life left in it yet, according to Effie.

Brian dismounted from his bike, leant it against the cottage wall, knocked his boots on the step – even though he'd polished them earlier he did this through force of habit – and, with a heavy heart, went into the kitchen.

Effie forced a smile onto her face. 'So how did you get on?' she asked.

Brian shook his head. 'You wouldn't credit it, but the job went late last evening.'

'You mean ...?' Effie trailed off.

'Aye, that's right. If I'd gone directly after yesterday's dinner instead of waiting till this morning I'd have got it.'

That was cruel, Norma thought. And resumed darning.

'My fault entirely. I shouldn't have waited,' Brian added, anger and bitterness in his voice.

Effie crossed over to the range and placed the iron in a place where it would be reheated. 'Was there a cottage going with the job?' she asked.

'Aye. A nice one too I believe.'

Effie and Brian's eyes locked, then she looked away. The slump of her shoulders betrayed her disappointment.

'Ach well, if it wasn't to be it wasn't to be,' she said, trying to make her voice sound light and unconcerned, and failing totally.

'I'll put the kettle on. I'm sure you could use a cup of tea,' Norma said to Brian.

Brian wanted to take Effie in his arms and comfort her, but didn't because the children were there. 'I certainly could,' he replied to Norma.

'What now Da?' Lyn asked.

'I'll have my tea and then take myself round about, see if anyone's heard of anything.'

'Make sure you buy a paper. There might be something advertised,' Effie said.

'I will. And I'll go into the pub and have a word with John Paul. He's a mine of information that man.' John Paul was the publican of Brian's local The Royal Arms.

Effie couldn't help her gaze straying to the calendar tacked to the wall. The first of June was uncomfortably close – six weeks away, that was all. And what were six weeks? Nothing whatever in their present situation. If only Brian had gone to Innellan yesterday afternoon! Brian blamed himself for that, but wasn't she just as much to blame. She should have thought to make him go straight away. But it hadn't even occurred to her. It was just that... well, their pace of life was such that they weren't used to doing things in a rush.

While Effie was staring at the calendar Norma noted that the deadness she'd seen in her da's eyes the previous night was back. And was it her imagination or did he seem to have aged?

'I'm glad you missed that job, I don't like Innellan anyway,' Eileen said suddenly, trying to cheer her da up.

Brian turned his attention to his youngest daughter. 'You know something Eileen?'

'What Da?'

'To tell the truth I don't either.'

They all laughed at that, with the exception of Effie.

'I'll make you some scones for later,' Lyn said.

All four females could bake, but Lyn's baking – which she didn't do very often as surprisingly she didn't enjoy doing it – was special. There wasn't another female in the district who could bake as well as her; she was in a class of her own. A lot of it was to do with her very cold hands, Effie had always said.

'I'll look forward to that,' Brian replied, giving a wee nod to show he appreciated the treat.

When Brian had drunk his tea he cycled away again, with Effie and Norma standing at the sink window watching him go.

'If only . . .' Effie started to say, trailing off to bite her lip.

Norma squeezed her mother's hand comfortingly. Then she returned to her darning; Effie to the ironing.

Early evening ten days later Norma was returning home with a pail of milk she'd been to Boyd's Farm for, when there was the ting of a bell behind her, and there was her da on his bike. On reaching her he dismounted.

'Any luck?' she demanded eagerly, knowing he'd been into nearby Dunoon to see the manager of the Marine Hotel. The hotel had large grounds attached and employed a number of gardeners and Brian had heard that one of them was shortly to retire.

'A *year* till the fellow retires, the manager told me,' Brian said ruefully and shrugged.

'So it was a wild-goose chase.'

'I'm afraid it was, pet.'

They walked along in silence.

'Da?'

He glanced sideways at her.

'What happens if you don't find something?'

'There's plenty of time left before we have to worry about that,' he replied quickly.

'But if you *don't?*' she persisted.

She waited for an answer, but none came. They walked the rest of the way home with the sort of silence between them that you could have cut with a knife.

Norma awoke suddenly, her eyes snapping open. She stared up into the heavy darkness wondering what had roused her.

She didn't need a clock to tell her it was late, very late. Well after midnight she guessed.

Outside a cat screamed, then screamed again. *That* must have been what had wakened her, she thought, smiling to herself. Snuggling down she prepared to go back to sleep.

Then she heard something else, a voice speaking from the direction of the kitchen. Her da's voice.

Norma frowned. What was he doing still up at this time? He was normally early to bed and early to rise. With the exception of Hogmanay she'd never known him be up after twelve.

Getting out of bed she threw her dressing gown round her shoulders and padded to the door. She opened the door quietly and, without making a sound, slipped out into the hallway.

The kitchen door was ajar and Norma could see her mother and father sitting by the range. A solitary paraffin lamp cast a soft yellow glow round their chairs.

Her mother was speaking now, but in such a low voice that Norma couldn't make out what she was saying.

The pair of them looked terrible, Norma thought. Her mother's face was haggard with worry; her da - this time it certainly wasn't her imagination - looked a dozen years older than before that fateful day when he'd been told of his sacking.

Brian put a hand to his forehead and leant forward in his chair. He was the very picture of despair.

For the first time in her life Norma felt really frightened. Her body tingled with gooseflesh; the inside of both thighs began to quiver.

She went back to bed and lay staring into the darkness. Fear filled her from head to toe, ice-cold, mind-numbing, terrifying fear.

Fear that was still with her when she woke again the next morning.

It was Friday night – bath night for Effie and the girls – and as was usual, Brian had gone to The Royal Arms to give them privacy.

The zinc bath was in front of the range and Eileen was in it. They always shared the same water, starting with the youngest and working their way through to Effie.

On the range itself various large pans were bubbling. After Eileen each new person into the bath got a hot top-up.

Norma glanced away from the book she was reading, over to where Effie was sorting through a pile of dirty laundry.

Effie, clutching a blouse Norma recognised as being one of Eileen's, was staring at Eileen in the bath. Suddenly a stricken expression crumpled her face, and tears welled in her eyes. With a sob she fled the room.

Lyn started to rise, but stopped halfway at a sign from Norma. 'I'll go,' Norma said.

She found Effie in the parlour weeping into a hanky.

'It's four weeks now, only four left,' Effie choked out.

'I know Ma,' Norma replied, lighting the lamp on the mantelpiece.

'Oh Norma!' Effie wailed. The pair of them came together and Effie hugged Norma tightly to her.

*She* mustn't cry as well, although she felt like doing so, Norma told herself. She must be strong. Usually it was Ma who was the strong one; this time it was up to her.

She stroked Effie's neck and waited for the weeping to subside, which it eventually did.

Effie wiped a nose that had gone red. 'I'm sorry for breaking down like that,' she apologised.

'It's understandable Ma.'

Effie held the hanky between her hands and twisted it.

'It was seeing Eileen in the bath and remembering the first bath I gave her as a baby that did it.' She twisted the hanky even more vigorously. 'If the worst comes to the worst – and it seems it's going to – the family is going to have to split up,' she said, the latter in a rush.

Norma was appalled. 'Split up? How do you mean?'

'Your da's already written to our relations and it's been agreed. You're going to Auntie Josie and Uncle Bill, Lyn to my sister Meg and her husband, and Eileen to Granny and Grandpa McKenzie. Brian and I will stay with his brother Gordon in Hunter's Quay.'

'But . . . I mean . . . surely there's some other way, a way the family can stick together?' Norma protested.

Effie shook her head. 'We have just over eleven pounds in savings – how far do you think that would get us without a wage coming in? No, your da and I have thought this through. Splitting the family for the time being is all we can do.'

Norma thought of Mr Hodgart, she'd never liked the man, now she positively loathed him for what he'd done to them. 'Everything was so happy and secure here till that Mr Hodgart bought the House,' she said.

'Aye, the Earl would never have got rid of your father. He thought the world of Brian and Brian's work. Said so often.'

Effie blew her nose with the now sodden handkerchief, then wiped her eyes which she knew to be puffy from crying. 'We weren't going to let on to you and the other two till next week, but then I had that wee breakdown just now and it all came tumbling out. You will keep it quiet till then, won't you? Your da and I decided that would be for the best.'

'I'll keep it to myself if that's what you want,' Norma agreed.

Effie kissed Norma on the cheek. 'I hadn't noticed till tonight how grown up you've become. It's good to have another woman to share things with.'

Norma's heart swelled to hear that. The two women clasped one another, never more close than they were at that moment.

'I'd better get on then,' Effie said when they'd released each other.

Norma put out the lamp.

Norma let herself out of the cottage, her mind in a turmoil. She'd lost all notion for having a bath, and Effie hadn't insisted.

It was a fine night, though somewhat chilly. She pulled her shawl more closely about her as she made her way down to the shore road which she crossed to get to the shoreline beyond.

The tide was in as she'd known it would be; the Firth placid, its waters gently lapping against the many big boulders and rocks hereabouts.

She had a favourite rock which she sought out now, and climbed onto. Across the Firth the Cloch Lighthouse winked in and out.

*The family to split up and she to go to Auntie Josie and Uncle Bill!* The thought made her feel sick. For apart from the split itself Auntie Josie and Uncle Bill were Wee Frees, meaning members of the Wee Free Church.

She didn't know too much about the Wee Frees, except they were very strict, with a lot of talk of hellfire and brimstone. It would be church, church and church again. How many times on a Sunday alone, was it twice or three times?

Auntie Josie and Uncle Bill were a dour and serious couple, as well as religious fanatics. Why, in the many times she'd been in their company she'd never seen either of them laugh. She knew without a shadow of a doubt she was going to loathe living with them.

It would be hard for her, but what about poor Eileen? It would break Eileen's heart to be parted from the rest of them, especially Ma, for at eleven Eileen was still very much tied to her mother.

For Lyn at thirteen, it wasn't quite so bad, but it was going to be an awful blow for her all the same.

Norma gave a sudden grin. Auntie Meg and Uncle Sammy who Lyn was going to were renowned for being tight, which was reflected in the way they ate - wholesome food, but not very much of it. Lyn would suffer there right enough.

But probably the one to suffer most would be Ma. Being parted from her children would be an open wound, daily salted by memories of the past.

As for her da, he wouldn't say much about it but she could imagine what he'd go through.

He was such a terrific man, her da, one of the best. She'd never known anyone not to like him. As Ma had said the Earl had thought the world of —

The idea came to her in a blinding flash.

*Thought the world of him,* she repeated slowly to herself.

It might be the answer. It just might be!

Sliding down from the rock she ran back towards the cottage.

When Brian returned home from the pub he found Effie, Norma and Lyn eagerly awaiting him. Eileen had already been sent to bed as it was past her bedtime.

'Norma's had an idea you should hear,' announced Effie.

'Oh aye?' He was a bit muzzy from beer, but not too much so. He sat down and began packing his pipe.

'The Earl of Arran and Clydesdale always thought the world of you and said so often.'

Brian nodded. That was true enough.

'And he's influential, right? Knows all sorts of people, many of whom must employ gardeners?'

Brian considered that as he tamped down his fill.

'It's worth a try. What have you got to lose?' Effie urged.

Not a damn thing, he thought to himself.

'Well Da?' Norma queried.

'Come here,' he said, beckoning her over.

He playfully punched her on the side of the jaw. 'I think it's a smashing idea. And you can write the letter because you've got the best copperplate.'

'I'll get pen and paper,' said Lyn, going to the drawer where these things were kept.

Effie was filled with excitement and new hope, as she'd been ever since Norma had told her of her idea. Surely the Earl, as kindly a man as had ever lived, would come to their rescue and find a way out of their predicament for them. Surely!

'Now what do you think you should write?' asked Effie.

'I'll explain what's happened, what my position is, and ask if he knows of anyone looking for a gardener,' Brian replied, furrowing his brow. He lit his pipe.

'We must emphasise the urgency of the situation – that we're being chucked out of here in a fortnight's time,' Norma stated.

In the end all four of them helped compose the letter.

The following Monday the girls returned home from school to find their parents in a lather of activity. Brian was putting on his best suit – the one he wore for going to church, weddings and funerals – while Effie was packing an overnight case for him.

'A telegram arrived not half an hour ago from the Earl asking your da to go and see him in Glasgow,' explained Effie.

Brian stopped what he was doing. 'And I'm going *right away* so that I can present myself on his doorstep first thing tomorrow morning. I lost that last opportunity through taking my time – I'm not about to repeat that mistake.'

Norma nodded her approval.

'Make your da up a piece to take with him; he'll probably feel like a bite before he gets to Glasgow,' Effie said to Norma.

'There's some of that fresh salmon left. Put that in the piece,' Brian added. He regularly got a fresh salmon from a game keeper he was friends with.

Lyn picked up the telegram which had been lying on the kitchen table, while Norma set to cutting bread.

'The Earl just says you've to go and see him, nothing else,' Lyn said.

'But it *is* a telegram. That speaks volumes as far as I'm concerned,' replied Effie.

Brian was knotting his tie, a job he always found difficult because of the thickness and hardness of his fingers. Fingers far more used to a trowel and hoe than to a tie. He stopped to stare at Effie.

'Let's not build our hopes up too high eh? The Earl might want to help, but that doesn't mean he's going to be able to.'

Effie's return stare bordered on being a glare. 'There's no need to be pessimistic about this,' she snapped.

'I'm not being pessimistic, realistic rather,' Brian replied softly.

'But he did send a telegram all the same,' Effie persisted.

Brian shut up, letting her have the last word. She'd got the message anyway, he could read that in her eyes.

'I've put a couple of nice tomatoes and a screw of salt in the poke as well, Da,' Norma said, changing the subject. With a deft twist she closed the brown paper bag containing her da's food.

Five minutes later Brian was ready for off.

'Now be careful where you stay the night – make sure it's respectable. You know the stories about Glasgow, it's the devil's own place,' Effie warned him as they made for the door.

'I'll be careful. Don't you worry about me,' he replied gently, his voice warm with emotion.

'Come and give your da a kiss and wish him luck,' Effie instructed the girls.

Norma was the last in line. 'Good luck Da,' she repeated as the other two had done.

Effie kissed him on the cheek – she'd never have dreamt of kissing him on the mouth in front of the children – muttered 'Good luck', and then Brian was on his way, out the door and striding down the path that would take him to the shore road.

Norma crossed two fingers.

Brian didn't return the next day, or the next. It was Thursday evening when he reappeared, wearing the most hangdog and woebegone of expressions.

Effie put a thumb in her mouth and chewed it. She felt sick.

'Well it was a good idea at least,' Brian said, and shrugged. He placed his case in a corner.

'So what happened?' Effie asked, her voice heavy with disappointment.

That was it then; the family would be split up after all and she would be going to stay with Auntie Josie and Uncle Bill, Norma thought to herself, feeling as sick as Effie.

'I brought you a wee minding back from Glasgow, lass,' Brian said, ignoring his wife's question. He produced a key which he handed to Effie.

She stared blankly at the plain, unadorned, gun-metal object in her hand. 'What's this?' she queried.

'A key.'

'I can see that!' she exclaimed, quite mystified.

Norma, knowing her da as she did and being very quick on the uptake, caught on first.

'Well, to be specific, it's a door-key,' Brian elaborated.

'What blinking door?'

Brian pulled a half bottle of whisky out of his hip pocket and placed it on the table.

'The front door of our new house,' he said, his hangdog and woebegone expression vanishing, to be replaced by a huge beaming smile.

Effie staggered. 'You mean . . .?'

'Aye, I've got a job, thanks to the Earl. I start the fourth of June!'

'Hooray?' Eileen yelled, jumping up and down.

'Oh see you, see you!' Effie said, shaking a fist at him for doing that to her. On impulse she went to him and hit him, but not too hard. There were bright sparkling tears in her eyes.

Lyn threw her arms round Norma and hugged her. Then Eileen joined in, the three of them all hugging one another.

'The house is in Bridgeton – the Earl helped me get that as well,' Brian continued.

Effie frowned. Bridgeton, she'd never heard of it.

'It's only a room and a kitchen, smaller than we've got here. But that was all the Earl's friend had available. It's not a bad tenement either – a lot nicer than many I saw.'

While Brian had been speaking he'd taken out two glasses and poured drams for himself and Effie. He now topped the glasses up with water.

'Where is Bridgeton?' Effie asked.

'Central Glasgow.'

'But ... You mean ... Are you saying we're going to live in Glasgow?' Effie demanded.

Brian sipped his drink. He'd known this was going to hit hard. 'My job is as a gardener with the Glasgow Corporation Parks Department, with me based at Glasgow Green. Bridgeton will be handy for my work,' he replied softly.

They were to go and stay in Glasgow! Norma hadn't even thought of the possibility when she'd made her suggestion to her da. She'd presumed the Earl would find Brian another position in a big house similar to Kilmichael House, a house in a rural or semi-rural setting. The sort of thing they were used to.

'Is this another of your jokes?' Effie queried, hoping it was.

Brian shook his head. 'No, I swear.'

'But Glasgow, Da! It's filthy there, and full of criminals,' protested Lyn.

'Well it certainly isn't as clean as it is round here, there's no disputing that. But not all Glaswegians are criminals; some of them are really quite nice, just ordinary, hard-working folk like ourselves.'

'You're telling us there's no choice, Da,' Norma said quietly.

Brian directed his reply to all of them. 'The Earl made a number of enquiries on my behalf, and this was the only one that came up. So it's either Glasgow and the Parks Department or else . . .' After a quick glance at Effie. 'Or else the family will have to split up.' He explained to Lyn and Eileen the contingency plans he'd made. When he'd finished the pair of them were as white as ghosts.

Brian took another sip of his drink. He was just as worried as the rest of the family about going to live in Glasgow, but had no intention of letting on he was. Not even to Effie later.

Effie appeared to be making a decision. Straightening up, she squared her shoulders and thrust out her chin. 'We must look on this as a challenge. If staying together means going to Glasgow, then go to Glasgow we will - and make the best of it,' she said, her voice iron with determination.

'That's the ticket lass!' Brian smiled and silently toasted his wife, his love for her, and the pride he felt for her creeping into his face.

Eight days till they had to vacate the cottage. They'd cut it fine, Norma thought.

But the family *was* going to remain together. That was all that really mattered.

Though God alone knew what they were going into.

All their friends and neighbours came to see them off at the harbour, a hundred folk or more. The gardeners and their families from the House, and the servants too, shopkeepers, school pals, old cronies - even a bevy of ladies from the WI of which Effie had been a keen member.

The paddle-steamer *Strathmore*'s gangplank was taken on board, the funnel hooter sounded, and that was it, they were away.

Norma, standing on the main deck with the rest of the family, was waving frantically to her friends: to Marion Cockburn and Isabella Doig whom she suddenly remembered owed her thruppence, to Mr Annan the baker - she'd aye been a special favourite of his, he slipping her fly buns and cakes for as long as she could remember.

There was Norman Rae, the first boy she'd ever kissed seriously, Norman waving to her fit to bust and looking sad as could be.

And there was Mrs McLure galloping onto the pier, late, but

not too late to have missed them. Mrs McLure ran the Post Office and had closed up especially to be there.

The *Strathmore* was stopping at Wemyss Bay where they'd get off and board the train to Glasgow.

Their furniture and all other belongings had left early that morning, being taken to Glasgow by the far longer inland route. the lorry carrying their things would arrive in Bridgeton some hours after they themselves had got there.

They waved and waved, only stopping when they came abreast of Kilmichael House and - just visible behind - the chimney-stack and -pot of what had been their cottage, and much loved home.

Finally the pier, Kirn and Kilmichael House disappeared astern.

Brian turned to Effie. 'A new beginning,' he said.

'A new beginning,' she echoed.

Rain had been threatening all day and now, heralded by a flash of lightening and a loud clap of thunder, it started bucketing down.

She hoped this wasn't an omen, Norma thought to herself as they raced for the nearest hatchway.

The rain was stotting off the deck as they went below.

## *Chapter Two*

Outside the Central Station they caught a tram that took them along Argyle Street and into the Trongate. Norma stared in fascination; she'd never seen so many buildings or people. As for the tram they were on, clanking and swaying, she found that just a wee bit frightening – like being aboard some metal prehistoric monster.

They left the Trongate to enter Gallowgate, with the district of Calton to the right of them.

Norma wrinkled her nose at the smell which suddenly pervaded the tram. It was a sooty smell, with other nasty odours mingled with it.

There was the smell of heavy industry – a bitter tang that left a bad taste in the mouth. That and the smell of unwashed bodies, excrement, urine, general dirt, decay and the rubbish bins. Together they formed the distinctive smell of the Glasgow slums.

'Ugh!' said Norma, pulling a face.

Effie sat tight-lipped staring at the tall, grey and – to her eyes forbidding – tenements of the Calton. They terrified her.

Lyn gawped at a wee boy strolling past the tram. His trouser legs were raggedy, stopping halfway between his knee and ankle. He had no shoes or socks on and his exposed feet were disgustingly filthy – not with the filth of the day, but with the accumulated filth of weeks.

They passed a street where two men were fighting in the gutter.

'Look Ma!' Eileen cried out, pointing.

There was the crash of a breaking bottle. One man fell to the ground, blood spurting from his face. The other began putting the boot in.

A teenage lad shot out of a closemouth, legs going sixteen to the dozen. He took off up the street like a runaway greyhound.

There was the piercing blast of a whistle, and a pair of policemen came charging out of the same closemouth to go thundering after the lad.

'I said they were all criminals here,' Lyn mumbled, but not loud enough for her da to hear.

'Bridgeton's not nearly as awful as this,' Brian whispered to Effie, giving her a reassuring smile. Her lips tightened.

Norma gazed in amazement at a man sitting on the pavement propped up against a tenement wall. From the way his head was lolling he was clearly drunk. Then, to her total horror, he threw up all over himself.

Calton gave way to Bridgeton, and as Brian had promised there was an improvement, but hardly a big one.

'Our stop!' said Brian, and they all got off, with Eileen clinging to her da's hand.

Norma thought of all they'd left behind: the fresh air from the Firth, the trees, flowers and plants, and the beautiful, glorious sea. All that for – *this?* A huge black cloud of depression settled over her.

They crossed over Gallowgate to a narrow street leading off. 'Cubie Street, where our house is,' Brian announced, thinking it looked a lot meaner and scruffier than he remembered it.

The tenements were grey; the street itself and pavements were grey; even the sky above was grey. The complexions of the children playing peerie in the street were the same colour, in complete contrast to their own healthy complexions.

They passed a broken window, taped up inside with a bit of cardboard. From the room behind came the sound of a woman's hacking cough.

'Here we are, number thirty-eight,' said Brian, stopping outside a close.

'Janice Morton has a big bum' had been chalked on the front of the building.

'That's not all she's got that's big!' had been chalked in a different hand below.

'We're two flights up,' Brian said, and led the way, Eileen still clinging to him as though for dear life.

On the half landing between the first and second flights of

stairs Effie insisted on stopping to inspect the communal toilet.

There was an ancient wooden seat that was scarred and scratched all over; it was even burnt in one place. The toilet bowl was yellow inside, but did give the appearance of having been regularly cleaned and disinfected.

The stone floor was badly cracked, as were the walls - walls painted a vile shade of green.

'It's not that bad,' said Brian quietly.

The toilet was better than she'd expected, Effie had to admit to herself. She'd feared something truly dreadful. It was the fact the family had to *share* it she found off-putting.

They continued on up the stairs.

There were three main doors on each landing, theirs the one on the left. Brian unlocked it and the door swung open.

'Now watch this!' he said, going into the small hall. He flicked a switch and the hall flooded with light.

'Electricity,' he smiled. There had been none at the cottage where they'd had to make do with paraffin lamps.

There were two doors leading from the hall, Brian led them through the one on the left.

They found themselves in a good-sized kitchen, which would also double as a bedroom for Brian and Effie, who would sleep in the cavity bed sunk into the wall that the kitchen shared with 'the room'.

'Modern fireplace, no more cooking on a range,' Brian said to Effie.

The gas stove was already installed, and stood in a corner. Gas was another convenience they hadn't had in the cottage.

Effie turned a brass tap, and immediately there was the hiss of gas. Cooking on gas was going to take getting used to she thought to herself.

Norma peered into the cavity bed. It was like looking into a wee cave she thought. It would be comfy though. She decided she liked it, and was disappointed she wouldn't be sleeping in it.

There was a good linoleum on the floor, while the walls had been distempered not long since. They were painted in a pretty primrose shade which cheered up what might otherwise have been a darkish room.

Norma crossed over to the window above the sink, facing the cavity bed, and peered out.

The communal back court was devoid of grass, except for a few forlorn tufts growing here and there. A great deal of rubbish lay scattered over the brown earth: tin cans, broken glass, old newspapers, these sort of things. The brick middens containing the bins were overflowing with refuse.

She turned on the cold water tap, cupped her hands, and took a mouthful of the water.

Her face lit up in surprise. The tap-water was almost as pure, and pleasant to drink, as the well-water they'd been used to.

She said so to Effie who came over and tried it for herself.

'You're right,' Effie said, agreeing with Norma. It was a relief to know she was still going to be able to brew a nice pot of tea.

At Brian's suggestion they all trooped through to 'the room'.

This was a little larger than the kitchen and its walls were papered. The paper was a floral pattern which Norma and Lyn said they didn't mind, but which Eileen declared to be horrible.

'Hard cheese,' Lyn said to her.

The mahogany-brown linoleum was on its last legs, with a gaping crack running right down its centre.

'That'll have to be replaced,' Effie said.

Brian nodded his agreement.

Norma went to the window and looked out. The window was clarty, just as the other had been. They both needed a right good clean.

Across the street two women were leaning out of adjoining windows, having a natter together. Both were wearing full-length pinnies and one had a scarf tied round her head.

There was the clatter of an empty can being kicked. The boy doing the kicking had on tackety boots, several sizes too large for him.

'I'm starving hungry!' Eileen suddenly announced. They had had sandwiches on the train but that seemed ages ago now.

'Well I can't cook anything till my pots and pans get here and that won't be for a while yet,' said Effie.

'Tell you what, why don't I nip out and buy fish suppers?' Brian suggested.

'That's a smashing idea!' Lyn enthused.

'While your da's getting the fish suppers you can get me some messages Norma. We'll need tea, milk and sugar for later tonight, and things for tomorrow's breakfast,' Effie said.

'I don't want to be out there on my own!' Norma replied in alarm.

'Don't be soft. We're going to be living here so you'll have to get used to going to the shops and round about. But as it is your first time Lyn can go with you,' Brian replied.

Lyn wasn't too keen either, but knew her da to be right. And like swimming, the sooner you took the plunge the better.

Effie reeled off the items she wanted, then extracted a ten shilling note from her purse and handed it to Norma.

'Mind check your change and not get diddled!' she warned, not trusting Glasgow shopkeepers one little bit.

Brian, Norma and Lyn walked back to Gallowgate where Norma immediately spied a wee place that would sell what she and Lyn had been sent out to get. The pair of them went in, leaving Brian to find a chippie.

There was a chap in a white apron behind the counter and another chap lounging in front of the counter talking to him. They broke off their conversation as Norma and Lyn approached.

The chap in the white apron couldn't have been nicer or more helpful, putting their messages in a cardboard box when he learned they didn't have a shopping bag.

While they were being served, the second chap, obviously a pal of the other, kept glancing at Norma. When their gazes met he smiled. She didn't smile back.

Lyn waited till they were outside the shop before bursting into laughter.

'I think he fancied you,' she teased.

'Who's that?' Norma replied, pretending innocence.

'You know who. The chap who kept giving you the glad eye.'

'Can't say I noticed,' Norma answered keeping up her pretence of innocence.

'You noticed all right. You'd have to be blind not to.'

'I must be blind then.'

'Oh come off it Norma McKenzie!'

He had been attractive, Norma thought. And wondered who he was.

On reaching what was now their home she promptly forgot all about him.

* * *

'What time is it now?' asked Effie.

Brian took out his pocket watch from his suit waistcoat. 'Ten past eleven,' he replied.

The entire family was sitting on the kitchen floor, their backs against various walls. Eileen had long since fallen asleep.

Effie exhaled sharply in exasperation, 'It's not coming to-night, I just know so,' she said, referring to the lorry bringing their furniture and other belongings. It was hours overdue.

'It must have broken down somewhere. That's the only explanation,' Brian replied.

Lyn yawned; she was dead tired. Completely whacked.

'So what are we going to do?' asked Norma.

'The four of you can crowd into that cavity bed while I doss down here. There's nothing else for it,' Brian answered. Luckily there was a mattress in the cavity bed.

'It may be June but it'll be cold during the night,' Lyn complained.

'It'll be colder for me than it will be for you. At least you can cuddle up,' Brian retorted.

'Lift Eileen in will you Brian, she can go to the back of the bed,' Effie said.

Brian went to Eileen and was just about to pick her up when there was a timid knock on the outside door. He looked at Effie who shrugged. She couldn't imagine who it was either.

Going into the hall Brian put the light on, then opened the outside door. A middle-aged woman in a purple cardy stood revealed. The door behind her was ajar.

'I'm Mrs Fullarton, your neighbour,' the woman said, smiling uncertainly.

'Pleased to meet you. I'm Brian McKenzie. We've just moved in, as you no doubt know,' he smiled back.

'Aye, well, that's why I'm chapping. I hope you don't think I'm sticking my nose in or anything like that, it's just that I saw you arrive but no flit with you. Is everything all right?'

'Come away ben and meet the wife and family,' Brian replied, and ushered Mrs Fullarton through to the kitchen where Effie, Norma and Lyn were now standing waiting to be introduced.

'Brian was just saying the lorry must have broken down,' Effie explained.

'It was coming from Kirn so it could well be stuck in the middle of nowhere,' Brian added.

Mrs Fullarton tut-tutted, then said, 'I went to Kirn on a mystery tour once. I thought it a lovely spot.'

'It is indeed,' Effie agreed.

Mrs Fullarton had a great many questions she was dying to ask, but now was hardly the time.

'And another lassie there fast asleep,' she said, nodding at Eileen.

'That's Eileen, my youngest. It's been a long day for her. For all of us,' Effie replied.

Mrs Fullarton's gaze swept round the kitchen taking in the messages that had been bought now standing on the board by the sink. 'Well, we can't let you spend the night like this. I'll organise sheets and blankets for you.'

'Can you do that?' exclaimed Brian.

'Oh aye. A wee knock here and a wee knock there and I'll soon have what you need. Leave it to me.' And with that Mrs Fullarton bustled from the kitchen and out into the house.

Ten minutes later she was back with a lad she introduced as her son Jacky. They'd brought two quilts with them, three large sheets, half a dozen beige blankets and four pillows. They'd also brought a kettle so the McKenzies could make tea.

Effie was visibly moved by all this kindness. 'It's awful good of you,' she said

'Ach away with you. It's what neighbours are for. We all give each other a helping hand round here. It's the only way to get by,' Mrs Fullarton replied.

'Is there anything else you need?' Jacky Fullarton asked. He was a lad in his late teens.

'Nothing I can think of,' Effie replied.

'We'll leave you to it then. Cheerio for now,' Mrs Fullarton said, shooing Jacky out the door.

'Would you credit that,' Effie said when the Fullartons had gone.

'I told you Glasgow folk weren't nearly as bad as they're painted,' Brian beamed.

Effie picked up one of the sheets and smelt it. 'Freshly laundered,' she said. In fact it and the others had been to the steamie that morning.

Norma and Lyn helped Effie make the cavity bed. Brian still had to doss on the floor where, although he spent an uncomfortable night, he at least was warm.

The lorry arrived in at one o'clock the next afternoon; the driver full of apologies. It was as Brian had thought; he'd broken down with engine trouble in an out-of-the-way spot and hadn't been able to get a tow and the engine fixed till that morning. He and Brian set to unloading the heavier things; the girls the lighter.

An oak wardrobe was proving something of a problem, being not only unwieldy but weighing an absolute ton, when two men came along the street to halt beside Brian.

'Mr McKenzie?'

'That's me.'

'I'm Jim Fullarton and this is Sandy Reid who lives the next flight up. Can we help?'

Brian smiled his gratitude. 'That would be tremendous. I'd be fair obliged.'

Jim and Sandy pitched in, and it wasn't long before the lorry was cleared, the entire flit indoors.

Brian was profuse in his thanks, but Jim and Sandy shrugged off what they'd done, Jim echoing his wife's words of the night before that that's what neighbours were for.

Back in the kitchen, Brian put an arm round Effie. 'Living in Glasgow isn't going to be as bad as we'd feared,' he said softly.

Effie agreed.

The Friday that marked their having been in Cubie Street a fortnight was Norma's fifteenth birthday. Effie made an Albert sponge with vanilla icing on top for her, and when Brian arrived home from work – where he'd settled in no bother at all – he was carrying a rectangular shaped parcel wrapped in brown paper.

'Happy birthday, girl,' he said, kissing Norma on the cheek and giving her the parcel.

His eyes twinkled as he watched her undo the string and unwrap the paper. She found a shoe-box inside.

Norma gasped with delight when she took the lid off the box. Nestling in a bed of tissue were a pair of blood-red high-heeled shoes.

'I hope they fit,' Brian smiled. Effie had told him what size and width to buy. But still, you never knew with these things.

Norma slipped first one on, then the other. 'Absolutely perfect,' she pronounced.

She walked up and down, showing them off. 'They're just fabulous Da! I hate to think what they cost.'

'Aye well, as it was your idea to write to the Earl, which saved the family from being split up, I thought you deserved something a wee bit special this year.'

'My first high heels,' she breathed, more to herself than anyone else.

'Can I try them on?' Eileen asked eagerly.

'No you cannot! And no fly goes behind my back. If you do you'll get a clout round the ear.'

Lyn didn't even bother to ask, knowing she'd get the same answer as Eileen.

After they'd had their main course Effie brought out the sponge she'd made and Norma cut it while everyone else sang 'Happy Birthday'. She put five pieces on to the plates laid out.

'My piece is smaller than the rest,' Lyn complained.

'They're all the same, I was careful about that,' Norma told her, thinking no matter what piece she'd given her Lyn would have seen it as smaller than the others.

Lyn didn't argue further, but wasn't at all convinced she hadn't been 'done'.

The table had been cleared; the dishes washed and put away, and Brian was talking to Effie about how different Glasgow Green was to the grounds of Kilmichael House, when suddenly the strains of music came wafting into the kitchen.

'Somebody must be playing a gramophone,' Effie said.

'Don't be daft, that's live or I'm a monkey's uncle. And it sounds like it's coming from the street,' Brian replied.

Eileen scampered through to the room to look out the window.

'You're right Da, there's a band out there!' she called through.

The rest of them went into the room to stare out, and sure enough, there was a band comprising two fiddlers and an accordionist playing just a little further down the street.

Several couples were dancing to the music, while others were standing by watching.

'I wonder what this is in aid of?' Brian mused aloud.

There was a knock on the outside door. Norma answered it to find Mrs Fullarton there, who asked if she could speak to her ma and da. Norma took her ben the room.

'Jenny Elder, who lives a few closes down on this side, has got engaged to Murray Muir who lives further up the street on the other side, and as both their fathers are idle they're having their engagement party in the street. I was instructed to tell you you're all welcome, and both sets of parents hope you'll come down and join in,' Mrs Fullarton said.

So that was the explanation, Norma thought. She glanced out the window again to see that more couples were now dancing. It looked like fun.

'It'll be a good chance for you to meet everyone, and they you,' Mrs Fullarton added.

It would too, Brian told himself.

'Would we be expected to bring anything?' Effie asked.

'Well those men who can afford it will probably take a few screwtops, but that's all,' Mrs Fullarton replied.

'Please Da?' Eileen pleaded.

Brian looked at Effie who gave him a nod. She also thought it a good idea.

'Right then, we'll be glad to accept. We'll be down shortly,' Brian said, knowing Effie would want to change her clothes and generally do herself up a bit. No doubt so would the girls.

'That's grand. Jim's just about to away up to the off-licence to get a few bottles and then we'll be going down.'

'Can I go with him? I'll get some screwtops as well,' Brian said, correctly thinking that what Mrs Fullarton had meant by those who could afford it being men in work, while those 'idle' wouldn't be expected to.

'Aye, he'll be out in a jiffy. You can meet him on the landing,' Mrs Fullarton replied.

Effie found it a daunting prospect having to go out and face so many new people. But she'd do it, and with a smile.

Norma was already rummaging through the wardrobe she shared with Eileen pulling out the dress she intended to wear. It was a cream colour, which would be set off perfectly by her new red shoes.

From outside came the sound of someone wheeching. The party was hotting up.

Effie dabbed on a wee touch of powder, then put a drop of the Evening in Paris perfume behind each ear. That completed her make-up. She never ever wore lipstick. Not that she had anything against lipstick, it was just that she'd always felt it was too much for her. She preferred things plain and simple.

There was a minor scuffle when Lyn discovered that Eileen was wearing a bracelet of hers, but Effie soon sorted that out, making Eileen return the bracelet to Lyn who put it on even though she hadn't intended wearing it.

'Can I have a dab of your powder Ma?' Norma asked.

Effie considered the request, then nodded. How grown up Norma was becoming. Why, it only seemed like yesterday that — She smiled to herself. Was there ever a parent who'd never had the same thought? She doubted it.

Effie took a final look at herself in the wardrobe mirror, and rearranged one of her tortoiseshell combs. She wasn't bad for someone of thirty-four who'd had three children and a miscarriage, she told herself. Not bad at all.

Brian returned with his screwtops to say that Jim Fullarton had suggested the two families go down together, which was what they did a few minutes later.

There was quite a gathering in the street now, with a good two dozen couples up dancing.

In quick succession the McKenzies met the Vicarys, Mathers, McNaughtons, Carrs, Galbraiths and Laidlaws. The Mathers and Laidlaws lived in their close.

'I was wondering if you'd care to have a birl?' Jacky Fullarton asked Norma, stammering a little.

Eileen giggled, and Norma glared at her, giving her a right sinker.

'I'd love to Jacky, thank you,' she replied and, taking his arm, crossed over with him to where the dancing was taking place.

The three-piece band, if you could call it a band, was playing a polka, and giving it big licks, the fiddlers sawing madly with their bows; the accordionist attacking his instrument with such vigour it might have been a demented bellows about to run amok.

While Norma was up with Jacky Fullarton, Brian and Effie met the Muirs and Elders, whose son and daughter's engagement hoolie it was.

The band took a break, so Norma and Jacky came off 'the floor', Norma rejoining Lyn and Jacky his parents.

'Look who was watching you,' Lyn said quietly, giving a sideways gesture of her head.

Norma glanced in that direction to see a vaguely familiar face staring back at her. He was tallish, with fair hair and - even noticeable at that distance - bright blue eyes.

'Recognise him?' queried Lyn.

The penny dropped. 'The chap in the shop we met that first night here. The one in front of the counter,' Norma replied.

'That's him, and he hasn't taken those gorgeous blue peepers off you the whole time you've been up with Jacky Fullarton.'

Norma had found him attractive before, and still did. In fact, he was quite a dish. She wondered if he'd ask her up? He must be interested if he'd been watching her the way Lyn said he had.

'He's on the move,' Lyn whispered

'Is he coming over here?' Norma asked, having immediately looked the opposite way.

'The Pride of Erin!' one of the fiddlers announced. The band struck up, and dancing resumed.

'He's gone over to speak to Jacky,' Lyn replied.

Eileen went dashing past, playing tig with some of the street's other children. She was having a whale of a time.

'I think he's coming over now, with Jacky,' Lyn whispered.

Norma put on her most nonchalent expression.

'Norma, I'd like you to meet a pal of mine, Midge Henderson - Midge, this is Norma McKenzie, and her sister Lyn,' Jacky said.

Norma focused on Midge, as if noticing him for the first time.

'Hello, pleased to meet you,' he smiled.

He had a typical Glasgow voice, grey with a hint of gravel.

'Midge? What sort of name is that?' she queried.

'It's short for Michael, and not because I used to play round the midgies as a wee boy,' he answered, his smile widening.

Norma's face went blank. 'What's a midgie?'

'They're new to Glasgow, flitted here from Kirn down the Clyde coast,' Jacky explained.

'I knew you'd moved here recently, but didn't realise it was from outside Glasgow. A midgie is a midden,' Midge replied.

'You learn something every day!' Lyn said and laughed.

'Would you like to dance?' Midge asked Norma.

She hesitated for a brief moment, not wanting to appear too eager. 'Yes, that would be nice. Thank you,' she said.

Lyn was hoping that Jacky would ask her up, and was disappointed when he excused himself, and went elsewhere. She watched in envy as Norma and Midge took to 'the floor'.

'What brought you here from Kirn?' asked Midge.

'My da landed a job with the Parks Department, he's a gardener.' She then explained about Mr Hodgart and Kilmichael House, but not about Brian writing to the Earl, thinking that a private matter. If her da wanted to tell people then that was up to him.

'Your da was lucky to get another job so quickly, unemployment being as rife as it is. And Glasgow's no better than the rest of Scotland - worse I'd say. Why, half the men in Cubie Street are idle, maybe even more than that.'

'What about yourself?' Norma asked.

'I'm an apprentice with the North Woodside Flint Mills on the Garriochmill Road. I finish my apprenticeship next year when I'm eighteen.'

Norma was intrigued. 'What happens in a flint mill?' she queried.

He grinned. 'Basically, we reduce the flint to a fine powder by a process of burning and grinding. It's then used in the making of glaze for sanitary earthenware. Right now I'm mainly concerned with the kiln where the flint is calcined, which is to say burned.'

'Sounds interesting,' Norma commented.

'Yes. And they're a good bunch that work there. But what about you, what do you do?'

'I was at school in Kirn, but left on coming here. I'm on the look-out for work, but haven't found anything so far.'

School! He'd taken her for older than that. He'd thought her his own age.

However, she was certainly a looker. Tall for a lassie, as tall as himself, with honey-blonde hair, a deepish voice and eyes that kept changing from grey to green and back again. He thought her a knockout.

'I like your shoes,' he said.

'I only got them today. They're for my birthday.'

'Your birthday!' he exclaimed. 'Congratulations. What does that make you then?'

'Fifteen,' she smiled.

Which meant she'd been only fourteen when he'd seen her in Chic's shop a fortnight previously. 'Ach you're no more than a bairn still!' he teased.

That annoyed her. Bairn indeed! She felt herself going right off him.

'I live in number six,' he said.

'Do you,' she answered coldly, making it sound as if that was of no importance whatever to her.

He burbled on till the end of the dance.

'Thank you,' she said the instant the dance was finished. Before he could ask her to stay up she strode off, leaving him standing.

'What happened there?' Lyn asked when Norma rejoined her.

'He was impertinent. I didn't like that,' Norma snapped in reply.

Lyn pulled a face. '*Impertinent was he! Dear me.*'

Trust Lyn to take the mickey, Norma thought. She was forever doing it, something she'd inherited from their Da.

The band struck up again, this time a schottische. Lyn looked round hopefully, but there was no lad making in her direction.

'I think I'm destined to be a wallflower,' she sniffed.

'What about me, will I do?' Norma said.

'I thought you'd never ask,' Lyn replied, and giggled, thinking what the heck! Your sister was better than nothing. Arm in arm, the pair of them took to 'the floor'.

Effie was thoroughly enjoying herself. It had been no ordeal whatever meeting all these folk; in fact it had been easy as pie. Right then she was having a fine old chinwag with Mrs Vicary who'd invited her in for a cup of tea the following day, an invitation she'd eagerly accepted.

Brian was drinking beer. The screwtops that had been brought had all been placed on a bench that had been set out, and anyone who wanted one just helped themselves, irrespective of whether they'd contributed or not.

Norma was dancing and laughing with Lyn when suddenly she found herself whisked out of Lyn's grasp and into that of a man. It was Midge.

'Lassies aren't allowed to dance with lassies here so we've come to split you up,' he said.

Lyn was with Jacky Fullarton, who'd been dragooned into this by Midge who'd wanted to dance again with Norma.

'You're persistent aren't you,' Norma said.

He gave her a cheeky grin. 'Did you take the hump because I called you a bairn?'

She'd give him the frozen treatment, she decided. She looked off to the side, and didn't reply.

'Ach come on, it was only a wee joke. No need to take it that way.'

She continued looking to the side.

'All right, I'm sorry if it upset you. That was the last thing I intended.'

She was stiff in his arms, like dancing with a stookie he thought. Her feet might be going through the motions, but apart from that she was totally unresponsive.

He felt his confidence draining away. He'd made a mistake in saying what he had, and a further mistake in splitting her from her sister. He stopped dancing.

'I didn't mean to force myself on you, and won't bother you anymore. I really am sorry you took such offence where none was meant. Thanks for the dance,' he said, and made to move away.

She didn't know why she did what she did next, but nevertheless she did. Perhaps it was something in his tone; perhaps it was because she really did like him and knew if he went now that would be the end of it.

She reached out and took hold of an arm, stopping him. 'I'll tell you what, let's start again shall we?'

His bright blue eyes sent a shiver through her insides. Then she was once more in his arms and they resumed dancing.

When that dance was finished she stayed where she was. She didn't have to be asked if she wanted to stay up. Both of them wanted to, and both knew that. It didn't have to be said.

A wee while later the band broke for a breather, and a woman called Belle McHarg got up to sing. She launched into a folksong called 'The Dundee Weaver'.

Oh I'm a Dundee weaver and I come from bonnie Dundee,
I met a Glesca fella and he came courting me.
He took me oot a walking, doon by the Kelvin Ha',
And there the dirty wee rascal stole my thingummyjig awa' ...

Norma tapped a foot in time to the tune, there'd been a lot of folksongs sung in and around Kirn, and she'd always enjoyed them. But this was a new one to her.

He took me oot a picnic, doon by the Rouken Glen,
He showed to me the bonnie wee birds and he showed me a bonnie wee hen.
He showed tae me the bonnie wee birds frae a linnet tae a craw,
Then he showed tae me the bird that stole my thingummyjig awa' ...

Norma frowned, she didn't understand the words.

So I'll go back to Dundee looking bonnie, young and fair,
Oh I'll put on my buckle and shoes and tie up my bonnie broon hair.
Oh I'll put on my corsets tight tae mak' my body look sma',
And wha' will ken with my rosy cheeks that my thingummyjig's awa' ...

Norma turned to Midge. 'What's her thingummyjig?' she asked.

He raised an eyebrow, saw she was serious, and wondered whether he should tell her or not. After all he'd only just met the girl.

He decided he would. Putting his mouth to an ear he whispered.

Norma's face flamed. How could she have been so dense! And how embarrassing. She felt quite mortified.

It was too much for Midge, he burst out laughing which made her face flame even more.

So a' you Dundee weavers take this advice from me,
Oh never let a fella an inch above your knee.
Oh never staun at the back of a close or up against a wa'
For if you do you can safely say your thingummyjig's awa.
For if you do you can safely say your thingummyjig's awa'.

'I shouldn't laugh but your expression after I told you was priceless,' Midge said.

Norma didn't know where to put herself. She wished the ground would open up and swallow her.

'I'd better get back to the others,' she mumbled, and started to go.

This time it was he who reached out and stopped her. 'Please don't?' he pleaded.

'I . . .'

'Please?'

'I feel such a fool.'

'You're anything but. You're the prettiest lassie here tonight, and you'll break my heart if you don't stay up.'

'Your heart must be easily broken then?'

He was amazed at his own audacity. He'd never said anything even remotely like that to a girl before.

The fiddler doing the announcing said they'd had a request for the 'dinky one-step'.

'Can you do it?' Norma asked. It was a favourite of hers, and a dance she'd learned at school. She'd had a teacher there who'd taught her a number of dances.

'Just try me,' Midge replied.

Right, she thought. She would.

It was a waltz-hold, with the man facing the line of dance, or direction in which the dancers move round the ballroom, which is to say anti-clockwise.

Afterwards Norma couldn't say how it happened, only that it did. She and Midge somehow fused, to become as one. She knew exactly what he was going to do, and how he was going to do it. And it was the same with him. They might have been telepathic.

When the dance ended there was applause, and the applause was for them alone. Glasgow is the most dancingest city in the Empire, and Glaswegians know good dancing when they see it.

'Well,' said Norma, lost for words.

'You're not half bad,' Midge told her.

'You're not half bad yourself.'

'Listen, there's a big dance on tomorrow night at the Magic Stick – Roy Fox and his band will be playing. Would you like to go with me?' Midge asked eagerly.

Norma laughed. 'What's the Magic Stick when it's at home?'
'It's the nickname for the Majestic, a dancehall in town.'
Roy Fox and his band, why they were famous! She'd heard them a number of times on the wireless.
'I'd love to but . . .'
'But what?' he queried anxiously.
'I really would have to ask my da first.'
'Then do that. Do you want me to come with you?'
'No, I'll speak to him on my own,' she replied, hoping Brian was going to say yes. Oh please God he would!
She told Midge she'd see him again in a few minutes, then left him to seek out her da whom she found amongst a knot of men chaffing one another.
'That was a fine bit of dancing there. You and the lad were quite a sight,' Brian said.
She drew her father aside. 'His name's Midge Henderson and he's asked me to go out with him tomorrow night. Can I Da?'
Brian's brow creased with doubt. She was just turned fifteen that day after all. If he agreed this would be the first time she'd ever been out properly with a lad.
'Take you where?' he queried.
'A dancehall in town.'
Brian didn't like the sound of that, not one little bit. He listened intently while she told him why Midge particularly wanted to go to the Majestic.
'Jim, can I have a word?' he called out to Jim Fullarton, who immediately came over.
He explained the situation, then asked Jim's opinion of Midge.
'Midge was born into the street, and I've known him all his life. Let me put it this way, if I had a lassie and Midge asked her out I wouldn't put the stoppers on it,' Jim replied.
'Would you let this supposed lassie of yours go into town with him though?'
'Norma will be all right with Midge, I assure you.'
'So can I go Da?'
She was clearly mad keen. It would be an awful blow to her if he did say no, and he didn't really see how he could refuse after Jim's strong recommendation of the boy.

His face cracked into a smile. 'I wouldn't mind seeing and hearing Roy Fox in the flesh myself. He's rare.'

Norma kissed him on a cheek. 'Thanks Da.'

Brian watched his eldest daughter walk away from him with a lump in his throat. This was the start of it, he told himself. She wasn't his wee Norma anymore.

'Well, what's the verdict?' Midge demanded when Norma joined him.

She nodded. 'It's on.'

'I'll pick you up at half six then.'

'I'll be ready.'

The 'dashing white sergeant' was announced. Brian got Effie up, and a chap asked Lyn if she'd care to trip the light fantastic with him.

Norma and Midge went back onto 'the floor'.

'How do I look Da?'

'A real treat,' he assured her.

Norma was wearing a black dress that Effie had found in a WI jumble sale, and which was the very thing for this occasion. She had her new red shoes on, of course, and a brand new pair of Ballito stockings which Effie had gone out that afternoon and bought for her.

'Will you kiss him when you get back?' Eileen asked wickedly, puckering up her lips and making kissing sounds - sounds that quickly degenerated into a fit of giggling.

Lyn laughed. 'And will it be in the back close?'

'There will be no kissing or back close for me!' Norma retorted sharply, thinking of the song from the night before.

'I should think so. And you two stop it!' Brian said, wagging a finger at Eileen and Lyn.

Brian was doing his best to put on a brave front, but was worried sick. It was all right Jim Fullarton saying Norma would be fine, but Glasgow was Glasgow.

'Home by ten thirty mind, no later,' he said to Norma.

'I'll tell Midge that,' Norma replied.

'Make sure you do.'

Brian tried not to think of the big gang fight that had taken place in Sauchiehall Street the weekend before last. The accounts of it in the newspapers had been enough to make your hair stand on end.

Effie glanced over at Brian. His brave front wasn't fooling her any and his eyes gave the game away. They told her how he was really feeling. Nor was she all that happy either, she had to admit it.

There was a knock on the outside door.

'I'll get it!' Eileen said, leaping up from her chair.

Lyn, just to annoy her, beat her to it.

'You're awful quiet the night,' Norma said to Midge. They were on top of a tram taking them into town. He couldn't have said more than a dozen words since picking her up.

'Am I?' he replied, pretending he hadn't realised he'd been.

He's gone right off me, Norma thought. He doesn't fancy me anymore.

But it wasn't that at all. He'd been looking forward all day to seeing her again, and then chapping her door he'd suddenly felt himself clamming up, going all shy. That had surprised him, shocked him even. For he was anything but a shy person. In fact he was normally quite the opposite. No girl had ever had this effect on him before.

He forced himself to make small talk till they came to their stop. From there, it was a short walk to the Majestic. They had to queue to get in.

The hall where the actual dancing took place was a gilt and plush cavern. Norma gaped, she'd never seen the like.

'It's gorgeous,' she breathed, quite overawed.

Roy Fox and his band were already playing. Al Bawley was the vocalist, giving his famed megaphone delivery. Thanks to the megaphone his words rang round the hall like bullets, each bullet crisp and clear.

'Would you like to sit for a bit, or get up right away?' Midge asked.

'Sit I think and ... well just take it all in,' she answered.

They had trouble finding a table, but when they eventually did, secured one that afforded them a good view of the bandstand.

Norma sat entranced, feeling as if she'd strayed into another world, a fairyland.

Eventually they got up to a foxtrot, and it was the same as the previous night. They fused together, to dance as one.

'I enjoyed that, I really did,' Norma enthused as they sat down again.

'I did too.'

She sighed with pleasure, having completely forgotten that he seemed to have gone off her.

For his part Midge was beginning to unclam, his shyness starting to disappear.

'Did you hear those American voices when we were on the floor?' he asked.

She shook her head. 'No.'

'Well I did.' His eyes took on a faraway, dreamy look. It was as if he was seeing something in the far, far distance, something she couldn't.

He went on, now speaking very softly. 'That's one place I'd give my eye-teeth to go to. And one day I will. I've promised myself.'

'What, America?'

'New York, Chicago, San Francisco and the Barbary Coast, all magic names to me, just as Sydney, Cape Town, Bombay, Cairo and many others are. It's not only America I want to see, but Australia, South Africa, India, Egypt and a dozen other countries I could name.'

'Sounds like you've got a real wanderlust,' she replied, smiling.

'I can't think of anything more exciting than travelling. Can you?'

'It doesn't really appeal to me all that much, I'm afraid. I should imagine it would get boring after a while.'

'Boring!' he exclaimed, shaking his head in disbelief. How could travelling possibly be boring!

'And how will you manage this travelling to all these foreign parts?' she asked.

'I don't know yet. But I will somehow. I'm determined.'

A young man's flight of fancy, she thought. And why not, it didn't do any harm to have dreams. It showed imagination, which was a good thing. But probably, like so many working-class Glaswegians, the only travelling he'd end up doing was 'doon ra watter fur ra Fair', which was to say down the Clyde for the Glasgow Fair holidays.

After a while they got up to dance again, and Norma couldn't help noticing that a number of pairs of eyes followed them round the floor. A compliment indeed in a Glasgow dancehall.

The following Wednesday evening, just as the McKenzies were about to sit down to tea, there was a knock on the outside door, which Eileen went to answer.

She came back into the kitchen. 'It's for you, Romeo himself,' she said airily to Norma.

Norma glared at her wee sister. 'Do you mean Midge?'

'Who else do you think I mean!'

'Didn't you ask him in?' Effie called out from the sink where she was draining the potatoes.

'He said he wouldn't as he was wearing his work boots. Maybe he didn't want to take them off because his feet smell,' Eileen jibed.

'Ssshh, he'll hear you!' Norma whispered.

She hurried through to the hall, closing the kitchen door behind her, which made Effie smile, and Brian frown. Her own da's work boots, covered in their usual clart, were just inside the front door where he'd left them on arriving home from work. He cleaned them once a week, on Sunday mornings after he'd had his bacon and egg and read the paper.

'Hello,' said Norma with a smile, wishing her hair wasn't so greasy-looking. She was going to wash it later on.

'I just met a lassie I know called May Hastie who works for the SCWS – that's the Scottish Cooperative Wholesale Society – in Morrison Street, which is off the Paisley Road. She's an office junior there – or at least was. She was informed this morning that she's been promoted and her promotion will take effect as from next week. That means her present job will be going vacant,' he said quickly.

Norma saw right away what he was driving at. 'And you think I should apply?'

'May says she's pretty certain they haven't got anyone lined up.'

There was a warmness in his voice when he spoke the girl's name that was a giveaway. A pang of jealousy stabbed through Norma. 'Is this May an old flame of yours then?' she teased.

Midge looked down and shuffled his feet. There she was making him feel, well, positively shy again. He found that profoundly disturbing.

'Aye she was, but it was a long time ago,' he mumbled.

'It's good of you to think of me Midge. Thank you.'

He cleared his throat. 'It's a huge warehouse in Morrison Street, you can't miss it. May says you should ask for a Mr Scully who does the hiring and firing.'

'I'll be there first thing tomorrow.'

'Good luck then.'

He was on the half landing when she called out. 'And thanks again Midge.'

He gave her a brief smile, then clattered away.

She flew back to the kitchen to tell Brian and Effie.

'How do you feel?' asked Effie.

'How do you think?'

Effie had come with Norma to Morrison Street and the pair of them were now sitting outside Mr Scully's office. Norma would go in alone.

'Now remember, only speak when you're spoken to, and don't ask any questions unless he asks you to.

'I understand,' Norma replied, nodding. Her insides were churning, for she was convinced she had a definite chance. She only prayed her face fitted.

Effie's gaze swept again over Norma, checking for the umpteenth time that she was neat and tidy; that everything was just as it should be. She didn't tell Norma, but she had the collywobbles herself.

'I wonder what the pay is?' Norma whispered.

'Whatever it is, tell him that's fine if you're offered the job. And tell him you can start right away, today if needs be. Let him see how keen you are.'

Mr Scully's door opened and his secretary emerged. 'Miss McKenzie, if you'll just step this way please,' the secretary said.

Norma rose. Her insides weren't just churning anymore, they were in her throat trying to jump out of her mouth.

'Good luck lass,' said Effie.

Norma went through the door feeling as though she was walking to her own execution.

She hung out the window, waiting for Midge to turn into the street on his way home from work. Then she saw him, talking to a couple of other lads he'd met in Gallowgate.

'Midge!' she shouted, gesturing that she was coming down.

When she reached the closemouth she found him waiting for her, the lads he'd been with having gone on.

'I got it! I start Monday,' she blurted out, hugging herself with glee.

'Oh that's smashing, it really is,' he beamed.

'Ma went with me. The warehouse was still closed when we arrived and we had to wait until it opened. Then we had to wait another half an hour before I got in to see Mr Scully, but when I did he was nice as pie. I just know I'm going to enjoy working there.'

'I'm pleased I was able to help, jobs being as scarce as they are and all.'

'Aye, like gold dust,' she agreed. For the chronic unemployment situation was something that had really come home to her since she'd started looking for work.

'Right then, good,' he said.

She placed a hand on his right arm, a gesture that said 'thank you' but in a more intimate way than just speaking the words, then turned, intending to run back up the close.

'Norma?'

She stopped, turning to him again.

'There's a dance on this Friday at Bridgeton Public Halls. The band won't be Roy Fox, but they shouldn't be bad all the same.'

Something flipped inside her. Flipped, fluttered and made her feel warm.

'I'd love to go with you,' she told him.

'Seven o'clock?'

'Seven o'clock. I'll be ready.'

Halfway up the stairs she started to sing.

## *Chapter Three*

It was February of the following year, 1933, and Midge was having a double celebration party at home. Firstly to celebrate his birthday - he'd turned eighteen the previous week - and secondly to celebrate the fact that his three-year apprenticeship was over and that he was now time-served. This meant that he would now be paid a full man's wage instead of a boy's.

Leslie and Alice Henderson, Midge's parents, had two rooms and a kitchen; the party being held in the larger of the two rooms.

The carpet had been rolled back, and a gramophone borrowed to provide music. Leslie had also laid on a couple of crates of beer and a couple of bottles of whisky.

Norma was there, for she and Midge had been courting all this while. So too was Midge's younger sister Katy, who was the same age as Norma, and there were other close friends from the street and round about, about twenty folk in all, a number Alice had declared to be just right for the amount of space they had available.

'Here, have some of this, you look like you could use it,' Midge said to Norma, handing her a glass of beer.

She drank some down, then handed back the glass. She'd just finished an energetic bout of dancing with Billy McManus, a neighbour who was also great pals with Midge.

'Enjoying yourself?' Midge asked.

She nodded. 'And you?'

'Thoroughly.'

She linked an arm round one of his, thinking how happy she was. She was always happy when she was with Midge, and she believed he felt the same way about her. At least that was what he said.

Bob Gillespie who was operating the gramophone now held up a hand and called for silence. The Gillespies lived in Graham Square adjacent to the Cattle Market; he and Leslie Henderson had fought side by side in the Great War.

'A wee bit of hush please!' he yelled.

The noise died away. 'That's better. Now as some of you might know, Midge and his girlfriend Norma there have been going a lot to the jigging lately, and a wee birdie has told me they're rather good. That being the case, and this being his party, I think he and Norma should give us an exhibition. So come on you two, it's a slow waltz.'

Midge looked at Norma. 'Well?'

'Why not,' she answered, and they took the centre of the floor to loud applause.

Bob Gillespie wound up the gramophone and placed the needle on the record. The music of the Savoy Orpheans filled the room.

It was as it always was when they danced together; they fused to become as one. As they swirled round the floor Bob and Beryl Gillespie nodded their appreciation.

When it was over Norma and Midge, more for a laugh than anything else, bowed solemnly first to one side, then to the other, then returned to where they'd been standing.

'That was smashing so it was,' Katy Henderson said to Norma, when the applause that had greeted the end of their exhibition was beginning to die away.

It was funny, Norma thought. It didn't bother her to perform in front of others, in fact she thoroughly enjoyed it. Whereas with other things, such as her interview with Mr Scully at SCWS, she'd go rigid with fright and embarrassment.

Later in the evening Bob and Beryl Gillespie came over to join Norma and Midge, Bob saying he wanted to speak with them.

'Did you know Beryl and I used to go ballroom dancing?' he asked.

'No I didn't.'

'Oh aye, for a number of years actually. We were nothing startling mind, but we both enjoyed it.'

Beryl Gillespie chipped in. 'We had to stop in the end because of my recurring hip bursitis. When something becomes a torture rather than a pleasure then you realise it's the time to give it up.'

'We still go spectating occasionally, but it's not the same thing,' Bob Gillespie said.

'You two have real talent, there's no doubt about it. Have you considered going in for proper ballroom dancing rather than the dancing you go to now?' Beryl asked.

Midge glanced at Norma. They had discussed it vaguely once, but never pursued the subject. 'Not really,' he said slowly.

'You'd find the standard a lot higher than those you're mixing with now, and of course, the most exciting thing about ballroom dancing are the championships. They give you something to aim for. And what an achievement if you could actually win a championship eh? Beryl and I would have given our eye-teeth to have done that, but we were nowhere near good enough,' Bob Gillespie said.

'Isn't it an expensive business though?' Norma asked.

'You mean buying the gowns?' Beryl queried.

'They must cost an awful lot.'

'They can do, if you buy them. But I used to always design and make my own. A lot of the women do that – it's a great deal cheaper that way. But if you were interested, to get you started, I could give you all mine - they're just taking up space in the wardrobe anyway, and your ma could alter them for you. Could she do that?'

'Oh aye, we have a Singer that she's a dab hand with. But I wouldn't have to ask her, I could do the altering myself. I can do everything except cutting out – for some reason I've never been able to get the hang of that so Ma always does it.'

'It can be very very glamorous. Out there with a spotlight on you is an experience that takes some beating,' Beryl went on.

Norma liked the idea of that, and so too did Midge.

'If you are interested why not jump right in at the deep end? This year's Glasgow Latin American Championship is to be held at the Albert Ballroom next month; why not put yourselves in for it?' Bob Gillespie suggested.

'It could be fun,' Norma said, smiling at Midge.

'Aye, but what about tails, he'd need a set of those and they must cost a small fortune,' commented Leslie Henderson.

'It's a pity but I sold mine after Beryl and I gave up, otherwise he'd have been welcome to them,' Bob Gillespie said.

'You certainly couldn't go ballroom dancing without a set,' Alice Henderson said.

'I'm afraid buying a brand new set of tails would be too much for my pocket. Even with my increase in wages it would be way beyond me,' Midge said.

'Then why not buy second-hand? Surely you could pick up a second-hand set somewhere?' Norma suggested.

'I could try.'

'Shall we put our names down then?'

'Do you want us to?'

'Do *you*?'

Midge laughed. 'Let me get the tails first. If I get them then we will.'

'I'm sure you'll find you'll really enjoy yourselves,' Beryl Gillespie beamed.

'And we'll come along to watch and give you support,' Bob Gillespie added.

'I'm looking forward to it already,' Midge said.

So was Norma. She was looking forward to it tremendously, and was glad the Gillespies had suggested it to them.

'I'll drop those gowns in to Alice and she can bring them over to you. You'll have them within the next few days,' Beryl Gillespie told Norma.

Norma couldn't wait.

Early evening two Saturdays later found Norma waiting for Midge to call – they were going out dancing at the Bridgeton Public Halls. She was anxious to hear how he had got on with his latest expedition to find a suitable set of tails.

Midge arrived on the dot of seven, wearing a glum expression.

'I've tried every second-hand clothes shop I know and not one of them has a single set of tails for sale. You'd think such things just didn't exist,' he announced.

'Aye well, it's Glasgow you see. Apart from your ballroom-dancers how many men would own the likes? Precious few I would imagine. And I suppose the toffs who do have them either wear them out or else pass them on to their sons, that sort tending to be mean,' Brian said from where he was sitting by the fireplace.

He had a point, Norma thought. Toffs – real toffs that is and not new money like the Hodgarts – did tend to hang on to things. They were known for it.

'Have you tried the Barrows?' Eileen piped up. The Barrows was a large street market near Glasgow Cross. She went on. 'They say you can get anything there from a stuffed parrot to French postcards.'

'Eileen!' exclaimed Effie. What did she know about French postcards!

Brian gave his youngest daughter a sinker, a look that plainly said, 'We'll have no more mention of things like that young lady, *or else*.'

Eileen smiled sweetly back, and wondered what they'd have said if she'd told them she'd seen half a dozen French postcards that Tommy Jack in her class had got from his brother in the Merchant Navy. But that was her secret, she wasn't telling anyone.

'I haven't tried the Barrows, that's a thought,' said Midge. It was possible he might just get a set there.

'I'll go tomorrow morning,' he told Norma, the Barrows being a Saturday- and Sunday-only market.

'And I'll come with you. I've never been.'

After Norma and Midge had left for the dancing Brian went back to his paper, to the news article about the German Reichstag having been set on fire.

Chancellor Hitler worried him, there was something disturbing about the man. Something very dangerous.

The Barrows was in full swing, with throngs of people surging to and fro on the hunt for bargains. There were a number of stalls that sold second-hand clothes. Norma and Midge began rifling through them.

It was she who found the set of tails, and a smashing set they were too. Hardly worn at all.

'Over here!' she shouted to Midge, and when he joined her she held them up against him for size. He tried on the jacket which was near as dammit to being a perfect fit. The trousers would need to be taken in a bit round the waist.

'How much?' Norma asked the stallholder.

'A fiver and you can take them away.'

Norma glanced at Midge; she knew three pounds to be his maximum. And that was a full week's wage at his new rate.

'That's daylight robbery. You should be wearing a black mask and carrying a pistol,' she replied to the stallholder.

The stallholder grinned. He enjoyed a bit of banter and suspected he was going to get some here.

'A fiver it is missus, and worth every farthing,' he said.

Norma smiled to herself to be called missus; it was really a term for an older woman. She knew he was getting at her.

'There can't be much call for a set of tails in Glasgow. You'll still have them here this time next year if we don't do you a favour by taking them off your hands,' she replied.

'I'll sell them all right, no bother at all.'

'Sez you!'

The stallholder stared at Norma. She stared straight back at him, holding his gaze.

He shrugged. 'Tell you what, as a gesture of goodwill I'll knock a dollar off the price. Four pounds fifteen, I can't say fairer than that.'

She laughed. 'Where do you think the likes of us are going to get that sort of money for a set of tails? We're only working-class folk you know, not blinking royalty.'

'Then why not a nice serge suit? I've got one here I can let you have for thirty bob.'

'I need tails for the dancing,' Midge explained.

'Oh aye?'

'Ballroom dancing,' Norma elaborated.

'I get you now. The real fancy stuff?' he said, and did a few quick steps behind his stall, much to the amusement of the others round about.

'Have you always had club feet?' Norma asked blithely.

The stallholder scowled; he considered himself to be a fairly good dancer. 'Those tails are worth four pounds fifteen. Why, they're almost new,' he said.

Norma looked down at the set of tails. She had her heart set on that Latin American Championship and these were the only set of second-hand ones they'd been able to find.

'I'll tell you what. I must be off my chump but I'll give them to you for four pounds ten. Now how about that?' the stallholder offered.

Norma had ten bob of her own money she could add to Midge's three quid, but that still left them a pound short. She looked again at the set of tails spread before them; she was determined she and Midge were going to walk away with them. *Determined.*

'Give me your three quid,' she said to Midge, holding out her hand. Taking the money from him she put it on the stall, then placed her ten shillings alongside.

'That's all we've got. I swear to you,' she said to the stallholder.

The man eyed the four crumpled notes. He was tempted – but not tempted enough. He was convinced he could do better.

'Sorry hen,' he said, shrugging his shoulders.

'Let's go,' Midge muttered, making to pick up the cash. But he was stopped by Norma tugging his arm.

'Four pounds seven and six, and not a penny less. That is my *final* comedown, I promise you.' the stallholder said, folding his arms resolutely in front of him.

Norma suddenly realised that a crowd had gathered round, all of whom were watching expectantly, waiting to see what was going to happen next.

'It's hopeless,' Midge said to her.

And so it seemed, for it was clear that the stallholder meant what he'd said about not coming down any further.

'Hell's teeth!' she swore, seeing the Latin American Championship fast disappearing down the plughole.

Then she spied a gramophone on an adjacent stall, which gave her an idea.

'Does that grammy work?' she called out to the owner of the stall, pointing at the machine.

He nodded.

'Then would you play it for us please? Something we can dance to.'

'What are you intending to do?' Midge asked in a low voice.

'We're seventeen and six short, so let's see if we can earn it,' she replied and, going over to an old gaffer in the crowd, asked if she could borrow his cap.

The owner of the gramophone was only too happy to oblige; what had he to lose after all? Someone might buy the gramophone as a result. Quickly he wound it up, and put a record on the table. It was a tango.

Realising that something unusual was happening, people were joining the ever-swelling crowd from all directions.

'Right, let's give them an explanation,' Norma said to Midge. Then, in a loud voice so all could hear, 'And all contributions will be welcome so that we can raise the seventeen and a kick we need!'

Glaswegians have a great sense of humour, and this ploy of Norma's appealed. It also showed originality and the refusal to be beaten, both qualities much admired by Mungo's children.

Midge entered into the spirit of the thing, what else could he have done? He bowed to Norma, she to him, and sliding into each other's arms they were off.

The glorious daftness of it all made the day for those watching; soon ha'pennies, pennies, wooden and silver thrup-pennies, and sixpences were flying through the air to land in and around the borrowed cap on the ground.

They danced the same tango again and again to a crowd that, forming in a semicircle round them and standing back to give them room, cheered, clapped, whistled and generally urged them on. They only stopped when it was clear that no more contributions would be coming their way.

Norma gathered up and counted the money. 'We're still one and two short,' she said to Midge.

'Ach tae hell with it. If you want that set of tails so bloody much, and because I enjoyed your dancing, you can have them for what you've got now,' the second-hand clothing stallholder announced, a comment which was greeted by a storm of applause from the crowd.

Norma's cheeks flushed with pleasure. She'd won – they'd got Midge's set of tails after all.

'As we're skint we'll have to walk home,' Midge said to her.

'I don't mind. Do you?'

He shook his head. 'Not one bit.'

The tails were wrapped in brown paper and the parcel tied with string.

The stallholder presented the parcel to Norma. 'You know

what lassie, you'll either end up being somebody in life, or being hung,' he told her.

'Hung probably,' she replied with a laugh.

When the Barrows were behind them Midge took the parcel from her. 'You're something special Norma, very special indeed,' he said quietly, with emotion.

Her reply was to take him by the hand. She was fair bursting with happiness and pride. Fair bursting with it to have had him say that.

'No!' Norma exclaimed and broke away from Midge. Her bosom was heaving, and she'd gone prickly all over.

They were alone in Norma's house, the rest of the McKenzie family having gone to the pictures to see Douglas Fairbanks in *Mr Robinson Crusoe*. Effie was a devoted fan of his.

Norma had stayed in to do some more work on the ballgown she'd decided to wear at the Latin American Championship. Midge had come over by chance to discover her alone.

'I only wanted to ...'

'I know what you wanted to do and you're not going to,' she replied hotly.

'There's no harm in me just ...'

'One thing leads to another, and before we know where we are we'll have gone the whole way. Kissing and cuddling are fine but that's it, that's where I draw the line,' she told him.

Midge threw himself into a fireside chair and put his head in his hands. His expression was thunderous.

'And there's no use doing a big moody on me, I won't change my mind,' she said.

'Other couples ...'

'I don't care what other couples get up to, that's their business, not mine. Or yours either come to that. And anyway, if they are doing such things they shouldn't say, which makes me wonder if they actually are or just pretending in order to impress.'

Midge took a deep breath.

'I know it's supposed to be more difficult for a man than a woman, but that's how it's going to be,' she said, softly this time.

She went to the kitchen window and looked out. It was

pelting with rain outside and bitter wind was blowing, rattling the window panes up and down the tenements.

She tensed slightly to hear him approach her from behind. His arms slid round her waist, and he nibbled her neck.

'That's lovely,' she whispered.

He blew in her ear, then kissed it, his tongue probing deep inside.

Norma's stomach turned to jelly; she felt positively weak at the knees. Her nipples started to ache.

'Don't kid me you don't really want to go any further?' he whispered.

'I didn't say I didn't want to. I said I wasn't going to.'

'Oh Norma!' He spun her round, his mouth seeking hers. As they kissed his left hand brushed against her right breast.

She pushed him away to hold him at arm's length. 'You don't take a telling do you?' she smiled.

'I didn't do anything!' he protested.

She didn't reply, letting the silence between them stretch out. She made her bosom heave as it had done earlier, and slitted her eyes.

'There is one thing I'll do for you,' she husked, her voice thick with passion. Her gaze flicked down to the front of his trousers, then back to his face.

Hope dawned in his eyes. 'What?' he breathed.

She pulled herself close to plaster herself all over him. With one hand she slowly drew his head down to her mouth. He shivered in anticipation.

'Make you a cup of tea,' she whispered into an ear.

For a couple of moments it didn't sink in. Then it did. 'Why you ...'

She laughed loudly, and just a trifle mockingly, as she released him.

'I'll make you a cup of tea,' she repeated, this time in her normal voice.

'See you!' he said, shaking a fist at her. He was more bemused than angry.

Still laughing she picked up the kettle and went back to the sink to fill it. She was doing that when he got his revenge.

There was a loud crack as the flat of his hand connected hard with her backside. She jumped, exclaiming with pain.

'That hurt!' she complained. And it did. Her bottom was stinging. She knew if she'd been able to look there'd be a red weal there.

'Want me to kiss it better?' he asked innocently.

This time it was Midge who laughed loudly.

It was by far the most exciting occasion Norma had ever been to. The atmosphere inside the Albert Ballroom was absolutely electric, the tension at fever pitch.

And the spectacle of the gowns was stunning. It was as if a flight of wildly exotic birds, all colours and combinations of the rainbow, had descended on the hall. The first sight of the gathering had literally taken Norma's breath away, so impressive was it.

The championship had started with forty competing couples, which had now been reduced to twenty. Those twenty were now in the process of being reduced to ten. Norma and Midge, each wearing the number eighteen, were up next.

Norma stared in admiration, and jealousy too, at one of the two couples now on the floor. That particular couple, number thirty-four, were simply magnificent. She was almost open-mouthed to watch them.

'They're terrific eh?' Midge whispered to her.

She nodded agreement. They were indeed.

Norma glanced over to where the Gillespies were sitting. Bob Gillespie gave her a wink, and a thumbs-up sign.

She was wearing the red shoes she'd had for her last birthday, the day she'd met Midge at the street party. She'd chosen the gown she had on specifically because it went with them.

The music ended, and both couples got a round of applause, as everyone did. The five judges sitting on a rostrum at the side of the ballroom went into a huddle. When all twenty of the remaining couples had danced, the chosen ten would be announced.

Norma and Midge rose as the two couples left the floor. Another couple rose also, the other part of their pair.

'Here we go then,' Midge whispered out the side of his mouth. Taking her by the hand he led her onto the floor.

It was a marvellous feeling to have a spotlight on you, Norma thought. It made her bubble inside. Whatever the outcome of the evening she knew she was hooked, and knew that Midge was too.

'Again a jive, this time to Cy Oliver's Opus 1,' the MC announced. As he was backing away the band struck up.

As was required in the jive Midge stayed in the one spot while taking Norma through a series of underarm turns and spins.

Their allotted time was two minutes and it whizzed by so quickly it seemed to Norma that they'd only been up for a handful of seconds. When it was over they bowed, accepting their applause.

'How do you think we did?' Midge asked her in a whisper when they'd sat down again and the next pair of couples were on the floor.

'Hard to say,' she whispered back. For in truth the general standard was very high. Far higher than she'd expected.

A little later the ten couples to go on were announced. They weren't one of them.

Norma bit back her disappointment. She'd hoped . . . Aye well maybe she'd been silly, not to say naive, to hope too much.

In the end the championship was won by the couple, number thirty-four who Norma and Midge had so admired, their final dance a paso doble to El Gato Montez.

Norma lay in bed staring up at the ceiling - Lyn and Eileen were sleeping in the other bed, a double, and Lyn was snoring - she was a terrible snorer, like her da.

Tonight had been a real eye-opener, Norma thought, her mind filled with the championship. She'd enjoyed it, oh thoroughly, but was ... what? She decided the word she was searching for was *frustrated*, yes that was it, she was frustrated that she and Midge hadn't done better, that they'd been so outclassed by many of the other couples taking part.

The way she and Midge danced was raw, simplistic and in many cases purely instinctive, she now realised. Which was well and good as far as it went. But if they were going to go in for other competitions - and she had every intention they would - they were going to have to build on that. In other words, a great deal of learning was going to have to be done by her and Midge if they were to achieve the sort of class they'd seen in the Albert Ballroom.

'What an achievement to win a championship,' Bob Gillespie had said the night of Midge's party. She now knew exactly what he meant, and swore to herself she was going to make that dream come true for her and Midge.

Eventually she fell asleep to dream of the championship, only this time it was herself and Midge who were couple number thirty-four, and who danced that final paso doble to win.

'If you want proper lessons then there's only one place to go, and that's Silver's over by the Citizens' Theatre,' Bob Gillespie said in reply to Norma's question.

'Have you any idea what the cost of lessons are?' Midge asked, worried about the money. Now that he was earning a full wage he was expected to contribute the same amount as his father did into the house. He wasn't left with hellish much after, though quite a bit more than he'd had as an apprentice.

Bob Gillespie looked at his wife Beryl who shook her head; she didn't know either.

'Sorry, can't help you there. I only know the place by reputation, nothing else,' Bob Gillespie said.

'And it's the Citizens' Theatre, that's in the Gorbals isn't it?' Norma queried.

Midge nodded.

'Not too far from where I work. I'll drop by tomorrow and find out what they charge,' Norma said.

She and Midge stayed with the Gillespies for an hour after that, talking about the Latin American Championship and how much they'd enjoyed it.

Finlay Rankine looked up from where he was sitting as Norma came in through the door of the studios. He was immediately struck by her, forcibly so.

A real cracker, he thought, eyeing her up and down. Deliciously nubile, just the way he liked them best.

She gave him a hesitant smile, and walked over to him. He noticed how sensuous her walk was – it was the walk of a born dancer.

There were three full-time instructors at Silver's, of which Finlay was one. Between them they virtually ran the place, the owners only appearing roughly every fortnight or so, sometimes not even as much as that.

'Can I help you?' he asked, rising to greet her.

Norma introduced herself, and explained why she'd come. Finlay replied that before they talked about money he'd show her round.

The smell of her made Finlay's nose twitch in appreciation. And those eyes, were they grey or were they green? They seemed to go from one to the other. He found them mesmeric.

Norma was impressed by what she saw, very much so. She'd thought that being in the Gorbals, Silver's might be quite tatty but she couldn't have been more wrong.

Finlay showed her all the facilities, ending up in the studio where he was about to teach. As they'd gone along Norma had explained about her and Midge having just taken up ballroom dancing, and how keen they were to improve.

'Let's see what you can do now,' Finlay said, and put a record on the gramophone. It was a foxtrot.

He'd been right, he thought as they glided round the studio, she was a natural mover. She was also very sexy; sexier than Trish whom he'd just broken off with. He'd met her at Silver's also.

When the record was finished Finlay reluctantly released Norma.

'There are three important considerations to remember when dancing the foxtrot: direction, follow-through and dance position. I would teach you to achieve all three to the best advantage. Also, amongst other things, the length of your stride is too long at the moment and because of this you're frantically losing control of your balance. And then there's contrabody – you're not employing that at all. If you're going to compete, it's essential you do,' he said.

'I'm afraid I don't even know what contrabody is.'

He gave her a thin, crocodile-like smile. 'Contrabody is when if I take a step with my right foot, for example, I swing the left side of my body towards that foot and vice versa. This action of turning the opposite hip and shoulder towards the moving leg facilitates the art of rotation. Understand?'

'I think so,' she said slowly.

Finlay glanced at the wall clock. His client would be arriving at any minute. He brought his attention back to Norma. She was so tempting, he could have gorged himself on her there and then.

'*You* have talent – what about your boyfriend?' he asked.

'Let me put it this way, if I've got talent then so has he,' she replied.

He grunted, believing her. A dozen steps or so is all it takes for one good dancer to recognise another.

'So what do you charge then?' Norma asked.

'We don't do individual lessons but courses. The minimum course is twenty lessons which for a combined lesson – that's you and your boyfriend together – would be thirty pounds,' Finlay replied.

Norma's eyes opened wide. 'How much?'

'Thirty pounds, payable in advance.'

Norma was staggered. After seeing the place she'd expected the prices to be steep, but nothing like that.

'And are those lessons an hour each?' she queried in a weak voice.

'No, half an hour.'

Worse still, she thought. Well that was it, Silver's was out for her and Midge, the prices were quite beyond their reach. Thirty quid! She wasn't just staggered; she was stunned.

'I'm sorry I've wasted your time,' she said to Finlay.

He'd already guessed she wouldn't be able to afford Silver's; it was unusual for them to have a client who was other than middle-class. Most of their clients were bored wives – often childless – who took the lessons as a hobby. Trish, a member of the childless contingent, had been one such, her husband a bank manager.

'A pity, you being so keen,' Finlay said slowly.

'Yes, I'll just have to find some other way to learn,' she replied.

'There are no alternative dance studios in Glasgow; we're the only one.'

She looked around to check where the door was, preparing to leave.

'However there *is* a way you can have a course here, for nothing,' he said silkily, treating her to another of his crocodile smiles.

Norma frowned. For nothing? What did he mean?

'I would teach you in the evenings, my final client of the day,' he continued, still smiling.

'And my boyfriend?'

'No boyfriend. Just you.'

'But we . . .' She stopped as the penny dropped. 'I wouldn't be paying?'

He nodded.

'And no boyfriend?'

He nodded again.

Outrage filled her. That and anger, and fear too. 'Are you propositioning me?' she demanded, voice tight.

'I find you exceptionally attractive. So I'll be nice to you if . . . you'll be the same to me.'

She couldn't believe she was hearing this. Why the dirty sod, what did he take her for!

'Enough lessons and I could make you, if not *the* best then certainly one of the best ballroom-dancers in Glasgow,' he purred. He had a flat in the West End with a big double bed in it, and could just picture her, naked, lying on it. He could feel himself getting excited at the thought. Excited, and he hadn't laid a finger on her yet.

'I wouldn't go with a slimy creep like you if you were the last man on earth,' she exploded in a vehement hiss.

He came forward very quickly to grab her by the waist. 'Don't turn my offer down out of hand – at least mull it over when you get home. I can always be contacted here should you change your mind.'

'I won't be changing my mind. Now let me go!'

He released her, still smiling his crocodile smile.

Heart thumping, she marched to the door and wrenched it open. She knew tears weren't far away.

'Your boyfriend's a lucky fella. I envy him,' Finlay said.

She turned in the doorway; she'd wipe that bloody smile off his face. It had just come to her how to do so.

'I didn't mention my boyfriend's name, did I?' She paused for effect, then said, 'Sammy McGuigan. His name's Sammy McGuigan. Maybe you've heard of him?'

The smile vanished as though by magic, and Finlay's face went a sick, milky-white. Sammy McGuigan was a notorious gang leader and razor king. Everyone in Glasgow had heard of Sammy McGuigan, he was regarded as a local Genghis Khan or Attila the Hun.

'Are you... will you...?' Finlay croaked from what were now bloodless lips.

'Tell him about your proposition? You'll just have to wait and find out, won't you?' she replied, and made off up the corridor that would take her to the reception area and out of the building.

She left a stricken Finlay behind her, so rigid from shock and terror he might have been carved out of stone.

She managed to reach the street before the tears came. What a horrible, dirty thing to have happened. And then with the tears came laughter, so that she was laughing and crying at the same time.

Oh by God she'd wiped that smile off his face all right! Sammy McGuigan, she'd been inspired to come up with that.

She'd left Finlay Rankine with a lot to think about. She must have scared him out of a year's growth.

It was several minutes before she was able to compose herself sufficiently to continue her way home.

'Aye of course we'll be happy to pass on all we know,' Bob Gillespie said.

After Silver's had fallen through – she hadn't told Midge about Finlay Rankine in case there had been a fight and he'd got into trouble with the police – they'd discussed what to do next, and it had seemed logical to them to approach the Gillespies to ask if they would help.

She and Midge had arrived at the Gillespies' about half an hour previously, but had to wait for Bob Gillespie to arrive home from work. He worked at the Cattle Market, a stone's throw away, where his job was to look after the cattle while they were on the premises, and herd them round during auctions, keeping them on the move so that bidders could satisfy themselves that none of the beasts were lame.

'That's very good of you, thank you,' Midge replied.

'We've already got a gramophone so there's no worry there,' said Beryl.

'Yes I think it best if we do it all here, at our home. Is that all right with you?' Bob Gillespie asked.

'Fine,' Norma nodded.

'How about two sessions a week, Tuesdays and Thursdays say?' Bob Gillespie suggested.

Norma glanced at Midge. 'Sounds excellent to me,' he said.

And so it was agreed, seven o'clock on Tuesdays and Thursdays - from then on Norma and Midge would present themselves at the Gillespie house to be taught what the Gillespies could teach them.

Friday night six weeks later Norma was in the room getting herself ready to go out with Midge. They were going to the Locarno Ballroom in Sauchiehall Street which had become something of a favourite of theirs of late. The night was going to be a big one; Victor Silvester and his band were playing.

Brian was away for a drink with Jim Fullarton and Sandy Reid; Lyn out somewhere, Norma didn't know where; and Eileen round at a pal's. Effie was through the kitchen knitting a new sleeveless pullover for Da.

Norma decided she needed the toilet and went. On returning to the house she went into the kitchen for a lipstick she'd left there, to discover Effie sitting in a fireside chair, knitting in front of her, tears rolling down her face.

'Ma! What's wrong?' Norma exclaimed, and hurried to Effie's side.

'Get me a clean hanky will you lass,' Effie said.

Norma went and got a hanky from the drawer where they were kept, came back to her mother and handed it to her. Effie wiped the tears away, dabbing her brimming eyes.

Norma knelt beside her ma. 'What is it? Is something wrong?'

'Not wrong, I was just...' Effie blew her nose, and wiped away more tears that had found their way onto her cheeks. 'Just thinking about our wee cottage at Kilmichael House, and what it used to be like living there. The flowers, the trees, the sea, the freshness of the air, and the cleanliness of it all.'

'I miss it too, I'm sure we all do,' Norma said quietly.

'You may miss it, but you and the other two have completely

settled in here. You're young you see, and the young can adapt a lot easier than us old ones.'

'If only there was a Womens' Institute branch hereabouts,' Norma said, Effie having been previously much involved with the WI. But there wasn't a WI in Bridgeton, it just wasn't the sort of area to support one.

Effie wiped away more tears. 'It's the countryside I miss more than the WI. A thousand and one things, the droning of the bees, the flitter of butterflies in flight, cows on their way home to be milked, daisies and clover – all the things I took for granted for so long, all of which have been totally removed from my life. And in their place? The sour stink of Bridgeton, filthy streets, soot-laden air, dirt and grime everywhere.'

Norma took one of her mother's hands and squeezed it. 'Have you spoken to Da about this?' she asked.

Effie shook her head. 'No, I don't have to tell him how I feel, he knows. Just as I know he doesn't enjoy working at Glasgow Green one iota as much as he did at Kilmichael House. He's never said, nor will I.'

'You're right about us younger ones getting used to Glasgow. When we first came here I used to think about our cottage at Kilmichael House and Kirn all the time, now I rarely do.'

'And that's how it should be if we're going to live here,' Effie replied.

Effie took a deep breath, then another. 'I'm all right now, I'm over my silliness. Have you got time for a cup of tea before you go?'

Norma glanced at the clock on the mantelpiece. Midge would be there at any moment, for he was always prompt. Well he'd just have to wait.

'A cup of tea would go down a treat,' she smiled back.

From somewhere nearby came the sound of voices raised in anger. There was a shout, followed by the crash of breaking glass. A window had either been put in or out.

Norma and Effie pretended not to hear a thing.

Norma and Midge came out of Green's Playhouse in the town. They'd just been to see Fred Astaire in *Dancing Lady*. They'd both been entranced, never once having taken their eyes off that mesmeric figure up there on the silver screen.

'Wasn't he just ... unbelievable!' Norma breathed.

'You can say that again.'

They walked a little way in silence, heading for their tram-stop, both lost in the memory of what they'd just seen.

'Imagine dancing alongside him, wouldn't that be the ultimate.' Midge said, awed at such a prospect.

A small smile curled Norma's lips upwards. 'No, to be as *good* as him, *that* would be the ultimate,' she replied.

Midge barked out a laugh. She was quite right of course. Trust Norma to see it that way.

They arrived at the tramstop and joined the queue. There would be a tram along soon. It was a regular, and busy, service.

Norma said in a quiet voice. 'You know that we've gone as far as we can with Bob and Beryl. We've learned a fair amount from them during these past four months. But that road's one we've come to the end of.'

'Yes, I agree. They've been floundering these last few weeks trying to think up something new to teach us,' Midge replied.

The Gillespies, bless them, had been helpful, but only to a degree, thought Norma. There was still much more, particularly in the realms of technique, for them to learn if they were ever going to win a championship.

So what to do next? What they really needed was to be taught by a top-ranking couple like the one, number thirty-four, who had won the Glasgow Latin American Championship. But Norma knew, as did Midge, that there was little hope of that. Bob Gillespie had explained to them that the top rankers never willingly passed anything on, such was the intense rivalry at that level.

'I suppose all we can do now is keep watching and pick up what we can that way,' Midge said.

Norma agreed reluctantly. She couldn't see any alternative, not for the moment anyway. But it was a very unsatisfactory, not to mention roundabout, way of doing things.

A tram rattled along, and they went on board, going on top to please Midge who preferred travelling there.

'I enjoyed the wee picture as well, it was a real bobby dazzler right enough,' Midge enthused. The *B* picture had been a travelogue on the Kalahari Desert.

'Wasn't that scenery breathtaking,' he continued. 'And what

about those bushmen with the big fat backsides who live there, weren't they absolutely fascinating.'

'I didn't think the scenery breathtaking at all, in fact I thought it looked pretty horrible. Sand and scrubland, what's breathtaking about that? And as for your bushmen with the big fat backsides...' She shuddered.

'But didn't you see that blood-red sunset. I've read about sunsets like that and always thought the description was an exaggeration. Now I know it isn't.'

He paused. Then, eyes miles away, added, 'I'd give anything to experience a sunset like that. To actually be there and watch it happen. It must be... well, it must be out of this world.'

Norma stared at Midge. Him and his wanting to travel, pipe-dreams he should grow out of.

After all how would he, a Glasgow flint mill-worker, ever get to the Kalahari? The idea was ludicrous.

She went back to thinking about Fred Astaire, and *Dancing Lady*. What he'd done with his feet and body had been poetry, sheer poetry. The man was a genius.

'I thought so, ten days overdue. Do you know how much that'll cost you in a fine? And it'll cost *you* young woman for neither your da or I will pay it,' Effie said, waving a library book at Eileen.

'There's no panic, don't worry,' Eileen replied, looked completely unconcerned.

'So you're not worried about money, you've found a tree that grows the stuff have you? For if you have I wish you'd show it to me, I could certainly use a handful of what it grows,' Effie went on waspishly. She hated money being wasted, and paying out fines on library books was a waste as far as she was concerned.

'I won't have to pay any fine,' Eileen said.

Norma glanced up from where she was doing some hand stitching on a new ballroom gown she was making, the first that was truly hers and not an alteration or remake. Not that there was anything wrong with those Beryl Gillespie had so kindly given her, just that in their design they were older than she would have wished. The material she was now working on had come her way from a lad at the SCWS who'd sold it to her dirt cheap, warning her not to mention where she'd got it from as it had 'fallen off the back of a lorry'. Nor had she told anyone, certainly not her ma. If she had told Effie it was nicked Effie would have had a canary.

'And why's that?' Effie demanded, thinking the girl was havering. But Eileen wasn't.

'Because of Charlie Marshall, one of the librarians. I often take books back late and he always slips them through for me,' Eileen replied.

Effie stared at her daughter. 'And why does he do that?'

'Why do you think Ma! Because he *likes* me, that's why.

Norma giggled.

'I'm not a baby anymore you know, though I'm treated as one round here often enough,' Eileen protested, worried now about Effie's reaction. Maybe she should have kept her mouth shut.

'And how old is this Charlie Marshall?' Effie asked quietly.

'Seventeen. He started in the library last year.'

Effie threw the library book onto the table, then went over to the sink so she could turn her back on Eileen. She didn't want her youngest to see her face.

'Does he know how old *you* are?' Effie queried.

'Oh aye, thirteen next month. That came out in a conversation I had with him a week past Thursday. We met in the street and stood chaffing for a while.

Effie rinsed through some cloths she had boiled, then wrung them out. Eileen was right, she was growing up fast, and a lot more quickly than the other two had done. She supposed she could thank Glasgow for that.

Effie looked at Eileen's reflection in Brian's shaving mirror that hung on a nail by the side of the window. She kept forgetting that Eileen was technically a woman now, and had been for a while.

'You just make sure that chaffing in the street and his slipping books by for you is all that happens,' she said ominously.

Eileen completely lost her bravado on hearing that, and blushed. 'Aye of course,' she muttered in reply.

It wouldn't be long before her youngest was courting, Effie thought with mixed emotions. How time flew, particularly where children were concerned.

She gazed out at the middens down at the back – their bins

overflowing as usual – only it wasn't the middens she saw, but a secret place in Bluebell Wood where she and Brian had done a lot of their courting. A beautiful spot, particularly when the bluebells were in bloom.

Why she could remember . . . She nodded at the memory, one of dozens that came flooding back.

Norma realised she needed to go to the toilet, and laid her stitching aside. She'd take it up again when she returned.

She was collecting the toilet roll from where it was kept in the hall when the outside door opened and Lyn came in.

'You've got chocolate on your mouche,' Norma said to Lyn who, brushing past, mumbled something about an éclair she hadn't been able to resist.

Her sister was getting bigger all the time, Norma thought as she went into the toilet and snecked the door. She was far more than a podge now; she was becoming a right fattie.

Norma sat and, having forgotten to bring something to read, her mind turned to the conversation that had taken place upstairs between Eileen and Ma.

Slowly a smile spread across her face. That could just be the answer to her problem. It could just be indeed.

Charlie Marshall was skinny, even by Glasgow standards, with a wispy moustache and a couple of plooks on his forehead. But he wasn't bad looking at all; Norma had seen a lot worse.

'How are you today Charlie?' Eileen asked coyly.

'Fine Eileen, and yourself?'

'Feeling guilty about this,' she replied, handing him the library book that was ten days overdue.

Charlie looked at the date page, then up at Norma, wondering who she was.

'This is my eldest sister,' Eileen explained.

The book disappeared under the counter. 'You're a naughty girl you know,' Charlie admonished Eileen.

'I know,' Eileen whispered in reply, and blinked her eyes at Charlie.

Why the little minx, she was flirting with the lad! Norma thought in astonishment. And Charlie, grinning foolishly back at Eileen, appeared to be loving every minute of it.

'My sister wants you to do her a favour, will you Charlie?' purred Eileen, then gave him an appealing smile.

Norma had never seen this side of Eileen before. Talk about a budding *femme fatale*! She had Charlie eating out of the palm of her hand.

'Of course I will,' Charlie replied.

With a hint of triumph in her eyes Eileen made a gesture to Norma indicating she should speak.

Norma explained to an attentive Charlie what she was after, and he replied that though he had nothing worthwhile on the subject in his library, leave it to him and he'd do his best for her.

A week later Norma left the library with half a dozen books on ballroom dancing that Charlie had obtained for her from other libraries. He'd tipped her the wink not to be too concerned about getting them back on their due date; just as long as they came back through him everything would be hunky dory. And when she'd done with those he'd have others waiting for her.

Hurrying home, Norma took the books into the room, stretched out on her bed and picked up the top one. The book was brand new, the first item it dealt with the rumba, a dance that had recently taken the United States by storm.

Basic box step, open cuban walk, side break, forward rock ... Brow furrowed in concentration, she began to read.

# *Chapter Four*

Norma felt sick; she had felt sick all evening since seeing who was on the panel of five judges – the instructor from Silver's, Finlay Rankine. Up until the moment of clapping eyes on him she'd thought that she and Midge had their best ever chance yet of winning a championship. Now she was convinced Rankine would do the dirty on the pair of them in retaliation for her turning him down and giving him such a fright about Sammy McGuigan.

The date was 5th November 1934, the venue the Plaza Ballroom in Glasgow's Southside where the All Lanarkshire Open Championship was being held. Norma was now seventeen and a half years old while Midge was nineteen, twenty that coming February. They'd been dancing competitively for twenty months now, and in that time had taken two second places and three thirds. But still the number one, that winning place, eluded them.

There were six couples left who would dance as individual couples one after the other. Rankine had let them come this far, Norma thought grimly. Now he'd slide the knife in.

For the umpteenth time that evening she glanced across to where Rankine was sitting, and for the umpteenth time he refused to meet her gaze.

She brought her attention back to the floor as the first of the six got up to dance.

The minutes ticked by as couple followed couple onto the floor, all of them turning in excellent performances. Then it was their turn.

As she stood up she suddenly relaxed, the tension, anxiety and disappointment caused by Finlay Rankine's presence suddenly draining out of her. It was all a formality anyway, their fate had already been decided, she told herself. But sod it, that wouldn't detract from her performance. She'd give it all she'd got - and then some more.

The dance was a saunter revé, the tune they would be dancing to 'In My Solitude'. The band struck up, and they were away.

As they took their bow she knew they'd done well, had been in cracking form. The magic between her and Midge had never been stronger. Bob Gillespie, sitting among the spectators with his wife Beryl, gave her a beaming smile and the thumbs-up sign.

Then it was all over, and time for the results to be announced. The MC returned from the judges to take the centre of the floor. He held up his hands for hush, and the excited buzz turned to silence.

He made a short speech, interspersed with a few not very funny jokes, thanking everyone connected with the championship. He made a special point of saying what a high overall standard there had been that night, which was absolutely true, there had been.

'And now the results,' the MC went on. 'In third place, couple number fourteen, Mr and Mrs John Garland!'

The Garlands got an enthusiastic round of applause as they walked over to the judges, where they were presented with a small medal apiece. Still to applause, they returned to their chairs.

'In second place, couple number forty-five, Miss Jane Milne and Mr David Liddell!'

This was another young couple, though older than Norma and Midge. They too got an enthusiastic response as they went up to collect a Waterford bowl.

She and Midge had been better than those two, Norma thought bitterly. She was certain of that. But now it was the winners' turn to be announced and she wondered who they would be?

'And now, in first place, winners of the All Lanarkshire Open Championship.' The MC paused, smiled tantalisingly, stretching the moment out. 'Couple number twenty-one, Miss Norma McKenzie and Mr Michael Henderson!' The last said in a rush of words.

For a second or two Norma didn't take it in, so convinced was she that Rankine would have done the dirty on her and Midge. Then she did.

They'd won their first championship. *They'd won!*

She looked at Midge who was flushed with pride and success.

'We did it,' he choked.

She nodded. They had. They'd done it. And the feeling was a glorious one, like being filled from top to toe with fizzy bubbles.

They rose and crossed over to the judges, where they were presented with a silver cup.

'Congratulations,' the five judges said in unison.

Norma and Midge shook each of the judges by the hand; Rankine smiling at her when she shook his.

Norma glanced over at the Gillespies who were both on their feet clapping furiously.

It was a popular win; that much was clear from the ear-battering applause. Midge waved a few times, and Norma nodded her head. Midge gave her the cup to hold which she did at shoulder height, then above her head. People laughed approvingly at that, and applauded even more fiercely.

The Gillespies came charging over to thump Midge's back and kiss Norma. The pair of them were babbling on nineteen to the dozen.

'I knew you could do it in time, I knew it!' Bob Gillespie raved excitedly to Norma, turning again to his wife, his voice a whole octave higher than it normally was. 'Didn't I always say that Beryl, didn't I?'

It was a little later when things had begun to calm down somewhat that Norma, temporarily separated from Midge, found Finlay Rankine at her side.

'Congratulations again, you and your partner fully deserved to win. It was an outstanding performance, and outstanding is a word I don't use lightly.'

'Thank you Mr Rankine,' she replied, embarrassed not by his praise, but by having to talk to him.

'There was no doubt about the outcome after that saunter revé. At least not in my mind.'

'I thought... Well, to be honest when I saw you on that panel I thought Midge and I didn't stand a chance.'

He treated her to one of his crocodile smiles. 'You were referring to that tale of yours about Sammy McGuigan?'

She nodded.

'Most effective it was too. I went around quaking in my shoes for the next fortnight, fully expecting McGuigan to come springing out at me with a razor in either fist, till I read that big article the *Evening Citizen* did on him.'

'I read it too,' Norma said.

Two weeks after she'd been to Silver's the *Evening Citizen* had done a full-page feature on McGuigan in which it had been stated that he had a long standing girlfriend whose name Norma couldn't now recall, but which certainly hadn't been hers. There had also been a picture of the girlfriend with McGuigan.

'And you thought I'd make sure you didn't get placed tonight because of that and because you refused me?'

She nodded again.

'I can understand you thinking that, but no, it's not my style. I may have faults, but cheap revenge isn't one of them. Anyway, I doubt I could have influenced the result against you even if I'd wanted to. You and Mr Henderson were simply streets ahead of the others. And I mean streets.'

'Thank you,' she whispered.

'I mean it, I assure you. By the way, did you tell Mr Henderson, Midge you just called him, about...?

'No,' she interjected.

'Well that's a relief. He might not be McGuigan, but I'm sure he's quite capable of doing his best to punch my head in. So tell me – I've been dying to know all night – who did teach you, bring you up to the level you're now at?'

'Some friends did help for a while, but we quickly absorbed all they could give us. After that it was me,' she replied.

He stared at her blankly, suspecting his leg was being pulled again. 'You? How so?' he queried.

'Me, and books on dancing. I must have read dozens of books on the subject, and still am. Books by experts, world champions. Books that specialise on the waltz, the foxtrot, the quickstep, the merengue, the mambo. Books on the history of modern dancing, books on various techniques and the application of these techniques.

'For example, let's take the history of the waltz. Did you know it originated in the country folk dances of Bavaria? Or that it didn't become popular among the European middle class until the first decade of this century? Up until then it was the cherished property of the aristocracy. Yet, in the United States, where they don't have a blue blood caste, it was being danced by the ordinary people as early as 1840.

'I can go on if you like?'

Finlay Rankine was dumbfounded, momentarily speechless.

She continued. 'Let's move from history to practice. When you dance the waltz you should do so with your entire body, all side-steps long and wide in order to obtain control and fluidity of movement. Knees should be kept flexed and never allowed to lock, otherwise your leg will move stiffly. However, when step patterns indicate you bring your feet together or cross them, your knees will not be as flexed as otherwise.

'Want me to go on?'

He shook his head, and found his voice. 'You're saying you learned everything from books?'

'Not everything. The books explain in detail how it should be done; we then watch others and see the translation from the page onto the floor so to speak, the realisation of the theory. We absorb both, then try to do better than the people we've been watching, or are competing against.'

'I'll be damned!' Finlay swore. He'd never heard of anyone doing it this way before. It was a novel approach. And very successful too, borne out by what he'd seen, and judged, earlier.

'And it was your idea to get these books and learn that way?' he asked.

'It was.'

'Aren't you the clever one. I'm impressed, very much so.'

'Thank you,' Norma replied, acknowledging his compliment.

'Of course doing what you did is one thing, but it wouldn't have amounted to what it has without the natural talent you and Mr Henderson have in abundance. It's a talent that comes right out and smacks one in the eye. In fact I'll go so far as to say the pair of you have the most potential I've personally ever come across. But . . .' He let the word hang in the air. 'You still have things to learn: nuances, the precisely correct line of a leg for example, that you won't get from a book, or pick up from watching because those you're watching – unless you're at top national and international level – won't be doing it. What I'd like to do is take you under my wing for a spell and teach you those little additions that can ratchet the quality of your performance up another notch or two.'

Norma raised an eyebrow. 'For free I suppose?'

'Yes, because you excite me. In the dancing sense that is.'

'And what about my boyfriend Midge? I don't suppose this generous offer includes him?' She asked sarcastically.

'The offer is to the pair of you as a couple, with no funny business attached. You have my sworn oath on that.'

He took out his wallet and produced a card. 'This is my home telephone number. Talk it over with Mr Henderson, and if you decide you would like my help then have him ring me. Which I may say, I hope he does.

Norma accepted the card. 'I'll talk to Midge about it later,' she replied.

'Goodbye for now then,' Finlay Rankine said, and walked away.

How about that, wasn't that a turn-up for the book! Norma thought. If Finlay Rankine could do as he'd promised, ratchet their performance up another notch or two as he'd put it, then this was an opportunity to be grabbed with both hands. And grab it they would, she'd see to that.

By golly she would.

Norma had just washed her hair in the sink and Lyn was in the process of doing so while Eileen was waiting to follow Lyn, when there was a rat-a-tat-tat on the outside door.

'I'll get it,' said Eileen, leaving the kitchen.

Brian, puffing on his pipe, was listening to Herbert Tatlock in 'Bitter Brevities' on the wireless and enjoying the rare fire that Effie had made. He was just getting over a cold, and still not feeling his best.

Eileen poked her head back into the kitchen. 'It's Midge; he wants to speak to you da,' she said.

'Wait up!' Lyn exclaimed from the sink, gave her hair a final quick rinse, wrapped it in a towel, and then hurriedly shrugged herself into a dressing gown.

By this time Norma had risen from the front of the fire where she'd been kneeling, drying her hair and combing it through. She too was in a dressing gown, as was Eileen.

Midge come to see her da and not her? She wondered what this was all about.

'I'll make a cup of tea,' said Effie who'd been tidying out the press. A visitor was always an excuse to put the kettle on. She switched the wireless off.

'You can come in now, she's decent,' Eileen said over her shoulder to Midge.

'I've got some news that might interest you, Mr McKenzie,' Midge announced the moment he was in the kitchen.

'Oh aye?'

'Do you know the Smarts who live in a three-room and kitchen on the next landing up from us?'

'He and I say hello and occasionally pass the time of day,' Brian replied.

'Well, I've just been talking to him. He's been unemployed for the past five months, got laid off from a firm over in Springburn, and was beginning to find things very difficult indeed. Anyway, to cut a long story short, he's landed himself a new job in Paisley which, because it's so far away, means he and his family are going to have to move.'

Brian blew out a stream of smoke, not seeing what Midge was driving at. 'That's very interesting son, and I'm certainly pleased for Mr Smart, to be idle being a terrible thing. But what's that got to do with me?'

'It's the house, isn't it?' said Norma, quick to grasp the point.

'If the Smarts flit, the house above us will be available, and it's a *three*-room and kitchen. I remember hearing Mrs McKenzie saying not long ago how cramped you were here,' Midge replied.

'I see now,' Brian said, stroking his chin. They were worse than cramped, bursting at the seams more like. A three-room and kitchen would certainly solve a lot of problems, and now that Lyn was working as well as Norma, and it wouldn't be long till Eileen was also, they could afford the larger house.

Norma had been promoted at the SCWS to filing clerk, and Lyn had been taken on in her old job as office junior. The two of them now went and came back from Morrison Street together.

'Anyone else after it?' Brian asked.

'Not as I've heard. That doesn't mean to say there isn't, mind you. But if you were interested then the quicker you speak out to the factor the better.'

'Oh I'm interested all right.' He looked over at Effie. 'First thing tomorrow morning it's the factor's office for you girl.'

'I'll be there when he opens up,' Effie promised, delighted at the prospect of a bigger place. It had become so that they all felt they were living like sardines in a can.

'Let's hope it comes off then,' Midge smiled.

Brian rose and shook Midge by the hand. 'It's very kind of you to come and tell us. It's not the first time we're indebted to you either,' he said, the latter referring to the fact it had been Midge's tip that had landed Norma her job at SCWS.

'Aye, well that's what friends are for,' Midge replied. He was that sort of person; if he could do a person a good turn he would.

He turned to Norma. 'There's something else. I've also been talking to Bob Gillespie - or I should say he's been talking to me - about the Edinburgh Veleta Championship which is coming up in three weeks time. He thinks we should go in for it and that we have a very strong chance of winning.'

'Let's have a go then,' Norma replied with enthusiasm.

'There's just one snag though. The evening won't finish until after the last train has gone, which means staying the night in a hotel in Edinburgh.'

'No,' said Brian firmly. 'That's definitely out.'

Norma pulled a face. 'I rather fancy the thought of a hotel, I've never stayed in one.'

'No disrespect to you Midge, but Brian's right. It just isn't on,' Effie said.

'I wouldn't ask if it was only Norma and myself, that would hardly be respectable, we've her name to consider after all. But the thing is the Gillespies, whom you've met, would be with us, and would be acting as chaperones.' Midge went on.

Brian took a draw of his pipe. That did alter matters considerably. He glanced across at Effie, and saw she thought so too.

'Please Da? The Edinburgh Veleta Championship is a very prestigious event. It would be a tremendous feather in our caps if we won it,' Norma pleaded.

'The Gillespies know a hotel in Newtown that's very reasonable and which they can recommend,' Midge added.

'What about work the next day?' Brian queried.

'It's a Saturday night event,' Midge explained.

The Gillespies were a fine respectable couple, Brian told himself, everything would be above board - and seen to be - with them in attendance.

'Effie?' he said, looking again at his wife.

'In the circumstances I'll agree if you do,' she replied.

Brian took another pull of his pipe. 'I went to Edinburgh once, didn't like it. The folk walk around with their noses in the air as if there's a permanent bad smell around them. Didn't take to them at all. A cold folk, very cold,' he said, and sat down.

'Does that mean we can go?' asked Norma.

'I'll expect you to bring me back a stick of Edinburgh rock. If there's one good thing ever came out of Edinburgh it's their rock, fair smashing so it is,' Brian said.

'Tomorrow night at my house for practice?' Midge smiled at Norma.

'Tomorrow night for practice,' she agreed.

Norma rewound the gramophone while Midge was away at the toilet, a gramophone he'd found and bought cheap from somewhere. They both bought records for it on a regular basis. They had two large stacks of them; some were new, some second-hand.

She and Midge had been practicing for the Veleta Championship which was now only four days away, and would practice every night until Saturday. Thursday and Friday nights they would be with Finlay Rankine who was proving a tremendous help to them. Norma had come to the conclusion that what Finlay didn't know about dancing just wasn't worth knowing.

She decided she was tired of the Veleta for the moment, and would put another type of music on, the merengue, which the Haitians, who claim to have originated it, call the singing dance.

Midge returned from the toilet. He and Norma had the house to themselves that night, Leslie and Alice having gone to a Burns Supper at the local Masonic Hall while Katy had gone to see and hear Geraldo and his band who were playing in town,

Geraldo's vocalist a young singer called Vera Lynn. Katy was also mad keen on dancing, but had nothing like the talent her brother had.

Norma decided on a wee bit of teasing. Sidling up to Midge she put her arms round him and whispered. 'Three Little Words, what does that mean to you?'

'Eh?' What was she havering about?

'Three little words,' she repeated. 'What does that mean to you?'

He stared at her, then a soft smile curled his lips upwards. 'I love you?'

She broke away from him. 'I thought you might say that. In fact it's a Yankee dance step, a new one we're going to try out. I found it in a book I've been reading.'

'You mean that's what this dance step is called, three little words?'

She nodded. 'So far I've discovered you can use it in the waltz, foxtrot, and merengue. It's a bit different, and a step no one else uses, at least no one I've ever seen. If you like it we can incorporate it into some of our performances.'

'Three little words,' he mused. Very Yankee.

'I love you – that's exactly what I thought when I first came across it,' she said, and went over to the gramophone to put a record on.

'Norma?'

She glanced at him over her shoulder.

His voice was suddenly husky, and far steelier than usual. 'I do, you know.'

She stopped up short. 'Do what?'

'Love you. I've never said before, but I have for a long time now.'

Norma's heart seemed to be turning over in her chest. She'd known for ages how he felt about her, but this was the first time he'd actually come out with it.

She went back over to him. There was a hint of tears in her eyes, and her voice had gone as husky as his when she whispered, 'Kiss me'.

It wasn't a passionate kiss, but one of great feeling on both sides. It seemed to her she could feel the warmth and intensity of the kiss in every part of her being.

The kiss went on and on, both of them reluctant to break the contact. Finally it was she who did so.

'And I love you too, but wasn't going to tell you until you'd said it first.'

'I've been meaning to... It's just, well, I felt embarrassed to say so.'

'Are you embarrassed now?'

He thought about that for a moment, then shook his head. 'Maybe that's because it just sort of happened naturally, without me planning it so to speak.'

'Maybe so,' she agreed.

He took a handful of honey blonde hair, and pulled it tight in his grasp, but not tight enough to hurt.

She stared into those piercing blue eyes of his, thinking how gorgeous they were. She knew why he'd taken so long in declaring his love. Glasgow men were like that, any emotional declaration – particularly love – being complete anathema to them.

'Tell me again,' she asked.

'I love you Norma. I love you.'

'And I love you.'

He took a deep breath, then drew her face close to his. He kissed her again, long and slowly and, as happened when they danced, it was as though they fused together to become as one.

When that kiss was over he took her in his arms. They stood there, holding tightly to one another.

After a while Norma put the record on and taught him how to do three little words.

The MC was a fat man whose face was streaming with perspiration, as it had been for most of the evening. The Usher Hall was jam-packed, so much so Norma couldn't even have begun to put a number to those present, most of them spectators come to watch.

She glanced at Midge. Second and third place had been announced – it was now the turn of the winner.

She caught sight of Finlay Rankine, and beside him the Gillespies. Finlay had insisted on coming through to Edinburgh with them, and had given them a quiet booster talk, as well as going over various technical details with them before the championship had begun.

Midge reached out and took her left hand, holding it clasped in one of his as the next few seconds ticked excruciatingly slowly by.

The MC was talking, but Norma wasn't really hearing what he was saying. They were just so many words that went in one ear and out the other. The only words that would register now was who the winning couple were.

'Couple number twenty-nine, McKenzie and Henderson!' The MC declared, leading the applause.

They'd done it, they'd taken the Edinburgh Veleta Championship! Somebody yelled very loudly. She learned afterwards that it was Bob Gillespie.

Still holding her by the hand Midge led her forward to the judges' rostrum where they would collect their prize. Oh but it was a proud moment right enough.

The prize was a silver salver, and two medals went with it. As the salver was large and heavy Midge held on to it in case Norma dropped it.

It took them ages to get away after that, but when they eventually did, they walked out into the chill night air to discover it had been snowing while they'd been inside, snow that covered the pavements and streets like a blanket.

Finlay managed to flag down a cruising taxi, and said he'd drop them at their hotel before going on to his own.

Norma, knowing Finlay, didn't believe he was staying in a hotel at all, but with some female he knew. A female who'd provide a lot more than he'd get in any hotel.

The taxi ride was a hilarious one, with Bob Gillespie cracking jokes and everyone laughing as though laughter was going to be banned come the morning. There was a certain amount of hysteria about the conversation, natural in the circumstances – winning the Edinburgh Veleta Championship was an enormous coup.

Arriving at the hotel they said goodbye to Finlay, arranging to meet him at the train in the morning. Midge, Bob and Beryl went straight into the lounge to order drinks – Finlay had refused the offer of one, his excuse being he might have trouble getting another taxi – Norma saying she'd join them after she'd been to her room. Midge showed all those present the silver salver he and Norma had won, and the three of them were bought a round by the hotel-owner as a congratulations gesture.

When Norma joined the others in the lounge it was clear that something of a party had developed. Midge was pouring Bob and Beryl whiskies the size of which you could have gone for a swim in. Norma said no to alcohol, settling instead for a glass of Irn Bru which was thirst-quenching, and just what she wanted.

She stayed for a little over half and hour, then left saying she was worn out and desperate for bed. Midge, the Gillespies and several others were in fine form when she took her leave.

Back in her bedroom she removed her make-up, had a good wash – an uppy and downy – then crawled into bed, which two hot water bottles had already made nice and cosy.

She lay in the darkness, going over the evening's events, analysing the better performances to see if there was anything she and Midge could pick up and use to their advantage. She was still doing this when she drifted off to sleep.

She awoke suddenly. What was that? Something had roused her, a noise of some sort, she was certain of it.

Tap tap tap.

There it was again.

She chewed a thumb, wondering who it was, and what she should do.

Tap tap tap.

Getting out of bed she tiptoed to the door. 'Who's there?' she demanded.

'It's Midge; let me in.'

Had something happened? Was something wrong? She quickly undid the snib and opened the door. Midge, wearing his dressing-gown and carrying a bottle, slipped inside.

'Jesus but it's freezing out.' As she shut the door and snibbed it again he flicked on the overhead light to get his bearings. When he had them he flicked it back off.

'Let's get into kip where we can be warm,' he said, and padded over to the bed.

She caught him by the arm just as he reached it. 'What do you think you're doing?' she asked in alarm.

'I've got a bottle of best sekt champagne here, and two tumblers. And as I haven't got any slippers on, my feet are like lumps of ice, so can we get into bed?' he replied.

'No you can't get into my bed! The Gillespies are just across the hallway for God's sake, they might have heard you come in!'

Midge chuckled. 'The state they're in neither of them will have heard anything. The roof could cave in an it wouldn't rouse them. I made sure of that.'

Norma frowned. 'What do you mean?'

'Can we get into bed first, please?'

'Oh all right,' she agreed reluctantly. What was he playing at? And why the sekt champagne? She'd never had champagne, nor did she want any right now. All she wanted was to go to sleep.

Being a single bed it was a tight fit, but they managed it. The pair of them pressed close up against one another.

'Hold these,' he instructed, and gave her the two tumblers, which he'd fished out of the pockets of his dressing gown.

'Just what is all this about?' she queried, totally mystified.

'Our own wee private celebration for what we did tonight,' he answered struggling with the cork. He pulled a face as he pushed as hard as he could with both thumbs.

With a pop the cork flew across the room just as the bedside lamp came on. With a low laugh Midge poured frothing champagne into the tumbler Norma was still holding.

'Terrific eh?' he said, and laughed again.

'What did you mean you made sure the Gillespies couldn't be roused?' she queried.

'I deliberately got them bevied to the gills, while actually taking it easy myself. I wanted them sparked out so that they wouldn't be aware when I came visiting,' he grinned in reply.

'You planned this then?'

'Whether we won or lost I intended coming to see you tonight. If we had lost I'd have got the Gillespies bevied out of disappointment. They're both pretty heavy drinkers anyway – I thought you'd have realised that by now.'

Norma hadn't.

Picking up the tumbler Norma had laid down he poured champagne for himself, stood the bottle by the side of the bed, and then raised his tumbler in a toast. 'To us!' he said, gulping down a mouthful.

Norma took a sip from her tumbler. It was bubbly and quite pleasant, if a trifle sweet for her taste.

'Oh Norma,' he whispered, his mouth seeking and kissing her breast.

She pushed him away. 'None of that now. I don't mind a celebratory drink as you've gone to all this trouble, but that's all.'

He downed what remained in his tumbler. 'Don't be daft,' he said, throwing himself on top of her.

His lips clamped on to hers, and his tongue snaked into her mouth. A hand found the breast he had kissed.

She managed to get her tumbler onto the bedside table without spilling its contents. As she was doing this his other hand shot up inside her nightie to grasp hold of her crotch.

'Stop it!' she exclaimed angrily, tearing her mouth away from his.

He groaned, both his hands working overtime feeling and prodding.

She hit him as hard as she could. A cracking slap that took him across the left cheek. His eyes, closed for the past few moments, snapped open in surprise.

'Let go of me,' she said, her voice hard and angry.

'But Norm...'

'I said let go. This instant, dammit!'

He released her, and she fell back against the pillow where she caught her breath.

He stared at her, perplexed. 'I thought... I thought you'd want me to come. That you'd want us to sleep together.'

'I never allowed anything like this to happen before so why should I suddenly do so now?' she snapped in reply.

'Because I've told you I love you, and you've admitted the same to me.'

So that was it. She was beginning to understand. 'You engineered all this so that you and I could sleep together for the first time, is that what you're saying?'

He nodded.

'You thought because we'd declared our love for one another that I'd sleep with you?'

'Staying in a hotel was a chance not to be missed. That's why I got the Gillespies bevied.'

She pulled the front of her nightie closer together, then reached for her drink. She really felt like one now.

'The answer's no,' she stated firmly.

Disappointment filled his face. 'But why not, I don't understand?'

She marshalled her thoughts, wanting to explain this clearly to him. Finally she said,

'I have no intention of going to my husband as second-hand goods; I want to be a virgin on my wedding night.

'Besides, if I did sleep with you now you might lose respect for me, and I'd hate that.'

'I wouldn't Norma, I swear!'

She gave him a cynical smile. 'I'm told men will swear anything to get you. Only afterwards, when they've had what they wanted, it's a different story.'

'Not with me, honest.'

'I think you'd better go back to your own bedroom now Midge. That would be best.'

'I don't want to go. I want to be here with you.'

'I want you to be here with me – only I'm not going to allow it. You'd just keep on trying, and I'd just have to keep on saying no, which seems a bit pointless when you think about it doesn't it?'

'I do love you,' he pleaded.

'I know, and I love you. But that's not enough. Not for me anyhow.'

He could see she wasn't going to change her mind, that she was determined to keep him at bay.

'I want you so much,' he said, balling his fists.

'And I want you too, but I won't give in to it, or you. I will not go as soiled property to my husband when the time comes because I feel, believe, that is his due.'

'I could force you,' he said.

She stared coldly at him. 'That would be a stupid mistake,' she replied levelly.

He hung his head. 'I'm sorry, I didn't really mean that. I would never force you. Never.'

She touched him very lightly on the arm. 'Goodnight then

Midge, see you in the morning.'

He got out of bed and stared down at her. He was twenty the following month, old enough to get married. And yet... What about his dream of visiting foreign places? If he got married those would have to go by the board. On the other hand what had he done to try and fulfil those dreams? Nothing whatever – so far it had been all talk on his part. All pish, wind and sugarally watter as his father would have said.

If he hadn't met Norma, if the two of them hadn't got so involved in this dancing; if he'd run away to sea as a boy as he'd always been going to instead of ending up as an apprentice at the North Woodside Flint Mills... Ifs and ands, pots and pans.

He lifted the bottle of champagne from the side of the bed. 'I'll take this with me and have a swig or two before I go to sleep,' he said.

At the door he stopped to look back at her. In that moment he knew what he was going to do, what his future would be.

It would be with Norma.

Success followed success. Already Lanarkshire Open Champions and Edinburgh Veleta Champions, they also became Glasgow Latin American Champions (having deposed the couple they'd so admired two years previously), Lanarkshire Ballroom Champions, Renfrewshire Latin American and Ballroom Champions, Stirlingshire Quickstep and Foxtrot Champions and Aberdeen Ballroom Champions.

That was their current standing when one night in August, they went to a new dancehall that had recently opened in Glasgow called Barrowland which overlooked the Barrows where Midge had bought his first set of tails.

'What do you think?' Midge asked as they waltzed round the floor.

Norma glanced about her. 'It has a good, friendly atmosphere. I like it,' she replied.

Midge nodded, that was his impression as well. They'd come again.

'Quite quiet though,' said Norma.

Midge looked at his watch. It was quiet for that time of a

Friday night, he'd have expected far more people to be there, particularly as the pubs had let out.

At the end of that waltz the band took a break, and they returned to their table. They were sitting there chatting when a middle-aged man in dinner jacket and bow tie approached them.

'I'd like to introduce myself. I'm Joe Dunlop, manager of Barrowland,' he smiled.

Midge rose, and had his hand shaken by Dunlop, who then shook Norma's hand.

'Mind if I join you?' Dunlop asked.

'Please do,' Norma told him. He borrowed a chair from an adjacent empty table.

'I saw you dance in the Lanarkshire Championship, I thought you were marvellous and well deserved to win the ballroom section.'

'Thank you,' Midge replied.

'I was wondering... Do you think you might give the patrons an exhibition tonight? Anything you fancy, I'd be most obliged.'

Norma glanced at Midge, and he shrugged back.

'How about a rialto two step to the tune of "Bladon Races"?' she suggested.

'Sounds great.'

'Then that's what we'll do.'

'You're a couple of toffs, thank you,' Dunlop said. 'I'll announce you myself, say in five minutes time?'

'Fine,' Norma replied.

Dunlop hurried off to talk to the band. 'I was hoping to practice our rialto two step tonight anyway, this gives us the chance,' Norma said to Midge, who agreed with her. It was a dance they did need to practice.

The band returned to the stand; then Joe Dunlop picked up a microphone.

'Ladies and gentlemen, tonight it is my great privilege to tell you we are going to be given an exhibition of a rialto two step by a young couple who are the hottest thing to hit the Scottish dancing scene for years.

'Ladies and gentlemen, will you give a big welcome to Miss Norma McKenzie and Mr Michael Henderson!'

Norma and Midge stood, inclining their heads to acknowledge the applause. They then walked out to the centre of the floor.

When the dance was over the response was rapturous, something they were becoming well used to. Audiences loved them, not just because they were top-notch dancers, but also because they positively exuded charisma, and were such a physically striking couple.

On returning to their table they were asked to sign a number of autographs, which they did. That was something else they were becoming well used to.

When the impromptu signing session was over Joe Dunlop came across and thanked them again. He then asked if they'd go with him to his office, for a word in private.

'Whisky?' he offered when the office door was shut behind them.

Norma and Midge both declined. Dunlop poured himself a small one, topping up the glass with lemonade.

'As I'm sure you know, Barrowland hasn't been opened that long and, as you can see from the numbers here tonight, hasn't really got going yet. My brief from the owners is to change that as quickly as possible, and make Barrowland one of the foremost, and popular – if not *the* foremost and *the* most popular – dancehall in Glasgow.

'I've already booked some of the big name bands, bands that have never been to Glasgow before. Billy Cotton for one, Henry Hall for another. I've also booked Stanley Black, Denny Dennis and Nat Gonella and his Georgians.'

'That's quite a line-up,' Midge acknowledged, for Dunlop had just reeled off some of the biggest names of the day.

'I'm also negotiating to have Glenn Miller appear here during his forthcoming British tour. If I can pull that off, and I'm pretty certain I can, it should really pack them in.'

Midge gave a low whistle. 'They don't come any bigger than Glenn Miller,' he said.

Dunlop nodded his agreement. He offered Midge a cigar, which Midge refused. Dunlop lit up, then went on.

'Watching the pair of you tonight I had a thought. What Barrowland also needs to bring people in is a regular exhibition couple, a couple who'd be in residence so to speak, and who'd perform, say, four times a night.'

'You mean professional dancers,' Norma said.

'That's it, a professional couple. What do you think?'

'I think it's an excellent idea. What couple did you have in mind?' Midge replied.

Norma, as usual, saw what was coming. 'I believe Mr Dunlop is thinking of us,' she said.

Midge looked from Dunlop to Norma, and back again to Dunlop. 'Are you?'

'Tuesdays through Saturdays, four exhibitions a night, and I'll pay a tenner,' Dunlop said quietly.

Midge swallowed hard. That was five pounds each, and for dancing! Work was work, but dancing was pleasure.

'I'll have a whisky after all please,' Norma said. She didn't really want one; it was a device to give her time to think.

'It would mean an end to our amateur status of course. It depends how important you feel that is to us,' she said to Midge.

'Certainly I enjoy, revel in, winning championships, I can't deny it. But a tenner a week between us, that's something that has to be considered seriously,' he replied.

He was right. It wouldn't bar them from all championships mind you, Norma thought, only the amateur ones. There were a few pro championships, but only a few. There was one notable exception, the All Scotland Dance Championship – all comers could enter that, pro and amateur alike. It was Scotland's most prestigious championship and the winners were acclaimed as the best dancers in Scotland.

She accepted her whisky from Dunlop. As she did so she searched his face, and what she saw there told her he was dead keen to have them.

Ten pounds was a lot of money, but then Dunlop – if he could afford whatever Glenn Miller would charge – certainly seemed to have access to plenty.

'It would be a huge sacrifice on our part. And once we relinquish our amateur status that's it, there's no going back,' she said softly.

'Do you want time to consider?' Dunlop suggested reluctantly.

'Would there be a contract?' she queried.

'I hadn't thought that far ahead. Would you want one?'

Now was the time to think of the future, Norma told herself. If they took the job and were successful, then who was to say this might not lead on to better, more lucrative things? In which case it would be better if they weren't tied by a contract.

'No,' she replied.

Midge glanced at her in surprise, but held his tongue. If Norma said no then she must have a reason.

Norma took a miniscule sip of her drink, and thought about being a professional dancer. The idea appealed, very much so.

'Fifteen pounds and we start next Tuesday,' she said.

Midge gaped at her. Fifteen nicker! Was she off her chump!

Dunlop stared at her. He hadn't expected to have to bargain. He shook his head; she was only a lassie after all, what did she know about business? And dammit, his offer was a good one.

'That's beyond me,' he replied.

Norma had another miniscule sip of whisky, and waited.

'Oh all right, eleven,' Dunlop said after a while, thinking that would be the end of it. But it wasn't.

Norma still didn't reply. She had looked into his face and seen how badly he wanted them. The seconds ticked by.

Dunlop frowned, he found it most off-putting the way she just sat there saying nothing. He began to believe she'd have sat there in silence for the rest of the night if he'd let her.

'Twelve pounds ten, and that's it,' he said, pouring himself another whisky.

Midge was jumping inside, and there was cold sweat on his forehead. Six pounds five a week each, it was a bloody fortune. Why didn't she agree? He considered putting his spoke in, then thought better of it. He had a lot of faith in Norma. Experience had taught him that when she took a stand she was invariably right.

Slowly and softly, but with a hint of steel, Norma said. 'If I may quote what you said about us in your introduction earlier on: "a young couple who are the hottest, and most exciting, thing to hit the Scottish dancing scene for years".

'Glenn Miller, Billy Cotton, Henry Hall – if you want the best you have to pay for them. You know that Mr Dunlop.'

He gave a grunt that was actually a laugh. Throwing his own words back at him! He liked that. It was what his Ikey friends called chutspah. He also liked the fact that, without actually saying so, she'd ranked herself and Henderson alongside Miller, Cotton and Hall. Now that was real chutspah.

'Fourteen pounds a week, and that *is* it. A matter of pride,' he told her.

This time she knew he meant it. He'd gone up four pounds, she'd have to concede one. As he said, his male pride demanded it.

'You have a deal Mr Dunlop,' she replied.

'Well, thank God for that!' he exclaimed, pulling a face. Which punctured the tension that had built up in the room, and made them all laugh.

When they left Dunlop's office a few minutes later Norma suggested to Midge that they call it a night and head back to Bridgeton, to which he readily agreed. He also wanted out of there, and fast.

He somehow managed to contain himself till they were away from the front of Barrowland, and down the street a bit. Then, giving vent to a loud Red Indian-type whoop, he caught Norma in his arms and, lifting her right off the pavement, birled her round and round.

'Fourteen pounds a week, it's unbelievable!' he croaked, setting her down again.

'You are certain about us giving up our amateur status? For once we do that's it, there's no going back,' she said anxiously.

'I'm certain, seven pounds a week certain. Why, that on top of what I'm earning now makes me rich, and you too.'

It did as well. She'd be the highest earning female in all Bridgeton, no doubt about it. From now on she'd be earning four times what she had been.

Midge let out another Red Indian whoop, and birled her round again. When he stopped Norma was smiling hugely, and her cheeks were flushed with a combination of euphoria, and self-satisfaction.

'Let's hurry home and tell our folks,' she said. She couldn't wait to see the look on her da's face when she broke the news. Or her mother's – the pair of them would be dumbstruck.

Hand in hand, laughing like a couple of dafties, she and Midge ran for the tram that had just pulled up.

* * *

They'd just finished their first exhibition of the evening when Norma spied the old man again, standing beside a pillar and staring at her.

'There he is again,' she whispered to Midge.

'Who?'

*'Him*, the old fella.'

Midge's expression creased into one of worry and concern. The old man had been coming in every night for the past fortnight. He always came alone, and never danced. Just stood, or sat, staring at Norma, his eyes glued to her.

'A joke's a joke, but this has gone far enough. I'm going to speak to Dunlop,' Midge replied.

Norma worried a crimson-painted nail. 'I think you should. He's starting to give me the creeps, that man, just staring at me the way he does.'

Midge was about to go and seek out Dunlop when the manager hove into view, doing his rounds, making sure everything was all right and going as it should.

Midge caught Dunlop's eye and gestured him over.

Norma and Midge had been resident professionals at Barrowland for just over three months now, and were loving every minute of it. Their exhibitions had become firm favourites with the patrons, as had they. Business at the dancehall was booming. And, as Dunlop was the first to admit, a lot of the credit of that was down to them.

When Dunlop joined them, Midge explained in low, hurried tones what was troubling Norma, and giving him cause for concern.

Dunlop glanced over at the old fella, wondering if he was dangerous. You never knew in Glasgow, and, as he had learned to his cost in the past, appearances could be very deceptive. He would take 'Spider' Webb, one of the two bouncers he employed, with him when he spoke to the man, just in case.

Dunlop left them in search of Spider, and shortly after that they watched Dunlop and Spider home in on the old man. A short conversation took place, at the end of which Dunlop led the way to his office with the old man following behind, and Spider behind him.

There were fifteen minutes till their second exhibition of the evening, the Doris waltz, when Dunlop reappeared with the old fella by his side.

'Norma, I'd like you to meet Mr Gallagher. He has an interesting story I think you should hear.'

If Dunlop had brought Gallagher to their table, he must be safe, Norma reasoned, and shook hands with him. Gallagher then shook hands with Midge.

Seeing Gallagher up close Norma realised he was even older than she'd thought. Late seventies? Eighties? He was positively ancient, though still spry on his feet.

'I must apologise for giving you a fright, I really am sorry. It just never dawned on me, with so many folk present, that you'd notice me watching you,' Gallagher said.

He was well spoken, Norma noted. Though hardly what you would have called a toff. His clothes had been expensive when bought, but that had been a fair while ago. The jacket cuff of his right sleeve had started to fray, and there was a distinct sheen to his trouser legs.

Norma invited Gallagher to sit, and Dunlop sat down as well. Norma and Midge always kept several empty chairs at their table, as some of the regulars liked to come over and have a natter, which they didn't discourage, looking on it as part and parcel of the service.

'Show Norma your photograph,' said Dunlop.

Gallagher reached into an inside pocket to produce his wallet. From the wallet he took a small photograph, about three inches square, Norma judged.

'My daughter,' Gallagher said simply, and handed Norma the photograph.

It was a sepia-coloured photograph of a girl in her late teens, or perhaps twenty or twenty-one. She was a very attractive girl, with long hair and smiling mouth. And she was somehow familiar.

Midge, leaning over, looked from the photograph up to Norma. 'It's you,' he said.

Gallagher nodded. 'The resemblance is remarkable. I noticed it the first time I saw your own photograph outside in the foyer, Miss McKenzie. It was that which prompted me to come in, and why I've been coming ever since.'

The photograph of Norma that Gallagher was referring to

was a huge blow-up one of her and Midge which was positioned in the foyer so as to be visible from the street. Gallagher had been passing when a glance at the photograph had brought him up short.

Norma stared at the small photograph in her hand. She could see it now. In a strange way it was like looking into a mirror, a mirror distorted by time. For the girl's clothes and hairstyle belonged to an earlier period. Before the Great War, Norma thought. Yes, sometime between the turn of the century and 1914.

'Her name was Morna - even the name is similar,' said Gallagher.

Norma glanced up at him. '*Was*?'

'She died young, of a brain tumour.'

'Oh I am sorry,' Norma said quietly.

Gallagher averted his gaze for a moment. When he looked back at Norma she could see a glint of tears in his face.

'When I saw you in the flesh I just couldn't believe it. It was as though Morna was still alive, though of course you wouldn't have been born until some years after her death.'

He groped for a handkerchief, a large, white, cotton one, which he blew his nose into.

'Excuse an old man his foolishness, but my Morna and I were very close, the way it is sometimes between a father and daughter.'

Gallagher stuffed the handkerchief back into his breast pocket. There were brown liver spots on his hands, hands that trembled slightly.

Norma gave the sepia photograph to Midge so he could study it more closely. It was Norma all right, he thought. Morna and Norma could have been identical twins. Identical, with just those few little differences to enable you to tell them apart. Morna's nose was a shade longer; her cheekbones somewhat more prominent.

'What colour eyes did she have?' asked Midge.

'Grey,' Gallagher replied.

Even that was similar Midge thought. Though Norma's weren't always grey but changed from grey to green and back again.

'And you say she died of a brain tumour,' Norma said.

'Yes, it was a most painful, and protracted death. Towards the end, she was sleeping most of the time, due to the huge doses of medication she was receiving. Then one afternoon she went to sleep and never woke up again.'

'And when was it she died?' Norma asked.

'1908.'

Nearly thirty years ago, Norma thought. Morna would have been fifty or thereabouts now, older than Effie.

'And Mrs Gallagher?' she inquired.

'Died giving birth to Ian, our son. He was killed in the closing months of the war. He was with Allenby when Allenby destroyed the last Turkish army at Megiddo.'

What a sad tale, Norma thought. And what a sad old man. She took the photograph of Morna from Midge, looked at it again, then passed it back to Gallagher.

'Thank you for showing your daughter's photograph to us,' she said.

'It was the least I could do after being so stupid as to frighten you. I never intended any harm, only to look, and remember, and . . .' He shrugged. 'Think of things as they might have been.'

Norma glanced at her watch. It was almost time for their second exhibition.

'Listen Mr Gallagher, we don't mind people coming over and chatting to us occasionally. If you'd like to from time to time then please feel free to do so,' Norma said.

His face lit up. 'You really mean that?'

'I do.'

'Is this acceptable to you Mr Henderson?'

Midge nodded. 'Yes of course.'

'From time to time then. And not for too long. I won't make a pest of myself, or outstay my welcome.'

Gallagher took Norma's right hand in one of his, and kissed the back of it the way a Frenchman would.

'Thank you,' he said softly.

There was silence round the table after Gallagher had gone, each of them thinking about the old man and his tragic story. Thoughts that had to be interrupted when the number being played came to an end.

'I'll introduce you,' Dunlop said, rising.

Norma fought back the lump that was in her throat. 'The Doris waltz,' she said to Midge.

From a dark, secluded part of the hall Gallagher watched Norma with tears rolling down his cheeks.

In the flesh he was in Barrowland watching Norma, but in his mind he was in a different place, with a laughing girl.

That Saturday afternoon found Norma and Midge, as they were now to be found most Saturday afternoons, in a hall in their local Bridgeton 'Pineapple' - the nickname used by Protestants when referring to a Catholic Chapel.

Neither Norma or Midge was Catholic, but both were friendly with Father Finn, the parish priest of St Mary Magdalen.

It wasn't common for Catholics and Protestants to be friendly in this way, particularly where one of the parties involved was a priest. But Father Finn was a man who rose above sectarianism, with time for everyone whether they belonged to the Catholic Faith or not. He was, as he'd often been described, a true Christian.

Up till then Norma and Midge had been practising at either her house - now the three room and kitchen - or Midge's. That was until Father Finn had suggested they use one of the halls in the 'Pineapple', which would give them a lot more space to practice in.

They'd been delighted to accept Father Finn's offer, and also the use of the 'Pineapple's' gramophone. They brought their own records along for each session as required.

'Well that's about it,' Midge said, releasing Norma, and going over to the gramophone to take the record they'd been dancing to - 'Kissin' Bug Boogie' with Sid Phillips and his Band - off the turntable.

Norma ran a hand through her hair. It was greasy; she'd need to wash it before she and Midge went to Barrowland that evening. They'd been practising a slight variation of the foxtrot basic one step which made the dance more exciting to watch. She was happy with it now, as was Midge.

She put on her coat, for it was cold in the unheated hall. She'd been dancing wearing a sweater and cardy on top of that. Enough when you were moving, but not when you'd stopped.

'Before I put the grammy away there's something I want to give you,' Midge said casually. He went to his own coat, fished in a pocket, and pulled something out.

Crossing to Norma, the faintest of smiles twisting his lips, he presented the something to her. It was a small black box. The unmistakable sort that rings come in.

Norma looked at the box, at Midge, then back at the box again.

'Open it,' he instructed.

There was white satin inside, and a black velvety panel. Embedded in the panel was an engagement ring consisting of a large diamond surrounded by smaller ones.

'I've been saving up for that. Wanted to give you a decent one,' Midge said, his smile widening.

Norma gazed at the ring. It was a smasher, a real humdinger. She doubted any other girl in Bridgeton had a ring as beautiful as this one. And it must have cost a fortune.

'So, are we engaged then?' he asked.

This was the last thing she'd expected, well, not in these circumstances anyway. It had taken her breath away.

'Engaged to be married?'

He laughed. 'What else do you think I mean!'

She gently pulled out the ring from the slit. As she did the light caught the big stone, sending out rays of flashing fire.

'This is an actual proposal?' she queried.

'An actual proposal,' he confirmed.

Norma was a bit miffed he'd chosen these very unglamorous surroundings in which to pop the question. It was so ... unromantic! And he might have asked her properly. 'So are we engaged then?' sounded like 'Would you like a fish supper for your tea?'

Devilment got into her. 'Aren't you supposed to go down on one knee to propose? Isn't that the tradition?'

Midge looked alarmed. Her tone might be jocular, but he knew her well enough to know she was serious. Down on one knee! He could feel his face colouring.

'No one would see. We're perfectly alone,' she purred.

He knew that was so, but glanced round the hall nonetheless. Just to be sure. 'I don't think I ...'

'Down on one knee,' she repeated, her tone still light,

but with an underlying hint of steel.

He took a deep breath. The things men did for women. Honestly! He went down in front of her.

'There,' he muttered.

'And you say . . .'

He groaned.

'And you say, Norma will you marry me?'

'Norma will you marry me?'

'Please.'

He took another deep breath. He felt a proper Charlie doing this, a right heid the ba'.

'Norma will you marry me *please*?' he asked.

She slipped the ring onto the appropriate finger, twisting it round one way, then the other, making it catch the light so that it shot off more flashing fire. During this she kept her face impassive.

Sudden alarm flared in Midge. She wasn't going to refuse him, was she! He'd never even considered the possibility. He'd thought her reaction would be to be all over him like the proverbial rash. Yet here she was, seemingly undecided.

'Norma?' he croaked. If she turned him down it would be a disaster, a catastrophe!

'A girl is supposed to take her time in answering that particular question. She musn't appear too eager.'

'So will you or won't you?' he demanded.

She grasped him by an elbow, and raised him back to his feet. She gazed into those gorgeous blue eyes of his, eyes she'd often thought would mesmerise her if she stared into them long and hard enough. 'Of course I'll marry you,' she whispered.

Relief flooded through him and he drew her close and kissed her. A kiss that made her squirm with pleasure.

When their mouths parted she kissed him back, on the neck, and under the chin.

'Three little words Midge,' she whispered.

He knew full well what she was after, but now it was his turn to tease.

'You want to dance?' he asked innocently.

She shook her head. 'The *other* three little words Midge.'

His expression became deadly earnest. 'I love you Norma,' he said softly.

'And I love you, Oh, how I love you!'

Their faces came together again, and their mouths closed on each other.

They were now officially engaged to be married. She was to be Mrs Midge Henderson, and she was overjoyed at the prospect. One she'd dreamt of for a long long time now.

*Mrs* Midge Henderson.

A warm, delicious prickle ran up her spine.

She'd been home long enough to wash her hair, dry it in front of the fire, and now get ready for Barrowland and still no one had noticed.

Norma looked over at Lyn. She was amazed old eagle eye hadn't spotted it. She brought her left hand up so that it was resting casual-like, on her left cheek.

'Everything all right Lyn?' she inquired nonchalantly.

Lyn was buried in a magazine of romantic stories she'd borrowed off a lassie at work. The story she was in the middle of was about a nurse, and set during the war. It was a cracker.

'Why shouldn't it be?' Lyn replied, glancing quickly in Norma's direction.

Norma waggled her engagement finger. Come on you stupid cow, the ring's bloody big enough she thought. 'Just asking, that's all,' she replied in the same nonchalant tone.

With a shrug Lyn returned eagerly to her nurse.

'Tea will be ready in a mo,' announced Effie from the stove, where she was making scrambled eggs, fried tomatoes, mushrooms and toast.

Norma looked over at her mother's back, then to her father engrossed in an *Evening Citizen*. She brought her gaze onto Eileen who was sitting staring into the fire.

'How's the job going then Eileen?' she asked. Eileen had left school that summer and was now working in a local bakery tending counter.

'Fine ta,' Eileen replied.

Norma, left hand still on cheek, waggled her engagement finger again. Making it a more pronounced waggle this time.

'The Mavors seem like nice people,' she said. The Mavors owned the bakery.

'Aye, they are.'

Norma glowered at Eileen. Her wee sister hadn't even so much as flicked her eyes at her, but continued staring into the fire.

'Oh dammit to hell, I give up!' she exploded.

Brian's head emerged from behind his paper. 'Something wrong?'

'No everything's right, except nobody's noticed that's all.'

She had everyone's attention now. Even Effie had paused in what she was doing to glance across at her.

'This afternoon Midge ...'

At which point 'old eagle eye' saw the ring. Squealing, Lyn jumped right out of her chair to point dramatically at Norma. 'She's wearing an engagement ring!'

At last! Norma thought with satisfaction. *At last*. She smiled as her two sisters crowded round.

'Let's see. Hold it up properly so we can get a good gander,' Lyn said.

I've been doing nothing but since I came in earlier. I was beginning to think you'd all been struck blind,' Norma retorted.

'Oh it's a brammer!' Eileen breathed.

'And the size of that stone, absolutely ginormous,' Lyn said, her eyes popping.

Brian was staring at his eldest daughter in astonishment, though he couldn't think why. He and Effie had long known this was on the cards. Maybe he'd thought they'd leave it a while longer. But at eighteen, eighteen and a half nearly, she was certainly old enough if that's what she wanted. Which it seemed she did.

Effie wiped her hands on her pinny. There was a catch in her throat as she walked over to a now beaming Norma. 'Let's have a look then,' she said, pushing a stray lock of hair away from her forehead.

'I've been flashing it like mad since I got in. Flash flash, sparkle sparkle!' Norma giggled. 'How you all missed it beats me.'

Effie studied the ring, then shook her head in admiration. 'Well he hasn't made a fool of you, that's for certain,' she said.

Norma suddenly found herself in her mother's arms, the pair of them holding each other tightly. There were tears in Effie's eyes when she finally let Norma go.

Brian shook her solemnly by the hand, his expression one of fierce pride. 'Congratulations lass,' he said, voice thick with emotion.

'Aye, congrats,' Lyn added.

'Can I try the ring on?' Eileen asked eagerly.

'No you cannot, that would be unlucky,' Norma replied instantly. She didn't know whether it was unlucky or not, she just didn't want anyone else, not even a sister, putting it on.

A few minutes later they all sat down to tea, laughing, joking and talking about the engagement.

Late that night Norma and Midge stopped on his landing as they always did coming back together from Barrowland. He'd just started to kiss her when his door opened and Katy poked her head out.

'If I could do a wolf whistle I would,' she grinned.

'Do you mind, this is private,' Midge replied, glaring at her.

'Sorry to interrupt the winching, but Ma and Da are upstairs with the McKenzies and want you to pop up there before you come in by,' she said.

'To the McKenzies, what for?'

'Search me. All I know is that I was to pass on the message.'

And with that Katy shut the door again.

Midge looked thoughtful, wondering what this was all about.

'Ach they're probably having a few drams in celebration and want us to join them,' Norma said.

'Aye, that's probably it right enough,' Midge replied. They continued up to the next landing where she used her key to let them into her house.

They walked into the kitchen, and were mobbed. 'Surprise!' shouted Brian, waving a whisky bottle in the air. His flushed cheeks told Norma he'd been hard at it for some while.

Norma's hand was grabbed and pumped up and down by Bob Gillespie; then Beryl was embracing her and saying how marvellous the news was.

After the Gillespies, it was the Fullartons' turn to offer congratulations; Jacky kissing her on the cheek, declaring that right from the word go, from the night he'd introduced Midge to her out in the street, he'd had the feeling the pair of them would end up tying the knot.

'We thought a wee party would be just the dab,' Effie said to Norma.

'This is tremendous Ma,' Norma enthused. Many of the friends from the street and round about were there, and several from further afield, including Finlay Rankine who'd been contacted by telephone.

Katy Henderson came into the kitchen, and gave Norma a fly wink. 'Your da wanted it to be a complete surprise.' she said.

'Well it was certainly that right enough. We didn't even have an inkling, just walked straight into it.'

Most of those present had already had a good drink while waiting for the newly engaged couple to return from Barrowland.

Norma spied Eileen with Charlie Marshall, the pair of them holding hands. Charlie's plooks had long since disappeared, and his once wispy moustache had thickened so that it now looked like a proper moustache instead of some very thin oose stuck to his upper lip.

He and Eileen made a handsome couple, Norma thought. How long till they got engaged? Not too long, she'd bet money on that.

Alice and Leslie Henderson forced their way over to tell her how pleased they were. Their Midge couldn't have found himself a nicer lassie, and that was the truth.

If there was one person not enjoying herself it was Lyn. When was *her* prince going to appear, she wondered despairingly. All the other girls had boyfriends and admirers, but not her. Of course if she wasn't so big it might have helped, but all she had to do was breathe to put on another pound. Well, maybe a wee bit more than breathe. But it was hardly her fault she had a healthy appetite!

Mr Laidlaw poured Norma a dram, having already given one to Midge.

'A toast! A toast!' the cry went up.

The general hubbub subsided. Brian came forward to do the honours.

Brian raised his glass. 'To the happy couple,' he said simply. Speechmaking wasn't exactly his forte.

'To the happy couple!' echoed from all sides.

Norma looked at Midge who grinned rather sheepishly back

at her. She'd never been so happy in her life. She was fair bursting with happiness.

She lifted her glass to him, and he to her. Everybody else present shouted and clapped as they toasted each other, and themselves.

It was late afternoon of Hogmanay and Norma and Midge were at the Central Station to see her family off to Kirn for a holiday. It was the first time ever that Effie and Brian had gone off on one, and it was their first visit back to Kirn.

Brian didn't get time off at Christmas - that was for weans and the English - but he got four days at New Year. That year, thanks to a bit of finagling on his part, he'd managed an extra afternoon, that afternoon, stopping at one o'clock instead of six.

They would be staying with an old friend of Effie's from the WI who owned a small guesthouse which, being out of season, was currently empty apart from herself and husband.

Norma couldn't go because of her commitment to Barrowland. Hogmanay was the biggest night of the year and, much as she'd have adored to go back to the place where she'd been born and brought up, it had never even entered her mind to let Joe Dunlop down.

Effie was full of going back to Kirn, as was Brian, though he refused to admit he was. He was being very casual about the whole affair, but underneath it all was just as excited as Effie.

Lyn was also looking forward to going back, though not nearly so much as her parents. As for Eileen, she hadn't wanted to go at all and was only doing so at her father's insistence. She wanted to be with Charlie over Hogmanay and, at sixteen, felt she was old enough to be left behind. Brian agreed she was old enough, but said it was only right and proper that they were all together for Hogmanay - those who could be, that was. Norma's exemption was strictly on account of work; otherwise he would have insisted she come as well.

Finally Effie, Brian, Lyn, Eileen and their assorted baggage were put aboard the train and a few minutes later the whistle sounded. Norma and Midge waved the McKenzies on their way.

'Let's get back,' Norma smiled to Midge when the train had

gone. She had an argument ready for him should he have suggested they do something else. But he didn't.

'Come upstairs with me, I've got an engagement present for you,' she said when they reached Midge's door.

His face lit up. 'A present? What?'

'Wait and see,' she laughed, and led the way up to the next landing.

She took him into the kitchen. 'Stay here, I won't be long,' she said, and left him standing in front of the fireplace.

She returned a few minutes later wearing a dressing gown and an enigmatic smile. She wasn't carrying or holding anything.

Puzzled, Midge frowned. What was going on? And where was his present?

Her heart was pounding at her own daring and audacity. If she wasn't absolutely certain there was still time for her to change her mind she told herself. But she *was* absolutely certain. She shivered in anticipation.

'Your engagement present,' she said throatily, and dropped her dressing gown to the floor to stand stark naked before him.

Midge gawped at her.

'I've been waiting for a suitable opportunity. Today, and the next four days are it.'

She took him by the hand, and he followed her through to her bedroom where the curtains were already closed, a bedside lamp switched on, and the bed turned down.

'Do I understand correctly?' he asked, finding his tongue again.

'Yes.'

'You want me to . . . I mean you and I to . . .' He trailed off.

'Yes.'

He swallowed hard. As the saying went, you could have knocked him over with a feather.

'But you told me . . . you told me that you'd go to your husband a virgin?'

'And so I am.'

'But I'm not your husband!'

'Not yet. But you're going to be. That's precisely what engaged means, engaged to be married. You're going to be my husband, I your wife. And I have a very expensive diamond ring to prove it,' she replied.

He stared hungrily at her. Taking in her full, well-rounded breasts. The satin sheen of her skin. The blonde tangle at the apex of two perfect legs.

'You're beautiful. Even more beautiful than I'd imagined,' he croaked.

She got into bed, waiting with the bedclothes pulled up to her chin while he undressed. Then he was beside her, his body cold against hers. The pair of them clutched each other for warmth.

His hands began to move. Touching, feeling, exploring, while she did the same. She whispered into his ear that he'd find the necessary under the pillow. She didn't want any 'accidents' happening.

As she'd known it would, the same magic that happened when they danced together happened now. They fused, to become as one. Completely one.

Later they both cried out. In unison.

## *Chapter Five*

Lyn was passing through the filing department at work when she came across Norma propped up against one of the large cabinets in the department. Norma's eyes were closed, and there was a strange expression on her face. Her complexion had gone all pasty, a sort of greeny colour.

'What is it? What's wrong?' demanded Lyn, putting a supporting arm round Norma's shoulders.

Norma's eyes flickered open. 'One moment I was all right, the next quite lightheaded. As if the inside of my head was trying to float out through the top of my skull.'

'Do you feel sick?'

'Aye, a bit.'

'Then let's get you sat down.'

Lyn helped Norma stumble to a nearby chair. 'Can you manage by yourself for a moment or two? I'll get you a glass of water.'

'Please.'

Lyn didn't like the look of Norma at all, and wondered if she should call a doctor.

When Lyn returned she found her sister slumped forward with her head in her hands. Norma glanced up at her approach, and gave her a wan smile.

Norma sipped the water Lyn had fetched. It was lovely and cold. She already felt better, her lightheadedness starting to recede.

'Do you think it's the flu?' Lyn queried anxiously.

'No. It's just tiredness. I'm sure of it. I was right whacked when I got out of bed this morning, totally drained. I'm certain that's what brought on this dizzy turn.'

Lyn's lips thinned. So that was it. She might have guessed.

Effie had been saying only the other week that she didn't know how Norma did it.

Norma drank more water, and her colour began to return. 'I'd like to wash my face. That would help a lot,' she said, her voice still a little weak.

On reaching the nearest ladies' toilet, having passed several concerned employees on the way, Lyn made Norma sit on the WC while she filled the basin. When Norma had washed and dried her face Lyn forced her to sit down again saying that she should stay there until fully recovered.

'This working what amounts to two full-time jobs just isn't on you know,' Lyn chided. 'You're at it from early morning till last thing at night. It can't go on for ever.'

Norma nodded. Lyn was right. She was doing far too much, and the strain was beginning to tell. Her dizzy turn was proof of that.

'Pack it in here, you don't need the money after all,' Lyn suggested.

'You forget I'm newly engaged. The sooner we get something behind us the sooner we can get married. Even if the money I earn here is nowhere what I bring in from Barrowland, it does make a big difference to what I put away each week.'

Lyn saw her sister's point. 'But with you and Midge both coining it surely it won't be that long before you can afford to get wed?'

'The sooner the better as far as I'm concerned. I can't wait to be Mrs Midge Henderson and have a wee house of our own.'

'Well it's up to you what you do, but if you go on like you are doing you'll end up in hospital. And that's a fact.'

Just then there was a knock on the toilet door. It was Norma's boss, a Mr Brown, come to inquire how she was, and was there anything he could do?

It was a thoughtful Norma who returned to work.

Norma and Midge were in Joe Dunlop's office, having requested to see the manager privately. Norma had told Midge to let her do the talking, she was a great deal better at this sort of thing than he was.

Norma stared levelly at Dunlop. Shortly after her dizzy turn at work she'd put the word out that she and Midge might be interested in moving dancehalls, if the fee was right. It hadn't taken long for the pair of them to have a 'bite'.

Norma had almost accepted this offer, and then she'd had a further thought. That was why she and Midge were there to see Dunlop. To find out if that further thought would work.

'So what can I do for you?' Dunlop asked with a smile. He took out one of the cigars he was addicted to, clipped it and lit up. When he'd finished Norma replied.

'The Locarno have offered us twenty pounds a week to go and be their professionals.'

Dunlop's smile vanished. Norma and Midge were a huge attraction at Barrowland. If they went to the Locarno they might take a lot of his clientele with them.

'I thought you liked it here?' he said slowly.

'We do. And we like you. But what's that got to do with it?'

Dunlop sighed, and puffed on his cigar. Truth was he'd rather been expecting something like this for a while. Neither Norma or Midge were fools, they knew the draw they were.

'All right then, I'll match the Locarno's offer. Twenty pounds a week as from Monday first,' he said.

Midge glanced at Norma, knowing what was coming next. Her 'further thought' as she'd put it.

'Let's say I go back to the Locarno and tell them about this conversation. What do you suppose their next move would be?'

Dunlop chewed the end of his cigar, regarding Norma through slitted eyes. 'You're saying that they'll offer more?'

'I think so. They're very keen to have us – they made that clear enough.'

Dunlop grunted. She was right, the Locarno would up the ante. The question now was what was the fee she'd decided on. For she obviously had a figure in mind.

'How much to keep you here?' he asked.

Her heart leapt within her. It had worked! It was amazing what a little bit of manipulation could accomplish.

'Thirty a week,' she stated boldly.

Midge choked. She'd told him she was going to ask for twenty-five.

'That's half again of what the Locarno are now offering,' Dunlop said quietly.

'I'm certain I can get them up to twenty-five. If you want us to stay here you'll have to top that, and top it by a reasonable amount.'

Dunlop stared hard at Norma, a cloud of cigar smoke surrounding his head and shoulders. 'How do I know you won't now go to the Locarno and try to get them to top thirty?'

'You think they might?'

Dunlop grinned. 'We shake hands and that's the end of the matter. Agreed?'

'For a reasonable period of time. Agreed?' she retorted.

Dunlop stood, and extended a hand across his desk. He shook first with Norma, then with Midge. 'Agreed,' he said.

Midge was opening the door for Norma when Dunlop suddenly went on, remembering, 'By the way, an American couple called Don and Zelda Caprice have been touring Europe – very successfully too I might add – and will be visiting Scotland before returning to the States. I've booked them for a fortnight next month. They'll be doing four exhibitions a night, alternating their performances with yours. All right?'

'We don't mind the competition if they don't,' Midge answered, and ushered Norma out of the office, shutting the door firmly behind them.

They looked at each other, both quite stunned. Fifteen pounds a week each – it was more than they'd been getting as a pair when they'd walked into Dunlop's office.

They walked down the corridor, away from the office, and turned a corner. There they fell into one another's arms.

'Tell me I'm dreaming!' Midge husked.

'It's no dream, it's for real.'

'It's a fortune, a King's ransom,' Midge enthused.

Norma gave a low laugh. 'Hardly a King's ransom, but it's an awful lot of money all the same.' She took a deep breath. 'I'm handing in my notice at SCWS tomorrow morning, what about you?'

'Aye. Why knock my pan out at the mills when I don't need to. I can live the life of Riley on fifteen quid a week.'

She gazed into his eyes, hoping he might suggest a date for their wedding there and then, but he didn't. She let it go for the moment. A date *would* be set for their wedding soon. She was determined about that.

'We need the daytimes free so we can practise. It's high time we enlarged our repertoire, and we need more than Saturday afternoons at Father Finn's "Pineapple" for that,' she said.

He nodded his agreement.

'Oh Midge!' she exclaimed, bubbling over with excitement and self-satisfaction at what she'd just pulled off. That, and love for this man now in her arms.

'I nearly died when you asked for thirty and not twenty-five as you'd said.'

'I suddenly thought, why not! And so I did.'

'You're a wee miracle worker Norma. And I adore you.'

When they returned to their table they found old man Gallagher waiting for them, come over for one of his chats. He talked about the dead Morna as he always did.

Midge was just about to pull the toilet chain when he heard the slam of a door followed by the click-clack of footsteps he would have recognised anywhere. He pulled the chain, and snecked open the cludgie door.

When Norma appeared he contrived to look mysterious, and crooked a finger, beckoning her to join him in the toilet.

'What is it?' she asked.

'Come here, inside,' he whispered back, and looked down behind the door as if something was there.

The moment she was inside he pulled her close with one hand and resnecked the door with the other.

'Got you,' he whispered, and gently bit her neck.

'What are you doing!' she exclaimed, struggling.

'Ssshhh!' he commanded. 'If you have to speak do so in a whisper.' He touched her breast. 'It's been so long,' he murmured, his eager mouth fastening onto hers.

So that's what this was all about, she thought as his tongue snaked and coiled round hers.

'No one will know we're both in here even if they try the door,' he said urgently when the kiss was over, dropping a hand to bring it up underneath her dress.

She pushed him back but, because there was so little room, couldn't break away from him completely.

'Are you mad! I'm not going to do it in the bog!' she whispered.

Midge was desperate – it had been weeks. 'But we so rarely

have the opportunity. Even though we're not working through the day now, your Ma is always around the house and so is mine. And we can't do it in the "Pineapple", that's completely out of the question.'

She forced his hand from under her dress. 'Stop that!' she ordered.

'But I want you so much.'

'Well it's your own fault. You could have me every night of the week if you wanted.'

He stared at her. 'How do you mean?'

It was the perfect opportunity and she wasn't going to let it go by. 'If we were married we'd have our own home and bed to go to.'

'But we've only been engaged two and a half months!'

'So where does it say you have to have a long engagement?'

Midge considered that. 'It doesn't I suppose. It's just that six or nine months or even a year is usual.'

'Long engagements are to give the engaged couple time to save up. But with what we're earning now that hardly applies to us, does it?'

She was right. What did they need to save up for! With thirty quid a week between them, and with what he had already put by – and her too no doubt – they could furnish a house as easy as pie. And furnish it damned well to boot.

'Let's set a date now,' she urged, her eyes bright with expectation.

The thought of Norma in his bed night and morning made Midge's blood race even more than it had been, which was saying something.

'As soon as we can arrange it then,' he agreed.

She sighed, and went tingly all over. 'How about directly after the All Scotland Dance Championship? That would be the perfect timing as far as I'm concerned.'

The All Scotland Dance Championship was Scotland's most prestigious championship and one of the few left open to them as pros. They'd been practising for it for months and it was now just a few weeks away.

'Directly after the championship then,' he nodded.

'Leave everything to me. I'll see the factor and arrange the house. And if there isn't a suitable one come available by that time we'll just stay in my room till it does.' Norma had been given her own bedroom when the family had moved into their three-room and kitchen. She paused. 'Oh Midge!' she exclaimed, and buried her mouth on his.

When the kiss was over he gave her a wicked grin. 'But only if . . .' His hand slipped back underneath her dress.

'Midge!'

'Please?' he whispered urgently.

At that moment she couldn't have refused him anything. Her lack of reply was his answer.

Thankful that he'd just happened to have 'the necessary' with him he turned her to face the door.

Don and Zelda Caprice got a thundering ovation at the conclusion of their first set of exhibition dances at Barrowland, an ovation Norma felt was well deserved.

Don was a man in his late twenties with cropped blond hair and a lithe, whipcord body. He was also handsome, but Norma didn't consider him as handsome as Midge.

Zelda was a little younger than her husband, and a Titian-haired beauty. She moved with the power-packed grace of a cheetah.

The rapturous applause reached new heights as the Americans left the floor. Again Norma was struck by the gown Zelda was wearing. It was couturier-made, Norma was certain of that. And absolutely gorgeous.

Joe Dunlop had introduced Norma and Midge to the Caprices at the beginning of the evening, but the two couples hadn't spoken since, as the Caprice's table was at the other side of the hall. Dunlop had thought it would look better if one couple came on from one side and then the other from the opposite side, rather than have the two couples concentrated at the same table.

Shortly after that it was time to go, and Norma and Midge met up again with the Caprices in the room where their coats, or wraps as Zelda referred to them, were kept.

'That was tremendous, top class,' Midge said to Don.

'And we were mighty impressed with you kids. We never expected anybody of your calibre up here in Scotland.'

Norma gazed in envy at the mink coat Zelda was shrugging

on. It was the sort of mink every girl dreams of.

Zelda caught her look. 'Want to try it hon?' she smiled.

'Oh no I couldn't!'

'Sure you could. Don bought it for me when we appeared in Ottawa last year. Didn't you Don?'

'I did indeed,' Don agreed.

The coat had a brown silk lining which rustled and whispered as Zelda helped Norma into it. When it was on Norma flipped up the collar so that it stood proud round her neck.

There was a full-length mirror attached to one wall. Norma crossed over to it and studied her reflection.

'How do I look?' she asked Midge.

'Like a filmstar.'

Zelda laughed. 'She does indeed. And Don and I should know, living in Hollywood as we do.'

'You live in Hollywood!' Midge exclaimed.

'We certainly do. And know lots of stars. Don't we Don?'

'Yeah,' Don agreed.

Midge thought that brilliant. Imagine, here he was talking to people who knew filmstars in the flesh! '*Who* do you know?' he asked eagerly.

'How about Alice Faye?' Zelda replied.

'Or Jimmy Cagney,' Don added.

Midge gulped. Those were two of the biggest names in Tinsel Town, a place he'd read a great deal about and would have given his eye-teeth to have visited.

'Or what about Jean Harlow – we know her real well,' Zelda continued.

'I like her,' Norma said, thinking of *Red Dust* that she'd seen Harlow in a few weeks previously.

'How about ... Garbo?' Midge asked.

'Sorry, there you have us,' Don admitted.

'We were once at a party she was at, but didn't get to meet her, I'm afraid,' Zelda said.

Don glanced at his wife; he was enjoying this, so why shouldn't they all continue the conversation back at the hotel? from Zelda's manner he guessed she'd also like that.

'Listen kids, we're staying at the Grand Hotel, which has agreed to lay on a dinner for us when we get back. Why don't you join us?'

'Yes, why don't you?' Zelda urged.

'Norma?' Midge queried, his expression and voice telling her he was mad keen to take up the invitation.

Norma thought of Effie and Brian, 'I'd love to have dinner with you, but if I don't turn up at the usual time my mother and father will worry themselves sick thinking something's happened to me. And I know Midge's parents would feel the same. It wouldn't be fair to either of them.'

Don frowned, he couldn't understand this. 'Why not just call and explain?'

Zelda saw Norma's lack of comprehension. 'He means telephone,' she explained.

Norma couldn't help the blush that stained her neck. What would these Hollywood people have thought if they'd seen Bridgeton? She shuddered to think.

'I'm afraid neither my parents or Midge's have a telephone,' she replied.

Don stared at her as if she'd just stated that her mother and father were a couple of orang-utans. 'No telephone! Well I'll be ...' He trailed off, lost for words.

'Perhaps another night then,' Zelda smiled.

'What about Friday?' Midge suggested, desperate to talk to the Caprices at further length.

Zelda glanced at Don. 'We've nothing special planned for then.'

And so it was agreed. The four of them would have dinner together that Friday night.

Midge couldn't wait.

They went to the Grand Hotel by taxi, to be greeted at the main entrance by a commissionaire in uniform and top hat. The man saluted, and helped first Zelda, then Norma, onto the pavement.

Norma had passed the Grand Hotel, reputedly Glasgow's finest, but had never been inside. As they headed for the dining-room, she made sure she took everything in – having a right good gander as Effie would have put it. In the dining-room they sat down at the table reserved for them.

A frown creased Midge's forehead as he studied the menu. It was almost incomprehensible to him. He swallowed hard, and his frown deepened as he continued staring blankly at words which, in the main, were French.

'I think I'll have the pâté followed by the *carbonnade de boeuf*,' Norma said.

'The same for me,' Midge told the hovering waiter. Norma smiled inwardly, she'd deliberately spoken when she had so that he could copy her order.

'And how about the wine, what would you recommend?' Don asked Midge, handing Midge the winelist.

Norma saw momentary panic in Midge's eyes. Like most working-class Glaswegians of the time he knew as much about wine as he did about riding a camel. It came either red or white, that was the sum of his knowledge on the subject.

'I wouldn't mind some claret. Or perhaps a Châteauneuf-du-Pape?' Norma said.

Midge blinked in astonishment.

'We have an excellent Châteauneuf-du-Pape,' the wine waiter said.

'Then we'll have a bottle of that. No, make it two bottles,' Don ordered.

Norma saw Midge's shoulders sag with relief. He hadn't foreseen what a posh dinner entailed (what had he expected to be on the menu, egg and chips!), but she had, and was prepared.

Bless Charlie Marshall and the Bridgeton Public Library! She'd explained her problem to Charlie who'd conjured up the appropriate books. It hadn't taken her long to learn the basics of what she'd find on the menu of a quality hotel, or to arm herself with some names and facts about wine. She was damned if she was going to look a fool, either in front of these Yankees or anyone else.

Midge shot Norma a glance that said not only 'thank you' but also 'where on Earth did you learn about Châteuneuf-du-Whatsit?' She smiled inscrutably in reply.

'And so we danced for King Leopold of Belgium,' Zelda was saying a little later – she and Don having been telling Norma and Midge about their European tour.

'A real king!' Midge breathed, his eyes popping out like organ stops.

'The second we've danced for on this tour. The other was King Carol of Rumania,' Don added.

'But when we hit Paris, now that really was spectacular,' Zelda went on.

Midge's meal grew cold in front of him. But that didn't bother him one little bit. All he wanted was to hear about the fabulous places the Caprices had been to.

The tales continued. Places, people, happenings, events. Midge drank in each and every word.

'Wasn't that just fantastic!' Midge said. He and Norma were in a taxi on their way back to Bridgeton. The taxi had been Norma's idea. Zelda had asked how they were getting home, and she'd immediately replied by taxi. It would have been humiliating to have answered otherwise.

After a while Midge fell silent, day-dreaming about the wonderful places the Caprices had been to. Oh how he wished . . .

Norma was thinking about the house they'd been promised in Greenvale Street, a stone's throw from Cubie Street. It was a three-room and kitchen, identical to the one she and her family were now in, and an unheard-of luxury for a childless couple. But as she and Midge could afford it, she hadn't seen any reason why they shouldn't indulge themselves with all that space. Why, they'd be the envy of the neighbourhood. She liked the idea of that. She liked it very much.

It was the following Tuesday afternoon and Norma and Midge were practising at the 'Pineapple'. They'd just broken for a breather and a cup of coffee from the flask that Norma always brought along.

'I've been thinking about the Caprices and that meal they treated us to. Don't you think we should return the gesture?' Midge asked.

'Is that necessary?'

'I feel we should. It's the polite thing to do,' he persisted.

Norma thought about that. She'd enjoyed the Americans' company, although it was Midge who'd gone overboard for them – he'd been talking non-stop about them all weekend.

'Perhaps we should do something . . .' she mused.

'What do you mean, something other than a meal?'

'Well, it is their first visit to Scotland. What we should do is take them round and about a bit. Show them the sights.'

'In Glasgow!' Midge laughed. 'And this, Zelda, is a ship-building yard, mind the oil on the deck and mind that low swinging crane doesn't take your head off. Or what about this blast furnace spewing dirt and filth into the air, and all over your nice dress. Maybe you'd like to write home about it?'

'Very funny,' Norma said drily.

'Glasgow's a working city, and a gey poor one at that. Slums and heavy industry, I can't see either Zelda or Don being dragged round any of that.'

Norma had an inspiration. 'Then let's forget about Glasgow and take them elsewhere. The Trossachs for example. It's one of Scotland's most famous beauty spots, and not that far away.'

Midge thought that a terrific idea. 'And we could lunch in a pub or hotel in the area,' he enthused.

'Lunch in a pub and high tea in a hotel.'

Midge nodded; that was even better. 'It would have to be next Sunday. They finish at Barrowland on Saturday and travel through to Edinburgh on the Monday.' Edinburgh was where the Caprices were appearing next.

'Sunday it will have to be then.' her face fell. 'The big drawback is getting there and back. It means taking a red bus.'

'They already know we don't have a car. And anyway, they'd probably love going on a red bus. Don't forget they don't have double-deckers in America.'

'Right then, we'll put it to them this evening,' Norma said.

They finished their coffee and returned to practising for the All Scotland Dance Championship, now only a short while away.

'Yeah sure, I think that would be real neat,' Zelda said, Norma and Midge having just proposed the day trip to the Trossachs.

'And we'll go by double-decker,' Midge added.

Don waved a hand. 'We don't have to bother about no bus. We'll travel in my car. Far more comfortable that way.'

'You have a car?' Norma queried in surprise.

'Well it's not really mine, I've rented it for the rest of my stay in Scotland. I'm lost without one you know. We Americans just ain't used to public transport.'

'Now you tell us your address beforehand and we'll stop by and pick you up,' Zelda said.

Alarm flared in Norma. The last thing she wanted was the Caprices coming to Bridgeton. It wasn't that she was pretending to be what she wasn't, rather that it would have caused her acute embarrassment for the Americans to see the district where she lived. And she was certain Midge felt the same way.

'Don't trouble yourself. We'll meet you at your hotel,' Norma replied.

'It's no trouble honey,' Don said.

Joe Dunlop popped his head round the door to ask if everything was all right. And tell them that even though it was a Tuesday, traditionally the slackest night of the week, there was already a fair-sized crowd in.

When Dunlop had gone Norma turned again to Don. 'As you don't know Glasgow you could have quite a bit of difficulty finding where Midge and I live. It would be a bad start to the day if you were to get lost and end up driving round and round looking for us. It'd be simpler if we come to you. And that's an end to it,' she said firmly.

'Okay then, if that's what you want,' Don conceded.

They agreed a time when Norma and Midge would turn up at the Grand Hotel.

Bremner's Warehouse in Glassford Street was where Norma decided to buy her wedding dress, and the bridesmaids' dresses for Lyn and Eileen.

'Isn't it exciting,' Lyn said.

Effie nodded. 'Aye, I must admit it is.' She was thoroughly enjoying the shopping and making the arrangements for the forthcoming wedding which was to take place the Saturday after the All Scotland Championship. The couple would be going away for a week's honeymoon, but only Midge knew where. Then they'd return to Greenvale Street which they were now in the process of redecorating.

'I remember my own dress. It wasn't an expensive one you ken, things being gey tight at the time, but bonny all the same.

Your da said I looked like an angel descending when I walked down the aisle,' Effie reminisced.

'You should have had photographs taken so that we could see now what you were like,' Lyn chided.

'Ah lass, there was no money for the likes of that. But I must admit, photographs would have been nice as a keepsake. Aye, they would've been right enough.'

Norma emerged from the cubicle where she'd been trying on yet another wedding dress.

'That's the one I'd go for. You're gorgeous in it,' Eileen enthused.

'I agree,' Lyn added.

Norma studied herself in a full-length mirror. She particularly liked the head-dress which was rather old-fashioned, with a cloche fitting. It was adorned with artificial orange blossom.

She smoothed down the ivory-coloured satin across her front. Eileen and Lyn were right, this was the dress for her. The dress she'd wear to become Mrs Midge Henderson.

'Ma?' she asked.

Effie nodded, tears of happiness in her eyes.

'I think it needs to be taken in a fraction here,' Norma said.

The assistant produced a measuring tape and some pins and they all fell to discussing the alterations that were going to have to be made.

Norma, Midge and Zelda waited at the front of the Grand Hotel while Don brought the car round. He tooted on the horn as he drew up beside them.

The car was green and called a Jowett Javelin. Norma and Zelda got in the back; Midge and Don in at the front. The car growled away with Midge giving Don directions.

There was a slight drizzle to start with, but they left that behind together with the horrible urban tangle that was Glasgow. They took the Bearsden/Milngavie road that would eventually bring them to Aberfoyle, and the Brig o'Turk beyond that.

This was Norma's first ever ride in a private car – the two taxis they'd taken the night of the meal in the Grand Hotel were her first experience of a motor vehicle at all – and she took to it like the proverbial duck to water. Long before they reached Aberfoyle she knew that she wanted a car for herself, and had made up her mind to take lessons directly she and Midge returned from their honeymoon.

When they stopped for petrol and everyone got out to stretch their legs she asked Don if she could sit in the driving seat. That was even better than being in the rear. Sitting there with the wheel between her hands she felt a tremendous sense of power and freedom. Not being in the least mechanical, she'd never have guessed she'd have fallen for cars this way. But she had. Hook, line and sinker.

At Brig o'Turk they parked, then strolled over to the water's edge. The Trossachs stretched from the shores of Loch Achray, where they were now standing, up through a richly wooded gorge – encompassing mountains, rivers and unparalleled landscapes – to that most beautiful of lochs, Loch Katrine. It was an area made famous by Sir Walter Scott in his poems *Lady of the Lake* and *Rob Roy*.

They walked along the lochside, Norma beside Don, and Zelda and Midge a little in front.

'Is it true there are orange trees in California. That you can just reach up and pluck an orange whenever you want one?' Midge asked Zelda.

'It's true enough, in some places there are orange and lemon trees stretching as far as the eye can see.'

'Gosh!' Midge exclaimed, wide-eyed.

'And you just wouldn't believe the sunshine we have there. Day after day, regular as clockwork. In fact we get so much sunshine there it gets boring.'

Midge shook his head in wonderment. 'After being born and brought up in Glasgow I don't think I'd ever get bored with sunshine.'

Zelda laughed. At times there was a little-boy quality about Midge that appealed to her. When they talked like this he made her think of a kid in a candy store.

'Maybe you'll come over and see those orange and lemon trees for yourself one day?' she suggested.

Midge took a deep breath. His heart was hammering; the blood pounding in his head at the thought. 'I've always wanted to travel, to see the world. That's been my dream for as long as I can remember. But ...' The light died in his eyes, and his shoulders drooped. 'That's not to be I'm afraid.'

'Norma?'

'Travelling doesn't appeal to her.'

'And so you'll settle down and be the good little stay-at-home hubby,' Zelda teased. And immediately wished she hadn't when she saw the expression of wretchedness that came over his face.

'I'm sorry, that was uncalled for,' she apologised.

Midge stooped, picked up a chuckie and threw it out into the loch where it plopped dully into the water.

'To be honest, I envy you and Don so much it hurts,' he said in a voice tight with emotion.

Zelda thought of the letter she'd seen Don furtively reading in their Munich hotel room, and how she'd ferreted it out of his case later when he was off having a massage. Going by Don's furtiveness she'd assumed it was a letter from another woman. She couldn't have been more wrong.

She hadn't been planning to do anything about that revelation until she got back to the States, but perhaps the answer to her problem was here beside her.

She looked at Midge with new interest.

They were all laughing at a joke Don had told as they drew up outside the Covenanters Inn, stopping there so that Don could pop in for some cigarettes.

Zelda finally stopped laughing to peer at the words chalked up on a blackboard just inside the main door.

'What's a dinner-dance?' she asked.

'Just that. You have dinner, and during the dinner, and afterwards, a band is playing which you can get up and dance to,' Norma explained.

A gleam came into Zelda's eyes. Turning, she addressed her companions. 'Listen you guys, today's been such a perfect one, why don't we extend it a while longer? I think this dinner-dance thing sounds just great.'

'It could be fun,' Midge said. He liked the idea.

'Are we dressed okay for it though?' Don queried, knowing how sticky the British could be about such matters.

That was a good point, Norma thought. Both men had

jackets and ties on, while she and Zelda were wearing reasonable skirts and tops. 'We should be acceptable,' she declared.

'Right then, in we go!' Zelda said, the gleam still in her eyes.

The inside of the Covenanters' Inn was done out in Jacobean-style decor. Claymores, two-handed swords, dirks, skean dhus, muskets, pistols and pikes adorned the walls. The carpets and curtains were in McGregor tartan, for this was the heart of McGregor country – that one time notorious outlaw clan whose name for years had been 'expressly abolished', the clan members forbidden the use of it.

They had a drink at the bar, where Don also bought some cigarettes, and then went through to where the dinner-dance was being held.

Norma judged there to be roughly forty people present; the tables they were sitting at grouped round three sides of the dancing area. On the fourth side, standing with their backs to a wall, was a six-piece band.

Zelda was right, Norma thought, it had been a perfect day. And what's more it had been extremely relaxing – just what she and Midge needed with the All Scotland Dance Championship coming up.

On this occasion Midge insisted that Don ordered the wine, looking slyly at Norma. Which Don did.

'We have some excellent wines in California you know,' Zelda said.

'Is that true!' Midge said, and gave a small, wondering shake of the head.

'Most palatable. Not quite up to the standard of the very best French and German wines mind you, but very palatable all the same,' Don added.

They all decided to order steak, and were waiting for these, having had their hors d'oeuvres, when the band started playing 'The Moonlight Saunter'.

'In the States we get T-bones – they're cuts of steak, which can be so huge they'll overhang the platters they're served on . . .'

Zelda switched her attention from Don to Midge, who was sitting beside her. She smiled, then glanced over to the dancing area.

Midge got the message. 'Would you care to get up?' he asked.

'Why yes. If you don't mind, that is, Norma?'

'Of course not.'

Midge escorted Zelda onto the floor, leaving Norma listening to Don holding forth about T-bone steaks.

By the end of the dance Zelda had found out what she'd wanted to know – and the reason why she'd suggested they go to the dinner-dance. As partners she and Midge were compatible, very compatible indeed.

From 'The Moonlight Saunter' the band went into 'Destiny Waltz'. Midge asked Zelda if she'd like to stay up, to which she replied she would.

As Midge and Zelda glided round the floor Norma thought how strange it was to see Midge dance with someone other than herself.

Later, when Don asked her to dance, she thought it even odder to be with someone other than Midge.

Brian, Effie, Lyn, Eileen and Charlie Marshall were there, so too were Leslie and Alice Henderson, Katy Henderson, Bob and Beryl Gillespie, Finlay Rankine accompanied by a stunning brunette, the Fullartons including Jacky's wife Sylvia, Joe Dunlop with his wife Margie, and Father Finn.

The All Scotland Dance Championship was being held in the Albert Ballroom, the venue of the first ever championship Norma and Midge had competed in, and the original number of entrants had been reduced to six couples, Norma and Midge among them. Of these, four were professional, two amateur.

Norma didn't normally get the jitters when competing, but she had them that night. If they were to win they'd be acknowledged as *the* best dancers in Scotland.

Before the final eliminations and the top three couples were decided there was to be an exhibition by the Caprices who'd come down from Dundee for the occasion.

'And now ladies and gentlemen, a big hand please for those international artistes who've been making such an impact during their tour of our country, and who are currently delighting audiences at the Dundee Trocadero – Don and Zelda Caprice!'

'How do you feel?' Midge whispered to Norma during the applause which greeted the Americans taking the floor.

'How do *you* feel?'

Midge grinned, but didn't reply. Instead he took her nearest hand and squeezed it.

He was jittery too; she could read it in his face. He was reassuring himself as much as her.

The Caprices were superb, quite outstanding Norma thought as they concluded their exhibition. She led what quickly swelled to an overwhelming clamour of appreciation.

Then it was back to the championship, and the MC called out the first of the six remaining couples onto the floor.

The minutes ticked by. Couple after couple performed, and sat down again. Finally it was their turn.

Their first dance was to be the cha cha cha, the second the lola tango. They acknowledged those watching, took their starting position, and were away.

The old magic that always happened between them was happening again, this time even more strongly than usual – Norma could feel the difference. Technically, everything went precisely as they'd planned and practised. They came over as a couple inspired.

They finished to a round of tumultuous applause – there was no question in Norma's mind that they'd won. It was not arrogance or ego on her part, but a frank appraisal of their performance. They'd left the other five couples standing for dead.

And was it proved. When the winners were announced it was them. They'd carried off the All Scotland Dance Championship, Scotland's most prestigious.

For a while there was pandemonium, with friends and relatives crowding round and hundreds of others offering their congratulations.

Effie was crying and Brian looked fit to burst with pride. Finlay Rankine repeated over and over that he'd known they'd do it, and Joe Dunlop was so ecstatic he was beside himself.

The prize was a crystal decanter and glasses to match, but these paled into insignificance compared to the kudos of winning. Norma would treasure the glory forever.

When the prize was presented Dunlop managed to get a private word with Norma and Midge. 'Listen, this calls for a party. All your people back to my place. And they're not to worry about booze or transport, Barrowland will be paying for those.'

When Norma and Midge were finally able to slip away they were taken to the waiting taxi that Dunlop had organised. They arrived at the Dunlop home to be greeted by Dunlop's wife Margie, and to find that nearly all of those invited had arrived before them. Norma learned that Dunlop hadn't only organised one taxi, but a veritable fleet of Black Cabs.

It was a smashing party, with the booze flowing and everyone enjoying themselves. With the exception of Lyn, that is, who, as usual, only enjoyed herself up to a point and had to seek consolation in the food.

Norma turned away from talking to Beryl Gillespie to glance over to a sofa where Midge had been sitting deep in conversation with Zelda Caprice. The two of them were still there with their heads together.

'You'd better keep an eye on her. She looks the carnivorous type to me,' Eileen said to Norma, having come across to join her.

'Who, Zelda?'

Eileen nodded.

'Don't be daft. She's a friend, and happily married. They'll be chaffing about dancing that's all.'

Eileen looked at her eldest sister. Norma might be nearly three and a half years older than her, but beside her she was naive at times. Often she felt the age difference between them was reversed, and that she was older than Norma. Not only older, but also more of 'a woman of the world'. 'I'll just say this, if it was my Charlie she had on that sofa I'd be over there like a shot,' Eileen said softly.

Norma had never heard anything so ridiculous. Why she and Midge were getting wed that Saturday!

However, just to be on the safe side, she did join Midge and Zelda after that. And they *were* talking about dancing.

Norma paused in her distempering. It was Tuesday afternoon, the day after the All Scotland Dance Championship, and she and Midge were in the Greenvale Street house working on what would be their bedroom.

Midge was standing with a can of distemper in his hand,

staring into space. There was a peculiar look about him, and his eyes had gone strangely glazed. There were beads of sweat on his brow, despite the fact it was chilly in the room.

'Midge?'

Wrapped in his thoughts, not hearing her, he continued staring into space.

'Midge!'

He blinked, then turned to her slowly.

'Is it last-minute panic? Is it just sinking in that by Saturday night you'll be a married man? That the knot will be tied between us?'

He swallowed. Made as though to reply, then changed his mind, and swallowed a second time.

Coming down off the ladder Norma went over to him and put an arm round his waist.

'I'm told that last-minute panic is quite natural, and that most people get it. I expect I'll get it myself. Come Saturday morning I'll probably be in such a paddy that I'll be wanting to take to the hills.'

He tried to smile, but it came out as a sort of lop-sided grimace.

'That's it. Don't think of it as the end of the world, but as a beginning.'

She buried her face in the crook of his neck. How she loved him.

She knew then what would cheer him up, make him feel better. It always did. Without fail.

Their new bed had just been delivered, and was in one of their spare bedrooms waiting to be brought through once they'd finished here. A spare bedroom with curtains up.

She took the can of distemper from his hand and laid it on the floor. She then led him through to the bed.

Dawn was breaking. Midge stood staring up at the shadowy shapes of the surrounding tenements. How horrible they were, he thought. And how squalid.

Somewhere close by a baby cried. A plaintive sound. And then a cat screeched – a screech to set the nerves on edge.

Midge yawned; he'd been prowling the streets for hours. He hadn't been able to sleep so he'd got up, dressed, and crept from the house. He'd never done such a thing before.

Dawn was now fully broken. Bridgeton revealed in all its splendour. A grey, evil-smelling slum.

A little later, when he walked back into his own close, he'd reached a decision.

It was Friday afternoon, the day before the wedding, and Norma was putting the presents away. The show of presents had been held the previous afternoon and the house had been chock-a-block.

It had been a grand show of presents. Effie had said how lucky she was to get so much – it was far more than she and Brian had received when they'd married.

Norma was placing a box of doilies from Jacky and Sylvia Fullarton in a drawer when there was a knock on the outside door. It would be Midge, at long last, she thought. But she was wrong. It was Don Caprice. He was clearly distraught.

'What's up?' she asked. Then, 'Why are you here and not in Dundee?'

Don stared at Norma. 'Can I come in?' he said, avoiding her question.

'Of course.' She shut the door behind them and led him through to the kitchen.

'Where's Midge?' he asked in a strained voice.

'I don't know. I was expecting him here hours ago, but so far he hasn't turned up. Now what is it Don, what's wrong?'

He lit a cigarette with shaking hands. 'I don't know why I came charging down to Glasgow. I suppose I thought... hoped...' He took a quick, nervous, puff of his cigarette. 'Have you got a drink in the house?'

'Sorry, no.'

He nodded. After which he inhaled deeply. 'I tried the Henderson house but there was no one home. Your mother said I'd find you here.'

Norma was bewildered. Don wasn't making any sense at all. 'Why did you go to the Hendersons?'

'You don't know do you?'

'Know what!'

He glanced away, unable to look her in the eye. 'I'm a dying man, Norma. When we were in Germany I started to feel unwell – loss of energy, constantly feeling drained, dizzy spells. I thought I'd been overdoing it, and that I just needed to ease off a bit. However, Zelda insisted I see a doctor.

'Well the doctor had his suspicions and said that tests had to be made. In the meantime I told Zelda that I'd been pronounced all right, and that the doctor had put me on an iron tonic —' He broke off laughing bitterly. 'I actually did buy a tonic in a drugstore to keep up appearances.

'When the results of the tests came through they were conclusive. I have leukaemia.'

Norma clapped her hands to her mouth.

'I've written a letter to my doc back home. Not that he'll be able to do anything. I'm literally under sentence of death.'

'How . . . how long?' asked Norma in a subdued voice.

'Three, maybe six months. Nine at the outside.'

How truly awful for him, Norma thought. Such a lovely man, cut off in his prime. 'And you haven't told Zelda?'

He shook his head. 'I wanted the tour to be finished and us back in LA before I did. But somehow she's found out – she's left me. Run off with a new partner.'

A sudden fear blossomed in the pit of Norma's stomach. She remembered the party at Joe Dunlop's, and what Eileen had said.

'No!' she whimpered. Midge wouldn't do that to her. He wouldn't!

'Zelda left me a note. Even though you haven't got it yet, or come across it, I would imagine Midge has done the same.'

Bile rose in her throat, and for a few moments she thought she was going to throw up. Then that passed.

'I'm sorry I had to be the one to tell you,' Don whispered.

'Where . . . Did Zelda say where?'

'London first, then the States.'

It was a nightmare, a horrible nightmare. She told herself she'd soon wake up and realise it was only that. But she didn't wake up; the nightmare was for real.

After a while Don left. Norma stood with her back to the front door, closed her eyes and finally let the tears come. Hot tears that coursed down her cheeks and fell on the linoleum below.

And with the tears, anger. Anger that exploded and roared within her.

Frantically she tugged at her engagement ring, ripping the skin of her finger as she pulled it off. Flying through to the kitchen she jerked open the window and threw the ring out as hard as she was able. With a sob she crashed the window shut again, cracking the glass in the process.

It couldn't be true, it just couldn't! And yet it was. Midge, *her Midge*, had run off with Zelda.

She screamed. A scream so powerful and intense it turned the back of her throat red raw. With tightly-clenched fists she beat her thighs. Again and again, as though her fists were hammers.

Then she remembered her wedding dress, hanging in their bedroom wardrobe. Running to the wardrobe she tore the dress and head-dress down from their hangers and screwed them up into a ball.

Then she spied, amongst a pile of her shoes that had been brought over from Cubie Street, a very old pair of red shoes. The red shoes she'd worn the night she'd met Midge, and which she'd kept ever since. She snatched up the red shoes as well and rushed out of the room.

She'd made up the fire earlier because it had been cold. She now tossed her wedding dress and head-dress onto the burning coals, throwing the red shoes on top of them. Using a poker, she rammed the lot down.

Norma watched with grim satisfaction as the dress and head-dress were set alight. The imitation orange blossom sizzled, and charred to a crisp cinder. The red shoes turned black first in places, then finally black all over.

Sinking to her knees, she gazed into the mini inferno. The anger had gone, its fury replaced by an aching emptiness. Where before she'd had a demon's strength, she was now weak as a kitten.

'Oh Midge!' she whispered.

The remains of the red shoes fell apart as she continued to weep.

# *Part II*

# DOUGLAS AND FANY
# 1940–43

## *Chapter Six*

It was late afternoon, getting on towards five o'clock. September 1940, and Norma was sitting in a car outside a private house in Muswell Hill. From this superb vantage point, high on the hill itself, she was watching a vast formation of German bombers droning past overhead.

It was a terrifying sight. Wave after wave, each wave consisting of a dozen squadrons, each squadron consisting of a dozen aircraft, heading east. It would be the Docks they were after, Norma told herself. And she was right.

The sky was perfect for flying, indeed it had been a perfect autumn so far, as the Battle of Britain continued to rage, and now the Blitz began. Spitfires and Hurricanes buzzed and darted among the *Luftwaffe*'s bombers, but there were so few compared to the numbers they were trying desperately to repel.

A parachute opened, then another. That cheered Norma, till it struck her that they might be British lads. She hadn't seen what plane, or planes, had gone down.

Norma tore her gaze from what was happening overhead to glance at the house into which Major-General Gilchrist had disappeared more than half an hour previously. She had no idea whom he'd gone to see, or indeed even what his business in the army was. He'd never volunteered any information about himself, and of course she'd never asked.

A strange, secretive figure, the Major-General. Another Scot like herself, only he was from the Highlands and spoke with the soft unmistakable lilt of the highlander. But that was all that was soft about Major-General Gilchrist. Although he had an intellectual, almost donnish, air about him, that didn't fool Norma any. She'd spent too long in Glasgow not to recognise a hard man when she saw one.

Norma had been Gilchrist's driver for a fortnight now, and he'd certainly kept her busy. Fourteen, sixteen hours some days, hither and yonning all over London and the Home Counties. They'd also been to Birmingham on several occasions, and once to Exeter.

At the outbreak of the war Norma had joined the First Aid Nursing Yeomanry, known as FANY. Formed in 1907, the FANY's original purpose had been to provide nurses on horse-back who could move quickly round the fringes of a traditional battlefield giving on-the-spot first aid.

During the Great War the purpose had been modified. The motorised ambulance had replaced the horse, and other aspects of 'on-the-spot' aid had been introduced, such as providing mobile canteens and mobile bathing facilities.

By the time of the Second World War the duties of FANY had changed still further. They were no longer part of the regular army, but worked in conjunction with it, amongst other things, supplying the army with drivers. Most FANYs worked along-side the Auxiliary Territorial Service, and were known as FANY-ATS, but Norma wasn't one of these. She was a Free FANY, which meant her loyalty was to FANY and FANY alone.

Norma looked again at the sky, where the waves of *Luftwaffe* bombers were still passing by. A Hurricane or Spitfire – she couldn't tell the difference – exploded even as she watched it. A ball of red and orange flame, smoke, then tiny bits of wreckage tumbled to earth. One moment the pilot had been alive; the next he was dead, blown to bits. Norma felt sick at the thought.

From far off came the dull boom of exploding bombs. A sound that rapidly grew louder and louder. The Docks, and surroun-ding areas, were taking a pasting.

Out the corner of her eye she saw the door to the house opening. It wasn't Major-General Gilchrist who emerged, but a Guards' Captain.

The Captain paused to stare up at the sky, then hurried over to the car. Norma rolled down her window.

'The Major-General wants you to go to this address and pick up several box files that will be ready waiting for you. You've to bring them straight back here,' the Captain said, handing

Norma a slip of paper on which the address had been written in best copperplate.

'I'll be as quick as I can,' Norma replied. She got out her *A to Z* as the Captain dashed back indoors.

She'd been in London for ten months, but the city was so huge she still had to look up every address before she set off.

This particular address was in Somers Town, adjacent to King's Cross. She decided to go down the Archway Road, down Holloway Road and then via Liverpool Road. It wasn't the shortest route, but the easiest as far as she was concerned.

She'd learned to drive after Midge had run off with Zelda, something she'd thrown herself into because it was a help to stop herself thinking, and brooding.

She'd never appeared at Barrowland again, nor had she wanted to, even though Joe Dunlop had suggested she might try and find another partner.

She'd given up the house in Greenvale Street that was to have been hers and Midge's, and stayed at home with the family. Without a job she'd been considering asking the SCWS to take her back, when Finlay Rankine had offered her a position - no strings attached he'd assured her, treating her to that crocodile smile of his - as a female dance instructor at Silver's. She'd grabbed the opportunity, and been happy and successful there, only leaving after the outbreak of war, when she'd come down to London to join the FANY at their headquarters in Lower Grosvenor Place.

Whilst working at Silver's an extraordinary event had taken place. She'd been helping Effie make the tea one evening when a man called Jardine had come chapping, asking to speak with her.

He was a Mr Martin Jardine of Jardine, Jardine, Hepburn and Deans, a firm of solicitors in Renfield Street. And acting on behalf of Mr Thomas Gallagher, recently deceased. A Thomas Gallagher whose son had been killed while serving with Allenby at Megiddo, and whose daughter Morna had died of a brain tumour. A daughter Norma was the spitting image of.

To cut a long story short, alone in the world, Mr Gallagher had left all his money and possessions to Norma. This consisted of a substantial amount of money in the bank, four jeweller's shops and a small flat in Kelvinbridge.

When she'd finally got over the shock of this totally unexpected windfall, Norma had instructed Jardine to sell the flat and shops. She knew nothing about the jewellery business, and wasn't interested in learning.

The capital realised from the sale, added to what was already in the bank made Norma a woman of considerable financial standing, financially independent for the rest of her life. Providing she didn't squander the money, that was – which she had no intention of doing.

Although she hadn't needed to go on working she'd elected to do so, and continued on at Silver's.

With this money behind her, Norma had been able to join the FANY, whose members were all unpaid volunteers.

Norma started to think about Midge. She'd never got over him and her heart still ached at the memory of what they'd had together. An ache she believed would be with her always.

The last she'd heard was that he was still in America and doing well. Don had died shortly after returning to Hollywood and Midge and Zelda had married soon afterwards.

After a while Norma had made herself go out with other men. Nor had there been any trouble meeting them since joining FANY. Officers were attracted to FANYs the way bees are to honey. It was said they had a special air about them.

She was going out with someone at the moment, a Major called Jeremy Dereham. But he – like the others – meant nothing to her. Love came once, and in her case that once was Midge Henderson. The rest were just good company – fun, jolly to be with, but no more than that.

She was snapped out of her reverie by a very loud bang fairly close by. That bang was followed by another, and then another.

Bombs, she thought grimly. Islington, where she was now, was well away from the Docks. There must be another target they were after.

She saw the side of a building momentarily bulge, then collapse inwards. Debris and dust whooshed into the air. She'd best get away from this, she told herself, and executed a few sharp turns that brought her into Risinghill Street. From there she could see the spires of St Pancras and King's Cross, which she judged to be about half a mile away.

She heard the bomb coming. Not a screech as she'd imagined

it would be, but rather as if coarse sand was raining down on a sheet of corrugated iron. A sound that steadily increased as the bomb hurtled groundwards.

And then the sound stopped, and for a split second there was an eerie silence. Suddenly she was enveloped in red and orange flame, exactly the same as that she'd witnessed in Muswell Hill when the plane had blown up.

The car went spinning through the air in a twisting, rotating motion. This is it, she thought, clinging on frantically as the car turned upside down.

How tinny the car now seemed. Quite the opposite to when its four wheels were on the ground.

Would death be instantaneous? she wondered. She prayed it would.

Finally, after what seemed like an eternity, an eternity during which everything happened in slow motion, the car hit the ground again, bounced, and went smashing into a street lamp.

There was the screech of metal being torn asunder. And for one horrifying instant a fountain of bright red blood. Her own? She was contemplating that when, as if a light had been switched off, she lost consciousness.

Norma came to to find a man's anxious face peering into hers. 'This one's alive,' the man said to someone in the background.

Norma groaned. Her chest was very painful, while her left arm was numb from the shoulder down. Then she remembered the fountain of blood.

Glancing quickly at her left arm she saw with relief that it was still there. She was lying in a pile of rubble – she guessed that she'd been thrown from the car. She touched her face, but there was no blood there. Whatever had happened, she hadn't gone through the windscreen.

A stout woman in the green uniform of the Women's Voluntary Service, the WVS, replaced the man. 'He's gone for a stretcher. We'll soon have you sorted out ducks,' the woman said.

Norma tried to take a deep breath, but couldn't because of the pain in her chest. She looked about her, and was appalled at what she saw.

When she'd turned into Risinghill Street it had been a short street with houses on both sides. Not any more. The houses were gone, completely flattened. There was no sign of her car. She could only assume it had been buried.

There were bodies everywhere. And . . . *bits* of bodies. Risinghill Street residents who'd been at home when the bomb had struck. She later learned that directly after the bomb a land mine had also hit the street, and it was the latter which had inflicted most of the damage.

She didn't know how she had managed to survive this carnage and awful destruction. But one thing she did know, and that was she was extremely lucky to have done so.

The man reappeared with another man and a stretcher. Together, with the help of the WVS lady, they manoeuvred Norma onto the stretcher.

At that point the pain in Norma's chest became so intense she passed out again.

Clouds, a haze of clouds extending in every direction. A puff of clouds parting to reveal . . . Was it? She couldn't be sure. And then she was. Midge had come back for her.

She ran to him, and threw her arms round his neck. Eagerly she pressed her lips onto his, her tongue into his mouth.

They were still kissing when the clouds rose up to envelop them. And with that oblivion once more.

She opened her eyes to stare at a white ceiling. She was in a bed, a very hard bed, and there was an antiseptic smell in the air.

'Hello,' a female voice said.

The girl was younger than her, and a nurse. 'Where am I?' Norma croaked.

'The Royal Free Hospital, Gray's Inn Road.'

'Am I . . .' She winced as pain stabbed her chest. 'Badly hurt?'

'Doctor will speak to you shortly. He'll answer all your questions,' the nurse replied with a smile.

The nurse left Norma to go off and fetch some screens, which she positioned round the bed.

Why did the girl keep looking sideways at her and smiling like that? Norma wondered. Was there something funny about her? She noticed for the first time that her left arm was in plaster.

That meant she'd been out for quite some time.

She was kept waiting for ages. Then a doctor and the same nurse as before came in through the screens.

'I'm Douglas Ross, the Assistant Surgeon. Sorry I've been so long. I was just about to come to you when they wheeled in an emergency. I had to attend to him first.'

'Will he be all right?' Norma asked.

'He died, I'm afraid.'

'Oh!'

Doctor Ross was a slightly built man with a sallow complexion and raven-black hair. He had liquid brown eyes and a slightly acquiline nose. He looked dead beat, as though he'd been on the go for far too long. Which he had.

'How do you feel?' he asked.

'Like I'd tangled with a road roller, and lost.'

He grinned. 'Any headache?'

'No. A sort of mental muzziness, but I wouldn't describe it as a headache.'

'Good,' he said approvingly.

He picked up her chart from where it was hanging on the bottom of the bed, and wrote on it. While he was writing he said, 'Your arm is broken in two places, the higher-up break a compound one. As you can see that's already been attended to.'

'I have an extremely sharp pain in my chest. As though someone was sticking a knife into me.'

He glanced at her over the top of the chart. 'I'd better have a look then. Staff, will you...'

The nurse was moving before he'd asked her to. She undid the top of the gown Norma had been put into.

'It's Miss McKenzie isn't it? There were some identification papers in what's left of your uniform. The uniform itself is only fit for the scrap bin I'm afraid,' Ross said.

By now Norma was bare to the waist. She felt embarrassed that this strange man could see her partial nakedness, and reminded herself he was a doctor. He no doubt saw breasts and other private parts every day of the week. Nonetheless, her neck still flamed when he came over to sit beside her.

'Where is this pain?' he queried.

She indicated. 'Here, and across here.'

His hand was cool, and very gentle. Gentle or not she yelped when he touched her, then yelped again.

'Is it sore when I do that?'

'Like Billy-O.'

'And you say it's as though someone was sticking a knife into you?'

'Sometimes it's as though the knife was being twisted this way and that.'

He regarded her thoughtfully. 'A broken rib, if indeed not broken ribs. But are the pressing bits pressing where they shouldn't? That's the question.'

He flipped first one side of her gown closed, then the other, so that her breasts were covered again. She was grateful for that.

'Tell Sister Roberts that I want Miss McKenzie's chest X-rayed from all angles as soon as possible, and to see those X-rays the moment they're available, Staff,' Ross said to the nurse.

He ran a weary hand through his hair. 'I'll speak to you again after I've viewed the X-rays,' he told Norma.

'Fine.'

What a nice man, she thought after he'd gone.

She was lying on a trolley waiting to be taken into X-ray.

There was a large mirror over to her left, behind a reception desk. Eventually her eyes drifted to it, and there, reflected, was Doctor Ross.

He was standing off to one side of her, in conversation with another doctor. Ross was listening to what the other doctor was saying, but his gaze was fastened onto Norma. He was watching her, but didn't realise she could see him doing so.

When, a few minutes later, a technician appeared to take her into X-ray he was still watching her.

'Darling!' Lynsey Dereham squealed, and ran up the ward to Norma's bed. Lynsey was also a FANY, and Norma's best pal. It was through Lynsey that she'd met Jeremy, her brother.

Jeremy was behind Lynsey, and with him William Trevalyn, and, with William, another officer whom she'd never seen before.

'For God's sake don't try and hug me – I've got four broken

ribs!' Norma said in alarm as Lynsey came round to her bedside. Lynsey was a great hugger.

Lynsey's arms dropped back to her sides. 'You look ghastly,' she declared.

'Oh thank you very much. That's a real confidence booster,' Norma replied.

'But you do darling. Quite, quite . . .'

'Ghastly,' Norma finished for her, and they both laughed. At least Lynsey did; Norma quickly stifled her laughter. It hurt to laugh.

'This is Freddy Harcourt, he was with us so we brought him along to meet the patient,' Jeremy said. Freddy was a major with The Royal Green Jackets, the same regiment as William. Jeremy was with The King's Royal Hussars.

'Jolly rotten luck what happened to you,' Freddy sympathised.

'Rotten luck that I was there at the time. But it was lucky that I survived. The street was blown to smithereens,' Norma replied quietly.

'We saw the street. What a mess,' Lynsey said soberly.

Jeremy pecked Norma on the cheek. 'This'll be you out of action for some while, I should imagine.'

She told them the extent of her injuries. 'When I first came in the doctor was worried that I might have a piece of broken rib touching a lung, which they tell me could have been very nasty indeed. However, that wasn't so, I'm happy to say.'

'I've brought you some chocs,' Jeremy said, plonking a box of Cadbury's best down on the bedside table.

'And I've brought you some of your personal things,' said Lynsey, taking a small case from William and placing it between the table and bed.

'I hope there's a nightie in the case?'

'There are two nighties. One of them's the pink, your favourite,' Lynsey reassured her.

They were a merry – if somewhat loud – crew. From the way Freddy and William carried on she suspected they'd been to a pub beforehand.

Freddy began in on an outrageous joke which had them all – with the exception of Norma who kept pleading 'Don't! Don't!' – falling about. In the middle of this hilarity Ross came striding into the ward. He came up short and frowned at them.

'Sssh! Quieten down, you'll get me into trouble!' Norma beseeched them, to no avail. Freddy was determined to deliver his punchline, which he did to the loudest laugh yet.

Turning on his heel, Ross stalked from the ward.

Norma fully expected Sister Roberts to come charging in to tell them to put a sock in it. But Sister didn't, nor did anyone else.

And then Freddy started in on another joke, this one even more outrageous than the one before.

The following day Doctor Ross was in the corridor leading to Marsden Ward when he ran into Sister Roberts carrying the largest bunch of flowers he'd ever seen. And being a hospital surgeon he'd seen large bunches of flowers in his time.

'I'm surprised you can carry that lot,' he said, gesturing at the flowers.

'Aren't they absolutely magnificent! They're for Miss McKenzie.'

Doctor Ross's heart sank a little on hearing that, which was stupid really. She was nothing to him after all.

'She's certainly popular, but then they say that FANYs always are,' Sister Roberts commented.

She was certainly popular all right, Ross thought sourly. Not a day went past without at least one male uniform by her bedside.

He changed the subject.

Norma got into bed, and lay back with a sigh. Her broken arm was throbbing dreadfully thanks to her having bashed the damned thing in the toilet. It was her own fault for being so clumsy; she should have been more careful of what she'd been doing.

Her head had spun with the pain, and she'd felt sick. If she'd fainted and gone crashing to the floor there would have been no one there to help her.

Despair welled up in her. How she hated all this. And how difficult everything was when one arm was incapacitated and you were strapped up like an Egyptian mummy round the middle.

She'd have given anything for a long hot wallow, but that was forbidden her. She was only allowed three or four inches of water and had to have a nurse in attendance to assist. There was no pleasure or relaxation in such a bath. None at all.

Then there was her hair – a complete mess. It needed a lot more doing to it than merely having a comb run through it, which was all she could manage in her present state. If only she could have gone to the hairdresser's, but of course that was impossible in the circumstances.

And now to top it all, just to add to her wretchedness, her period had started. Her despair turned to self-pity.

A murmuring voice caught her attention. The voice belonged to Sister who was further up the ward with Doctor Ross. And there he was, doing it again, *staring* at her. Why was the damned man forever staring at her, she was beginning to find it downright creepy.

Sister left Ross and went over to a nearby student nurse. Seconds later the student was putting the screens round Norma's bed.

And then Norma remembered her comb, an ivory one with an overlaid silver grip that had been a present from Finlay Rankine when she'd left Glasgow to join the FANY. She'd left the bloody thing in the toilet. She'd have to go back for it straight away otherwise it would take a walk, if it hadn't already. She was about to swing her legs out of bed when Ross came through the screens.

'And how are you today?' he smiled.

'Don't tell me I remind you of someone else too?' she snapped at him.

'I beg your pardon?'

'There was another man I used to know who watched me the way you do. Turned out I was the spit of his dead daughter. So is that it, do I remind you of someone else? Is that why you're always staring at me?'

The smile disappeared. His face froze.

'Well?' she demanded, her voice harsh and grating.

'I didn't realise...' He broke off in confusion.

She wanted to take a deep breath, but couldn't thanks to her strapped-up chest. Another irritation. Today, was just full of them.

'I'm sorry. I really am...' He trailed off, gulped, then blundered out through the screens, knocking them skewiff in the process.

'Damn!' she muttered angrily. She hadn't meant to do that, attack him almost. As doctors went he couldn't have been nicer or more attentive to her.

It was just one of those days. And he *was* forever watching her when he thought she wasn't aware.

She'd had a bad night, partly because of the pain in her arm where she'd bashed it, and partly because of her guilty conscience at having said to Ross what she had. She'd been waiting all morning for him to come onto the ward so she could make amends. Her outburst had been most unlike her.

Just before lunch he made an appearance in the company of Sister Hennessy, the junior Sister.

'Could I have a private word please Doctor?' she called out to him when he made to pass by the bottom of her bed.

He stopped, then turned to regard her impassively. 'Certainly Miss McKenzie,' he replied, and came round to stand beside her.

Sister Hennessy continued on down the ward.

Norma cleared her throat. 'I'm sorry for snapping at you yesterday. It was completely uncalled for.'

She'd expected him to unbend, perhaps for a smile to come onto his face. No such smile, or any other indication of forgiveness, was forthcoming.

'I mean it. I am sorry.'

He nodded. 'A few more days and I don't see any reason why we can't discharge you. After being discharged you'll still have to attend hospital as an out patient until your arm and ribs are fully mended. Then there will have to be a period of convalescence before you can take up your duties with FANY again. I shall write to your CO to explain the situation.' He glanced at his watch. 'Now if you'll excuse me I must be getting on.'

He strode up the ward to rejoin Sister Hennessy.

She felt like picking something up, preferably something heavy, and chucking it after him. Arrogant silly man! She'd been in the wrong and admitted she had, why couldn't he accept her apology!

When he went off the ward sometime later he was careful to never once let his gaze stray in her direction.

To give herself something to do she'd been helping Staff hand out the afternoon coffee and biscuits, the same Staff who'd been with her when she'd regained consciousness after Risinghill Street. The pair of them were now in Sister's office tucking into the remains of a cake that had been given by the relative of a departing patient.

'Hmm, delish!' Staff crooned, wiping cream from the corners of her mouth.

Norma had to agree, the cake was delish. She wondered how long they'd continue to enjoy such luxuries – already there was talk of food rationing having to be introduced.

'Tell me about Doctor Ross, Staff. What's he like?'

Staff glanced sideways at Norma. 'You mean in his private life?'

'Yes.'

'Very quiet and shy. He doesn't have a girlfriend if that's what you're asking. In fact the last thing he is is a ladies' man. That's why it was so hysterically funny when you . . .' Staff broke off abruptly and groped for her packet of Black Cat.

'When I what?' Norma demanded. Was Staff referring to the words she'd had with Ross. And how could they be interpreted as hysterically funny. She was lost.

'Forget me, I'm not supposed to say,' Staff replied, and lit up. Thinking, her and her big mouth.

But Norma wasn't the type to let go. There was a mystery here, she wanted an explanation. 'Come on, don't be mean,' she prompted.

Staff blew a stream of smoke towards the ceiling and didn't reply.

'Has he been saying something about me?' Norma queried.

'No, it's nothing like that,' Staff answered in alarm.

'Then what is it like?'

'Oh buggeration!' Staff thought. When would she ever learn to keep her big yap shut.

'Doctor Ross and I were called down from the ward when you

arrived in Casualty. He was examining your broken arm when you suddenly threw your other arm round him and gave him a real passionate kiss.'

'I what!' Norma exclaimed.

'Threw your good arm round his neck and gave him a real passionate kiss. And while you were kissing you were making the sort of sounds... well you know the sort of sounds a girl can make at certain times.'

'Oh my God!' Norma whispered, completely stunned by this revelation. Her face and shoulders all the way down to her breasts turned a bright shade of pink.

She remembered the peculiar smile Staff had given her after she'd regained consciousness, and wondering if there was something funny about herself. No wonder Staff had been amused after witnessing that.

And then it all came flooding back; she'd completely forgotten about it until now.

She remembered her dream. The haze of clouds extending in every direction and a puff of cloud parting to reveal Midge. She'd thought Midge had returned to her, gone rushing up to him and ...

She'd kissed Doctor Ross believing she was kissing Midge. That had to be it. She knew now why the dream had seemed so real. Passionate wasn't the word, she must have stuck her tongue halfway down the poor man's throat. It was clear to her now why Ross had been staring at her the way he had. Only too horribly clear indeed.

'How embarrassing,' she muttered to Staff.

'You should have seen how embarrassed *he* was. We thought he was going to expire on the spot. Particularly when you wouldn't let him go. You may have only one working arm but you certainly used it to good effect. In the end it took four of us to prise him free.'

It got worse and worse, Norma thought. 'Did I mention a name at all?' she asked weakly.

Staff shook her head.

Norma wasn't sure whether that was a relief or not.

'Things happen in hospitals, usually under anaesthetic, that we normally keep to ourselves. That was why I was reluctant to tell you about it.' Staff explained.

Norma gave a brittle laugh. 'It was a dream I had. I thought he was someone else.'

'Your chap?' Staff asked with interest.

'No, my ex.'

'You still care for your ex then?'

Norma sidestepped that one. 'He and I were professional ballroom-dancers. We danced as a couple,' she replied instead.

She then went on to tell Staff about Barrowland and the pinnacle of their achievement when they'd won the All Scotland Dance Championship.

She lied a little as a face-saver. She said Midge had always wanted to see the world and had gone off to do just that. She didn't mention that he'd jilted her the day before the wedding to run away with a cold-hearted bitch called Zelda Caprice.

Should she or shouldn't she? She'd been debating that with herself ever since the bombshell Staff had dropped. Now Doctor Ross was back on the ward she had the opportunity to speak to him if she wanted to.

'Doctor? Could I have another word?'

He stopped, to eye her coldly. 'Is something the matter Miss McKenzie?'

'No I eh . . . ' She glanced at the nurse with him who got the message. The nurse moved on to another patient several beds further down the ward. He came over.

'I'm told I . . . That when I . . .' She trailed off. This was damnably difficult.

'Yes?'

She looked into that cold gaze, and withered inside. He was being so off-putting. She knew then that she'd lost her nerve, That she wouldn't go through with making, or trying to make, another apology.

'Nothing. Nothing at all,' she mumbled.

He picked up her chart and studied it.

'You're Scots aren't you? I didn't twig it for quite some time as you're so well-spoken.'

He glanced up at her, but didn't answer.

'Am I wrong then? Is it the north of England perhaps?'

'I am Scots,' he said slowly.

'Thought you were. Where from?' she asked in a friendly manner.

'I don't consider that information relevant to your case Miss McKenzie,' he replied.

It was like being slapped in the face and doused with iced water at the same time. If she could have curled up and vanished she would have done.

'You can be discharged after breakfast tomorrow,' he said, replaced the chart, and walked away.

Fuck you too! she thought, which was hardly a ladylike expression. But nonetheless said exactly what she felt.

*Fuck you too*!

'Thank you for the flowers, they're gorgeous,' Norma said to Major-General Gilchrist, for it was he who'd sent her the huge bunch of flowers that Doctor Ross had commented upon. The flowers, somewhat past their best now, still took pride of place on the window-sill to the right of Norma's bed.

'I should have been to see you before now, but honestly Norma I haven't had a moment. I shouldn't really be taking this time off, but then I realised I could mix business with pleasure so to speak, and so here I am.'

Business? She waited for him to elaborate.

'When will they let you out?' he queried.

'Lucky you came today, otherwise you'd have missed me. I'm to be discharged tomorrow directly after breakfast. I should have been discharged earlier except that my doctor is a very cautious man.'

'And which doctor is that?'

'Doctor Ross. Douglas Ross. He's the Assistant Surgeon on this ward.'

A strange expression came over Gilchrist's face; an amused glint into his eyes. 'That's extremely interesting to hear,' he replied, but more to himself than Norma.

'Is it?' She couldn't think why on earth that should be of interest to the Major-General.

'What will you do when you leave here?' Gilchrist asked, changing the conversation.

'It'll be another seven to eight weeks till my broken bones mend, and I've to have a spell of convalescence after that. I thought I'd spend the time in Glasgow. I haven't been home since I joined the FANY.

'Good idea.'

They talked for a few minutes longer, then Gilchrist reluctantly excused himself to go back to his work.

After Gilchrist had gone Norma went over to choose a magazine from the collection kept for the patients' use. She was leafing through a copy of *My Weekly* when she happened to glance out of the window. From there, she could see the corridors leading to and from Marsden Ward, and framed in one of the windows she could make out the heads and shoulders of Major-General Gilchrist and Doctor Ross. The pair of them were talking together.

Now what was that all about? Norma wondered. Were they discussing her? And if so why? And what was the business Gilchrist had mentioned but failed to elaborate on?

The two men moved away out of sight.

East West, home's best. The old saying was right, Norma thought to herself standing outside the Central Station at the Gordon Street entrance. That familiar smell stung her nostrils. Soot, dirt, the wind off the Clyde. Glasgow, how she'd missed it while down south, and how good it was to be back.

'Here's a taxi now,' the soldier who was helping her with her luggage said, waving at the Black Cab that had suddenly appeared. She'd had to ask the soldier to help her as there hadn't been any porters around. All called up, she'd presumed. Thank goodness at least one taxi driver wasn't.

But she was wrong about the latter. The taxi driver had been called up and the person now driving the taxi was his wife.

'Cubie Street in Bridgeton, just off the Gallowgate,' Norma instructed. 'I'd be obliged if you'd drive slowly. I've got four broken ribs strapped up underneath my uniform.'

'Oh aye, what happened to you then, hen?' the female taxi driver asked as she set the vehicle in motion.

Norma smiled to herself. Typical Glasgow. Straight to the point. It had slipped her mind just how blunt and abrasive Glaswegians were. Other folk, less kindly disposed towards Mungo's children, might have put that another way.

When the taxi drew up outside the McKenzie close the taxi

driver knew all about Risinghill Street and the Royal Free Hospital. Norma also knew about the woman's husband with the Seaforth Highlanders and the couple's wee son who went to a day nursery.

The taxi driver carried Norma's two cases up the stairs for her, and refused a tip, saying she wouldn't take a tip from someone wounded in the course of duty. Norma hadn't thought of herself as being 'wounded in the course of duty' before. Now that she did it made her feel rather proud of herself.

Effie answered the door. Her face lit up with incredulity and joy. 'Norma! I was just this minute writing to you!' And then the face fell. 'But what's wrong with your arm?'

Norma had deliberately not written home about being blown up as she hadn't wanted to worry the family. 'Let's go in and I'll tell you all about it Ma. And could you lift these cases for me. Besides this broken arm I've got four broken ribs as well.'

'Help ma bob!' Effie exclaimed, a hand going to her mouth.

Effie put Norma's cases in her bedroom, then listened wide-eyed as Norma, for the second time that day, but now in more detail, recounted what had happened to her in Risinghill Street and of her subsequent hospitalisation in the Royal Free.

'Oh lass!' Effie whispered when Norma finally came to the end of her tale. Going to Norma she took her very gently in her arms. For almost a minute they remained like that, standing in complete silence. Then Effie, giving her nose a wipe, broke away.

'I thought it best you didn't know, Ma. You'd only have made yourself ill with worry. Or come down to London which is the last place to be while the Blitz is going on.'

'Is the Blitz as bad as they say?'

'It's bad all right, and from all accounts going to get worse. Gerry is determined to bomb London into submission, which he'll never do of course. And certainly never while Mr Churchill is Prime Minister.'

'Aye, Churchill may be a Tory, but he's the man for this job right enough,' Effie admitted grudgingly.

Now she'd had a chance to look at her Norma thought her ma had lost weight, particularly in the face. 'How's Da?' she asked. Brian had gone into the Pioneer Corps earlier on that year.

'Fine according to him. He's currently in North Queensferry building gun emplacements there.' North Queensferry was on the Firth of Forth at the spot where the two great Forth bridges were sited. The bridges joined North Queensferry on the north bank with Queensferry itself on the south. Because of the Firth's narrowness there it was a most strategic spot, and the best place to defend the naval base at Rosyth.

Effie pointed over at the table on which writing materials were laid out. 'I've just done a letter to him and was in the middle of one to you to say that Eileen is marrying Charlie Marshall this coming Saturday.'

'Oh that's terrific news!' exclaimed Norma. 'I've come back just at the right time.'

Norma remembered that they had originally intended to get married early on last year, but then Charlie shied off when it became apparent there was a war in the offing, saying that he had no intention of leaving Eileen a teenage widow. Eileen had been terribly upset, having been desperately keen to get wed to Charlie and set up house together.

'When you left for London he hadn't been called up, nor was he for some months after. He thought he'd go into one of the fighting regiments, but the army in its wisdom decided otherwise. They put him on a temporary clerking attachment, working out at Maryhill Barracks where he's been since his basic training. Which has been grand for him and Eileen as it's meant they can get together twice and sometimes three times a week.

'Well, yesterday he got the news that his attachment has been made permanent. He's to see out the war from behind a desk – a very safe desk in Aldershot – and he's being transferred there late next week.

'Of course Eileen was ecstatic to know that he's not going to come to any harm, but she was also most upset to lose him to Aldershot. Anyway, to cut a long story short, she convinced him that his argument about leaving her a widow no longer holds water, and so he's agreed to their marriage this Saturday. They're taking out a special licence for it.'

'I really am happy for them. Those two were made for one another,' Norma replied.

'And now you can get to the wedding as well. Eileen will be very pleased about it.'

'What about Da? Will he manage to come?'

'I shouldn't think so. He'll do his damnest, needless to say. But it's very doubtful indeed. It's a top priority job he's on, the men of the Corps there working flat out to get those gun emplacements finished before Gerry takes the notion to have a sail up the Forth. I just can't see him getting away, even more so when it's at such short notice.'

It would break her da's heart to miss his Eileen's wedding, Norma thought. But there you were, war was war. All sorts of sacrifices had to be made.

'Let's go through and put the kettle on,' suggested Effie.

'I was beginning to think you'd never ask.'

Effie laughed at that, but it was a glum laugh. Her mind was still on Brian.

'And how are Lyn and Eileen getting on in their new jobs?' Norma asked in the kitchen. Lyn had left the SCWS and Eileen the baker's she'd tended counter at and they'd both joined an armaments factory where they now worked as machinists.

'Just fine. They say it's gey hard graft, but they were expecting that. And just wait till you clap eyes on Lyn, you're going to get a shock I can tell you.'

'Why's that?'

Effie gave a mysterious smile. 'Wait and see. I don't want to spoil it for you.'

Norma was intrigued, and couldn't for the life of her think what her mother was referring to.

It wasn't long after that Norma heard the scrape of a key in the outside door, followed by the voices of Lyn and Eileen chaffing to each other. She rose from the chair in the living room where she'd been sitting to greet her two sisters.

Eileen was the same, but her mouth literally dropped at the sight of Lyn. Gone was 'podge' of old, in her place a svelte young lady with a curvaceous figure.

Eileen squealed on realising who it was, and Norma had to quickly warn the pair of them about her ribs as they flew at her.

Kisses were exchanged. 'Congratulations!' Norma said to Eileen. 'Ma's told me about Saturday.'

'And to think you'll be here for it. That's absolutely terrific!' Eileen enthused.

'But what's all this broken arm and ribs bit?' Lyn queried.

Lyn and Eileen listened soberly as Norma went through her story yet again.

'Jings but you were fortunate there right enough,' Eileen said when Norma was done.

'If you could have seen what was left of that street you'd appreciate just how fortunate,' Norma replied, and shuddered. It sometimes gave her the willies to think of the narrowness of her escape.

She turned to Lyn. 'I can't believe this. Look at you, you're beautiful! What the hell happened?'

'I suppose it just all boils down to the fact I got sick to the back teeth of being fat and the eternal wallflower. I decided I was going to diet, and that's exactly what I did. The weight just fell off. Didn't it Ma?'

Effie nodded her agreement.

'And what about boyfriends now?'

'I have to beat them off with a club, and that's a fact,' Lyn grinned in reply.

'Oh I'm so pleased, really I am. I come back to find you looking like a fashion model and Eileen about to be wed. I couldn't have had a better homecoming.'

Eileen swung on Effie. 'How long will tea be Ma? I've got so many things to do and organise if the wedding is going to take place on Saturday.' She glanced at her wristwatch. 'I'm meeting Charlie in less than an hour. We're going round to Dow's pub to discuss the arrangements for the reception.' To Norma she said. 'Dow's is hardly ideal but it's the best we'll manage in the time available.'

Norma had been to functions there before. It was a barn of a place, and not exactly the cheeriest of environments. But as Eileen said, time was against her and Charlie.

'The people will make the occasion, not the venue,' she replied, which bucked Eileen up. For that was true enough.

Effie got on with the tea while Eileen laid the table. Norma and Lyn sat in front of the living-room fire.

'Speaking of chaps, what about you?' Lyn asked.

'I have one. His name is Jeremy Dereham. He's all right.'

Lyn raised a well-plucked eyebrow. 'Just all right?'

Norma shrugged.

'Still Midge eh?'

Norma just gazed into the depths of the fire.

Lyn was full of advice on the subject, but wisely didn't offer it.

'So tell me about all these swells you're with nowadays? They are swells aren't they?' Lyn asked instead.

Norma gave a subdued smile. 'They are that. All FANYs are monied, and usually come from top drawer families - yours truly being one of the few exceptions to the latter.'

Norma then told Lyn of an escapade that she and Lynsey Dereham had got up to that, well before she was finished recounting it, had Lyn reduced to tears of laughter.

She'd been right about folks making the occasion and not the venue. You couldn't have had a better reception than Eileen and Charlie's. It was a cracker.

Eileen was radiant, in that special way only a new bride can be, and Charlie was flushed with a combination of drink, pride and happiness.

Norma watched them dance past. She'd been asked up a number of times but had pleaded in each instance that her broken ribs weren't up to it. That was only partially true, for she could've managed a slow waltz like the one now being played. The truth of the matter was that she didn't want to get up because here, amongst all these dear friends and neighbours, the pain of Midge was worse than it had been for a long, long time. To have gone on the floor would only have made that pain even worse.

She sipped her whisky and thought of the wedding that never was, the one that was supposed to have taken place between her and Midge. Many of those now present would have been there, and it would have been she who would have been the radiant bride; Midge the happy groom.

Emotion clogged her throat. She could just see herself and Midge out there, that old magic sparking between them as they swept and glided round the floor.

Eileen's wedding reception faded, replaced by a collage of other places, other times. Competitions they'd been in, exhibitions they'd given. The pair of them at Barrowland, the Plaza, Locarno; the different gowns she'd worn; the ways she'd done her hair; the routines they'd devised together.

She remembered what it was like to be in Midge's arms, to

have the warmth of his body burning against hers. The way the two of them were as one, both on the dancefloor, and in bed. This time she didn't sip her whisky, but took a large swallow.

Her thoughts were interrupted by a great cry going up from the main doorway into the room. She craned her neck to see what was going on.

The knot of people there parted to reveal her da clad from neck to toe in motorbike leathers, gloves and boots, and carrying a crash helmet. The bottom part of his face was filthy from dirt thrown up by the roads he'd been travelling on.

Effie went hurrying over to him. As did Lyn, Eileen and Charlie. Because she'd been furthest away Norma was the last of them to reach Brian.

Eileen threw her arms round her father. 'You did it. You managed to come,' she choked, quite overcome.

Effie, her eyes shining, was staring at Brian. She took his hand when he reached out to her.

The reception had been a cracker before, Norma thought. With her da here it was now perfect. Just perfect.

'I've only got a few hours as I have to be back on site first thing the morn's morn. But I'm here, that's all that matters,' Brian said.

'All that matters,' Effie agreed.

A large dram was thrust into Brian's grasp. 'To the happy couple. Lang may their lum reek!' he toasted.

He downed the dram in one, kissed Eileen on the cheek, then shook with Charlie. 'Welcome to the family, son,' he said.

Eileen began to cry, but they were tears of joy. Charlie hooked an arm round her waist, and pulled her close.

'I should have known you'd move hell and high water,' Effie said to Brian.

'Aye, well it's no' every day you have a daughter get married. I was determined that if there was a way to get here I'd find it. And I did. I'm just disappointed I couldn't get here for the actual ceremony itself.'

Effie gave him a big hug, thinking to herself there weren't many better than her Brian. She'd have walked over broken glass for him, so she would.

Brian looked at Norma, taking in her plastered arm. He knew

all that had happened to her from Effie's letter. They'd talk in a bit, but not right now. 'Hello lass,' he said.

There were more hugs and kisses, then Brian went off to remove his motorcycle gear and give his face a wash. Effie went with him.

'Trust the old man,' Lyn said to Norma.

'I didn't know he could ride a motorbike.'

'Neither did I. I wouldn't put it past him to have learned just to get here.'

Neither did Norma. Later, when she asked him, that transpired to be the case. He'd had half an hour's tuition before setting off from North Queensferry and had borrowed a motorbike. He'd more or less learned to handle the machine *en route*.

'I want a word with you,' Norma said to Eileen and Charlie, having at last managed to get them in a corner alone. She handed Charlie an envelope she'd prepared earlier.

'What's this then?' he asked.

'I know with all the frantic rush and everything you haven't been able to fix up a proper honeymoon and had intended to just take a few days here and there. Rather than that I'd like you to book into a hotel and have those few days complete with all the trappings at my expense.'

Charlie was dumbfounded. 'We can't . . .' he started to protest, but Norma cut him off.

'Yes you can – and will. I can well afford it. It's my wedding present to you.' To Eileen she added. 'And a *posh* hotel mind, the very best.'

Eileen smiled her gratitude. 'That really will be something. A honeymoon to remember.'

'It's awful good of you,' Charlie said.

'The pleasure's all mine. Just you two enjoy yourselves. That's all I ask.'

Charlie glanced down at the envelope. When he came to open it he would find to his astonishment, and delight, that it contained fifty pounds in used fivers. Norma didn't believe in doing things by halves. 'I never said at the time, but I will now. You're a smashing bird Norma, first class. You never deserved what Henderson did to you. That was criminal so it was.'

She somehow forced a smile onto her face. 'That's history now Charlie. Character-building we would call it in the FANY.'

Eileen's heart went out to her big sister. Sod that Midge Henderson for a selfish pig. He'd gutted Norma, that's what he'd done. Gutted her.

The next morning, some hours after Brian had left to return to North Queensferry, Eileen and Charlie boarded a tram for town where they booked into a suite in the Adelphi Hotel. There they spent four glorious days, and four ecstatic nights. As it turned out, their entire married life together.

Effie and Norma reached their close having just returned from the steamie where they'd been doing the washing and mangling. It was a fortnight since Norma had been given the all clear by the hospital, a fortnight during which she'd remained in Glasgow to convalesce.

As they let themselves into the house they saw that the afternoon post had been. An official-looking, buff-coloured envelope was addressed to Norma. She read its contents standing by the living room window.

Effie didn't have to ask what the letter said. She knew. 'When?' she queried.

Norma glanced up at her mother. 'Tomorrow. I've to report in as soon as possible.'

Effie nodded. 'It's just as well we went to the steamie the day then. Everything will be clean to take back with you.'

Effie helped her pack.

## *Chapter Seven*

The train was still a good many miles from London when a sailor in Norma's carriage suddenly exclaimed, pointing out the window. 'Bloody Norah, look at that!' he said, his tone a combination of amazement and awe.

The rest of the passengers in the carriage crowded round his window. The night sky, in the direction of the capital, might have been the sky over hell itself. At the centre it was a deep bloody crimson shot through with white and yellow streaks, the crimson changing colour to red, and then pink when it finally reached its periphery.

'Listen!' another sailor said.

The sounds were faint but there was no mistaking what they were. The dull crump of bombs exploding. So many bombs it was like a long string of Chinese crackers going off, one after the other. And when the end of the string was reached there was a brief pause, and then another string started.

'She's taking a proper pasting from the looks of it,' an Indian officer said unnecessarily.

There was a huge explosion that momentarily drowned out all other sounds, then the Chinese cracker effect was back.

They'd got something big there, Norma thought to herself, and wondered what. From the magnitude of the explosion it might well have been an armaments factory. Her mouth suddenly went dry with the thought that Lyn and Eileen worked in one of those. Thankfully the *Luftwaffe* had stayed away from Glasgow so far.

They resumed their seats to talk and speculate amongst themselves. The nearer they got to London the louder the explosions became. At one point just past Watford they all held their breath as a plane's engines droned overhead. A large heavy plane that had to be a Gerry bomber.

Norma broke out in a cold sweat. She couldn't stop her mind flashing back to Risinghill Street and her left arm began to ache as though from the memory.

The train stopped twice, but only for a few minutes on each occasion. Then it arrived at Euston Station, where they all hurriedly disembarked.

The white lights Norma had seen from afar were in fact searchlights. Besides the noise of bombs exploding there was also the distinctive boom-boom of anti-aircraft ack-ack guns, a number of these directly surrounding the station, and the other nearby stations of King's Cross and St Pancras. At the end of the platform she discovered a miniature lake of water, the result of a burst main, which she had to paddle through.

There were no taxis to be had for love or money, so it would have to be the Underground. She was pleased she'd only brought one suitcase with her, having left the other one in Glasgow.

If it was hell on the surface it was the Black Hole of Calcutta below. There were so many people huddled together that she could hardly get down the stairs, and out on the platform the story was just the same.

It was a pathetic sight: men and women dossing down uncomfortably for the night, some sitting propped up against a wall, others lying prostrate with blankets or other coverings over their faces in an attempt to block out the light. At one place she passed a baby bedded down in an open suitcase. As for the smell – luckily she was used to the Glasgow slums otherwise it might have turned her stomach. It was clear that the poor blighters all around her had become used to it.

Nor was Euston the only station jam-packed in this way. So was every station her tube came to, including the stop where she got out.

It was 10.34am, so her wristwatch told her, as Norma entered Baker Street. She'd come from 10 Grosvenor Place – FANY HQ had moved there from Wilton Place in October – where she'd had a face-to-face with Commandant Hopewell. The Commandant, after welcoming her back and inquiring about her health, had been mysterious, to say the least. She was to report to an address in Baker Street where a VIP wanted to speak to her. That had been all. No explanation as to who the VIP was, or what he wanted to speak to her about.

She arrived at number 64 where a plate bore the legend Inter-Services Research Bureau, whatever that was.

The woman at reception wasn't wearing a uniform, but had an air of cold efficiency about her. Her gaze fastened onto Norma the moment Norma walked through the door, a gaze Norma likened to an eagle's when it sights its prey. A little shiver ran up her spine.

'Are you McKenzie?' the woman asked in a neutral voice.

'Yes.'

The woman rose. 'You're expected. Come with me.'

They went into a corridor which, within a few yards branched hard left and hard right. They took the left-hand way, which in turn soon branched again, this time into three. The place is a rabbit warren, Norma thought to herself. And she was right.

'Wait in there,' the woman said, pointing to a door painted a bilious shade of green. Then, without waiting for a reply, she left.

Norma went through the green painted door to discover a surprise waiting for her on the other side in the shape of Lynsey Dereham. 'Lynsey!' 'Norma!' they exclaimed simultaneously.

Lynsey was about to hug Norma when she suddenly stopped. 'The ribs?'

Norma grinned. 'Mended. But don't squeeze them too tight, just in case.'

They hugged, then kissed each other on the cheek. 'You look tremendous, fit as a fiddle,' Lynsey said.

Norma couldn't say the same about her friend. If asked to describe Lynsey it would have been as death warmed up.

'When did you get back?' Lynsey demanded.

'Last night. I tried several times to ring you to come and meet me at the station, but you were never there.'

'If I said life's been hectic that would be the understatement of the year. I was in the City when the bombing started. It was a nightmare. I thought a dozen times I wasn't going to survive. But I did, and here I am to tell the tale.'

'I heard that they'd concentrated on the City.'

'That was their target all right, and they certainly succeeded in hitting it. Being Christmas, many of the buildings didn't have any fire-watchers, and then the water failed. They tried to take water from the Thames but it was at a very low ebb.'

'You were driving someone?'

'A brass hat from the War Office. As I said, we were already in the City when the raid started. When he realised the City was the designated target he began organising. Suffice it to say it was well after dawn before I saw my kip.'

No wonder Lynsey looked terrible thought Norma. 'So when were you ordered to report here?'

'Early yesterday. And you?'

'About an hour ago when I spoke to Commandant Hopewell.'

The two women stared at one another, puzzlement reflected in their eyes. 'Any idea what it's all about?' asked Norma.

Lynsey shook her head. 'None at all.'

'It can't be coincidence that you and I are here together.'

'Shouldn't think so,' Lynsey agreed, lighting a cigarette.

'I wonder who this VIP is? The Commandant was most mysterious about him.'

'She was exactly the same with me.'

Norma sat on one of the wooden chairs that had been provided, and Lynsey followed suit. 'How was Glasgow?' Lynsey asked.

Norma gave Lynsey a quick rundown on all that had happened to her at home, including an account of Eileen's wedding to Charlie Marshall. She'd never hidden from any of her fellow FANYs the sort of background she came from. Nor had they ever been the least bit sniffy to her. But then the sort of girl who would have been sniffy wasn't the type to join the FANY.

'Jeremy mentioned he'd written to you.'

'Yes. Twice. In his last letter he told me his regiment was being posted abroad. He didn't say where.'

'They left four days ago. He had been trying to contact me and had not been getting through. A message finally reached me via one of his chums, by which time he'd gone.'

'Did the chum say where the regiment was off to?'

'No. But then it was bound to have been a secret.'

'I'll miss him,' Norma said. Which was true enough. She might not love Jeremy, but he was good fun.

The door opened and a FANY came in. 'They're ready for you now. Please step this way,' the FANY said, a FANY neither Norma or Lynsey had ever encountered before. But then that wasn't too surprising, there were quite a number of Free FANYs (if nowhere near the number of FANY-ATS) after all. Lynsey stubbed out her cigarette; then she and Norma followed the FANY out of the room.

'Who are we going to see?' Lynsey queried as the three of them turned into yet another corridor. Her only reply - she hadn't really expected one but it was worth a try - was an enigmatic smile.

When it did come, the answer astonished Norma. 'Hello. I'm glad we managed to get the pair of you here together. That's what we wanted,' said Major-General Gilchrist, rising from behind his desk. There was another female present, Peggy Boughton, Commandant Hopewell's secretary.

The Major-General introduced himself to Lynsey then said to Norma, 'The hospital you were attending in Glasgow tells me you're fighting fit again. Is that correct.'

'Yes sir,' Norma replied weakly. Gilchrist was the last person she'd expected to see.

'Good. Now would the pair of you like to sit down.'

Norma and Lynsey did as they were bid. The Major-General remained standing. 'At the moment you're both being used as drivers. How would you like the opportunity to do something more, *substantially* more, for the war effort?' he asked.

Norma and Lynsey glanced at one another, intrigued. 'What did you have in mind, sir?' Norma answered for the two of them.

'Before I go any further you must both swear to me that nothing you are told inside this room will go further should either of you decide to decline my offer. It's very important.'

'I swear,' Norma said.

'And I,' Lynsey added.

'Right then.' Gilchrist walked a few steps one way, then retraced them. He chuckled suddenly. 'I imagine you've been wondering what the Inter-Services Research Bureau is?'

'Yes sir, we have,' Lynsey replied.

'Well it's a façade, a front for another organisation - an

organisation Peggy and I belong to, and which I was in the process of setting up when you were acting as my driver Norma.'

Norma sat forward in her chair. Gilchrist had her absolute attention.

He went on. 'With the fall of France it became apparent to some of us that we needed to organise movements in enemy-occupied territory comparable to the Sinn Fein movement in Ireland, or the Chinese guerrillas now operating against Japan, or - one might as well admit it - to the organisations the Nazis themselves have developed so remarkably in almost every country in the world.

'Halifax approached Churchill last July and he gave us the go-ahead. Neville Chamberlain arranged the details, the last important act of that man's life as he went into hospital a few days later. And so Special Operations Executive was born. An entirely new formation to co-ordinate all action, by way of subversion and sabotage, against the enemy overseas.'

Gilchrist paused. Norma and Lynsey waited with bated breath for him to continue. This was fascinating.

'Churchill's directive to Hugh Dalton - the Minister in charge of SOE when we came into being - was, "And now set Europe ablaze!" Which is precisely what we intend to do. We are to create and foster the spirit of resistance in Nazi-occupied countries, and try to establish a nucleus of trained operatives - a fifth column you could call them - who will be ready to assist in the liberation of the country concerned when we, the British, are able to invade it.

'We will also, as I have already mentioned, be instigating acts of subversion and sabotage. Suddenness, subterfuge and flexibility are the principle characteristics of such operations. They will be stiletto attacks to harry and confuse the enemy, hurting it in both military and economic areas.'

Gilchrist stopped and took a deep breath. 'I think that gives you a fair idea of what we in SOE are up to. We have discovered that FANYs, partly because they are not in the regular army, and partly for various other reasons, are ideal for our purposes, and we have been recruiting a great many over the past few months.'

He looked directly at Norma. 'I was most impressed with you when you were driving for me, and that day I came to see you in the Royal Free decided to ask you to join us when you were better again. I want you to be a WT, that is, a wireless telegraphy operator for us. You will be based in England with contact into France.'

He turned to Lynsey. 'When I spoke to Peggy about Norma she told me you two were fast friends. I've studied your file and records and would like you also to join us. I want you and Norma to train and work together. That is most important.'

Peggy Boughton spoke for the first time. 'Norma, would you mind waiting outside for a few minutes. This next part of the interview is between Lynsey and ourselves.'

'Yes of course,' Norma replied immediately, and left the room.

Outside in the corridor she tried to collect her thoughts. Exciting, that was her initial reaction. The whole thing sounded so exciting. She wondered if she'd be any good as a wireless operator, and didn't see why not. She resolved there and then what her answer was going to be.

The few minutes stretched to five, then Peggy Boughton opened the door and asked Norma to come back in.

'Lynsey's agreed to join us. What about you Norma?' Gilchrist queried.

'Yes please.'

'That's the ticket.' He smiled, and Peggy Boughton smiled as well.

Papers were produced, and both girls had to sign the Official Secrets Act. 'As far as anyone outside SOE is concerned you're still drivers,' Peggy Boughton said.

Norma and Lynsey nodded.

'Now I want you to go off and pack.' Gilchrist glanced at his wristwatch. 'A car will pick you up between seventeen and eighteen hundred hours this evening and take you to your place of training.'

'As quick as that!' Norma exclaimed.

'Why, is there something in London you wish to settle before leaving?' Gilchrist queried.

Norma shook her head.

'I'll probably be seeing you again then fairly soon,' Gilchrist said.

Although Norma hadn't seen it happen Gilchrist or Peggy

Boughton must have pressed a concealed buzzer, for the door opened and the same FANY who'd brought them to the room came in.

'I'll show you out,' she said.

Norma followed the FANY in somewhat of a daze. Lynsey walked beside her looking even paler than previously.

Norma was curious about that part of Lynsey's interview at which she hadn't been present. But as Lynsey didn't volunteer any information about it she didn't ask.

The car came to collect her at quarter to six. Besides Lynsey there were two other girl passengers, a Pamela Parkinson and a Violette Hart. The latter two were both Free FANYs, both vaguely known to Norma and Lynsey. The driver, a FANY-AT, informed them that Norma was the last one she had to pick up. Violette inquired where they were going, what their destination was? The FANY-AT gave Violette a brief glance in the rear-view mirror, but made no reply.

After a while Lynsey fell asleep. A little later so too did Norma.

Bombardier Gutteridge was regular army, and tiny. The first thing you couldn't help noticing about him were his crossed eyes. He reminded Norma of Ben Turpin, the American film comedian.

'Get fell in ladies!' Gutteridge barked. The four girls lined up with their cases at their feet.

'Riiiight turn! Quick march!' He strode off smartly. The girls hastily snatched up their cases and followed. Just before they reached the building he was taking them to it started to snow. The date was 30th December 1940. The following night would be New Year's Eve.

The barrack room contained a dozen beds and was freezing despite there being a coal-burning stove in the centre of the room. They would very quickly learn that the stove only heated the area directly surrounding it. Six feet away and the temperature plunged.

'Those beds with empty lockers beside them are free. Take your choice. Unpack; there will be someone here shortly to take you to the mess for a meal. Welcome to Fawley Court,'

Bombardier Gutteridge barked out, and abruptly left them.

Norma and Lynsey chose beds that were side by side. Pam and Violette, who were also friends, did the same, but in another part of the room.

The FANY who came to take them to the mess had been at Overthorpe Hall, where all FANYs trained, at the same time as Norma, so there was a reunion. Her name was Helen Rolfe.

Pleasantries were exchanged, and introductions made. Helen said she'd been detailed to settle the four of them in, and first of all how about some food?

'I'm ravenous,' Violette proclaimed, and the other three admitted they were hungry too.

The mess was in the main building, a manor-style house. In the mess, dinner being over, a meal had been set aside for each of them.

'There are sixteen FANYs in residence at the moment, including yourselves. The rest are men, and regular army. Some of them our chaps; some not,' Helen explained as they ate.

'When you say "our chaps" do you mean . . .?' Norma trailed off deliberately, not at all sure it was a name she should mention.

Helen smiled. 'SOE?'

Norma nodded.

'Yes, that's exactly what I mean.'

'And the other?' Pam inquired.

'Training in Morse and WT for use within their own units.'

'And how long will we be here for?' Norma asked.

'Until you're competent in Morse and the use of a WT set. The usual time is about four months.'

'Do you get failures?' Violette asked.

'There haven't been any while I've been here. But there were several just before I arrived. Both were regular army chaps and were returned to the outfits they'd come from. I'm happy to say that so far no FANY has failed.'

The four girls were still eating and talking when another FANY burst into the mess. This newcomer was wild-eyed, her hair awry. It was obvious she'd been crying heavily. For a handful of seconds she stared distraughtly at the girls and

Helen. Then whirling round, fled out the same entrance she'd come in.

Helen sighed. 'That's Ineke, a Dutchwoman we recruited. Her fiancé is a "joe" for us, working in N Section. She received a message this afternoon that the SD – that's the Sicherheitsdienst, the Nazi Party Security Service who're every bit as awful as the Gestapo – have picked him up. Poor sod, the best he can hope for is that they kill him quickly. Which is most unlikely knowing them.'

Silence reigned round the table. 'What's N Section?' Pam asked eventually.

'The Section dealing with the Netherlands. T Section is that dealing with Belgium, and F Section that dealing with France. You'll all be in F Section when you graduate from here, I believe.'

'And a "joe"?' This time the questioner was Lynsey.

'Our name for an agent in the field.'

Lynsey lit a cigarette. The others continued chatting, but she was now lost in her own thoughts. Every so often she glanced at the doorway through which Ineke had fled.

Fawley Court was surrounded by fair-sized grounds. After dinner Lynsey announced she was off for a stroll; she wanted some fresh air. Norma said she'd tag along.

The moon was up, and very bright. From a part of the main building came the sound of male and female laughter. In the distance a motorbike engine revved, then quickly faded out of hearing range. Lynsey shivered, and pulled the lapels of her greatcoat up round her neck.

'Last night the Blitz; tonight peace and tranquillity,' she said softly.

'Yes, quite a contrast.'

A few steps further on Norma suddenly exclaimed. 'Look!' And pointed to the sky.

A shooting star burned and blazed its way across the heavens, to be finally consumed by its entry into earth's atmosphere. It died in a shower of golden sparks.

'Did you make a wish?' asked Norma.

'Oh yes.' Lynsey's reply was so quiet Norma had to strain to hear it.

'So did I.' She'd wished for happiness, the same thing she always wished for, be it shooting stars, chicken-bones or whatever.

'This morning, with Major-General Gilchrist and Peggy Boughton, it was only words. Tonight, hearing about that Dutchman and his capture by the Germans it all became horribly real,' Lynsey said, lighting yet another cigarette. She'd been smoking heavily all day.

Norma frowned. 'How do you mean?'

'I don't suppose it matters that I tell you now; you'd find out soon enough anyway. The reason you and I are to train together, work as a twosome, is because I'm going to be your "joe". When I'm finished here there will be further training for me, then it'll be into France.'

Norma came up short. 'You speak French?'

'Like a native. When I was a child I always had French nannies. Besides which, Pa has a villa in the Dordogne, where we spent every summer holiday up until the war. I was already bilingual when I started school.'

'And Gilchrist found this out when he went through your file?'

'That's it.'

Norma didn't know what to say. As Lynsey put it, what had been mere words was now horribly real, for Lynsey anyway.

Lynsey gave a brittle laugh. 'It's all too funny really. Too funny by half.'

They walked a little while longer, then returned to their room where they met, between then and the following morning, all the other girls they'd be sharing that particular barrack room with.

As Norma commented more than once, learning to be a proficient WT operator, to the standard demanded by Bombardier Gutteridge, was damned hard work. The Bombardier had been a WT operator in civilian life, and was a natural teacher. He was also a holy terror if he thought his pupil was giving less than a hundred per cent.

The required speed for the Morse Code was twenty-five words a minute. That meant, as all messages in code were in five-letter groups, one hundred and twenty-five letters a minute – slightly more than two a second.

The tricky part was that when you were writing down one letter you had to be reading three letters ahead. There was a technique to this which, Gutteridge assured them early on, once you'd acquired you'd never ever lose again.

Bombardier Gutteridge was in charge of all their technical training and what he said went. Being an SOE establishment – as opposed to regular army – eccentricities about rank prevailed. Ability counted, not rank. At Fawley Court, lieutenants, captains, majors and even a lieutenant-colonel deferred to Bombardier Gutteridge – something that would never have happened in any other unit. But then, as Norma and Lynsey soon discovered, SOE wasn't like any other unit in the British Army. It was unique.

'I'm looking forward to this,' Norma said to Lieutenant Philip Bodington as the car they'd borrowed from Fawley Court brought them into Henley. Henley was the nearest civilised spot to FC (as the inmates referred to it), there being roughly a mile and a half between the two. FC kept a pool of cars, all ancient but still roadworthy, for general use.

Norma and Philip were in the front seats; Lynsey and another Lieutenant called Simon Rafferty in the back. Philip and Simon had arrived at FC a few weeks previously, and had already been out with Norma and Lynsey several times, the two couples having hit it off together. Norma always paired with Philip; Lynsey with Simon. It was a Saturday night in March and they were *en route* to catch the first house of the new Busby Berkeley that the Kingsway in Henley was showing.

*Pathe News* was just starting as they entered the auditorium. They watched scenes of the recent British raid on the Lofoten Islands, followed by President Roosevelt signing a Lease and Lend Bill which the commentator said was going to be a huge boost to the British war effort. Then the news was over and it was time for the main picture *Strike Up The Band*.

Philip produced a box of chocolates which was clever of him as sweets were becoming harder and harder to get hold of. They were delicious chocs too.

It was about halfway through the film when a dancing

number came up on screen. Norma found herself staring up at Midge. It was as though a hand had taken hold of her insides and was squeezing them. Another her brain. She was suddenly breathless, and there was the foul acid taste of bile at the back of her throat.

Midge, huge up there on the silver screen. And with him Zelda, the pair of them dancing up a storm.

Three little words – Norma saw the step quite clearly. And then they repeated it.

She swallowed, and swallowed again. But the taste of bile wouldn't go away. She wondered why Midge and Zelda had gone hazy at the edges, then realised there were tears in her eyes.

The number finished, and Midge and Zelda were replaced by a host of girls swirling in patterns. She blew her nose, then discreetly wiped her eyes.

'Absolutely spiffing eh?' Philip whispered.

'Absolutely,' she agreed in a voice that was cracked and raw.

Philip glanced at her, a questioning glance which she ignored. She continued staring up at the screen as though totally absorbed in what was happening there. In her mind she was rerunning the Midge and Zelda sequence.

They were good together, there was no denying it. In fact they were more than good; they were excellent. But *not better* than she and Midge had been. She derived grim satisfaction from that.

When the picture was over and the credits began rolling she eagerly looked for his name. She'd expected to see Michael Henderson, but he was billed as Mike. Zelda was still Zelda Caprice. So although Midge and Zelda had married she hadn't taken his name, at least not for professional purposes.

When, after the full programme was over, Simon suggested they go for a drink Norma was all for it. A drink might dull the pain a little.

'Excuse me, I'll be right back,' Norma said, rising from the marble-topped table at which they were sitting. She walked the length of the pub, though not past all that many people as business was surprisingly slack, to the door marked Ladies, and went inside.

Discovering she was alone, as she'd hoped she'd be, she let

herself go. She started to tremble, and then shake all over. Going to the sink she splashed cold water over her face, and felt a little better. So she splashed some more.

Lynsey came through the door, her expression one of concern. 'Are you all right? You've been looking ... well, strange to say the least ever since we came out of the picture-hall.'

There was no towel. Norma took out a hanky and dried herself with that. When she was finished she noted the hanky was streaked with what little make-up she'd been wearing. She'd have to repair that before going back through again.

'I've stopped shaking,' she said in surprise. 'I was shaking like a leaf just a few moments ago.'

Lynsey, deeply worried now, took Norma by the arm. 'What is it?' she asked gently.

Lynsey knew that Norma had been a professional dancer in the past, but nothing about Midge or Midge running off with Zelda Caprice the day before he and Norma were due to be married. Norma told Lynsey all about that now, and how they'd just watched Midge and Zelda in *Strike Up The Band.*

'Poor darling,' Lynsey said softly when Norma eventually finished her story.

The tears were back; Norma could feel them stinging her newly washed face. 'I'm sorry I'm making such a fool of myself,' she choked.

'No you're not. You're just getting it off your chest to a friend - that's what friends are for.'

'Oh Lynsey,' Norma said, and hung her head.

Lynsey took her into her arms and held her there, comforting her, till finally the tears stopped and Norma was once more in control of herself.

'Find a spot off the road and let's draw in there for a while,' Norma said. On returning to their table with Lynsey she'd pleaded a headache and so Philip was driving her back to FC. Lynsey and Simon had stayed on at her insistence.

Philip shot Norma a questioning look. What did she mean by that? He liked Norma, but was never quite sure what to make of her. 'Head better then?' he asked.

'Yes.'

He remembered a dirt track turn off that he'd noticed on

another excursion out in a car. It meandered past a pond, and then on up to a farm. He turned into that, to stop by the pond.

'You're in a funny mood tonight,' he said.

'Am I? I wasn't aware of that,' she lied.

'Have I done something?'

'Nothing at all I assure you. You've been your usual sweet self.' Leaning across she kissed him on the cheek. Next moment he'd pulled her to him and his lips were on hers, his tongue deep inside her mouth.

He smelled of old leather, she thought. That and boot polish. An odd combination, but one she didn't find at all offensive. In fact it was rather pleasant. And certainly very masculine.

It hadn't been in her mind to do what she did next, not her conscious mind anyway. He stiffened when she took a hand and guided it to her right breast. She'd never allowed, far less instigated, such intimacy before.

He kneaded and squeezed, cupped and caressed. First one breast, then the other. She didn't protest when he sought and found the outline of her mound.

'Let's go in the back?' he suggested, his voice thick with desire. For he fancied Norma rotten, had done since he'd first clapped eyes on her. But he'd never dared hope what he was daring to hope now. That had never seemed a possibility.

Without replying she removed the hand between her legs, and got out of the car. She was in the back before him.

Her thoughts and emotions were in a turmoil. She hurt so much inside, the old wound had been ripped wide open again. Damn Midge for what he'd done to her. Damn herself for still feeling about him the way she did. And most of all damn Zelda, damn Zelda to roast forever in everlasting hell.

She closed her eyes as Philip entered her. It was the first time since the last occasion she and Midge had made love. Jeremy had often tried, but she'd never let him.

In her mind she pictured Midge watching her and Philip. Yes, she thought, that's what she wanted. Him to watch. To see everything.

Watch! you bastard she shouted at him. *Watch!*

She used the small torch she kept under her pillow to glance at the clock by the side of her bed. Another hour and it would be dawn; she hadn't slept a wink. She was hot and sticky, and there was sweat on her forehead, underarms and thighs. She felt wretched.

She turned over for the umpteenth time since coming to bed. Why had she done what she had, why? The answer was revenge of course. She'd imagined she was somehow getting back at Midge, cocking a snook at him.

She wished now she hadn't done it with Philip. It had solved nothing, made nothing better. If anything it had made things worse. She was filled with regret, and remorse, and . . . yes, she had to admit it, even revulsion.

Not that there was anything wrong with Philip. He was a nice enough chap – she'd never have gone out with him in the first place if he hadn't been. But she shouldn't have done it with him because she just didn't have those sort of feelings towards him.

She felt she'd cheapened herself. Cheapened and demeaned herself by doing what she had.

She turned over again, saw a mental picture of herself and Philip in the back of the car, and shuddered. First thing she'd do when she got up was have a bath, she promised herself. A piping hot one. And when in it she'd scrub herself hard with soap and loofah, scour her skin clean again. For she felt dirty all over.

Dawn was rising when, at long last, she finally fell into a fitful sleep. A sleep during which she continued to toss and turn, and from time to time mutter reproachfully to herself.

Next morning Norma and Lynsey, as had become their Sunday habit since coming to Fawley Court, took out horses from a nearby riding stable. Norma had learned to ride at Kilmichael House, and, under FANY tutelage, had greatly extended her experience and expertise while training at Overthorpe Hall. For although FANY no longer used horses in the execution of their duties they were still a very horsey-orientated service.

Norma was exhausted after her terrible night, completely drained. Nor had her bath helped; it had neither revived her nor taken away that sensation of dirtiness. Touching her horse with her heels she urged it into a canter.

Lynsey followed suit.

The ground was rock hard, still frozen in its winter sleep,

perfect for riding. Norma touched her horse again, and the canter changed to a gallop. Lynsey came with her.

Hooves drummed the earth; wind sang in her ears. She touched the horse again urging it to go faster.

The gallop became a mad one; the girls remaining in control, but only just. Neither looked at the other, yet each was aware that the other was there, as their horses further lengthened their stride, stretching themselves to their limit.

Still side by side they jumped a hedge. Norma bit the inside of her mouth as her mount landed with a bone-jarring thump. They continued on without let up.

They plunged into a small wood where low hanging branches brushed and whipped their bodies, one branch ripping open a cut on Lynsey's right cheek. And then they were out of the wood and charging up a hill.

'Faster! Faster!' Norma whispered, this time not touching with her heels but positively digging them in. Her beast snorted as it laboured to obey.

Another hedge reared before them which they successfully cleared. Then it was another hedge, this one taller than the previous ones. They jumped that successfully too, though it was a near thing in Norma's case.

On and on they went, flat out. And then just as suddenly as it had started, the madness that had gripped them both was over. They began reining in.

The horses were blowing heavily when they came to a stop overlooking the very pond that Norma and Philip had parked beside the night before. Lynsey, chest heaving, dabbed with a balled handkerchief at the cut on her cheek. 'I suppose the truth of the matter is you can run as hard and fast as you like, but you can't run away from it,' she said softly.

Norma glanced at her friend, knowing exactly what she was talking about. 'I suppose not,' she replied.

Norma watched a crow wing over the pond, and then fly off in the direction of FC. For some reason she thought it looked extremely sinister, though she couldn't have said why. It was only an ordinary crow.

'What were *you* trying to run away from?' she asked Lynsey.

Lynsey's face sort of twisted and crumpled in on itself to

become the face of a little girl. A little girl scared out of her wits. 'Whatever lies in wait for me over there, in France.'

Norma had guessed it was that. 'You could tell M you've changed your mind.' M was the symbol by which Major-General Gilchrist was known in SOE. As M he was director of operations and training.

'I can't; it would be letting the side down. I agreed to go, and so I must.'

Norma patted her horse's neck. It was a chestnut mare, a fine animal. She didn't know what to say in reply to that, so said nothing.

'I'm twenty-three you know. Not very old is it?'

Norma shook her head.

'Normally I'd have an entire life ahead of me. A husband, babies, that sort of thing.'

'You still can,' Norma protested.

Lynsey gave Norma a sad, knowing smile. As if she was in on some secret Norma wasn't. Wheeling her horse round she started back towards the riding stable, and Norma followed.

Somewhere close by, perched in a tree probably, a crow cawed, and it seemed to Norma that the caw had a mocking quality to it. The same sinister-looking crow she wondered?

The crow cawed mockingly again, causing Norma to break out in gooseflesh.

It was raining, a fine drizzle that would soon turn into something nastier if the colour of the sky was anything to go by. The four of them came out the barrack room together. Norma and Lynsey, Pam and Violette. There were two cars waiting for them, each with a FANY-ATS driver at the wheel. One car for Norma and Pam, the other for Lynsey and Violette. Norma and Pam were off to F Section to begin their duties there; Lynsey and Violette to an establishment where they would receive field training.

Norma stowed her suitcase in the boot, then helped Pam with hers. The moment of parting had arrived. Goodbyes had already been said to Bombardier Gutteridge and others at FC.

Lynsey threw her arms round Norma, hugging her tightly. When the two girls pulled slightly apart, still holding onto each other, they both had tears in their eyes.

'I don't know if I'll see you again before I go "over by". If not, good luck,' Lynsey whispered.

'And you, all the luck in the world.'

Norma kissed Lynsey on the cheek, and Lynsey did the same to her. A few feet away Pam and Violette were entangled in an emotional embrace.

The drizzle had got heavier. Over to the east there was a jagged flash of lightning.

'Take care,' Norma whispered.

Lynsey hugged Norma again, then abruptly released her friend.

Norma got into her car, and a couple of seconds later was joined by Pam. Their car started off with the other car following behind. They stayed like that till they reached the main road where Norma and Pam's car turned left, Lynsey and Violette's right.

Norma and Pam watched the other car through the rear window as it gradually receded into the distance. Finally they went round a bend and the other car was lost to view, and they to it.

Norma closed her eyes and offered a brief prayer asking God to keep Lynsey and Violette safe.

They drew into the grounds of an imposing country house that had a hutted encampment off to one side. They would shortly learn that the house was called Grendon Underwood and that the hutted encampment was the wireless station.

There was a FANY standing on the steps leading up to the house's front door. Norma recognised the figure – it was Helen Rolfe who'd left FC shortly after she and Lynsey had arrived there.

The car stopped, and Norma and Pam got out. Norma went straight to Helen who shook her by the hand.

'I thought you'd like a friendly face to meet you. Welcome to F Section,' Helen said.

The modified twin-engined Whitley bomber belonged to 138 Squadron and had taken off from Newmarket racecourse with two passengers aboard, one of whom was Lynsey Dereham.

Lynsey sat staring in fascination at the aircraft's modification which was a hole that had been fitted to its floor. When she was given the signal she was going to have to jump through that hole. A Whitley had no side-doors; the hole was a parachutist's quick exit point.

The aircraft would be flying at five hundred feet when she left it. Her parachute would be opened automatically by static line, and, providing it was packed properly - and she'd packed it herself earlier - would be opened fully for only a few seconds before she hit the ground. The landing shock would be roughly the same as if she'd jumped from a first-floor window. The entire procedure, from jumping out the hole to picking herself up off the ground would take a quarter of a minute. As quick as that.

She held her breath and counted fifteen seconds. It was no time at all. But time enough to go from being very much alive to very, very dead if something did go wrong, which it occasionally did. They hadn't kept that from her. It occasionally did.

She could have jumped from a greater height of course, but that would only have produced risks of a different nature. It was a case of the devil and the deep blue sea.

She fumbled for her cigarettes, then wondered if it was allowed. No one had said.

'Go ahead, it's permitted,' her companion said in perfect French, the first time he'd spoken.

*En route* to the plane the pilot had informed her that there would be another 'joe' making the journey with her, but that she'd be jumping before him. His destination was further inland.

She'd already been in the Whitley and selected a spot for herself when a car had driven alongside and he'd got out. The moment he was aboard, the Whitley had started its engines, then began getting ready for take-off. He had remained silent throughout the journey, not even saying hello, so she had thought he had wanted it that way.

She offered the packet to him. 'You?'

He shuffled over and took one. When his lighter blazed she saw that he had sallow skin and liquid brown eyes. 'Thank you', he said, and sat beside her.

He'd spoken again in French. Was he French or English? She couldn't tell. She puffed on her cigarette and noted that her hand was trembling ever so slightly. She was aware that he'd also noticed.

'First time in?' he asked.

'Yes.'

'It's my third. DF took me out last month. And now I'm going back in again.' DF was the SOE escape section which every SOE field operative knew about in case he or she had to use it.

She took another drag of her cigarette, drawing the smoke deep down into her lungs. 'I'm Marie Thérèse,' she said on the exhale.

'I'm Gabriel.'

She wondered what his real name was. Marie Thérèse was her code name, just as Gabriel would be his.

'Fresh from Arisaig?' he asked. Arisaig was on the western coast of Scotland a little to the south of Mallaig. That wild and beautiful countryside of South Morar and neighbouring Moidart was ideal for field training, and had been selected by M himself for that very reason.

'I came down by train last night,' she acknowledged. Her eyes strayed back to the hole in the aircraft floor. How long to go now? Not too long she didn't think. A cold shiver ran up her spine. 'Can I ask you something?' she queried softly.

He knew what it was going to be. 'Go ahead.'

'What's it really like down there?'

'You want the truth?'

'Yes.'

He sighed. 'Pretty scary at times. In fact, pretty scary a lot of the time. But what you mustn't ever do is let fear get the upper hand. To let it do so is inevitably fatal.' He paused, and his eyes took on a faraway look. 'The trick is to keep a cool head and, no matter what, never panic. Fear and panic, those are the enemy just as much as the Germans. Conquer them and you stand a fair chance of keeping out of the hands of the latter.'

'I'll remember what you've just said. Thank you.'

The faraway look faded from his eyes, and he brought his gaze to bear on her. 'Are you being met?'

'Yes, by members of the Circuit I'm joining. I'm a replacement WT operator; they lost their previous one the week before last.'

He nodded. 'It's good you're being met, particularly as it's your first time in.'

The co-pilot appeared from up front. 'Three minutes to drop point. You'll get a red on the minute, green for go,' he said to Lynsey. Her answer to that was a weak smile. She waited till the co-pilot had disappeared back up front before turning again to Gabriel.

'Will you do me a favour? Will you stand behind me and give me a push if I freeze?'

She'd gone very pale, the colour of curdled milk. She looked so young and vulnerable, and fragile. How could they ask a girl like this to jump into enemy-occupied territory? And yet they did ask because they had to, and the girls did jump. It was a rotten war. 'I'll stand behind you,' he agreed.

The red light winked on and they both came to their feet. She crossed to the hole, hooked up – her parachute would be activated by static line – then stood on the hole's rim. There was nothing to be seen below, only darkness.

'*Bonne chance*, Marie Thérèse,' he whispered, and a moment later the red light winked out and the green on.

His mouth stretched into a thin slash of a smile when she was gone. He hadn't had to push her; he was glad about that.

Norma glanced at the clock on the wall. Lynsey was now two minutes late in coming through for her first contact with Grendon Underwood.

The room she was in was long and bare. The transmitter-receivers and Morse keys were set on benches, the girls who operated them seated on swivel chairs. The slogan *Remember the Enemy is Listening* dominated one wall.

M was present, talking to Helen Rolfe. Then he walked over to Norma, glancing at the wall-clock. Lynsey was now three minutes overdue. The first contact was always the most nerve-wracking one; for all they knew Lynsey could already be dead and buried, not having survived the parachute jump.

M thought of Frère Jacques, the leader of Penelope Circuit which Lynsey had been sent in to join. Nothing but trouble that man; at times it seemed as though he had every single bad trait of the French race. The only Frenchman he knew who was more overbearing was De Gaulle himself. But despite his faults Frère

Jacques *was* good; he excelled at both organisation and sabotage. But was incredibly overbearing and bumptious with it.

'Would you like a cup of tea? I can have one brought to you,' M said to Norma.

She shook her head. 'After Marie Thérèse comes through, yes, but not till then. To be honest, I don't think I could swallow it.'

He placed a comforting hand on her shoulder, and glanced again at the wall-clock. Lynsey was now five minutes overdue.

If she was dead that still meant Frère Jacques would have the plastic explosive that had gone in with her. It was explosive the Penelope Circuit desperately needed. And he'd have the S-phone he'd requested. The S-phone being a device that enabled a person on the ground to make a verbal contact with an aircraft in the immediate vicinity. It was a fairly new invention, and one that was bound to prove extremely helpful.

The minutes ticked slowly, agonisingly by. Nine, ten, eleven, twelve. M's expression was grim; Norma's was filled with despair.

And then suddenly Norma's earphones were beeping with the incoming signal they'd been waiting for. Marie Thérèse calling, Marie Thérèse calling.

Norma's hand flashed to the sender key. Home base receiving, Home base receiving.

Snatching up a pencil she began hurriedly writing down the message Marie Thérèse was sending on behalf of Penelope Circuit.

When the incoming message was over Norma sent the outgoing one. And then that was it, their first exchange was completed.

Norma took off her earphones to discover that M had already left with the incoming message for the decoding room. She joined him there.

'How did Marie Thérèse seem?' M asked Norma.

'Nervous as all get out. Her sending wasn't a patch on what she's capable of. But then I suppose there's a big difference between doing it in Fawley Court and German-occupied France.'

'Now you know why we trained you and the others as

twosomes. Each knows his or her partner's 'fist' so well it makes life a great deal easier all round.'

He studied the decrypt that the decoder handed him. It was full of sending mistakes, but still intelligible.

'Good,' he said, and walked away.

Norma left the wireless station for the main house where she'd now have that cup of tea. What a fifteen minutes that had been, waiting for Lynsey to come through. Each minute had felt like a year in length.

Before tea though, she'd go and root out Pam, to tell her Lynsey was all right and operational. The following week it was going to be Violette's turn to go 'over by'. She was joining Autogiro Circuit.

Lynsey lay on her bed staring up at the fly-blown ceiling. She'd been with Penelope a fortnight now and already she'd come to loathe and detest that little pipsqueak Frère Jacques. He was a horrible man who stank of unwashed armpits. Just to be near him made her want to throw up. She doubted he'd had a bath that year. Or the previous year come to that.

But it wasn't merely his lack of personal hygiene, it was his manner. His air of superiority. His sheer bloody arrogance. The Germans had a reputation for arrogance but that Frenchman beat them by a mile.

She stopped thinking to listen to the approaching sound of jackboots. Tramp, tramp, tramp, a dozen or so soldiers, she judged.

Her heart leapt into her mouth when, at a barked command, the marching ceased directly beneath her window. *They'd come for her, they'd found out who she was and where she was and come for her!*

Don't let fear get the upper hand, don't panic! she commanded herself, remember Gabriel's advice. She'd almost certainly be shot if she tried to make a bolt for it, and it might just *not* be her they were after.

Her groping hand sought and found the phial she'd been given in Arisaig. She looked back up at the ceiling as she placed it between her teeth. If it was her they were after, and they came breaking into her room, a corpse was all they'd find. Death would have been instantaneous, with no pain. The people in Arisaig had assured her of that.

Somewhere nearby a door crashed shut, followed by another barked command from the officer in charge. The detachment was continuing on its way.

Lynsey didn't know why the soldiers had stopped where they had, but it hadn't been for her. There were tears in her eyes as she removed the phial from between her teeth.

Lynsey stared coldly at Frère Jacques, who stood with the inevitable cigarette dangling from his lower lip. With his cigarette, beret and bright red neckerchief he was like something out of a comic opera, except there was nothing comic about the business he and the rest of those present were involved in. She wouldn't have believed it possible, but he stank even worse than usual.

'No, I will not transmit from there again,' she said.

His eyes slitted meanly. 'You will do as I tell you.'

'We've used that house twice running. It would be stupid to do so again.'

His eyes slitted even more. 'I say it is safe. That's all that need concern you.'

'Like hell. It's my neck that's on the line, not yours.'

He drew himself up to his full height, which wasn't saying much. 'I am leader of Penelope, you will do as I command. As *I*, Frère Jacques, command. Is that clear?'

'You know the rules, we're supposed to change the place of transmission every time ...'

'Those are London's rules,' he interjected dismissively. 'In the field I can change them if I see fit.'

Lynsey continued staring coldly at him. To go back a third time to that house would be sheer lunacy. The German directional finders were bound to have at least a general fix on the area, probably a fix on the street itself. Give them another chance and they'd have the house surrounded, with herself inside. A rat in a trap. 'No, and that's final,' she said.

Several of the others present were smirking. Frère Jacques wasn't exactly well loved by them. It was amusing to see the Englishwoman defying him.

Frère Jacques scowled. He would have his way with this, even if it meant using force on the bitch. The Germans in that section had been heavily reinforced and were now everywhere, like summer flies round a pile of *merde*. He was at his wit's end trying to find new safe premises, but wasn't going to explain that to Marie Thérèse. A strong leader didn't need to explain. To explain was a weakness, and he was strong, not weak. He puffed out his chest, and stalked over to her.

He was so quick she never even saw it coming. She yelled in fright and pain as he smacked the side of her face. As she staggered backwards he leapt after her and hit her again.

She went completely still when the knife point pricked her throat. 'You transmit in half an hour. And from where I have said. Understand?'

The stink of him in her nostrils was unbelievably vile. 'If you're so convinced that house is safe to be used again then you come with me.'

He gave a Gallic shrug. 'If you want.'

The knife vanished, and he swaggered across to where a jug of wine stood on a table. He poured himself a large tumblerful which he drank straight off.

'We go now,' he said.

She decided to tell Norma she wanted out, and as soon as possible. The dangers were horrendous enough without having to work for a lunatic such as Frère Jacques. DF would get her away, just as it had done Gabriel.

She followed Frère Jacques out of the room.

Norma was busily writing down the incoming message when the Morse coming through on her earphones suddenly changed to a continuous buzz. Nothing like this had ever happened before. Her hand went to the sender key.

Calling Marie Thérèse, calling Marie Thérèse.

The buzzing ceased abruptly, followed by an eerie silence.

Calling Marie Thérèse, calling Marie Thérèse.

There was no answer.

'Let's take a walk Norma,' M said.

She knew from his face what it was all about. Six days had passed since they'd lost contact with Lynsey, six days during which her set had been manned round the clock, mainly by herself, waiting for contact to be re-established. Praying for it. There had been only silence.

They left the wireless station, and headed out across the grass. It was a beautiful August day, the sun cracking the sky.

'She's dead,' M said simply.

In her heart of hearts Norma had known all along, but it was still a shock to hear it confirmed. 'How?'

'The Gestapo surprised her at her set. They ...' He paused, then added softly. 'Shot her through the back of the head. The buzz you heard was caused by her falling forward onto her Morse key.'

Norma could just picture the scene. Lynsey hunched over her key, and then ... She swallowed hard. 'Was anyone else with her?'

'Frère Jacques. He was killed as well. We finally got word of what had happened from Autogiro Circuit. Josephine's signal came in only fifteen minutes ago.' Josephine was Violette's codename.

'I think you should have some time off, perhaps go home for a few weeks. I can arrange to let you have a car,' M said.

'Yes, I'd like that.'

Norma left for Glasgow early the following morning.

## *Chapter Eight*

Norma chapped the door for the fourth time. Someone was in all right, she could hear whoever it was shuffling about. So why didn't they answer? She didn't have a door key on her, having left it behind when she was last up.

The shuffling was coming slowly nearer. There was a bump, followed by a moan of pain that she recognised as coming from her mother.

'Ma, it's Norma, open up will you!' This time she didn't chap the door but pounded it. What on earth was going on!

Finally the door swung open to reveal Effie swaying weakly. Her hair was down and wet with sweat, as was her forehead, and her eyes had a strange, hard, glassy look about them.

'Oh Ma!' Norma whispered. Then leapt forward to catch her mother as she collapsed to the floor.

'Headache, terrible headache,' Effie croaked feverishly.

Effie was far too heavy for Norma to pick up. She had to drag her through to her parents' bedroom where she put her on the bed.

'Ma it's Norma, can you hear me?'

The glassy eyes tried to focus. 'Norma?'

'Aye, it's me Ma. What's wrong with you?'

'Headache, all last night. Got worse after . . . after Lyn and Eileen left for work.'

Norma felt her mother's forehead, it was fiery-hot. Her temperature was clearly way up. She pulled the quilt over Effie, then said she wouldn't be gone more than a minute. She hoped. Well, one of the neighbours in the close had to be in!

As it transpired Alice Henderson, Midge's mum, who lived on the next landing down, was. Hurriedly Norma explained the situation, and asked Alice if she'd telephone the family doctor from the nearest payphone. Alice immediately threw her pinny aside and said she'd run to Bell's the newsagents; they had a phone they'd let her use.

'Mind impress on the doctor that it's an emergency,' Norma shouted after Alice as Alice clattered down the stairs.

She rushed back to Effie who gasped that she wanted water. Effie gulped down a glassful, and asked for another. She gulped that one down too.

Effie was soaked through with perspiration, her clothes ringing. With great difficulty Norma stripped her ma, then got her into a clean nightie. When she'd done that she manoeuvred her between the sheets.

At which point Alice Henderson arrived back to say she'd eventually managed to get through to the doctor, his phone had been continually busy, and that he was on his way. He'd be there shortly.

'Is there anything else I could do to help?' queried Alice.

'Put the kettle on while I sit here with Ma. I could fair use a cup of tea after my drive up from England.'

Norma glanced at her wristwatch, and wondered what time Lyn and Eileen would be home from work. She knew from the correspondence she'd had with Effie that they were putting in longer and longer hours at the armaments factory to help boost production, as was everyone who worked there. As for her da, in her last letter to her Effie had mentioned that he was now in Berwick-upon-Tweed constructing a shore defence system there.

She heard Alice go out of the house, and upstairs. When Alice brought through her cup of tea she also brought several fingers of home-baked shortie. It was good shortie too, but not a patch on Lyn's.

Every few minutes Norma wiped Effie's face down with a towel. Where *was* the doctor she thought, glancing yet again at her watch.

'I'll show him ben,' Alice said when there was a tap on the outside door.

Doctor Dickie was old, out of retirement for the war. He and Norma had never met before.

'Let's see what's what then,' Doctor Dickie said, sitting on the edge of the bed.

'Can you hear me, Mrs McKenzie?' he asked.

Effie's eyes fluttered open. Norma had thought her to be asleep as she hadn't uttered or moaned since being put into the clean nightie.

'Can you speak, woman?'

'Headache, awful headache. Like a vice, you understand? A vice.'

'I understand, Mrs McKenzie.' He put a thermometer into her mouth, and in the meantime took her pulse.

Her temperature was a hundred and three. He put an arm behind her shoulders, then brought her upwards in a semi-sitting position. 'Can you drop your head so that your chin touches your breastbone?' he asked her.

She whimpered when she tried. Her head and chin only moved fractionally. 'Sore, too sore,' she complained. He gently eased her back to the vertical.

His expression was grim; his face lined with concern when he turned to Norma. 'One thing's for certain. I'm not moving your mother in her present condition. She's an extremely ill woman.'

'What's wrong with her, doctor?'

Dickie produced an opthalmascope which he shone first in Effie's right eye, then her left. He snapped the light off again. 'It could be either of several things. I'm not really sure which.'

'Then can you get someone who would know?'

He stared at her in surprise, for this was a slum area and he knew nothing at all about her inheritance. 'You mean a specialist? They cost a great deal of money, Miss McKenzie.'

Effie gave a hollow groan, and her eyes rolled upwards. She'd slipped into unconsciousness.

'It doesn't matter what the specialist costs. Get him,' Norma said with authority.

'With all due respect, Miss McKenzie. Can you afford him? If I ask who I have in mind to come to a tenement in Bridgeton he's going to laugh in my face.'

She'd had a cheque book for some time. It had been Lynsey's idea. 'It's an absolute must, darling!' She took it out now. 'The specialist's name?' she queried.

'Rodney Creighton. He's the top neurologist in Glasgow.'

She wrote out a cheque, then tore it from the book and handed it to Dickie. 'Tell him if it costs more than that, all he has to do is say. But I want him here as soon as it is humanly possible.'

Dickie stared at the cheque in astonishment. A cheque for a hundred pounds written out by a Bridgeton lassie. Wonders never ceased.

'And don't worry about your own time, that'll be amply rewarded,' Norma added.

Dickie slipped the cheque into his wallet. 'I'll get onto Creighton right away. In the meantime continue doing as you have been with that towel.'

'Can I change her again? This nightie is already soaked through.'

'By all means. If she comes round and asks for water give her some, as much as she wants.' He rose. 'I'll be as quick as I can.'

'Expense is no object. If this Creighton needs to bring anything with him, tell him to do so.'

'I will, Miss McKenzie,' Dickie replied, and hurried from the bedroom. Alice Henderson went with him to show him out.

'Would you like me to help you change Effie?' Alice asked on her return.

'Please.' Norma went to look out another nightie.

Rodney Creighton was younger than Norma had expected – in his early forties she judged. He wore a pin-striped suit and black Homburg, and had a very grave manner about him. Those who knew him well said he had no sense of humour whatever.

He handed Norma his Homburg (a bit pompous that, she thought, he could have just laid it down), and sat beside Effie, who hadn't regained consciousness. His examination, using various instruments and testing devices, was thorough.

'You were quite correct not to move her, doctor,' he said to Dickie when the examination was over.

'Is it meningitis?'

'No, encephalitis. The symptoms are very similar.'

Norma had never heard of encephalitis. 'What is it?' she queried.

'Infection of the brain caused by a virus. It was first noted in Vienna in 1916, and there was an epidemic of it in London in 1918. It's relatively uncommon today,' Creighton replied.

'Can you cure it?'

'Mrs McKenzie has a most severe case of encephalitis, a most severe case indeed. In my opinion there's only one thing can pull her through and that's a drug called M&B. It's a drug that's fairly new and, what with the war on, extremely difficult to come by.'

'You're saying it's expensive?'

Creighton's expression never wavered. 'Yes. But also difficult to come by.'

'Can you get some?'

He opened his black bag and extracted a sealed bottle. 'From Doctor Dickie's account of the patient's symptoms I realised that M&B might be needed, and so, being in the fortunate position of already having some on the premises, I took the precaution of bringing it along.'

He talked like a textbook, Norma thought. His words were all neutral, without emphasis. It was a little creepy to hear.

'Could you assist please, doctor,' he said to Dickie, taking a metal container from his black bag. He opened the container to reveal a hypodermic syringe.

Doctor Dickie rolled up Effie's right sleeve as Creighton filled the syringe with a dose of M&B. Dickie held Effie's upper arm as Creighton first swabbed it with cotton wool and spirit, then slid in the needle.

'You said only M&B could pull my mother through. Does that mean without it she'd have died?' Norma asked.

Creighton fixed Norma with an unwavering stare. 'Almost certainly. Encephalitis is, when the infection is as severe as your mother's, a killer. I doubt she'd have lasted the night.'

Norma shuddered to hear that. Thank God she'd come home when she had. 'And now she'll be all right?'

'In medicine nothing can be taken for granted. Let's just say she now has a real fighting chance, and that one can be optimistic about a recovery. I shall return later to administer another injection, by which time we should hopefully have signs of improvement.'

Creighton repacked his black bag, then Norma saw him and Doctor Dickie to the front door. Creighton told Norma to expect him around 10pm.

When the doctor and specialist had disappeared down the stairs, Norma went back to her ma. Alice Henderson had gone upstairs before Dickie and Creighton had arrived, to make Leslie and Katy's tea, but had said that if Norma wanted her again all Norma had to do was knock and she'd come running.

Norma wasn't sure whether it was her imagination or not but Effie seemed less fevered than she had been. Was the injection already taking effect? She certainly hoped so.

It wasn't long after that the outside door opened and Norma heard the voices of Lyn and Eileen, the two of them chaffing away to each other about an incident at work.

'Ma, where are you? I'm starving hungry!' Eileen called out from the kitchen. She gaped when Norma appeared in the hall. 'When did you get back?' she queried, then flew at Norma to give her a big hug.

Lyn appeared from the living room, if anything looking even more attractive and curvaceous than the last time Norma had seen her. 'I should have guessed when I saw that army car parked in the street,' she said. She and Eileen were still in their factory overalls.

'Ma's badly ill. I've had a specialist here,' Norma announced.

'What are you havering about?' Lyn demanded with a frown.

Norma then recounted all that had happened, and the three of them went through to their parents' bedroom.

'She mentioned at breakfast that a headache had kept her awake for most of last night, but I never dreamt it was anything more than just that,' said Eileen.

'Do you think we should contact Da?' Lyn asked Norma. 'Can we?'

'There's a telephone in the house where he's billeted, but he's rarely there before nine or ten in the evening,' Lyn replied.

'We'll wait till later then, and see what we think,' Norma said.

The three of them looked down at Effie who was still sweating profusely, but otherwise seemed peaceful enough.

'You never know the minute till the minute after,' Eileen said. A prophetic statement regarding her own circumstances as she was shortly to discover.

A quarter of an hour later Effie started to scream.

Eileen opened the door to Creighton who hurried past her into Effie's bedroom. Effie was in a terrible state, thrashing this way and that; moaning like a stricken animal one minute, screaming in a demented fashion the next.

Creighton felt her boiling forehead, then took her pulse. Effie wasn't unconscious anymore, neither was she properly awake. She was somewhere in between: half unconscious, half awake.

'Damn!' Creighton swore softly.

'The M&B isn't working?' Norma prompted.

'No, it's not that. I'm afraid she's allergic to the drug. What we're witnessing here is her reaction against it.' He looked Norma straight in the eyes. 'It does happen occasionally, and can't be foreseen. I'm sorry.'

When Norma spoke next her voice was quavering. It was the question she'd been dreading having to ask. 'You're saying she's going to die after all?'

'I'm afraid so. Between the encephalitis and her allergy to M&B death is . . .' he broke off, and shrugged.

'Surely there's something can be done? Something else you can give her?' Eileen urged frantically.

'I'm afraid not, Miss McKenzie. M&B was her only hope. All we can do now is wait for the end.'

Lyn sobbed, and stuffed a balled fist into her mouth. She just couldn't imagine Ma dying. Ma, like Da, had been there forever. And should continue to be so.

'She'll pass into a coma very soon and when the time comes she'll just sort of drift off,' said Creighton.

Effie screamed again, the loudest scream. Lyn covered her ears.

'I'll come first thing in the morning . . .'

'Why bother if she'll be dead by then,' Eileen interjected tartly.

Creighton looked at Norma. 'I can send Doctor Dickie if you prefer. But a death certificate will have to be signed.'

'You come, Mr Creighton. Despite what's happened I know you did your best. Her being allergic to M&B was . . .' Norma trailed off.

'Thank you.'

Effie jerked all over, then jerked again. Her body and limbs seemed to relax.

'That's her starting to go into a coma. Within a few minutes it'll be as though she's just fallen asleep.'

'I must know, could *anyone* have done anything for her?' Eileen asked bluntly.

'No, I assure you. M&B was her only known lifeline. I give you my solemn word on that.'

Eileen gave a reluctant nod; she believed him. He reeked of sincerity.

Norma saw him out.

It was just as Creighton had said, Effie appeared to be in a deep sleep. Even the sweating had stopped. Apart from being pale she looked quite normal. Except that she was at death's door, about to pass through.

Norma glanced at her wristwatch to see that Eileen had been gone more than thirty minutes now. Was she having trouble getting through to Da? Or was Da still not back at his billet and Eileen was hanging on at the phone box?

Lyn came into the bedroom. She'd changed into her pyjamas and a pink candlewick dressing gown. Her face was puffed from crying. 'I hope Da gets here before . . . before . . .' She broke off, unable to say it. The tears started flowing again.

Da was going to take this hard, Norma thought. He and Ma had been a proper couple, as one. They would all take it hard of course, but Da most of all. 'I hope and pray he gets here in time too,' Norma replied.

Norma brought her attention back to bear on Effie. How she was going to miss her ma. It was a terrible blow, particularly coming so soon as it did after Lynsey.

And then Eileen was back with them. 'I finally spoke to Da. He says you're not to bother going for him in your car, Norma. He's going to come on his motorbike, he says he'll make better time if he leaves straightaway on that.'

Norma relaxed a little, she'd been all keyed up ready to drive to Berwick-upon-Tweed to pick up Brian and bring him back here. But he was probably right about making better time on his motorbike.

'He broke down and started to cry. I've never heard Da cry before,' Eileen added.

Neither had Norma. All the years of her life she'd never known her da cry. Effie often, but never her da.

Eileen made a pot of tea which no one drank. Then she too

got changed into pyjamas and dressing gown. Not that any of them intended sleeping, but it was more comfortable like that.

They hadn't intended to sleep, but as the hours passed the long hard day at the armaments factory caught up with Lyn and Eileen. Lyn was the first to drop off. Sitting in the living room staring off into space she was awake one moment, snoring the next. Eileen put a travelling rug over her. A little later she too had dozed off, leaving Norma alone with Ma.

It was that time in the early hours of the morning when everything is hushed and still, Norma was dog tired, and thinking that Brian should be arriving at any time now, when Lynsey appeared in the bedroom to stare sorrowfully at her.

She stared back, not frightened or alarmed in the least. Lynsey had come to help, she somehow knew that to be so.

'I lost you, Lynsey, I don't want to lose Ma too,' Norma whispered. Lynsey's still sorrowful stare transferred itself to Effie.

'A life for a life. Hers for yours. I beg it,' Norma pleaded, again in a whisper.

Lynsey walked closer. There was a faint luminous glow surrounding her. And every so often she sort of shimmered, as if it was only an act of supreme willpower that was keeping her there.

Lynsey looked back at Norma, and the hint of a smile touched the corners of her mouth. 'Your hands,' she mouthed.

Norma held her hands out in front of her. 'What about them?'

Lynsey's smile widened a fraction, and as it did a strange tingling invaded Norma's hands. She later described it as like a pins and needles sensation, only pleasant rather than painful.

'On your mother, lay them on your mother.'

Norma did, placing her hands on the exposed flesh between the neck and breasts. The tingling intensified, and it was as though the energy which was causing the tingling flowed from her into Effie.

And then, as suddenly as she'd appeared, Lynsey was gone. So too was the tingling. Everything was back to normal.

Norma lifted her hands off Effie and stared at them. Had she momentarily nodded off to dream what had happened? What had *seemed* to happen? She shook her head, then took a deep breath. She'd either been dreaming or hallucinating, that had to be the case.

She snapped out of her reverie when she heard the sound of boots on the outside landing, followed by the grate of a key going into the lock.

She met Brian in the hall. 'Is she . . .?'

'Ma's still with us.'

Eileen appeared, wiping the sleep from her eyes. 'What time is it? she asked. Norma told her as Brian brushed passed on into the bedroom. Lyn also appeared, she too had been woken up by her da's arrival.

The three sisters went into their parents' bedroom to find Brian sitting beside Effie gazing down at her. Norma noticed right away that Effie's colour had improved, and that her breathing had deepened.

Effie sighed, and then her eyes opened. 'Hello dear, what are you doing here? This is a pleasant surprise.'

With the exception of Norma everyone else was totally stunned to hear Effie speak as she just had, at the transformation in her. Effie glanced across at Norma. 'I feel awfully weak, but that terrible headache's better. Completely gone.'

Norma didn't need a doctor to tell her that Effie had recovered, was going to live. She looked down at her hands – it hadn't been a dream or hallucination after all. It had actually happened.

When she looked up again her da was embracing her ma. It was a sight that brought a lump to her throat so big it threatened to choke her.

She'd expected Creighton to pooh-pooh her story, but he didn't. He listened intently, occasionally nodding his head in affirmation as she recounted what had happened. When she finished there was a silence between them.

'Can I see your hands?' he asked.

She lifted them up and he took them in his own. 'Has anything like this ever occurred before?'

'No.'

'Perhaps . . . perhaps you have healing hands, the hands of a healer.' He stared her straight in the eyes. 'That's not so fantastic as it might at first seem. It's well-documented that some people have this ability to cure by merely placing their hands on an inflicted or diseased person.'

'You believe that?' she queried.

'Oh yes. We've never been able to pin-point a scientific reason why it should be so, but it is. I myself met just such a person in India, a holy man, who could cure by the laying on of hands. I was a sceptic up until then, but not after I'd witnessed him do what he did.'

'And Lynsey?'

Creighton's brow furrowed into a frown. 'It could be that your healing ability – and there can be no other reason that I can think of why your mother has recovered when by all the laws of medicine she should be dead by now – is latent and Lynsey was a device, or catalyst, used by your subconscious to bring that ability to the surface.'

'I thought myself it was more of a miracle.'

'And what's a miracle? Life, death, healing hands, they're all miracles.'

He rose, and reached for his Homburg. 'I'll tell you this, I'm not an envious man, but if you do have this ability within you – which I'm sure you must – then I envy you it. Very much so.' He gave her a sudden smile, something he did rarely. 'It's good for us physicians to feel humility from time to time. At this moment I feel extremely humble indeed.'

Norma went out onto the landing with him. 'Your mother's illness has taken a lot out of her. See that for a while to come she gets plenty of rest; she's not to over-exert herself in any way,' Creighton said, fumbling in an inside pocket.

'I understand.'

He took out a diary-cum-notebook, from which he extracted a piece of paper. This he gave to her. 'You must have that back. I couldn't possibly accept it in the circumstances.'

It was her cheque for a hundred pounds. 'No I...'

'And I insist,' he said with finality.

He made a small, old-fashioned bow, then placed his Homburg on his head. 'I can't tell you how pleased I am about your mother. And it's an honour to have met you Miss McKenzie.'

She liked him, Norma decided as he went down the stairs. She hadn't up until then, but she did now. Who'd have thought he'd believe in healing hands? She certainly wouldn't. Which only proved the saying that you couldn't always judge a book by its cover.

She held her hands up in front of her, remembering the tingling sensation, and the energy that had caused it flowing from her into her mother.

'Thank you Lynsey,' she whispered. Then, in a reverential tone. 'And thank you God.'

She went back inside, closing the door behind her.

By the beginning of the following week Effie was up and about, though still taking it easy. To aid her recuperation Norma took her for a drive in the car to Largs, and the following day to Helensburgh. The third drive was a surprise; she drove Effie to Berwick-upon-Tweed where they met up with Brian, the three of them managing to have dinner in a fish restaurant there. Effie pronounced the trip to Berwick-upon-Tweed as the best treat of all.

Arriving home from Berwick-upon-Tweed Norma and Effie found that the postie had left a letter addressed to Eileen in his afternoon delivery. Effie recognised the writing as Charlie's and placed the letter on the mantelpiece to await Eileen's return from work.

Norma was preparing tea when her sisters came in from the factory. 'There's a letter from Charlie on the mantelpiece for you Eileen!' Effie cried out from her bedroom where, at Norma's insistence, she was having a wee lie down before tea.

Eileen ran to the mantelpiece and snatched up Charlie's letter. Impatiently she tore it open. A handful of seconds later she squealed with joy.

'What is it?' Lyn demanded.

'Charlie's got some leave. He'll get into the Central Station late tonight!' This was the first leave Charlie had been given since going south.

Lyn beamed, that was good news. 'Och I'm awful pleased,' she said.

Norma came into the living room. 'What's up?' An ecstatic Eileen repeated the news. Effie joined them, knowing something was going on and not wanting to be out of it.

'That's tremendous,' she said when she heard what the commotion was all about.

A fire was hurriedly laid so that Eileen could have a bath, and while the water was heating she ransacked her wardrobe trying to decide what to wear. Finally she selected a dress that she herself wasn't daft about but which was a great favourite of Charlie's. She was dressing for her man after all, not herself.

Lyn contributed a pair of silk stockings she'd been keeping for a special occasion (since the start of the war silk stockings had been murder to come by) and Norma lent Eileen a bottle of perfume given to her by Jeremy Dereham. The perfume was French, and had cost Jeremy a small fortune. It smelled heavenly.

Norma went into the bathroom while Eileen was in the tub. 'This is only a suggestion, but as Charlie is getting in pretty late would you like me to drive you to the station and the pair of you back? If you don't want a third party present I'd quite understand.'

'That's a marvellous idea, Norma. Thanks, I'll take you up on it.'

As Norma left Eileen her sister started to sing.

'Ten minutes late,' said Eileen.

'There's a war on you know, everything doesn't just run like clockwork as it used to,' Norma replied.

Eileen had worked herself up into a lather of impatience. She couldn't wait to see Charlie again. To touch him, to be kissed by him, to be safe and warm in his arms. Several times during the journey from Cubie Street she'd shivered all over in anticipation.

Norma glanced up at the arrivals board, but there was no indication as to how much longer the train was going to be. And then the tannoy crackled into life.

'Due to a derailment at Lockerbie . . .'

Eileen's expression changed to one of panic. She clutched Norma by the arm, squeezing the arm so hard Norma grimaced with pain. They looked at one another when the brief message was over. There had been a derailment at Lockerbie and because of this the line from London was blocked. Further news would be relayed as it came through.

'I must know if Charlie's train was involved. I must, and right away,' Eileen said, her voice tight with fear.

'We'll find someone, come on,' Norma replied.

A sign guided them to the station master's office. They knocked, and a voice bid them enter. They discovered the station master chalking a message on a blackboard – a message about the derailment. Norma explained why they'd come.

The station master looked at them from behind thick pebble glasses. He was about to reply when a phone, one of several, rang. 'Excuse me,' he muttered, picking up the receiver. A man appeared behind Norma and Eileen to make the same inquiries that they had. The station master hung up.

'What train was your husband on again, hen?' he asked Eileen. She told him.

'I'm afraid that is one of those involved in the derailment. That phone call was from Lockerbie naming the trains.'

'Is anyone hurt?' Norma demanded.

'I've no idea. I haven't been informed yet.'

'There's more than one train involved you say?' the man behind Norma and Eileen queried.

'Aye, the other was a goods.'

'When will you know more about what's happened?' Norma asked.

'Haven't the foggiest, hen. But I promise you this, if you hang around then when I know you will.' He returned to the blackboard to finish writing his message.

As Norma, Eileen and the man who'd come in behind them left the station master's office they passed a number of others heading where they'd just been.

Eileen had gone strangely quiet, and seemed to have somehow shrunk in on herself. 'Let's go to the buffet and wait there,' Norma suggested. Eileen didn't reply, but just followed her sister to the opposite side of the station where the buffet was situated.

They found a table no bother. 'What will I get you?' Norma asked. She had to repeat the question when Eileen didn't reply.

'Tea, coffee, whatever, it doesn't matter,' Eileen said.

Norma bought two teas; she would have bought a couple of drams as well as she thought they could both use a drink. But it was after hours and the bar was shut.

'Norma, I'm awful scared. Really I am,' Eileen said when Norma was sat beside her.

'I know, but the chances are he's fine. He might even have joined another train beyond the blockage and could be once more on his way.'

Eileen brightened fractionally. 'Do you really think so?'

'I think we should think positively until we find out otherwise.'

Norma glanced at a wall-clock. It was now twenty-five minutes past the time that Charlie's train had been due to arrive.

Every so often the station master repeated his original message over the tannoy, adding that there was still no further news. At half past midnight he used the tannoy to ask those waiting for word about the derailment to assemble in front of his office. About two dozen anxious folk gathered there.

'I've just had a phone call to say the line will definitely not be cleared tonight, and will probably not be until later on tomorrow morning. I suggest therefore that you all go home and come back again sometime then.'

'So it's a serious derailment,' a woman said.

'Must be if it's going to take them that long to clear it,' the station master conceded.

'Are there any casualties?' a man asked.

'I believe there are a few. But I have no idea as to how many or who they are.'

'Is there nothing more you can tell us?' Norma queried.

'I swear to you hen I've relayed everything that I've been told. I'm not holding anything back.'

'Is Lockerbie?' a middle-aged woman asked.

'I don't think they're deliberately doing so, I just think they're busy.'

That sounded ominous to Norma, but she didn't say so to Eileen.

There were a few more questions which the station master answered; then the crowd broke up to head for home.

As they dispersed the station master went into his office and slumped down in an old dilapidated leather armchair he kept there. He'd been over twenty-five years in the railways and knew only too well that in railway matters of this kind no news was bad news. He feared the worst about the derailment at Lockerbie.

The first thing Eileen did when she got up the next morning was turn on the wireless to see if there was anything about the derailment on the early news. There wasn't. Nor was there anything in the paper when it was delivered.

'Right then, let's be on our way,' Norma said when she judged it was time for them to go. She was driving Eileen back in again to the Central Station having said she would do so the night before.

Eileen opened the outside door to discover a policeman with fist raised just about to chap. Her heart plummeted at the sight of him.

'I'm looking for Mrs Charles Marshall,' he stated.

'You'd better come away through,' Eileen replied, and led him ben.

On reaching the living room the policeman took up a position in front of the fireplace where he stood holding his hat. He coughed, then coughed again. Although he'd done this many times before it never got any easier.

'My Charlie's dead isn't he?' Eileen said, staring straight at the policeman.

'I'm sorry Mrs Marshall, the answer's yes.'

Norma's hand flew to her mouth, Effie made a sort of sighing sound that was really a long release of air.

'I knew, I somehow knew,' said Eileen, her face frozen with shock.

Effie started to rise to go to her youngest. 'It's all right Ma, just sit where you are for the moment,' Eileen said. Effie sat again.

'Do you know anything about this derailment, any of the details?' Eileen asked the policeman, her eyes bright with tears.

'There was a head-on collision between the passenger train carrying your husband and a goods train. The derailment was as a result of the collision.'

'How many died?' asked Eileen.

'Thirty-six that we know of. There are still some bodies feared to be in the wreckage.'

'And other casualties?'

'Over a hundred hospitalised. It was a terrible crash apparently.'

'Was Charlie... Did he...' She bit her lower lip. 'Did he suffer much?'

'According to what I was told he must have died instantly. They all must have in the coach he was in, the coach nearest the engine.'

'He'd have chosen that coach specifically because when the train arrived in at the Central that coach would be nearest the barrier, and me,' Eileen said, the tears now streaming down her cheeks. She whimpered, then turned her back to the policeman. Her shoulders sagged, her body drooped. Up until then her crying had been silent; it wasn't anymore.

Norma got to her first, Effie second. 'Oh my wee lassie,' Effie said, and swept Eileen into her arms. She too was crying.

'Four days, that's all the time we had together as man and wife, four days,' Eileen sobbed.

The policeman let himself out as Effie and Norma were putting Eileen to bed.

The funeral was in Riddrie Park Cemetery within sight of Hogganfield Loch. Eileen hadn't been allowed to see the body – the remains they cried it – as it would have been too distressing for her. She was told it was best she remember Charlie as he'd been and not what was going underground in the coffin.

The minister began in on the final part of the service. Eileen was standing with her parents on one side of her, Norma and Lyn on the other. She was holding Brian's hand as she'd been doing ever since the coffin was lowered into the earth.

Facing the McKenzies across the grave were the Marshalls, Mrs Marshall in a state of collapse and being held upright by her husband who was extremely anguished himself. A knot of relatives stood beside them.

It was a small turn-out, Norma thought. But that was only to be expected with a war on. From what Eileen had told her Charlie had had plenty of pals but there were only a couple of them present. The rest, she assumed, were away with the Armed Forces.

There were a handful of girls from the library where Charlie had worked before going into the army. Several of those were blubbing into hankies.

She glanced sideways at Eileen. How she felt for her sister remembering the sheer purgatory she'd gone through when she'd lost Midge. Midge hadn't died true enough, but the severance had been just as final as if he had. Eileen was now suffering all the agonies she'd suffered then.

She looked further across at Ma. Only the previous week they'd all thought they were going to be burying her. But Effie had recovered and it was Charlie they were burying instead. Poor bugger, poor Eileen.

Effie stared down at the coffin top, thinking of Eileen. At least Eileen was still young. Another lad was bound to come along eventually – not to replace Charlie but rather take the place that had been his. The minister started to sing and she joined in. 'The Lord's my shepherd...'

Eileen didn't sing, she couldn't have sung to save herself. She was recalling the happy times she and Charlie had had together, the days of their courting. And of course those four glorious days and ecstatic nights in the Adelphi Hotel, their honeymoon.

How ironic it was that Charlie had only agreed to marry her believing himself to have a safe billet in Aldershot. Well, the billet might have been safe enough, but the journey home hadn't been. He'd left her a widow after all, if not a teenage one. She was twenty years old.

Charlie was dead, her dear darling Charlie was dead, and as far as she was concerned so too was she. Oh she might be breathing and walking about, but she was stone dead inside where it mattered. If Effie had mentioned her thoughts, and hopes, about there being someone else eventually, she could have told her mother there never would be. Just as Effie and Brian were as one, so too had she and Charlie been. There would never be another man in her life, her heart was forever Charlie's.

Before she'd been a flesh and blood person. Now only a shell remained, an empty hollow shell waiting for her own death when she could rejoin Charlie.

When the singing was over the minister intoned. 'Ashes to ashes...'

# *Chapter Nine*

On her return to Grendon Underwood Norma went straight to the room she shared with Helen Rolfe and Pam Parkinson, something Helen had arranged prior to her and Pam's arrival at F Section, to find Pam, off duty, stretched out on her bed reading a novel.

'So how was Bonnie Scotland?' Pam asked, laying the novel aside and swinging her legs onto the floor.

'I had an eventful time to say the least. My mother nearly died of a brain infection and my brother-in-law did, killed in a train-crash.'

Pam's face fell. 'Oh I am sorry.'

Norma put her suitcase onto her bed, then sat beside it. 'Death seems everywhere these days. It's horrible.'

Pam knew Norma was also thinking of Lynsey. 'Autogiro was penetrated while you were away. We lost three "joes".'

'Violette?' asked Norma in alarm.

'She was lucky. Twigging, literally in the nick of time, that the Gestapo were onto her and about to pick her up, she did a bunk over the Pyrenees. DF took her through the Perpignan and Ceret route. The Spaniards connected with her in their Frontier Zone, taking her from there to Figueras and finally to Barcelona where she is still awaiting transport home to England. We're hoping to take her out by sub at the weekend.'

'If the Gestapo have identified her then she won't, thank God, be sent in again. That's the end of Josephine.'

'You can imagine how relieved she must be, as I am. When she returns she and I will go on leave together. After that it's Fawley Court again and a link-up with a new partner. And I suppose that's what'll be happening to you.'

Norma nodded, that's what she also believed would happen.

'I'm really pleased about Violette. If I don't see her then give her my love when you do.'

'I will,' Pam smiled. 'But listen, I musn't keep you here chatting. You're to get cleaned up and report to DR's office, he wants to see you as soon as possible.'

'And who's DR when he's at home?' This was a new one on Norma.

'There have been changes made while you've been in Glasgow. SOE has been expanding at such a rate of knots that M felt the need to delegate some of his responsibilities. As a result the position of regional controller has been created, to be known by the symbol DR, a position directly below M in the hierarchy. Our DR is called Lieutenant-Colonel Roe and as well as being in charge of F Section he is also in charge of DF, RF, N and T Sections. His office here is the one M used to use.' RF was the Free French, or Gaullist, Section while N and T were Holland and Belgium respectively.

'Does that mean we won't be seeing M around as much as we have been doing?' Norma asked, for she'd become quite fond of Gilchrist, viewing him as a paternal figure.

'I don't expect we'll see that much of him, although I would imagine he will put in an appearance from time to time.'

That disappointed Norma. 'So what's this Roe like?'

'Pleasant enough, and very, very efficient.'

Norma went to have a wash and brush-up. When that was completed she took herself along to what had been M's office.

DR was a medium-sized man with a receding hairline, bushy eyebrows and a thick moustache. He shook Norma by the hand, which surprised her; she hadn't expected that.

'Sit down. Looking forward to getting back to work?' he asked. Waiting to sit himself until she'd done so.

'Yes sir.'

'Bad business about Marie Thérèse, bad business indeed. We recently lost three other agents with Autogiro, but the circuit is still managing to function despite that, though I doubt if for all that much longer.'

'I heard about the three "joes", Pam Parkinson told me. She wanted me to know that Josephine is safe in Spain. Pam and Josephine, Marie Thérèse and myself all trained together at FC.'

At Grendon Underwood it was quite permissable for the

people there to talk 'shop' freely amongst themselves. What was strictly forbidden was to talk about F Section and the SOE in general outside the organisation.

DR came to the point. 'I have a challenge for you. Does that appeal?'

She grinned. 'Yes sir, it does.'

'I want you to work with a new partner. He's a very experienced agent who's already been into France, and out again, a number of times. He's going back there shortly to commit various specialised acts of sabotage for us, after which he'll be setting up a new circuit to replace Autogiro when that inevitably collapses altogether. Have you heard of Arisaig?'

She shook her head. 'No.'

'We have several field training establishments there, one of which will be teaching him the special techniques that will be required for the first part of his mission.'

'May I ask something?'

'Of course.'

'What happened to his original partner, the one he trained with?'

'Cigarette?' DR asked, offering his packet.

'No thanks.'

DR lit up, to give Norma a hard stare through a cloud of blue smoke. 'Did you know Mary Cluff?'

'Only to say hello to in passing.' Mary was another WT operator at Grendon Underwood.

'She was his partner. I say *was* because she suffered a minor heart attack, brought on by the stress of the job two nights ago. She's in hospital now, and going to be perfectly all right. But if she does return to duty it'll be FANY mobile canteens for her from here on - for obvious health reasons she's finished with SOE.'

'And I'm to replace her. So when do I get to meet my other half?'

DR gave a thin smile. 'That's the challenge - you don't. As soon as he's finished at Arisaig we're whipping him back to France. From now until he goes you and he will transmit to each other daily, several times daily if he can manage it. You'll get to know each other's "fists", and develop your transmitting relationship that way.'

It was novel, Norma thought. But a viable proposition. After all there was no reason why they *had* to meet.

'I'll contact Arisaig and organise your first session. Any objections, time being of the essence, if that's later on today?'

'None whatever,' Norma replied.

'Right then, I'll send you word after I've spoken to Arisaig.'

Norma could see she was dismissed. She rose. 'Thank you sir. I'll be waiting to hear from you.'

'His code name's Gabriel. That's all you need know about him,' DR said.

Home base calling, Home base calling.

Gabriel receiving. Gabriel receiving.

Hello.

Prepare to take message.

Abrupt, Norma thought, picking up her pencil. No pleasantries and 'how's your father?' it would seem. The message started to beep at almost unbelievable speed in her earphones. Her pencil flew.

> Now is the winter of our discontent,
> Made glorious Summer by this sun of York
> And all the clouds that lower'd upon our house
> In the deep bosom of the Ocean buried.
> Now are our brows bound with victorious wreaths,
> Our bruised arms hung up for monuments;
> Our stern alarums changed to merry meetings...

Norma lost him there. She doodled round what she'd written down while the rest of the message beeped at bewildering speed in her earphones. She'd never known anyone to transmit so quickly. Bombardier Gutteridge must have loved Gabriel. He must have been a star pupil.

Transmission ceased.

Gulp! – she tapped out slowly.

And then there was a new signal in her ears. One that wasn't Morse and didn't make any sense at all. No sense, but something. What? She listened intently as the jumble continued. Then the penny dropped. Jesus he was clever! If she was right that was.

Are you laughing at me?

Very good. Most wouldn't have understood. It shows you have 'feel'.

Right now I feel a bit of a twit. Your message, was it Shakespeare?

Richard the Third.

Was way too fast for me.

How far did you get?

Merry meetings.

Mary would have got all of it.

I'm not Mary. I'm Norma.

I transmitted that quickly because it's something I've had to learn to do in the past due to the conditions I've been transmitting under. It's one of my tricks for continuing survival.

So do I take it you always transmit that quickly when in the field?

No, only when it's necessary. Which it occasionally can be.

I understand.

Hello Norma.

She smiled, there were to be the pleasantries after all. Hello Gabriel.

Shall we try again?

Give me the same message, but slowly. If you start slowly and increase your speed a little day by day then eventually, I hope, I'll be able to cope with you at your fastest.

Right, I'll do that. Are you pretty?

The unexpectedness of his question startled her. Some men think so.

Blonde or brunette?

Why do you want to know?

I want to build up a picture of you in my mind. It'll help with the business in hand.

Baloney! she thought. He was just downright curious. Honey-blonde.

Are you small?

Fairly tall for a woman.

How tall is that?

Six feet six.

She smiled again when the sound of his 'laughter' filled her earphones.

Come on Norma, the truth?

Five nine.

And what colour are your eyes?

Sometimes grey, sometimes green. They change back and forth all the time.

Sounds fascinating. What size bust?

Get lost!

Oh come on?

No! And that's final.

Spoilsport. What are your legs like?

I've got two.

You know what I mean!

Do you want me to stop sending?

(Pause) All right, I'll behave. Are you ready to receive a message?

Ready Gabriel. By the way, what colour are your eyes?

> Now is the winter of our discontent,
> Made glorious Summer by this sun of York ...

Three days later a letter arrived for Norma. When she opened it she discovered it was from Jeremy Dereham. She sat on the edge of her bed to read it.

His regiment was back in England, but only temporarily. He'd been devastated to learn of Lynsey's death from his parents. Did she know what had happened? For his parents certainly didn't. They'd been notified that Lynsey had been killed, and that was all.

He'd tried contacting her at her old address, but she'd gone, nor could (or would) anyone, including FANY HQ give him a forwarding one. All FANY HQ would say was that if he wrote care of them she would get the letter.

If she was in London or in reasonable striking range could they meet? He very much wanted to see her for herself, but also to find out what she knew about Lynsey.

His parents had taken Lynsey's death extremely badly, and this mystery surrounding her death certainly didn't help. If only mater and pater could find out what actually did happen then perhaps that might ease their pain a little. It was terrible for them not knowing how their daughter died after all. If it had been in a car crash – and with her being a driver that seemed the likeliest cause of death – then why the evasion and secrecy?

Damn! Norma swore when she'd finished the letter. The War Office had made a right hash of things. An explanation should have been given of Lynsey's death, even if it wasn't the truth. You just didn't do this sort of thing to people. The fact a war was on was no excuse. Not only was it insensitive in the extreme it was, even worse in her book, downright sloppy.

She would reply to Jeremy, but what to say? She was going to have to talk this over with DR.

She had to wait till the following afternoon to see DR as he'd been away at RF Section. 'Come in!' he called out when she knocked on his office door.

She told him what her problem was, then handed him Jeremy's letter to read for himself.

'So what's Dereham to you?' he asked when he'd finished reading.

'We went out together for a while sir. Then his regiment got posted abroad. That's nearly a year ago now.'

DR shook his head. 'Bad show by the War Office. I'll have a word with M, he'll see to it this doesn't happen again.'

'And what do I tell Jeremy, sir?'

DR had a think about that. 'The car crash is probably the best and most likely tale. Embellish it by saying she was carrying a high-ranking foreign brass hat on hush hush business when the crash occurred, and that it was because of the nature of the man's business that the War Office, being over-diligent and cautious, clammed up on the Derehams. That should do the trick eh?'

'Yes sir.'

'Good. And I . . .' DR stopped in mid-sentence as the thought struck him. Rising, he crossed to a filing cabinet and opened the third drawer down. He extracted a file from inside, returned to his seat, sat again and began leafing through the file.

Norma squinted to make out the name typewritten on the front of the file. The name was Lynsey Dereham. It was her dead friend's file that DR was reading.

'It states here that Miss Dereham spoke perfect French as a result of a succession of French nannies she had as a child and because she spent every summer up until the war at her father's villa in the Dordogne.'

'Yes sir.'

DR looked up at Norma. 'What about the brother?'

'You mean what's his French like? I've no idea sir.'

DR's eyes took on a hard, calculating gleam. 'Chances are high that it's as good as his sister's was. After all, they would have shared the nannies and the summers in the Dordogne. What's his physical appearance?'

'Mousy coloured hair, brown eyes...'

DR grunted; that was what he wanted to hear. Jeremy would have been ruled out immediately if he'd been extremely Anglo-Saxon in appearance. 'What's your opinion of him Norma, would he make a good "joe"?'

Her stomach turned over on being asked that. The incidence of mortality amongst "joes" was so incredibly high, and not only in F Section but throughout all the sections. They were said to have a fifty-fifty chance of returning from a mission, but in fact the odds against were now higher than that. And as the war progressed those odds could only increase.

Should she say no? The Derehams had lost a daughter already; it wasn't fair to put their son, and sole remaining off-spring, in jeopardy as well. Then again, being in a fighting regiment he was already in jeopardy. She decided after a few more moments of mind tussling that the only answer she could give was an honest one. 'I think it's possible he might sir. He's a fairly cool person, the sort that's good in an emergency I should imagine.'

That was precisely what DR had been hoping Norma would say. 'Which regiment is he with?'

'The King's Royal Hussars.'

DR made a note of that. He would instigate some inquiries right away. 'Normally I'd get him along to Baker Street but right now we have a bit of a flap there.' DR's expression became grim. 'We suspect a leak, only *suspect* mind you, but until it's either discounted or plugged it would be best for potential agents to stay clear of the place. So I'll tell you what, as he himself suggested that you meet, write and invite him here. Say you'll tell him all you know about his sister's death when you see him.'

'I'll write today sir.'

'Let me know when you have a date for his visit so that I can set up a preliminary testing out session for him.'

'Right sir.'

On leaving DR's office Norma went straight to her room where she wrote the letter.

Jeremy Dereham stared at Grendon Underwood, thinking it was a most handsome building. He glanced over at the hutted encampment which was the wireless station to note the various clusters of aerials and antennae pointing skyward. He wondered what went on there. Then Norma was striding towards him, waving a hand in greeting.

'It's marvellous to see you again,' he said, and kissed her lightly on the mouth.

'It's been a long time.'

'A lifetime in Lynsey's case.'

Her smile disappeared. 'We'll talk about that shortly. But how about a little fortification first? I could certainly use a drink.'

'Top-hole idea.'

She forced a smile back onto her face. 'Then I'll take you to the bar.'

'This country living certainly seems to agree with you. You look terrific Norma,' he said as they went inside.

'Thank you.' She couldn't say the same for him. There were bags under his eyes and hollows in his cheeks. His skin seemed somehow stretched, and lifeless.

'How was abroad?'

'Far too hot for my taste. And I had recurring bouts of dysentery which wasn't exactly pleasant.'

'I can imagine.' That could explain why he appeared so tired and generally run-down, she thought. From what she'd heard dysentery could really take it out of you.

There was a man and woman standing at the bar. He was called Monckton, she Renée Dufrenoy and they were both there on DR's instructions. Apart from Norma, Jeremy and the barman they were the only others present.

'I think I'll have a G & T. What about you?' Norma asked Jeremy, taking up a position beside Monckton and Renée where Jeremy naturally enough joined her.

'A G & T sounds fine.'

Norma ordered, for it would go on her mess bill, then asked Jeremy if he'd excuse her for a few moments; she'd just remembered something she urgently had to attend to. As she was leaving the room Monckton and Renée started talking in French.

She gave them fifteen minutes, then returned to the bar. 'Sorry about that, took longer than I thought it would,' she apologised to Jeremy who'd been deep in conversation with Monckton and Renée.

Renée was standing behind Jeremy and there, where Norma could see but he couldn't, shook her head several times. For whatever reason – Norma later found out that, unlike his sister, he spoke French with a pronounced English accent – Jeremy had failed the crucial language test.

Norma was filled with relief. Thank God for that! After a while she took him over to a table by a window and there told him the lie DR had concocted about Lynsey's death.

What's wrong?

What makes you think something's wrong?

I can tell by the way you're sending. Your mind isn't fully on what you're doing.

Norma put the end of her pencil in her mouth and chewed it. She hadn't been aware there was any difference in her sending. But Gabriel was right, her mind hadn't been fully on the job

The brother of the girl I trained with at FC came to see me today. He wanted to know how his sister died. I wasn't allowed to tell him the truth of course. I said that she died in a car crash, as we were both drivers before she and I joined the SOE.

Gabriel had never asked about Norma's previous pairing, nor had she mentioned anything. Up until now he hadn't even known whether the pairing was a man or woman. And why hadn't he asked? Because he saw it as personal. An area you only walked into when invited – I take it she died on a mission?

The Gestapo surprised her at her set while transmitting and shot her through the back of the head.

(Pause) At least it was quick. Many aren't so lucky.

I know.

Did the brother believe what you told him?

Totally. I was very convincing.

Would I have known her?

I shouldn't think so. Her code name was Marie Thérèse.

(Pause) I have to stop transmitting now. I'll come through again at twenty-one hundred hours.

He lifted the hand from his Morse key and ran it over his face.
'Shit!' he swore.

He left the transmitting hut to stride down to the beach. There he lit a cigarette and stared out at the island of Eigg, now only partially visible because of the sea mist.

He recalled that she'd offered him a cigarette which he'd accepted, and thinking how young, vulnerable and fragile she'd looked. It was a rotten war he'd thought at the time - and how right he'd been.

It wasn't just a rotten war. It was rapidly becoming a bastard of one.

Dead on the second of twenty-one hundred hours Norma's earphones began to beep.

Hello Norma.

Hello Gabriel.

Sorry I 'rang off' so abruptly earlier. It was just that, well, you gave me a shock.

I did?

Your pairing, Marie Thérèse. I met her.

(Pause)

Norma?

There were tears in her eyes, pain in her heart. She was looking at her Morse key but it was Lynsey's face she was seeing.

How did you meet her?

We shared the same ride when she went in. She asked me to stand behind her and give her a push should she freeze when it came time for her to jump.

Did she freeze?

No. I was glad about that.

We were friends before FC, in fact she was my best friend. It was because of me that she was asked to join SOE and become a "joe".

And now you feel responsible for her death?

If she hadn't been my friend she'd probably still be a driver, and alive.

You're being too hard on yourself. Man only proposes, God disposes. It was her karma.

What's that?

Her fate.
(Pause) Her real name was Lynsey.
Nice name. She seemed a nice girl. I liked her.
Norma dashed away some tears. She'd been so composed when talking to Jeremy, but then she'd been prepared for that. She hadn't been for this. I'm glad you met and liked Lynsey. She was a smashing person. A real gem, and a good pal to me.
(Pause) I've got some news Norma.
?
I'm going back over in ten days time.
She took a deep breath. Your training's almost finished then?
Almost.
Plane?
So I'm told.
She remembered she had a hanky on her, fumbled for it, and blew into it. She then dabbed at her wet cheeks.
In that case we'd better get cracking on some speed work. I'm still not as fast as Mary was.
You will be in ten days time.
So what have you got for me this evening, Shakespeare again? She knew he liked using Shakespeare because of the difficulty and complexity of the language. It made a first-class exercise to send and receive.
*A Midsummer Night's Dream.* Do you know the play?
No.
It's a great favourite of mine. I've seen it lots of times. Tell you what, when the war's over why don't we meet up and I'll take you to see a production. (Pause) Well?
Sounds fun.
And if the production is in London I'll take you to the Savoy Grill for supper afterwards. I adore the Savoy Grill. Ever been there?
Never.
If we go you'll enjoy it, everyone does. We shall meet for drinks before the show. I shall carry a rolled-up copy of *The Times* and bring you a single red rose. I shall say hello Norma, and you shall reply hello Gabriel. Savoy Grill or not, it shall be a splendid night out.
I'm looking forward to it.
So am I.

It'll give me something to think about when... Ready for message Norma?

Ready to receive message Gabriel.

> I know a bank where the wild thyme blows,
> Where oxlips and the nodding violet grows,
> Quite overcanopied with luscious woodbine,
> With sweet musk roses and with eglantine...

Her pencil flew as he sent at his quickest. She got eighty percent of the message, her best result yet. But she was going to need those ten remaining days - she wished it was longer.

He stood staring out to sea, a sea that was pounding ashore in fury. There was a fierce, cutting wind blowing, while overhead dark clouds were scudding against the moon. He shuddered, a shudder brought on not only by the cutting wind.

Shot through the back of the head Norma had said. He hoped, no he prayed, that when his end came it was as quick and final as that. He had a horror of falling into the hands of the Gestapo or SD, a horror that kept him awake nights and brought cold clammy sweat to his forehead.

He knew only too well what the Gestapo and SD were capable of. The bath of icy water they stuck your head into, keeping it under till you were on the point of drowning. Again and again the ducking till in the end even the toughest lost all will and blabbed.

The torture with the pliers, pulling out your fingernails one by one. And when they ran out of fingernails they started on your toes.

He'd told Marie Thérèse never to let fear get the upper hand, but by God what a monumental effort that could be. When over there fear was always with you, day and night, every waking moment. Fear that could become so intense he'd known an agent die of it, literally scared to death.

He'd have given anything not to go back, to stay on in Britain. But when the time came he'd go, just as he'd gone before. Just as Marie Thérèse and the others had gone.

Bending over he threw up.

It was the same Whitley bomber belonging to 138 Squadron

that had taken him and Marie Thérèse the last time he'd gone in, only on this occasion it left from Stapleford Abbots rather than Newmarket racecourse. The pilot and co-pilot were also the same. The only difference was that he wasn't sharing this journey with another 'joe'.

He lit a cigarette, then looked at the duffel bag attached to his right ankle by a length of rope. There were a million francs in that bag which he'd be using to set up Oberon Circuit.

He smiled to himself. He'd asked Norma what he should call the Circuit, and Oberon had been her choice. Oberon was the fairy King in *A Midsummer Night's Dream* which she'd been in the middle of reading. So she'd know the play when they went to see it, she'd said. He'd been flattered by that.

He wondered what she was like? He did have a mental picture of her, but it was probably quite different to how she really looked. She certainly sounded a smasher. And intelligent, far more than Mary had been.

A production of *A Midsummer Night's Dream* and supper at the Savoy Grill afterwards? What a lovely dream that was.

The co-pilot appeared and gave him the thumbs up sign. 'Three minutes to drop point. You know the drill,' he said.

Gabriel gave the thumbs-up sign back, then stood up. As he ground his cigarette out underfoot he wondered what Norma was doing at that moment? She certainly wouldn't be at her set, he wasn't due to transmit till the following night. Maybe she was out with a boyfriend? He'd never asked her if she had one, but if she was a good-looking lassie then probably she did. That thought depressed him, though there was no reason why it should. She was nothing personal to him after all. Why, they'd never even met!

The red light came on and his stomach knotted. The breath caught in his throat. He fought to control the fear that flooded through him. Fear that would be with him till he was either dead or out of France again.

He stepped to the rim of the hole and waited. The red light winked out and the green came on.

He was smiling as he jumped into the darkness.

Norma chewed a thumbnail that was already half bitten. Seventy-two hours had gone by and still no signal from Gabriel.

Where was he? What had happened? Was he ...? She refused even to think of that dread word.

She glanced up at the clock. Another few minutes and it would be past the agreed time during which she would be standing by her set.

Come on Gabriel, where are you! She didn't so much as think but shouted inside her head.

And then her earphones were beeping. Gabriel calling. Gabriel calling.

Her hand flashed to the Morse key. Home base receiving. Home base receiving.

The message was short, delivered at his quickest. A dozen seconds was all it took her to jot it down. It was in code of course – they'd switched to code during the final days of their sessions together – so she had no idea what it said. She would only find out after it had been decoded.

She took a deep breath. He'd survived the jump, and was alive. Though under pressure it would seem from the quickness of his sending.

Tearing the top leaf from her pad she took the message through to the decoders.

He was trapped. If he turned round and tried to get back on the train he'd just come off, the Gestapo man at the barrier would spot him doing so, come after him and that would be that. As he was carrying the wireless set he'd picked up on arrival, not to mention the duffel bag containing the million francs, he hadn't a hope in hell of getting past them undetected. They were checking everyone, every suitcase and every bag.

Never ever panic! There may just be a solution, a way out. Don't panic, think. *Think.*

It was an absurd idea. Yet was it? He held aloft the suitcase containing his wireless and headed straight for the barrier.

'I have a captured British wireless set here! Make way, I have a captured British wireless set here!' he shouted. When one poor woman didn't move out of his path quickly enough, he thrust her aside, she stumbling and nearly falling, only being saved from measuring her length on the platform by a workman who grabbed her by the shoulder. Someone spat. It was a gesture of contempt towards a collaborator.

He arrived at the barrier with a face filled with triumph and excitement. 'I have a captured British wireless set here. Take me immediately to your superiors,' he said.

The Gestapo men looked at one another. 'Let me see this wireless,' the older of the two said.

Gabriel dropped the duffel bag to the ground, then heaved the suitcase onto the barrier and snapped open its locks. He lifted the top of the suitcase to reveal his set.

'How did you come by this?' the same Gestapo man demanded.

He made a tutting sound of impatience. 'I haven't got time to stand here talking, I must speak to your superiors immediately. Besides this set I have important information for them. Information that must be acted upon right away.'

Would his bluff work? His heart was hammering as he waited to find out.

'*Merde*,' someone muttered, meaning Gabriel. There were about twenty other passengers crowded round the barrier staring hostilely at him.

'I'll take you,' the younger Gestapo man said. 'Come.'

He sagged slightly at the knees, but they didn't see that. Snapping his suitcase shut again, he heaved it down off the barrier, snatched up the duffel bag and strode after the younger Gestapo man. Behind him the older Gestapo man continued to search.

The Gestapo man took Gabriel to a Mercedes, instructing him to slide the suitcase into the back seat, which he did, casually tossing the duffel bag on top of it. Then the pair of them got into the front.

'How far to your headquarters?' Gabriel asked as they drove off.

'About a kilometre and a half.'

He would have to make a move soon. For of course he daren't try to extend his bluff to Gestapo HQ. Once in there he'd never come out again - alive that is.

He slid his hand underneath his coat and jacket to touch the hilt of the stiletto he had strapped below his left armpit. Slowly he pulled the knife free.

His opportunity came as they stopped at a set of traffic lights which had changed just before they'd arrived at them. He'd already gone over in his mind how he would do this, the precise spot he'd strike for.

The steel was painted black so there was no flash or glint. The Gestapo man stiffened, eyes bulging, as the slim knife punched home. He was dead almost the moment the blade went into his side.

Gabriel released his hold of the stiletto, opened the car door and stepped out into the street. Taking his time, giving no appearance of hurry, he closed the door again. He then retrieved the suitcase and duffel bag from the rear seat, shut that door also, turned, and walked off. As he walked he looked neither to the left or right.

Behind him a car horn sounded, then sounded again. A few seconds later another car horn sounded, this one very impatiently. He presumed correctly that the lights had changed to 'go'.

He turned into an intersecting street where he caught an autobus. It didn't matter where the autobus was going, just as long as it was away from the Mercedes and dead Gestapo man.

'A little warmer today,' the woman who took his fare commented.

He nodded his agreement. 'Yes it is. It certainly is.'

This time the message, the third he'd sent, came through at a leisurely pace. She tore the top leaf from her pad when it was finished, and was about to rise from her chair to take it through to the coders when he started sending again. She put her earphones back on.

Hello Norma, how are you?

She blinked in astonishment. Not only was he sending in plain language but appeared to want to chat.

I'm fine. Should you be doing this? It's most irregular. The sound of his laughter filled her ears.

It's teeming down with rain here, and earlier on there was fog. The combination is very depressing.

We've also got rain. Are you sure it's safe for you to do this?

Don't worry. Caution's my middle name. There isn't a direction-finding team in the area, I know that for a fact. And if the krauts *are* listening in, so what? They won't learn anything to their advantage. (Pause) Do you like wine?

What an unusual question she thought.

I enjoy a glass though I'm hardly a connoisseur.

Right now I'm drinking a bottle of Grand Vin de Château Latour that I've personally liberated. Sheer nectar.

It sounds a very grand wine.

It is. Premier Grand Cru Classé.

Do you know much about wine?

A fair bit. My mother taught me. She ...

No, don't!

(Pause) What's wrong?

We've never really divulged personal details about one another, apart from me giving you a physical description of myself that is.

And talking about Marie Thérèse.

Yes.

And you don't want to?

Correct.

(Pause) I think I understand your reasons. And you're right, I'm sure of it. (Pause) But will you still go and see *A Midsummer Night's Dream* with me after the war?

And have supper in the Savoy Grill afterwards if the production is in London. Yes, I said I would, and I will.

(Pause) Goodbye then, for now.

Gabriel?

Yes?

Did you ever do this with Mary? Chat when you were in the field I mean.

(Pause) No.

(Long Pause) Do be careful.

I told you, caution's my middle name.

Enjoy the wine. Goodbye.

Goodbye for now Norma.

She took her earphones off. Wherever he was, whatever he was up to he was lonely. She knew that as surely as her name was Norma McKenzie. Lonely, and probably scared. But she *was* right to keep some distance between them, not to let their relationship become too close and intimate. It had been bad enough losing Lynsey, she didn't want to go through that ever again.

She took his message through to the decoders.

There was a click, and the lock was sprung. Gabriel smiled to himself, it was easy when you knew how, and he knew how thanks to the locksmith who'd taught him in Arisaig. He went through the door he'd just opened and relocked it. He padded forwards.

Further into the factory there was yet another door he had to deal with, this one yielding as easily to his pick as the others had done. A few minutes later he found the safe, which was where he'd been briefed it would be.

It was a new safe made just before the war by Schlage Brothers of Berlin, one of Germany's best safe-makers. The safe he'd practised on in Arisaig had been identical, if a little older. Kneeling before it, he went to work.

He was frowning in concentration when he heard the sound of approaching feet. The armed nightwatchman making his rounds.

Swiftly he switched off his torch, gathered up his bits and pieces and hid behind a filing cabinet. The silken cord he now held between his hands had a single knot at its centre. The nightwatchman would die quietly. He didn't want to be interrupted again.

The nightwatchman didn't put the overhead light on, which made it easier for Gabriel. He was carrying a torch that he shone round the room. The first he was aware of Gabriel's presence was when the cord looped round his neck.

When the man was dead, garrotted, Gabriel laid him on the floor. He switched off the fallen torch, and returned to the safe.

Finally the safe swung open. Inside he found what he'd come for, and what the Admiralty in London were most anxious to get hold of.

He spread the plans on the floor, and shone the thin beam of his torch over them. *Schnorchel* was what the Germans had named the device, an underwater breathing system, still in a state of development, that would allow a U-boat to run continuously at periscope depth.

To Gabriel's eye it appeared that development was nearing completion which was going to give the Admiralty a great deal to think about, and act upon. They would also of course incorporate the system, or their version of it, into His Majesty's submarines.

He gathered up the plans, carefully refolding them one by

one, and slipped them into the briefcase he'd brought along. Then he made his way to the shop floor itself, seeking out the area where the tools and dies were kept, may of which were bound to be originals created especially for *Schnorchel*. Unfortunately the plans weren't originals – those would be in Germany along with various other copies.

He'd brought six pounds of plastic along with him, this particular plastic's distinctive almondy odour strong in his nostrils as he broke the six-pound mass into two of roughly three pounds each. He slid a time pencil, preset for thirty minutes, into the first section, and activated the pencil by pressing it. The now primed bomb he placed amongst the tools and dies.

He did the same with the second section of PE, placing that beside what looked to be the most important piece of machinery on the shop floor. When that was done he stealthily left the factory by the same route he'd entered it.

The time pencils he'd used had been known to act up, and even fail, from time to time, but they did neither on this occasion. The two very satisfactory bangs were within seconds of one another.

There must have been a large amount of inflammables and combustibles in the factory because almost immediately it turned into a raging inferno. It was like some huge Guy Fawkes bonfire as whoosh after whoosh of flames leapt skywards.

Next morning the plans he'd stolen began their journey to London and the Admiralty.

Norma was getting ready to go on duty when Madge Philips, one of the decoders, knocked on her door and said she was to stop by and see DR in his office before she did. He wanted a word.

'Come in!' he called after she'd tapped.

When she saw the bottle of scotch on his desk her smile wavered, then disappeared altogether. When DR asked you to his office and produced a bottle it only meant one thing. 'Do you mind if I sit?' she said, for her legs were suddenly weak and in threat of buckling under her.

'What happened?' she asked as DR poured them both hefty ones.

'Gabriel got picked up by the Gestapo last night, and he didn't have his death phial on him. It seemed he'd lost the damned thing and was waiting for a replacement. The rest of the Circuit, knowing the inevitable results of interrogation and torture by the Gestapo, immediately contacted DF and are even now on their way to Spain.'

She took a deep breath, then swallowed half her whisky. She didn't taste a thing. 'How do they know he was picked up by the Gestapo?'

'Another member of the Circuit actually witnessed it happen.'

'So he finally ran out of luck.'

'I'm afraid so.' DR paused, then added softly. 'He was one of our best. In fact I'd go so far as to say he was *the* best.'

'Six months, he lasted six months and it was his fourth trip in. That was quite an achievement,' she said with a choke in her voice.

'Yes. We should really have brought him out some time back but... well he was doing such a first-class job.'

She leant forward, bending over slightly so that DR couldn't see her face. It was contorted with all manner of emotions.

'You appreciate there's nothing we can do for him. Now that he's in the Gestapo's clutches he's quite lost to us.'

She sat up again and drank off the remainder of her whisky. This time it burned going down. 'So that's that, the end of the Oberon Circuit.'

'Yes.'

'And the end of Gabriel.'

DR took her glass and refilled it. 'How about a spot of leave, eh? You might like to go home?'

Almost the exact same words M had said to her after Lynsey's death. Only Lynsey's death had been quick, over in a second. It wouldn't be like that for Gabriel. His death would be long, drawn-out and agonising. Those fiends in the Gestapo would make certain of that.

'Yes, I think I would,' she replied.

'You can go on leave starting from now. I'll fill out the necessary bumf to make it official.'

'Thank you sir.'

'I am so dreadfully sorry,' DR said in a voice filled with compassion.

'Yes sir, so am I.'

She left for Glasgow the following morning.

# *Chapter Ten*

Norma was asleep in the cabin she shared with Helen Rolfe and Violette Hart when the torpedo struck. She awoke to find herself in mid-air, catapulted from her bunk. She landed on the floor with a jarring thump, and promptly blacked out.

The *Scythia* heeled, and juddered. There was noise and confusion everywhere. A short distance away their escort, a corvette, whooped as it raced for that area of sea its captain had judged the torpedo had come from. As the corvette knifed through the water the captain wished for the umpteenth time that he had the new asdic aboard; what a difference that must make to the locating and killing of U-boats. He gave a terse command and the first of his depth charges were released. The sea behind him fountained as one after one they went off.

Norma came groggily round to find Helen lying moaning beside her and Violette sitting on the floor looking totally and utterly bewildered. She turned to Helen who, from the sounds she was making, was in considerable pain.

On the *Scythia*'s bridge Captain Howat was being given the initial damage report. It wasn't nearly as serious as he'd at first feared, but serious enough nonetheless. Two seamen were dead, but the hole in the *Scythia*'s side was patchable. Thank the Lord they were so close to Algiers, their destination.

Norma left Helen to crawl over to Violette. A quick examination showed that Violette hadn't been physically injured. 'Violette, are you all right? Come on snap out of it, Helen's hurt.'

Violette made a strange animal-like sound at the back of her throat. Norma slapped her, then slapped her again. Violette cried out at this treatment, but it worked, bringing her back to her senses.

'Helen's hurt you say?'

'There don't appear to be any broken bones so it must be something internal.'

Their cabin door flew open. 'Everyone fine in here?' a very young and fresh-faced seaman demanded. He bit his lip when Norma told him about Helen.

'What happened?' Violette asked.

'Torpedo. Took us aft.'

'Are we going to sink?'

'Not according to the First who's up now telling the old man that.' First was the First Officer, the old man Captain Howat.

Jonty Wrolsen and Pat Tunbridge-Briggs, two more of the ten FANY's who were aboard, and the other two bunking on the port side, crowded round the young seaman. 'Awfully exciting what!' Pat exclaimed enthusiastically.

'Helen's hurt, fairly badly I suspect,' Norma said.

Pat's face fell, and she cursed herself inwardly for being so gung ho! That was just typical of her, saying the wrong damned thing at the wrong damned time.

'I'll report what's happened here to the captain. That's all I can do for the moment,' the young seaman said.

'Anyone else hurt?' asked Norma.

'That's what I'm doing the rounds to find out. This lady is the only one so far, though a couple of our chaps who were standing right at the point of impact were killed.' Having said that, the young seaman turned and hurried off down the passageway.

Norma bent again to Helen who'd gone a dirty yellow colour. She didn't like the look of that at all.

Helen's eyes flickered open. She'd been unconscious all this while. 'Excruciating pain in the small of my back,' she whispered.

Violette came over with a towel and wiped away the blood trickling from the left-hand corner of Helen's mouth. As soon as she wiped the blood away it appeared again.

'Should we try and move her onto one of the lower bunks?' Violette asked Norma. There were four bunks in the cabin, two lower and two higher. Norma and Violette had the lower bunks, Helen one of the higher. The second higher was empty. Helen, like Norma, had been asleep when the torpedo had struck, and she too had come flying off her bunk. Only in her case she'd had further to fall than Norma.

Norma wasn't at all sure about that. It would certainly be more comfortable for Helen. But was it the right thing to do?

More depth charges exploded, rocking the *Scythia*. Norma suddenly had a horrible thought – what if they were torpedoed again? She listened to the corvette whoop-whooping like a mad thing, and prayed that one of those depth charges had found its target. 'Let's try and lift Helen,' she replied.

All four girls lent a hand. Helen gasped in agony as she was raised from the floor, and the trickle of blood became a small river.

Captain Howat, still on the bridge, was also considering the possibility of a second torpedo. The *Scythia*, with its speed reduced to four knots – as opposed to its usual ten – was a sitting duck if the U-boat managed to get another crack at them. He glanced round as his Third Officer appeared on the bridge.

'We've started jettisoning the deck cargo sir. Once the hole is clear of the waterline we'll begin on the patch. The entire operation shouldn't take all that long,' Third reported.

Captain Howat grunted; that was good news. He'd go down to the damaged area himself shortly to see what was what. They were extremely lucky the torpedo had hit them where it had – any lower and a patch would have been impossible. The wireless operator came up onto the bridge.

'Escort says she's convinced the U-boat's done a bunk. She wants to know our situation.'

That was even better news, providing it was correct. He gave the wireless operator the answer, then turned to the young seaman to find out about the casualties.

'No more dead other than the two you already know about sir. But there is one serious injury, a FANY. She's in a bad way according to her mates.'

Captain Howat swore. 'Which FANY is it?' he demanded, for he'd made friends with all of them.

'Ensign Rolfe sir.'

'She's in with Ensigns McKenzie and Hart isn't she?'

'Yes sir.'

'Well, away back to their cabin and tell them I'll be down just as soon as possible.'

Captain Howat looked out over the green sea at the corvette

now astern of him on the starboard side. He hoped the corvette's captain was right about the U-boat. He made some mental calculations, then went over to the blow tube and had a word with the First Engineer. As soon as the hole was patched up they could bring their speed back up to seven, maybe eight, knots. Dawn was half an hour gone – if all went well they should reach Algiers somewhere round about midday. He took his medicine chest with him and went below.

'Come in captain,' Norma said when Howat appeared at the door of their cabin. He went over to where Helen was and stared grim-faced, down at her. He thought she looked extremely ill.

'She came to for a short while to complain of an excruciating pain in the small of her back. Then she passed out again, Norma said.

Helen twisted one way, then the other. Her low moaning was pitiful to hear.

Captain Howat replied. 'We don't have a doctor aboard, but I can give her a morphine injection to deaden the pain.' Suddenly there was an enormous splash outside the porthole. It was followed by an even bigger one. The Captain explained about the *Scythia* having to jettison its deck cargo, then brought his attention back to Helen. 'I'll radio through to Algiers and tell them to have a doctor standing by. I'll make it clear it's an emergency.'

'I'll give her the injection if you like? I'm quite good at them,' Norma volunteered. Giving injections had been part of her original FANY training.

Captain Howat was only too pleased to agree to that. He hated giving injections almost as much as he hated having them. He put his medicine chest on the bunk above Helen's and rummaged inside. 'Right, carry on,' he said, handing Norma the necessary bits and pieces.

The others watched as Norma loaded the syringe, then slid the needle home. The morphine was quick to take effect and soon Helen stopped moaning and twisting about. By which time Captain Howat was back on his bridge giving the wireless operator the message he wanted radioed ahead.

Norma and Violette were with Helen when the *Scythia* limped into Algiers and gently bumped the quayside where it was to berth. Almost instantly there was the rattle and bang of a gangplank going into place.

Captain Howat personally brought the doctor to their cabin. The doctor, without any preliminaries or introductions, went straight to the still unconscious Helen. Bending over her he prised open one eye. While doing that with his left hand he took her neck pulse with his right.

He was a slightly-built man with sallow skin and very dark hair shot through with grey. He had a neatly clipped beard and a thick moustache, also streaked with grey. He'd seemed vaguely familiar to Norma from the moment he'd appeared in the doorway.

Having peered into her eye and taken her pulse he gently lifted Helen up and over onto her side so that he could feel the small of her back. She moaned, the first time she'd done so since the morphine injection. 'An excruciating pain, she said?' he queried of Norma who was closest to him.

'Yes, those were her precise words.'

The doctor, probing very gently, then laid Helen flat again. 'And how long did the bleeding from the mouth go on for?'

'A good hour, maybe more,' Norma replied.

The doctor frowned. 'Was that continuous bleeding?'

'No, it would stop from time to time. Then she'd vomit and it would start up again.'

'Was there blood in the vomit?'

Norma nodded.

'And when was she given the morphine?'

It was Captain Howat who answered, giving the exact time which he'd had to note for his log. The doctor then produced a syringe and proceeded to give Helen another measure of morphine.

'Any idea what's wrong?' queried Norma.

He looked her directly in the eye, and again she had that nagging feeling there was something familiar about him.

'I think it's pretty certain there's been internal haemorrhaging which may still be going on. I'll have to open her up to find out.

'You suspect something other than internal haemorrhaging then?'

'I can assure you that haemorrhaging is serious enough. But

yes, I do have my suspicions. Though nothing I'm going to commit myself to here and now.'

Prickly character, Norma thought. Prickly to the point of being rude.

'I want this young woman in the hospital right away,' the doctor said. The two orderlies who'd come on board with him and had been lurking outside the cabin appeared in the doorway. 'The patient is going to have to be strapped to your stretcher to get her up the companionway. Strap her securely, but as comfortably as you can. And not over the mid-area,' the doctor told them.

Norma touched the doctor on the arm. 'I'm a great friend of hers. Can I go with her? Please?'

A frown of irritation creased his face. 'Please?' she pleaded a second time. He tried to think of a reason why he should refuse her, and couldn't. The frown relaxed a little. 'Oh all right, if you must.'

'Don't worry about anything here. I'll attend to it,' said Violette.

'And we'll help her if she needs it,' Jonty added.

The tricky part was getting the stretcher up the companionway – the stairs leading from that deck to the next. There was no other way that the stretcher could be taken. But this was eventually accomplished, with one orderly pulling and the other pushing and with the stretcher at an angle of about seventy degrees. After that it was through a hatch onto the outer deck, and the gangplank beyond.

Norma said a hurried goodbye to Captain Howat, whom she, and all the other FANYs had come to think very highly of. Then she was off down the gangplank to where an army ambulance was waiting.

Helen's stretcher was loaded in the rear of the ambulance by the two orderlies, who then got in at the front of the vehicle, one of them doubling as driver. The doctor climbed in the rear with his patient, and Norma followed suit. The driver engaged gear and the ambulance pulled away.

Norma glanced out the window beside her. It was her first visit to a foreign country – apart from England that is – and how different it all was. The smell of the place struck her forcibly. Warm, pungent, definitely exotic and... dangerous. Yes that was it, dangerous. But it was bound to feel like that after the heavy fighting that had taken place a few weeks previously when the combined Anglo-American force had landed here to take the town and surrounding countryside as part of the invasion of North Africa.

'Are we going to the local hospital?' she asked the doctor.

He looked at her as though she was daft. 'I wouldn't take my dog to the local hospital to have its claws trimmed,' he replied caustically.

There it was again, that feeling of *déjà vu*. Did she know him, and if so from where? She wracked her memory.

'We're going to an army field hospital that's been established fairly close to where you'll be billeted.'

'And where will we be billeted?'

He gave her a sideways look, his eyes narrowing fractionally as he did. It was a look that had something chilling and deadly about it. It made her shiver. 'I was informed that you and the other FANYs aboard that ship are SOE. Is that correct?'

'Yes'

'Then you'll be billeted at the Club des Pins along with the other members of the SOE already here.'

'Club des Pins? Sounds very grand. Is it in the town itself?'

'No, it's a group of villas roughly fifteen miles west of Algiers. It overlooks the beach where the main assault came in.'

'A group of villas. So it's not an actual club then?'

'More what you might call a tiny holiday resort. It was used by wealthy Algerians before the war. It's a rather pleasant spot, I like it.'

'Are you billeted there as well then?'

'I have a bed there. Also a room in the St George Hotel which is in Algiers. I flit between the two as work demands.' He pointed out her window. 'I don't know if it'll interest you but that shell of a building over there was the famous Al-Hani Mosque till it was hit directly by a bomb during the landings.'

She glanced out the window, remembering the bomb in Risinghill Street which had so nearly done for her. And with that association in her mind it suddenly clicked with her who the doctor was.

'You're Doctor Ross,' she blurted out.

His left eyebrow crawled up his forehead in surprise. It stayed there as he regarded her quizzically.

He hadn't had a beard or moustache then, nor had there been any grey in his hair. And gosh, he did appear so much older now, years older than she recalled him. Was she wrong?

'*Are* you Doctor Ross?' she desperately tried to remember his Christian name. Douglas, that was it. 'Doctor Douglas Ross?'

He was thinking back to the cabin on board *Scythia*. He hadn't mentioned his name there. He rarely did unless it was absolutely necessary, something he did from force of habit.

'How do you know me?' he asked quietly.

'I was your patient once, in the Royal Free Hospital in Gray's Inn Road. I was a FANY driver at the time and my car was blown up in Risinghill Street right at the beginning of the Blitz. I had a broken left arm and four broken ribs which you treated in Marsden Ward.'

Recognition dawned on his face. 'Miss McKenzie, yes I remember you now. You were the one who...' He broke off, and coloured.

Still as shy as ever, she thought. 'I kissed you while I was unconscious, thinking you were my boyfriend.'

'So you found out about that?'

'Yes, Staff told me.'

He glanced down at the floor of the ambulance, clearly embarrassed.

Norma went on. 'I remember I tore a strip off you one day because you were forever staring at me. It quite upset you.'

'Did it?' he said casually, as if he couldn't recall that bit.

'If it's not too late, sorry. It was just a bad day for me, a culmination of things.'

'That's all right, no need to apologise.'

'You were very off with me after that. In fact, not to put too fine a point on it, you were downright uncivil.'

'Now it's my turn to say sorry.'

She laughed. 'It was a long time ago – two years would you believe. A lot of water under the bridge since then.'

'Yes, a lot of water,' he agreed.

She recalled something else. 'If you were at this Club des Pins you must be SOE as well?'

'I am.'

'The day M came to visit me I remember seeing him talking to you afterwards and wondering what it was about. Was that when he recruited you?'

'That was when he first approached me. I saw him in Baker Street after that,' Ross said slowly.

'So what do you do in SOE?' she asked.

'What do you think?'

She nodded. 'I suppose SOE needs doctors like everyone else.'

'We take care of our own whenever possible. That's why it was me who came to see Miss Rolfe and not another army doctor.'

'It's a small world,' Norma mused.

'It is indeed.'

When they arrived at the army field hospital – a vast tent – the two orderlies came running round to the rear of the ambulance and threw open the doors. Ross supervised their taking Helen's stretcher out, and once that had been safely accomplished he and Norma followed. Ross gave an order and the stretcher was taken inside. He turned to Norma. 'What will you do now?'

'Wait if you don't mind.'

'It could be quite some while.'

'I'll wait anyway.'

'Right then.' He turned on his heel and strode into the hospital.

Norma couldn't get over bumping into Ross again, or how much he'd aged. He must have had a hard war, poor thing, she thought.

She glanced around. There were several other tents, smaller than the main one, and buildings beyond, several hundred yards away she judged. She spied a wooden bench with some empty wooden crates beside it. She'd sit and wait there.

She'd been sitting a while when she was approached by a Queen Alexandra nurse. 'Can I help you?' the QA asked.

Norma explained why she was waiting.

The QA smiled. 'How about a cup of tea or coffee?'

'Either would be marvellous.'

The QA left Norma to vanish into one of the nearby tents. She reappeared a few minutes later holding a steaming mug of coffee and, of all things, a jam-filled doughnut. It was the first nourishment Norma had had since dinner the previous night.

She stared at a camel that had appeared in the distance, the first she'd ever seen. A number of what she thought must be Shetland ponies appeared behind the camel, then she realised they were donkeys. They were another first.

Two soldiers walked by wearing uniforms she didn't recognise. A thrill ran through her when it dawned they were Americans. The one who'd started to speak sounded just like Clark Gable!

She glanced at her watch, it was an hour and three quarters now since Helen had been carried inside. She'd been worried all along, now her worry intensified. It seemed an awful long time. She just prayed that everything was all right.

A convoy of four ambulances drew up, and a number of wounded were taken from them to be stretchered into the hospital. One squaddie had half a leg blown away, the grotesque, obscene, blood-soaked bandaged stump sticking up into the air. Norma averted her gaze as he went past – she couldn't help herself.

A gaggle of QAs came out of one of the smaller tents to go dashing into the hospital tent. From somewhere inside came a great shriek of agony. It covered Norma from top to toe in gooseflesh.

She'd been sitting for a fraction over three hours when Ross suddenly re-emerged, glancing about him. Norma hurried over.

'Besides the internal bleeding, which is still going on, Miss Rolfe had a severely damaged kidney. So damaged in fact I had no choice but to remove it,' he reported.

'Will she live?' Norma asked softly.

He took a deep breath, then stared off into the distance. 'The next twenty-four hours will tell. It depends on how strong a fighter your friend is, and of course, it has to be said, conditions round here are hardly ideal. So we'll just have to wait and see.'

'But you have done your best for her?' That was a statement, not a question.

That could have been interpreted as impertinent by some, but not by him. He understood her concern. 'Yes Miss McKenzie, my very best.'

'Then thank you Doctor.'

He offered her a cigarette. 'I don't,' she smiled. He put one in his mouth and lit up. He drew smoke deep into his lungs, held it there for the space of a few seconds, then blew it out in a long thin blue stream. 'I have to go to Club des Pins to collect a few items, can I give you a lift?'

'That would be kind of you. Have you finished for the day?'

'Not quite, I'll have to come back. There are several patients who need my attention. My car's this way.'

He led her to a camouflage-painted Standard car and they climbed into the front seats. 'What will you be doing at Massingham?' he asked as they drove away.

'Massingham?'

'Inter-Service Signals Unit 6, codename Massingham. In other words our lot at Club des Pins.'

'Oh I see!' she smiled. 'I'm a WT operator. Three of our party are, the others are coders and decoders.'

'There's a lot hoped for Massingham. I think you'll find it's going to be pretty lively there during the coming months. And it'll be even livelier once we've booted the axis powers out of North Africa.'

'And *will* we be able to do that?'

'Before El Alamein I would have said our chances were sixty–forty against. Now I would put it at seventy-five–twenty-five in our favour.' The British victory at El Alamein had taken place the previous month.

'You believe El Alamein meant that much?'

'Not only me, but Monty and Ike. They believe it.'

'You move amongst such exalted company do you?'

He barked out a laugh. 'You'd be surprised whom you meet in the bar of the St George Hotel. Ike was there just the other day.'

'He was?'

'In the flesh.'

'And Monty?'

'I haven't met him. But I know he believes what I've just told you, Eisenhower told me that.'

'Win or lose, there'll be a lot of casualties,' she said, thinking of the soldier with half his leg blown away and that terrible shriek of agony she'd heard directly afterwards.

'There always are during wars,' he replied darkly. And it

seemed to Norma that his mood changed to become as dark as his tone had been.

They didn't speak again till they arrived at Club des Pins, Inter-Service Signals Unit 6, Massingham. 'Why it's gorgeous!' Norma cried out in delight.

There were more villas than she'd thought there would be, together with other pre-fabricated buildings that had been erected since the invasion. The sea was a beautiful bluey-green washing a bone-white shore. The villas were all white with various coloured roofs.

'Let's find out where they've put you,' Ross said, bringing the Standard to a halt beside one of the villas. He got out and vanished into the villa. When he re-emerged there was a French Lieutenant with him. They both came to Norma's side of the car where the Lieutenant flashed her a beaming smile, then saluted.

'Lieutenant Rene Bonnier de la Chapelle at your service, Mademoiselle McKenzie. You have been billeted at Casa Bon-Bon where your friend Mademoiselle Hart – *très charmante*! – is already installed.'

Norma giggled. 'Is it really called Casa Bon-Bon?'

'*Oui mademoiselle.*'

The sweetie house, was how she translated it. How could she not enjoy living in a place like that. 'Thank you Lieutenant,' she said. In reply to which the Frenchman became ramrod stiff, and bowed. Ross, the ghost of a smile hovering round his lips, walked round to the driver's seat, got in, and they continued down the dirt street.

'Who on earth was that?' Norma demanded.

'One of the instructors.'

'What does he instruct?'

'A number of things – you'll find out.'

Casa Bon-Bon had a pantiled roof and looked like something straight out of a story book or picture postcard. Norma gave a laugh when she compared it to Cubie Street and Bridgeton.

'What's so funny?' Ross queried.

'I was just . . .' She broke off. She wasn't going to tell him about Bridgeton. Why should she? 'Nothing,' she said, and got out the car.

The door opened and Violette came flying onto the verandah. 'How's Helen?' she demanded anxiously.

Norma asked Ross to repeat to Violette what he'd told her outside the field hospital, which he did. 'And now I must away,' he declared.

'Which villa are you in?' Norma asked.

He hesitated for a moment, then pointed behind her and Casa Bon-Bon. 'Over in that direction. The one with the green roof, it's the only one with a roof that colour.'

'Thank you for what you've done.' She stood watching him drive away, and then he turned a corner and was lost to view. 'Damnest thing, I knew him from before,' she said to Violette.

'Really?'

'Let's go inside and I'll tell you about it.'

Once through the doorway Norma came up short. Her initial impression of the inside of Casa Bon-Bon was that it was bare as Mother Hubbard's cupboard.

'We've got a bedroom each. I've stached your gear in one of them, and Helen's in another. As you can see there isn't exactly a lot in here.'

'Do we have beds?' Norma asked, not at all fancying the idea of sleeping on the floor.

'Three iron-framed canvas ones. Also some blankets, storm lanterns and paraffin.'

'No sheets, pillows or pillowcases?'

Violette shook her head.

Norma went to the closest window and stared out over the sea. It was a tremendous view, and so peaceful! She just couldn't imagine the hell it must have been when the invasion had come storming ashore. She turned again to Violette. 'What about eating?'

Violette's face lit up. 'There's a canteen run by – would you believe – a couple of Kenyan FANYs, so we're going to be just dandy there. The chap who brought me out here said that at night the canteen doubles as a club and bar for those who don't want to go into Algiers or are tied here for some reason.'

Norma knew of the Kenyan branch of the FANYs of course, but had never met any.

'I think I'll go out on the scrounge. I'm the world's best scrounger, did you know that?'

Norma laughed. 'No I didn't.'

'When God doled out the talents, one of the main ones he

gave me was the ability to scrounge. Give me a few days and, if it's humanly possible, I'll have this place transformed.'

'What about bathing facilities?' Norma queried.

'No baths, yet, but there are showers.'

Norma suddenly felt extremely tired. It had been a long, not to say, eventful day. 'I think I might just lie down and have a couple of hours shut-eye. I'm deadbeat,' she said.

'I'li show you your room.'

The room was a decent size and alive with light. Norma liked it immediately. There was the scent of flowers in the air, a heavy musklike smell. She had no idea what sort of flowers it came from, and wondered if her da would have known. He probably would have done. He had a tremendous knowledge of flowers and plants, not only of British domestic ones, but foreign plants as well. Gardening hadn't only been his job, it had also been his hobby. And no doubt still was.

When Violette had left her to go out scrounging she closed her eyes and prayed for Helen's recovery. Then she shook out her blankets, spread them over the bed, and lay down. Within seconds she was fast asleep. She dreamt she was back in Barrowland dancing with Midge.

The nine new FANY arrivals met up and went to the canteen for dinner together. There they were given an enthusiastic welcome by the two Kenyan FANYs who were eagerly waiting to say hello. The two Kenyans had already met Violette, who'd spoken to them during her afternoon scrounge, a scrounge which had produced a feather bolster, two cans of paint, some very useful wooden boxes that would double as furniture, together with a decorator's pasting-up table. She hadn't a clue how the latter had come to be where she'd liberated it from, but there it had been.

While they were eating, the French Lieutenant, René Bonnier de la Chapelle, came into the canteen. Before joining the small cluster of other Frenchmen he came over for a few words with Violette and Norma, and was introduced to the rest of the party. He informed them that a Major Fulford would come by shortly to speak to them, so would nobody please leave the canteen until the Major had put in an appearance.

Norma spied Doctor Ross sitting by himself at the far end of the canteen. She thought he might look over and smile, or give her a small wave of recognition. He did neither.

When dinner was finished they lingered over coffee waiting for Major Fulford. There were only the nine of them left in the canteen, and the two Kenyan FANYs who were out in the kitchen doing the washing up.

The Major introduced himself, then said in a soft Dorset burr, 'First thing tomorrow morning, seven hundred hours, assemble here for breakfast, after which I'll take you to where you'll be working. Hopefully the nine of you are the advance guard for many more like yourselves, for although we're starting small at Massingham we have great expectations for it. Great expectations. And you girls are in on the business right from the beginning.'

He paraded round their table, tapping his swagger stick against a leg. 'It's been decided that one of you is to be promoted in rank to be in charge of the others.' He stopped beside Norma. 'Congratulations *Captain* McKenzie.'

Norma's mouth dropped open in astonishment. 'Me?'

'*You*, Captain. You may consider yourself to hold the rank of captain as from now.'

Norma didn't know what to say. She was totally dumbfounded – this was the last thing she'd expected. Why, if anyone should have been put in charge it was Helen. And then she remembered that Helen was in hospital, fighting for her life.

'Three cheers for Captain McKenzie!' Violette said, and led the other FANYs in three rousing cheers, for Norma was popular with all of them. Norma blushed.

Major Fulford took Norma aside. 'All your equipment has been set up, all the equipment you'll need for the moment anyway. Tomorrow you're to establish contact with our wireless station in Tunisia, and F Section in Britain. You're also to establish contact with Gibraltar and Baker Street. You'll find that as the days go by a fair volume of signals will be passing between the five stations.'

'Yes sir,' Norma replied, nodding that she understood.

'Right then, see you at seven hundred hours,' Major Fulford said, and strode off.

'Well,' Norma said to Violette, 'wasn't that a turn up for the book? I'm sure Helen was the one originally earmarked for promotion, only they had to change their minds after what happened to her.'

'It could be, she is the most senior of us. But if it couldn't be her I'm glad it was you.'

'Would you like to speak to Pam tomorrow?'

'You mean Pam Parkinson!'

'We're to establish contact with F Section; if she's on duty during the establishing process the pair of you can have a coded exchange.'

'Let's just hope she is,' Violette beamed.

Next day Norma wasn't able to get to the hospital till early evening. She met Ross on his way out.

'I've got some good news for you. Miss Rolfe is doing absolutely splendidly,' he said before she could speak.

It was as if a huge load had been lifted from Norma's shoulders. 'She is going to be all right then?'

'No doubt about it. In fact I'm so pleased with her progress I'm having her transferred to the wards. She's very weak of course, but quite out of danger. It's simply a matter of rest and recuperation.'

'You've no idea what a relief it is to hear you say that.'

His lips slashed into a thin smile. He felt like teasing her, 'I think I do understand Miss McKenzie. This sort of situation isn't exactly new to me after all.'

'I'm sorry, I didn't mean that literally. It was just . . . well a way of expressing myself.'

He nodded, but didn't reply. He thinks I'm an idiot! she thought, and felt a warm stain rise in her neck. She indicated the canvas bag she was carrying. 'I've brought in some of Helen's things that she'll probably want. Can I see her to give them to her? Or is that out of the question for now?'

'On the contrary, I insist you see her. It's the best medicine I can prescribe. Tell Sister Littlejohn, on my instructions, that you're to have a full ten minutes with Miss Rolfe. I can't allow more than that for now as it would tire her too much.

'Thank you doctor.'

He walked away without saying anything else. As she went inside to seek out the Sister she felt she'd made a right fool of herself. Then again, there was no need for him to have picked her up as he had. It should have been obvious she hadn't meant what she'd said literally.

Doctor Ross confused her. He could be so charming and pleasant one moment, a real aggravating sod the next.

The following day Ross entered the room that Helen had been moved to. There were only two female patients in the room, Helen and a QA who'd suffered a burst appendix, and the pair of them were the only female patients the hospital had. The wards were filled with men, ninety-five percent of whom were casualties of the fighting that had taken place at the invasion and was continuing as the Allied forces advanced.

Helen was pale but cheerful. She'd made excellent progress, Ross thought as he examined her.

'How long will I be here?' Helen asked, already anxious to be up and about again.

'Between a month and six weeks, it all depends on how you do. Though I must say with your constitution it's much more likely to be the month than the six weeks.'

It bucked Helen up to hear that. 'Then what?'

'Do you want to return to England? If would be easy for me to arrange if you do.'

She shook her head. 'I would feel I was letting everyone down - myself included - if I went back when it wasn't absolutely necessary. If it's possible I'd prefer to stay on here.'

'Then you shall. After you've been discharged you'll still need a few more weeks of convalescence, but after that you should be able to get on with your duties.'

He glanced across at a photograph in a metal frame standing on her bedside locker. It was a photo of a trio of laughing girls, one of whom was Helen, the other the McKenzie lass, and the third . . . He frowned, the face was vaguely familiar.

Helen saw what had caught his attention. 'That came with the other things Norma brought me. It was taken at Fawley Court where the tree of us trained.'

'Norma?'

'McKenzie. Norma McKenzie who's just been promoted to Captain. She came in the ambulance with you when you brought me here.'

'And the third girl?'

'Lynsey Dereham. She's dead now. She . . .' Helen's voice thickened with emotion. 'She went to France as a "joe" and never came out again. Norma was her WT operator; they were particularly close.'

'May I?' he asked, and picked up the photograph. A strange expression played across his face as he stared at it. Slowly, and very carefully, he replaced it on top of the locker.

He rose to smile down at Helen. 'You're doing very well, I'm extremely pleased.' He left the room without waiting for a reply.

Norma glanced at her wristwatch - twenty minutes till Violette relieved her. With Helen out of action she and Violette, the remaining WT operators, were having to work extra long shifts, but another two FANY operators were *en route* from Grendon Underwood and should be with them during the next day or so, coming out by plane as opposed to ship as they had done.

Jonty Wrolsen handed her a coded signal for Tunisia which she sent. Things in Tunisia weren't going as well as had been hoped. The winter conditions - mainly in the form of a tremendous amount of mud - and the stiff resistance were proving considerable problems.

She glanced at her wristwatch again, thirteen minutes to go now. And then her earphones beeped with an incoming signal. A signal in plain language!

Calling Massingham. Calling Massingham.

Massingham receiving. Massingman receiving.

(Pause) Hello Norma.

Little prickles ran all over her skin. She found she was holding her breath. It couldn't be, it was impossible, and yet 'the fist' was identical.

Who is this?

Who do you think?

She rocked back in her chair. This had to be some sort of practical joke, had to be. Except 'the fist' *was the same*!

Gabriel?

Prepare to receive message.

Her shaking hand picked up a pencil. She could hardly see her pad for the tears blurring her vision.

Ready to receive.

I know a bank where the wild thyme blows,
Where oxlips and the nodding violet grows,
Quite overcanopied with luscious woodbine,
With sweet musk roses and with eglantine ...

She wrote none of it down, she didn't have to, she knew the words off by heart. To confirm it really was him he'd sent it at his fastest.

(Pause) Norma?

It is you.

Yes.

Laugh for me. He did, the sound of his 'laughter' filled her ears.

How's that?

I was told the Gestapo picked you up?

They did.

So how is it you're still alive?

Meet me for a drink and I'll tell you all about it.

Where?

The bar of the St George Hotel.

In Algiers!

Yes.

You're in Algiers?

Yes. Are you free tonight?

I can be.

Would 8 pm suit?

Where?

The bar of the St George Hotel?

I'll be there. How will I recognise you?

I'm only four feet three.

Fibber! Anyway, that was my joke originally.

So it was! Six feet six didn't you say?

Seriously, how will I recognise you?

I'll know who you are, the honey-blonde with grey-green eyes and the enormous bust.

I never said it was enormous!

Didn't you?

No I did not!

Then you'll be the honey-blonde with grey-green eyes and two legs. Any honey-blondes with grey-green eyes and three legs will be ruled out immediately. (He laughed.)

Very droll. Till 8 pm then.
Till 8 pm.
Goodbye Gabriel.
Goodbye Norma.
She took her earphones off and laid them beside her sender key. When she looked up and round Violette was staring quizzically at her.
'You don't half look odd. As though you'd just seen a ghost,' Violette said.
Norma gave a semi-hysterical laugh. 'Not seen, "spoken" to.'
Violette frowned. 'I don't understand.
'You'll never guess who just signalled me?' Norma said.
'Who?'
'Gabriel.'
Violette's jaw dropped. 'But he's dead!'
'No he's not, he's in Algiers. And I'm going to meet him tonight for a drink.'
And having said that Norma fainted clean away, Violette just managing to catch her before she hit the floor.

She was shaking as she walked into the bar. What on earth would Gabriel be like in the flesh? She was dying to know. And how on earth had he managed to pop up in Algiers? She'd been wondering about that ever since he'd come through to her earlier on.
She glanced about. There were a number of people present including the famous American aviator General Doolittle. She stood for several moments waiting for Gabriel to approach her, when he didn't she went over to the bar itself.
'Let me buy you that,' a voice said, from someone who'd come up behind her. It was Douglas Ross, the doctor.
'Thank you, but I'm meeting someone,' she smiled back.
'He's not here already then?'
'I eh . . .' She didn't know what to say. Was Gabriel here? She certainly didn't want to say that she'd no idea what the person she was meeting looked like, that would have sounded most peculiar.
'He doesn't seem to be,' she said evasively.
'Then I insist on buying you that drink.' Ross beckoned the

barman over and asked Norma what she'd like. She said she'd have a gin sling. He ordered a cold beer for himself.

'Out to paint the town red, eh?' he prompted.

She wished she hadn't run into Ross, the last thing she wanted was to talk about Gabriel. Except to Gabriel himself that was. 'Just a quiet drink that's all.'

'A friend from Massingham?'

'No.'

He nodded as though that held some significance for him. She smiled, and he smiled back. She found that irritating. In fact she was beginning to find him irritating.

The barman laid their drinks in front of them and Ross said to put them on his tab. 'Cheers!' he toasted. 'Cheers!' she responded, and they both took a sip from their respective glasses.

'I saw your Miss Rolfe this morning, a big improvement from yesterday. I've told her I can probably discharge her in about a month.'

'Good.'

'She had a photograph on her bedside locker that caught my eye. You, her and Marie Thérèse.'

'It was taken at Fawley Court where we did our WT and Morse training.'

'Yes, she said that.'

Another customer, a male civilian, entered the bar. He was short, swarthy and extremely fat. Surely that wasn't . . . She turned to stare at Ross in astonishment. 'What did you just say?'

'About what?'

'The photograph I took in to Helen.'

'That it caught my eye.'

'And . . .?'

'And what?'

'You named the three of us. Do it again.'

'Let me have one of your hands,' he said.

'I beg your pardon!'

'Let me have one of your hands.'

She looked into his liquid brown eyes and saw amusement there, that and something else, something she couldn't define. Tentatively she extended her right hand which he took in his. Using the forefinger of his free hand he rapped out in Morse on the back of the hand he was holding. Hello Norma.

She recognised 'the fist' instantly. 'You?' she whispered.

'I see there's a table going free over there. Shall we use it?' he smiled in reply. He lifted both drinks, and led the way. She followed him, dumbstruck by this revelation. Douglas Ross of all people!

He put their drinks down, pulled out a chair for her, and pushed it in again as she sat. He sat facing her. 'I never knew you were Norma till I saw that photograph. I didn't recognise Marie Thérèse at first – well, the only time I saw her she was kitted out for a jump which can make quite a difference to the appearance. And then the penny dropped. Miss Rolfe told me that you'd been her WT operator, and that your Christian name was Norma, which of course made you my Norma also,' he explained.

'How...' she cleared her throat. Her mind was still whizzing round and round. 'How did you signal me this afternoon?'

'That wasn't difficult. I borrowed a field set from stores and, having already found out what frequency you were transmitting on, the rest was easy. I contacted you from my villa.'

'Excuse me,' she said, taking a deep breath, 'You must appreciate how big a shock this is for me. I was expecting, well I don't know what I was expecting, but certainly not you. You're a doctor.'

'I was also a "joe".'

'Gabriel,' she said amazed.

He swallowed some beer, and she took a sip of her gin sling. 'You asked about the Gestapo,' he said.

She nodded. The mystery was about to be explained.

'When I went in on that last mission I very nearly got caught at Nantes railway station. I came off the train with my wireless in its suitcase to find two Gestapo men, an older and a younger, at the barrier checking everyone and every piece of luggage. I couldn't turn back, or run, so I bluffed it out. I told them I had a captured British wireless set and important information – information that had to be acted upon right away, and that they were to take me to their headquarters immediately. They bought my story, and the younger Gestapo man said he'd drive me there. I managed to kill him *en route* and made my escape.'

Ross paused to light a cigarette, then went on, 'When I was finally picked up by the Gestapo all those months later it wasn't because they were onto me or the Oberon Circuit, but a piece of damned bad luck. The older of the two Gestapo men from Nantes was driving past, saw and remembered me, and that was that. In the bag.

'They drove me straight to their local headquarters and threw me in a cell. That night Bonzo, as I nicknamed the older man, came to my cell with a couple of his chums. They told me it was going to be a long process, that they intended enjoying themselves, and that this session would only be the start.'

Ross swallowed more beer. His stomach heaved at the memory, and he'd gone chill all over. He could see the look in Bonzo's eyes the first time Bonzo hit him, a combination of sadistic pleasure and malicious glee.

'So they tortured you,' Norma said in a quiet voice.

'Only the once. Before they could indulge themselves any further a message arrived from the big cheese himself, Heinrich Himmler, head of the SS and Gestapo, saying that he personally wanted to "interview" me. I have no idea what about.

'I was bundled into a car with Bonzo, another charmer and a driver, with me in between Bonzo and his pal, and off we set. I don't know what our destination was – I did ask and got a clout round the mouth for my trouble, but it was a helluva long drive.

'Hours passed, and night came. We stopped off for food and our third refill of petrol, then set off again. A little past midnight the one on my right dozed off, and about half an hour later Bonzo, on my left, did the same.

'To be truthful I never dreamt I'd get away with it. What I did intend was being shot in the process of trying, killed, so that it would be over and done with, and there would be no more torture. I threw my full weight against Bonzo, at the same time grabbing the door handle. Bonzo gave a yell of surprise, the door flew open, and we both went tumbling out.'

Ross shook his head in disbelief. 'It's the sort of thing you see in the pictures and which wouldn't work in real life. Except on that occasion it did. Bonzo and I bounced on the road while the driver jammed on his brakes and slewed to a stop. Completely unhurt, I jumped to my feet and sprinted for the trees – we were passing through a forest at the time. A number of shots rang out, but none hit me and I was away.'

'That's incredible,' Norma breathed. 'What happened then?'

'I ran and ran till I was nearly sick. There was a full moon that night. Having shaken off pursuit I continued on walking as fast as I could, wanting to put as much distance between me and my captors as possible. I knew that come the dawn the whole area would be crawling with Germans, and that Bonzo and the other two would do everything they could to recapture me to avoid having to go to Himmler and report my escape.'

He drew on his cigarette, and blew out smoke. 'I walked till the first light, then hid out along a riverbank until the next night when I started walking again.

'I had no idea where I was, except that I must be halfway across France, in some direction, from where I'd been picked up; had to be from the number of hours we'd driven. I wasn't worried about the other members of Oberon. Their identities were safe as I hadn't talked, and once they realised I'd disappeared they'd be onto DF like a shot to be taken out of France.

'That second night, starving hungry, I decided to reconnoitre a farm to see if I could find anything to eat. Well I found more than that, I found the Maquis.'

He paused. 'Do you know about the Maquis?'

'A little, not much.'

'They're young men avoiding the STO, which is the compulsory labour service in Germany. They form into bands, often taking to the extreme high ground where they camp out. The group I had fallen in with belonged to a band seven hundred strong that had an encampment on the Glières plateau near Annecy. That particular group had come down off the plateau to collect some arms and ammunition, which they were desperately short of. When I explained to the group who and what I was, and that the Gestapo had taken my papers and money, they said it was best, for the time being, that I went with them. And so, thinking that it was for the best, I did.'

'Why didn't SOE hear you were still alive?' asked Norma.

Ross pulled a face. 'When the Maquis discovered I was a doctor, they were overjoyed, it solved a great many of their medical problems. Again and again they assured me they were trying to get in touch with DF so that I could be taken out of

France but in reality they were doing no such thing. It suited their purpose to have me stay with them, so I was trapped.

'When I finally twigged that they weren't making any effort to contact DF I argued the toss with them hoping they'd change their mind, but they didn't.

'Did you escape from them in the end?' Norma queried.

'There wasn't a hope of that, I was too closely watched. And so the months passed with me thinking I was going to be there, on that damned plateau, for the duration of the war. Then one day one of their leaders, a man called Henri Delmas, caught a bullet that lodged close to the heart. Only a skilled surgeon could remove that bullet, and if it wasn't taken out soon Delmas would die. I realised that was my opportunity and told them, even if it meant my own life, that I wouldn't operate unless they promised me they would do as they'd said originally and contact DF.

'The leaders gave me that promise, and just to make sure they kept it, for they were all devout Catholics, I made each and every one of them swear it on a statue of the Virgin Mary and Infant Jesus.

'I operated - damned tricky it was too given the conditions - and Delmas survived. This time they did keep their word. A fortnight later I had a rendezvous with a DF agent.'

'When was this?' asked Norma.

'Early on this month, five days before the invasion came ashore here.'

'So DF brought you here then?'

'I thought they'd take me out into Switzerland, the Glières plateau being close to the Swiss border, but no, they took me south to the coast close to St Tropez where I was put aboard a felucca and taken to Algiers. I arrived in Algiers two days after the invasion.'

'Why weren't you taken back to England?'

'Various reasons. Now I'm known to the Gestapo I won't be asked to return to France, so my time in the field is over. M knew that I'd be very useful here as a doctor, particularly while the fighting is going on, which it will do until we recapture all of North Africa. It is also better for the SOE to have their own doctor here, a doctor who's SOE himself. The other part of my brief is that when the fighting in North Africa is over I'm to take up duties as an instructor. I'll be teaching parachuting and unarmed combat.'

'To whom?'

'Not regular SOE agents as that's all done for them at Arisaig, so it can only be irregulars of some sort. But that's just a guess on my part, the hierarchy haven't confided in me yet. Only to say that I will be taking up such duties in the course of time.'

'It was a shock to see the grey in your hair,' she said suddenly, then blushed. It was a rather personal comment to make.

He stroked his beard. 'Life in the field does that to you. At least it did to me,' he replied quietly.

An uneasy silence fell between them. 'Would you like another gin sling?' he asked eventually. 'I'd like another beer myself.'

'Please.'

He left her to go to the bar, while she finished her drink. When he returned there were more silences between them, and what conversation there was had become stilted. She felt he'd put up a mental barrier against her.

After a while he offered to drive her home, and she accepted. She'd cadged a lift to the hotel from someone else at Massingham, there was always to-ing and fro-ing between there and Algiers.

'Goodnight then,' he said rather formally at the door of Casa Bon-Bon.

She wondered if she should ask him in, and decided against it. 'Goodnight,' she answered, and shook the hand he extended to her.

She thought he was going to say something further, but he didn't. Leaving her he returned to his car and drove off.

'Damn!' she swore. She'd been so looking forward to meeting Gabriel, and the whole thing had fallen flat. She shouldn't have made that remark about his greyness, everything had been all right up until then.

Violette, waiting up for her, shrieked when she told her who Gabriel had turned out to be.

Norma was sitting on the beach, staring out to sea, thinking about Jeremy Dereham. She hadn't heard from him since he'd visited Grendon Underwood fourteen months previously. But then she hadn't written to him either. War was strange; it brought some people together, made others drift apart. There had been nothing serious between them anyway. It had been fun to go out with him, that had been all.

'Hello.'

She glanced up to find Ross smiling down at her. 'Hello.'

'I saw you were on your own and thought I'd come and join you. Is that all right?'

'It's a free beach.'

His smile vanished. 'Well, if you'd rather I didn't.'

There she was saying the wrong thing again. She seemed to make a habit of it where he was concerned. 'I'd like it if you would,' she stated firmly, and patted the sand beside her.

He sat, pulled his knees up to his chest, and put his arms round them. The years seemed to drop away to make him look young again, boyish almost. He also looked extremely vulnerable. Norma's instinct was to take him to her breast, cuddle him close, and tell him not to worry about the Bogey Man. He was safe from the Bogey Man while she was there.

'Fancy a jeep?' he asked.

'I beg your pardon?'

'You haven't got your own transport yet, so you're having to rely on lifts when you want to go anywhere. I can get a Yankee jeep for you if you want.'

Doctor Ross was just full of surprises. First he reveals himself as Gabriel, now he was offering her a jeep. 'Where's the catch?'

He gave her one of his sideways looks. 'No catch Norma. I'm only trying to be helpful to a . . . friend.' He paused. 'We are still friends aren't we? Like when I was Gabriel?'

She'd been wondering about that in bed the previous night, and her conclusion had been that they weren't. 'Yes,' she said, and meant it.

'I'll have it round at the Casa Bon-Bon tomorrow sometime.'

'As easy as that?'

'As easy as that,' he confirmed.

'How can you . . .' She broke off when he held a finger to his lips. 'It's not stolen is it?'

'Would I give you a stolen jeep?' he replied, in mock outrage.

'You might. How do I know what you'd do?'

He laughed. 'It isn't stolen, I promise you.' He paused, then added as a throwaway. 'At least not around here it isn't.'

'Doctor Ross!'

He laughed again. 'Nor anywhere else. And please, the name is Douglas.'

'All right, Douglas,' she said, almost shyly.

'Do you swim?'

Now what was this about? 'I can do, though I haven't swum in years. I was born by the sea, and learned to swim in it.'

'Where was that?'

'A little place called Kirn on the Firth of Clyde.'

He looked away. 'How about us getting together for a swim tomorrow? I know it's winter here but the sea is warm. Of course I'll understand if you're busy and it's not on.'

Defensive, she thought. But then the last thing he was was a ladies' man, she remembered the Staff in the Royal Free telling her that. 'That would be nice.'

He looked back at her. 'What time?' he asked slowly.

Norma thought of her schedule, and wished those other two FANY WT operators would hurry up and get there. Life was so difficult with only herself and Violette to man their set.

'3 pm?'

He screwed up his face in thought. He had a ward round then but could rejiggle that. 'Yes, that's fine with me. Will this spot do?'

'It's as good as any other.'

'Then three o'clock here.' He ran a hand through bone-white sand. 'Tell me about Kirn, and yourself. I know nothing about you after all. Or very little anyway. Certainly nothing about your background.'

She amazed herself by telling him everything. About her parents, sisters, Bridgeton, Midge, her dancing, and Midge running off with Zelda Caprice. The only thing she didn't spell out was that she and Midge had been lovers, but then that must have been obvious from the way she spoke about him.

Douglas listened intently.

She glanced at her wristwatch. Ten past three, he was late. She was already wearing the costume she'd borrowed underneath her uniform. All she had to do was take her uniform off and she'd be ready for their dip. She had a huge towel with her, one of Violette's scroungings, and could change underneath that when it was time to get dressed again.

Three fifteen now, and still no sign of him. She ran her hands through her hair. She was really looking forward to this, and had been since he'd proposed it. She kicked off her shoes and scrunched sand up between her stockinged feet. It was a good feeling and reminded her of Kirn and those far off, happy, childhood days.

When it reached the half hour her spirits started to sink. Where was he? Then she had a terrible thought, had he changed his mind? Surely not?

Could it be that he'd gone off her when she'd told him her family lived in the Glasgow slums? After all he was what in Bridgeton they'd always called a 'toff'; well-educated, well-spoken, undoubtedly monied to some degree.

She knew her background was totally different to all the other FANYs – theirs were more or less similar to what Douglas's must be. When he realised she was a slummie had that been it? Anger flared in her, if that was the case he might have broken their arrangement or made some excuse – not just left her standing there.

At quarter to, feeling angry, let down, and a little sick, she began walking back to Casa Bon-Bon.

She opened her eyes, what was that? There it was again, a knocking. Someone was knocking on the outside door. She fumbled for the matches she kept by her bedside and lit one. She saw it was gone midnight. The knocking started again.

She lit the storm lantern by her bed, then slipped into her dressing gown. Violette put her head round the bedroom door.

'Who do you think it is?' Violette asked, wiping the sleep from her eyes.

'Search me. But we'd better answer it. It could be something to do with work.'

'At this hour?'

'Since when did the army consider the time?'

Violette nodded, Norma had a point. 'Wait a mo' though,' she said, and returned to her own bedroom. When she met up with Norma in the sitting room she was carrying a .38 Webley revolver.

'Where did you get that from?' Norma whispered. She hadn't known Violette had a gun.

'It was issued to me when I was a "joe". I just never handed it back again,' Violette explained.

The storm lantern Norma was holding cast weird and grotesque shadows on the ceiling and walls as they walked to the outside door. Just before they reached it the person knocked again.

'Who's there?' Violette demanded.

'Field Marshall Rommel,' a male voice replied.

Violette glanced at Norma. Somebody was playing funny buggers. 'I've got a gun here; if Field Marshall Rommel tries anything he shouldn't the krauts will be looking for a new Field Marshall to replace a very dead one,' Violette said, and gestured to Norma to open the door.

The door swung open to reveal a walking stick with a piece of white material tied to its tip. The person holding the stick was hiding round the side of the door.

'Peace. I come in peace and bearing gifts,' Douglas said, having disguised his voice before. He stepped out and smiled at them. Besides the walking stick he was carrying two bottles of wine.

Violette dropped the gun. 'I think it's for you,' she said to Norma.

'My fullest apologies for standing you up, but there was a very good reason which I've now come to tell you. I thought we might have a drink together,' he said, and brandished the wine bottles.

'I'll leave the pair of you to it. I'm going back to bed,' Violette said diplomatically.

'Not until you've seen Norma's jeep,' Douglas told her.

Norma looked at the street beyond, and sure enough there was an American jeep parked in front of the house. 'I thought that . . .' She stopped herself, deciding she didn't want him to know what she had thought.

'It really is for me?' she said.

'Hold this please,' he replied, and gave her the walking stick. He put a hand in a trousers' pocket and pulled out an ignition key. 'As from this moment it's all yours,' he smiled, and exchanged the key for the walking stick.

'Shall we inspect it?' he proposed.

The three of them went to the jeep which was an almost new one with only five thousand miles on the clock. It was left hand drive of course, something Norma was going to have to get used to. 'I don't know what to say,' Norma told him.

'How about "come on in and let's open that wine you've got there"?'

Norma gave a low laugh. 'All right, come on in and we'll open that wine you've got there.'

He smiled broadly. 'Why Miss McKenzie, I thought you'd never ask.'

They returned to the villa and went inside. Violette left Norma and Douglas, saying she needed her beauty sleep.

Douglas sat on a wooden box while Norma lit a second lantern, then opened the wine. 'We've no glasses I'm afraid, we'll have to make do with mugs.'

'That's fine by me.'

The wine was a local red, the labels on the outside of the bottles written in Arabic and English. As Norma was pouring Douglas said, 'I really am terribly sorry about this afternoon, but it was unavoidable.'

'Oh yes?' She let a hint of coolness creep into her voice.

'I was just about to leave the hospital when suddenly we had a flap on. A Stuka dive bombed a fuel dump and the whole shebang went up. We had umpteen survivors brought in, many with the most frightful burns.'

She handed him his mug of wine. She could see now how tired he was, he reminded her of the first time she'd ever seen him at the Royal Free; he'd looked desperately tired then too.

He went on, 'I only left the hospital half an hour ago and went straight to pick up your jeep which I'd intended bringing along this afternoon.'

She felt terrible, she should have realised it was something to do with the hospital that had kept him away from the beach. She'd been stupid to think what she had.

He drank some wine, and a strange, haunted, expression came onto his face, and into his eyes. 'I had three men die on me, one after the other, in the operating theatre. It's horrible when that sort of thing happens. You feel so ineffectual.' He swallowed what was left in his mug. Without his asking she took the mug from him and refilled it.

When he lit a cigarette she noticed his hands were trembling. It was a complete transformation from the chap who'd knocked the door only a couple of minutes previously.

She sipped her own wine. 'Yesterday I told you all about me. What about telling me something about you now?'

He gave her a sideways look, the haunted expression still on his face and in his eyes. 'What sort of thing would you like to know?'

'Whereabouts you come from in Scotland for a start?'

'Glasgow.'

She blinked in surprise. She wasn't sure where she'd expected him to name, but not there. There was absolutely nothing 'Glasgow' about him. 'Do you really?'

'A place called Burnside. It's out on the road to Rutherglen and Cambuslang.'

'I'm afraid those are only names to me, I don't know the south side very well at all. I don't think I've ever been beyond the Plaza Ballroom in Victoria Road.'

'You danced there when you were a professional?'

'And as an amateur. We danced all the ballrooms in Glasgow as both.'

He puffed on his cigarette. 'My father's an eye specialist in the Victoria Infirmary, not far from your Plaza. He's the leading eye specialist in Scotland.'

'And what about your mother?'

'She's French, from Paris.'

'And you speak the language perfectly which was why M asked you to be a "joe".'

'I'm completely bi-lingual. Because of my mother I grew up speaking French as naturally as I did English. I can even vary my accent if I want to, which was handy at times when I was in the field.'

Similar in a way to Lynsey's background she thought. But then it was bound to have been. 'What's your mother called?'

'Solange.'

That was a lovely name, Norma thought. It had a romantic aura about it, but then so many French names did. 'And your father?'

'Forsyth.'

Forsyth Ross, there was nothing romantic about that. It sounded to her like a brand of whisky, or a district in the Western Highlands. 'Is your mother terribly attractive?' she asked, thinking to herself, like you are.

'She certainly was when younger, in fact she was something of a beauty. She and my father are still as in love as when they first met when he was in Paris studying for a short while after the Great War. He worships the ground she walks on.'

'And you take after your mother in looks?'

He stared at her. 'How did you know that?'

'It wasn't too difficult to work out. Your mother's French, and you don't look at all Scots, which I suppose is why – taking into consideration that you're so well spoken with only a hint of accent – that I always have trouble remembering that you actually are.'

He rubbed a hand across his face. 'It's my sallow complexion that's so un-Scottish. At school they used to call me fish-face.'

Norma laughed. 'And what school was that, Kelvinside Academy?'

'Glasgow Academy actually. There's nothing really to choose between the two. I went where I did because my father had gone there before me. They're both frightfully elitist of course.'

'Frightfully,' she agreed in a mocking tone. She was enjoying this, it was somehow terribly intimate, drawing them closer together. 'I went to a local school myself. It wasn't strange to see a bare bum hanging out of a threadbare pair of breeks there, or for children to have no shoes at all, even in deep mid winter.'

'*Not* elitist,' he smiled.

'Most definitely not.'

'But you were happy? That's the most important thing.'

'Oh yes! I had a wonderful family around me and we never went without proper food, clothes or shoes. Da was always in employment.'

'And now you've got money of your own.'

'Thanks to dear old Mr Gallagher and his daughter Morna.'

Douglas drank more wine. It was cheap, far too sweet, and not at all to his taste, but all he'd been able to lay his hands on at such short notice and so late at night. He wished he'd been able to buy something really nice for Norma, a Pauillac perhaps. Yes, a Pauillac would have been the very dab.

'Will you live with your parents after the war, or buy a place of your own?' he asked.

'I don't know. I could buy a wee place, I might enjoy that. What about you?'

'That all depends on where I get a job. I'd like to return to Glasgow, and if I did it would be silly to buy my own place when the house we've got already is so huge we rattle around in it like a handful of peas in a drum.'

'It's that large is it?'

'Absolutely enormous. We have nine bedrooms, which doesn't include those belonging to the servants.'

Norma was intrigued. 'You have servants?'

'Oh indeed, you need them to run a place that size. We have a butler, cook, three maids and a gardener.'

'Your father must be extremely rich?'

'Stinking. He did inherit a great deal mind, but he's added to that considerably. It's very lucrative being the leading eye specialist in Scotland. Anybody who's anybody comes to him, and pays top whack for the privilege.'

'How about brothers and sisters?'

Douglas shook his head. 'There's just me. I did have an elder brother but he died when he was only eight days old. Although they wanted more of a family mother never got pregnant again after she'd had me. It just wasn't to be.'

'It must have been lonely being an only child,' Norma said, thinking how she'd always had Lyn, and later Eileen, to play and fight with.

'I suppose it's a case of never missing what you've never had. I can't say I remember being particularly lonely, though presumably I must have been at times.'

It struck her then that his having been an only child had a lot to do with how he was as an adult. There was a sense about him of being apart from everyone else, it was even noticeable in company. That would also account for his shyness and general reserve. He hadn't had the physical and mental rough and tumble of brothers and sisters to knock that out of him.

He talked about himself some more, and she learned about Burnside and the house in Blairbeth Road which his grandfather, another eye specialist, had had built when the old Queen was on the throne.

Douglas drained his mug, the last of the wine he'd brought. 'I've really enjoyed our chat, it's quite unwound me. And I apologise again about this afternoon.'

'As you said, it was unavoidable.'

He placed his mug on the floor, and stood up. 'You really have done wonders with this place in such a short while. I've been meaning to mention that ever since I came in.'

Norma laughed. 'Not me, Violette. She's a terrific scrounger – as you can see.'

There were all sorts of items in the sitting room that Violette had come up with, though as yet no proper chairs. She'd promised that those, and a settee, would be forthcoming in the near future, but refused to say from where.

Douglas turned to Norma. 'There's a NAAFI dance on Friday night and I was wondering if you'd care to go with me. Hardly the Plaza mind you, and I'm more of a shuffler than anything else, but it might be fun.'

'I'm working till eight, though the two new girls will be here by then so I could rearrange my duty period if it was necessary.'

'No need. I'll pick you up here around nine which should give you time to get yourself ready, and get us there just as things are beginning to hot up.'

'Right then, it's a date as our American friends say.'

'It's a date.'

'And can we go in my jeep? I'd like that.'

'The jeep it is, with you driving.'

It had turned out to be a smashing day after all, she thought when he'd gone. She sang quietly to herself as she washed and dried their mugs, an old favourite of hers that she'd often danced to in Barrowland.

It was the third time they'd taken the floor together, and he was as stiff and unyielding as on the first. Stiffie the goalkeeper he'd have been cried in Glasgow. She suspected he was a better dancer than he appeared, if only he'd relax and let himself go.

'Can I tell you a secret?' she smiled.

'What?'

'I won't bite.'

He smiled painfully back. 'Sorry.'
'Relax.'
'I thought I was.'
'Nonsense, you know full well you're not.'
He unloosened a bit, but only a bit. 'It's funny you know,' he said.
'What is?'
'I'm all right when I "talk" to you on the WT. But like this I sort of clam up.'
'You don't have to be embarrassed because you're the bashful type where women are concerned. Lots of men are. And I'll tell you something else: I'd much rather go out with a man like that, who shows some respect, than with many of the Lotharios around.'
'You would?'
'Without a shadow of a doubt.'
He perked up visibly to hear that, and even unloosened a little bit more.
The band were chronic, Norma thought. Even the worst Glasgow dancehalls would soon have given them the order of the boot. As for the standard of dancing, it was on about a par with the band's playing. Which wasn't saying very much at all.
Despite everything, Douglas never did relax properly, but Norma had a good time and was sad when the last Waltz was played. As they climbed into the jeep she contemplated asking Douglas if he'd like to go for a drive along the seafront, but decided not to. She'd have jumped at the chance if he'd suggested it though.
'You're an excellent driver,' Douglas said as they headed for Massingham.
'I like driving, and I suppose if you like doing something you tend to be good at it. Generally speaking anyway.'
He leant back in his seat and closed his eyes.
'Penny for them?'
'I was just thinking how different all this is to . . .' He trailed off.
'France?'
'Yes,' he said softly.
'At least that's all behind you now. You'll never be asked to go back.

Thank God, he said inwardly. 'If I told you what a relief it was to know that, you'd think me quite a coward.'

Norma looked at him, what a bundle of contrasts he was. And so sensitive – a huge streak of sensitivity ran right through him. 'How could Gabriel be a coward after what he did? DR told me after we learned you'd been picked up by the Gestapo that you were the best agent we had.'

'DR said that?'

'And meant it, I can assure you. He also said he kept you in far longer than he should have done because you were doing such a first-class job. He greatly admired you – as I did.'

'Cowardice and bravery, there's a very thin dividing line between the two. Very thin,' Douglas said, so softly Norma had to strain to hear.

'Then how much more of an achievement for the coward to be brave than for the naturally brave person who fears nothing.'

'The ones who fear nothing soon end up dead, heroes or otherwise.'

Silence fell between them till, coming into Club des Pins, Norma cracked a joke which made them both laugh. Immediately the atmosphere lightened.

She parked in front of Casa Bon-Bon behind Douglas's Standard. He was about to get out when she placed a restraining hand on his arm. 'Thank you very much for tonight.'

'Sorry I'm not much of a dancer.'

'Stop apologising, you do so too often. It was a lovely evening.'

He stared at her in the darkness. 'Would you like to go out again?'

'When?'

He hesitated. 'Is tomorrow night too soon? Or inconvenient?'

'Where to?'

'The bar in the canteen?'

'What time?'

'Nine.'

'Do you want to meet me here or there?'

'Here.'

'Right then, I'll be waiting.'

'If I don't turn up, or am late, it'll be because of the hospital,' he said quickly.

'I understand.'

'If you had a phone I could ring, but you haven't.'

'If you don't turn up or are late I'll know that it's the hospital that's to blame,' she repeated. Perhaps it was because of the darkness, there was only a sliver of moon showing in the sky, but it was almost as though they were 'talking' to each other on WT. The old easiness was suddenly back between them.

'Norma?'

'Yes?'

'I know this probably sounds juvenile and trite, but I like you, I like you very much.'

'I'm glad about that. I like you very much too.'

Come on! she thought. Don't just sit there, take me in your arms and kiss me. Can't you see I'm dying for you to do that!

'Goodnight,' he said huskily.

'Goodnight.'

He reached for the doorhandle. 'Is that all?' she asked quietly. He stopped reaching, and turned to her again.

He placed a hand on her cheek, and slowly drew it down her cheek and the length of her neck. She shivered and her insides flared with a sudden excitement. The same hand went to the nape of her neck, and drew her to him. She went willingly.

He kissed her deeply, for a long time. When it was finally over she found herself limp, drained almost. It had been that kind of kiss.

'Tomorrow night,' he breathed.

'Tomorrow night,' she confirmed, in a high-pitched squeak, and wondered at her voice having come out like that. She certainly hadn't intended it to.

She cleared her throat. 'Tomorrow night,' she repeated in what was more like her normal voice.

She continued sitting in the jeep while he went to his Standard, got in and drove away.

She took a deep breath, then another. She stared up at a sky mainly obscured by low scudding clouds. The sliver of moon was still visible, while over to the northeast a small scattering of stars had appeared.

Closing her eyes, she smiled. She hadn't felt this way in a long time. A long long time. Not since ... Breaking off that line of thought she got out the jeep and went inside.

Norma and Douglas were in Algiers doing some Christmas shopping, when, on coming out of a souk, Norma spotted a man on the opposite side of the street, the sight of whose face brought her up short. The man was the double, an absolute *doppelgänger* of ... 'Da!' she screamed, and dropped the parcels she was carrying.

Arms thrown wide she flew across the road. That was no *doppelgänger*, that was the real thing, her father.

Brian was staring at her in a combination of astonishment and joy. As she crashed into him he picked her up and birled her round again and again.

'It really is you, it really is,' she said through the tears of delight and happiness that were streaming down her face.

Brian put her back on the ground. 'Oh lassie!' he whispered, a glint of wet in his eyes. By now Douglas had joined them.

'Da, I'd like you to meet Douglas Ross. He's a friend of mine. Douglas this is my father.'

'Pleased to meet you sir,' Brian said, having taken note of Douglas's rank.

Douglas would have shaken hands but couldn't because of the parcels he was loaded down with. 'And I'm pleased to meet you Mr McKenzie.'

'But what on earth are you doing in Algiers?' Norma asked Brian.

Brian released her. I'm *en route* to Tunisia with the Pioneers. We're to link up with the Royal Engineers there and build various roads and bridges.'

'So when did you arrive?'

'Three days ago. We've another two days in Algiers I'm told, then it's on to Tunisia. If only I'd known you were here! Your letters home are all censored so we didn't have a clue where you were, only that it was someplace hot. And us just bumping into each other, what a coincidence, eh!'

Norma couldn't believe it. Her da, here in Algiers, standing in front of her beaming at her out of that weather-beaten face of his. It was incredible.

'Wait till your ma hears about this,' Brian said.

Norma glanced at her wristwatch, she was due on duty in forty minutes, and it was too late now to rearrange the duty.

Douglas saw her look at her watch and guessed correctly what was going through her mind. 'May I make a suggestion?'

'What?' she replied.

'As you're due back on duty why don't you make an arrangement to meet up with your father this evening. Are you free then Mr McKenzie?'

'I am indeed.'

'How about if I organise a private room for the pair of you in the St George Hotel. You can eat there together, and can be assured the food won't poison you as it would in many Algerian restaurants.'

'That's a terrific idea!' Norma enthused.

'Leave everything to me then.'

Norma gave him a grateful look. She knew there was more to his suggestion than the fact that Algerian restaurants tended to have a very bad reputation – it was because her da was a private and she an officer. It wouldn't be at all correct for her to socialise in public with someone from Other Ranks, even if it was her father. The British Armed Forces could be very sticky indeed about that sort of thing. (Not that it would have done her any damage, the SOE didn't care a fig about such matters, but if they were seen together and it was reported it could rebound on her da.)

'You'll join us of course,' Norma said to him.

'I wouldn't want to intrude,' Douglas replied.

'You wouldn't be.'

There was something in his daughter's voice that made Brian glance from her to Douglas. So that was how the land lay he thought to himself.

Douglas could see this wasn't merely a gesture on Norma's part, that she really did want him to join them. 'All right then, I'd be delighted to.' To Brian he said, 'Do you know where the St George is?'

'Aye, I've walked past it several times.'

'Let's say nine o'clock then. I'll be waiting in reception.'

Brian, his eyes shining, turned again to Norma. 'Who'd have credited it eh lass?'

'Who'd have credited it,' she echoed.

Brian appeared first in reception to find Douglas waiting for him. Douglas took him to the reserved room where he left him with a bottle of malt whisky while he returned to reception. Norma showed up, breathless with excitement, five minutes later.

'Is he here?' demanded Norma.

Douglas nodded. 'Yes.'

'All through my duty period I kept thinking I'd been day-dreaming and that it was all a figment of my imagination. I'm afraid I made a right hash of several signals. A sender in Gib got quite cross with me at one point.'

Douglas had taken her by the crook of the arm and was leading her to where their room was located. It was a smallish, wood-panelled room and was ideal for their purpose.

On entering the room Norma came up short, a smile blossoming on her face to see her da standing there with a glass of whisky in his hand and that same old battered pipe that she could remember from time out of mind stuck in his mouth.

'First decent dram I've had in months,' he smiled back, waving his glass at her.

'You can thank Douglas for that.'

'And I do,' Brian replied, giving Douglas a nod. He held out his drink in front of him. 'To you Norma, God bless and keep you safe during the rest of this terrible war.' He drained his glass.

Besides the whisky Douglas had laid on brandy and wine. He opted for the wine while Norma joined her father with 'the cratur'. 'Slainthe!' Douglas toasted.

Brian rounded on him in surprise, for the Gaelic pronunciation had been perfect. 'You're Scots? I mean, you're Scots sir? I'd never have guessed.'

'While we're alone like this it's Douglas, and yes I am Scots, from Glasgow.'

'You certainly don't sound it.'

Douglas laughed. 'That's what Norma always says.'

Brian's eyes flickered between the two. 'Is she your driver then?'

With a start Norma remembered her father knew nothing about her being in the SOE – as far as he and the rest of the family knew she was still a FANY driver. It was the same with Douglas's parents, they knew nothing about his involvement with SOE either.

'No, I'm hardly important enough for that. I'm just a doctor,' Douglas replied, appreciating the situation.

'I should think doctors are as important as anyone out here, and more important than many,' said Brian.

'True, but you know what I mean. FANYs drive for VIPs, and doctor or not, I'm certainly not that.'

A waiter appeared with some bits and bobs to munch on, a prelude to their meal which would be appearing shortly. When the waiter had gone Brian asked, 'So how did you two meet then?'

It was Norma who answered. 'Remember when I got blown up in London? Well it was Douglas who attended me at the Royal Free Hospital.'

'And a rotten patient she was too,' Douglas joked.

'Nonsense, I was ideal!' Norma retorted.

The undertones of this little exchange weren't lost on Brian; they told him a lot. Hadn't he and Effie had exactly the same sort of exchanges way back.

'Anyway, the ship Norma came in on was torpedoed and her friend had been hurt. I turned up to help and that's how we met a second time,' Douglas explained.

Brian's eyebrows shot up his forehead. 'Torpedoed? This is the first I've heard of that.'

'Well I did mention it, but my letters home are all censored. However, I came to no harm – as you can see.'

'But your pal did?'

'Helen Rolfe, she's making marvellous progress though. Isn't she Douglas?'

'I hope to discharge her for Christmas. She's come on by leaps and bounds.'

'She lost a kidney,' Norma said to Brian.

'Let's just be thankful it wasn't you,' Brian muttered, taking another swallow of his malt.

'How's Eileen? Ma rarely mentions her in her letters.' Turning to Douglas she explained, 'That's my wee sister who lost her hubby in the train crash.'

Brian shook his head. 'I was home just before I left for here, and to be frank Norma that lassie worries the pants off me. She's lost weight, completely let herself go, and most of the time just sort of wanders around looking lost. It fair broke my heart to see her.'

'She was very much in love with Charlie. It's going to take her a long time to get over him.'

'Let's just hope she does. She's still a young woman with her whole life ahead of her. I'm bitter sorry about Charlie, but she mustn't let it sour her for ayeways.'

'Do you think it might Da?'

He shrugged. 'It could well, and that's a fact. As you say, Charlie Marshall was sun and moon to that girl.'

'And what about Lyn?'

'She's hunky dory. Looking lovelier than ever.'

'What a transformation that was eh?'

Brian nodded. 'Talk about the ugly duckling.'

Norma said to Douglas, 'Lyn's the middle sister. She was a right fatso when young, podge I used to call her when I was being nasty. Then suddenly she went on a diet – while I was in London with the FANY – and wham bam! I hardly recognised her. She'd turned into a real glamour puss with the sort of figure that makes other women turn green with envy. Including yours truly.'

'Maybe I'll get to meet them all one day,' Douglas smiled.

'Maybe,' she smiled back.

They chatted on about Glasgow for a while longer, and then the same waiter returned with a trolley and their food. A circular table with three chairs round it had already been set for them.

There was a seafood dish to start with, followed by fillet steak and a choice of vegetables. The hotel did very well out of the Americans who stayed there, the Americans making sure they and their chums didn't go without.

There were some bottles of Pabst and Blatz American beer to go with the steaks, as the hotel was out of British beer for the time being. Brian tasted a Blatz, screwed up his face in disgust and said thank you very much, but he'd stick with the malt whisky.

Halfway through the main course Douglas excused himself to go to the toilet. When he was gone Brian looked levelly at Norma. 'It seems serious between you two.'

She pushed a piece of sautéd potato round her plate. 'It could be Da. I don't know for certain yet,' she replied evasively.

'Well that's what comes across.'

She pushed the potato some more. 'Do you like him?'

'Oh aye, he's a nice enough chap. But he's a different kind to us Norma.'

'You mean that - despite me being in the FANY and an officer - I'm still working-class and he isn't?'

'It's not just between you and him, there are also his parents and friends to take into account. Can you go up to his and their level? For that's what you'd have to do.'

She laid down her fork and took a swallow of whisky. What her father was saying wasn't new to her; she'd already thought along those lines herself. 'I know this Da, that he's the only man I've felt anything for since Midge.'

Brian lowered his eyes, unable to gaze into the old pain that had suddenly appeared in hers.

After a few seconds silence he changed the subject.

It was Christmas Eve 1942 and Norma and Violette were eagerly awaiting the arrival of Helen from the hospital. Douglas was arranging the details of her discharge and would then bring her on to Casa Bon-Bon, where her room was all ready waiting for her. Violette had even managed to scrounge some proper beds - three of them, so they had one each. A vast improvement on the iron framed canvas jobs which had been sheer torture to sleep on.

Norma and Violette had made multi-coloured paper chains which they had strung across the sitting room. A Christmas bell hung suspended from the ceiling.

The tree was a five foot fir provided by Douglas. They hadn't been able to get hold of fairy lights so the tree was decorated with puff balls of cotton wool and various sparkly bits and pieces that Violette had come up with.

Pride of place in the sitting-room, next to the tree, was a three-piece suite that had made its appearance several days previously. It was an old suite, junkable by any standards, but an awful lot better than the wooden boxes they'd been making do with up until then. Violette had refused to say where it, and the beds, had come from. That was her closely-guarded secret.

Underneath the tree were the presents, while on the decorator's pasting-up table, covered with a local fancy-worked tablecloth bought in Algiers, were a host of festive goodies, including a number of bottles of wine and spirits that Douglas had laid on.

Norma glanced at her watch. 'Shouldn't be long now,' she said.

'Fancy a sherry?'

'Why not!'

Violette did the honours, using two of their 'new' glasses, something else she'd recently scrounged.

'Deck the halls with boughs of holly ...' Norma sang to herself as Violette poured. She was really looking forward to Christmas, mainly because she'd be spending a lot of it with Douglas. The following morning, after breakfast, she, Violette and other FANYs (there were now over fifty at Massingham), were going carol singing at the hospital. She'd enjoy that, even if she didn't have a particularly marvellous singing voice.

Violette handed Norma her drink. 'Absent friends,' Norma toasted. Violette knew that Norma was referring to Lynsey and Pam Parkinson, the latter still in F section.

'Absent friends,' Violette agreed, and they both sipped their sherry.

'They're here!' Norma exclaimed on hearing a car drawing up outside the villa. They both laid down their glasses, rushed to the front door and flung it open.

Douglas helped Helen out of his Standard, and up into the house. Once inside, with Norma and Violette fussing about her, she was taken to the settee and told to rest there. They'd show her round the villa when she'd caught her breath. And meanwhile, how about a celebratory sherry?

'Oh yes please,' Helen replied.

'Just what the doctor ordered.' Douglas said. 'And I'll have a large brandy if you don't mind.'

Norma gave him a sharp look. There was something in his

voice that wasn't natural, something disturbing. 'What's wrong?' she demanded.

He lit a cigarette. 'Admiral Darlan was assassinated a couple of hours ago.' Darlan was a collaborator, deputy to Pétain in Vichy France, who'd been unlucky enough to be in Algiers when it was taken by the Allies. At that stage the French political situation in North Africa was basically a tussle between the Darlanists who advocated non-resistance to the axis powers, and the de Gaullists who were determined to fight.

Norma's face lit up. 'But that's good news!'

'Except for one thing.'

'What's that?'

'It was René Bonnier de la Chapelle who shot him.'

Norma thought of the dashing French Lieutenant whom she and many others at Massingham had become so fond of. 'What will they do to him?' she asked quietly.

'It's a capital offence. But they may commute it to a prison sentence, hopefully a short one.'

Norma had a sudden thought. 'Did SOE set this up?'

'He used an SOE pistol, but apart from that I couldn't say.'

'It's certainly to the Allied advantage that the traitor Darlan is dead. And if SOE organised it, good luck to them, they did the right thing,' Violette said venomously.

'Has René been arrested?' queried Norma.

'Yes.' This time it was Helen who answered.

'There'll be a court martial, though no one knows exactly when,' Douglas said.

That was a dampener right enough, thought Norma. Poor René. Time in prison, no matter how short, what a horrible prospect for him.

Violette poured sherry for Helen, and a hefty brandy for Douglas. Then they all sat and talked quietly about Darlan's death and the effect it was going to have on the Allied cause in North Africa, a cause that was still, in the main, bogged down in the mud of Tunisia. The new offensive would be in the spring when the ground would be hardened again, and when wheeled and tracked vehicles and guns could continue advancing.

It was Boxing Day. There had been a non-stop traffic of signals in and out of Massingham. At 8 pm Norma and the three other WT operators on that shift knocked off, handing over to the caretaker shift – two girls, who'd be working through till midnight. The coders and decoders also changed shift at this time, also handing over to a reduced number.

When Norma got back to Casa Bon-Bon, she found that Violette had gone for a drink in the canteen bar, and Helen was preparing to go to bed. Helen was finding it tiring being out of hospital and was, wisely, having early nights.

It was about an hour later when Norma, in pyjamas and a dressing gown, heard a car drive up and park outside the villa. A minute later there was a tap on the front door.

'Can I come in?' Douglas asked when she opened the door.

He took off his hat and threw it onto the settee. 'Is there any of that brandy left?'

'Plenty. Do you want some?'

'Please.'

He sat on the settee beside his hat, and bent forward to put his face in his hands, his elbows resting on his knees. He didn't look up again till Norma handed him his brandy.

He gulped down half the glass's contents, took a couple of deep breaths, then gulped down what remained. 'They shot René half an hour ago,' he said quietly.

Norma was shocked to hear that. 'But he was pardoned by General Giraud!'

'The Darlanists worked on Giraud till they persuaded him to withdraw the pardon. René was then taken out and executed.'

'Vengeance I suppose,' she said heavily.

'It won't do them any good, de Gaulle's the man for the French in North Africa now. But they had to have their pound of flesh for their Admiral.'

Norma poured herself a brandy, and refilled Douglas's glass. She could see now how wretched he looked. His face was taut and he had dark shadows under his eyes.

He shuddered all over, from head to toe, then slumped in on himself. 'So many people, so many dead, gone since the war started,' he whispered in a voice that was riven and raw.

Norma thought of Lynsey, and Charlie Marshall and all the others who had died, all as a direct result of the conflict. 'Yes,' she whispered.

'I only thank God I don't have to go back into the field again.'

She went and knelt beside him. 'At least with Rene it was quick, soon over with. Not like it would have been with you, and has been for so many others, if you hadn't succeeded in escaping from the Gestapo.'

'Sometimes I wake up at night convinced that Bonzo is in the room with me. It's absolutely terrifying.'

She placed her glass on the floor, and took him into her arms. His body was hard against her softness. Holding him seemed the most natural thing in the world. She felt that she'd known him always, that in her arms was where he belonged. It was at that moment, that they first truly became as one.

'Would you like to stay the night?' she asked.

'With you?'

'With me,' she confirmed. 'In my bed.'

He shuddered again, a long racking shudder that left him limp in her embrace. 'I can think of nothing that I'd like more.'

She released him, picked up her glass, rose and extended a hand to him. 'Luckily it's a three-quarter bed so we won't be too squashed,' she said.

He grasped hold of her hand, and rose. 'Hello Norma.'

'Hello Gabriel.'

She led him through to the bedroom.

They stripped together, each watching the other as they did. He finished first, and went to the bed from where he continued to watch Norma. When she too was completely naked she came to lie beside him.

She ran a palm along his leg, a leg that was firm with muscle. His belly too was firm when she touched, then caressed that.

'I eh . . . feel I should say something,' he said in a low voice.

She knew what it was going to be. 'You've never been with a woman before have you?'

His embarrassment gave way to surprise. 'Is it that obvious?'

She kissed him lightly on the lips. 'The only thing that's obvious is how right this is between us.'

'That's how I feel Norma. I never because . . . well I suppose because I've always been rather shy where women are concerned. Then the war happened, and even if I'd wanted to there wasn't any time for that sort of thing anymore.'

'I'm glad I'm the first, that you waited for me.' She paused, then added softly. 'I won't try and lie to you and pretend that I too am a virgin. I'm not.'

'The boyfriend in Glasgow, the one you danced with?'

'Yes.' She didn't see the point in mentioning that single encounter with Philip what's-his-name at Fawley Court. 'Midge and I were engaged to be married.'

He nodded, understanding and accepting what she'd told him.

She gathered him into her arms again, as she'd done in the sitting room. And for a while they were both sublimely content to lie there just like that.

Norma lay listening to the sound of his breathing. He was breathing shallowly in sleep, every so often giving a sort of snort.

She felt whole again, complete. It was how she'd used to feel with Midge, and she hadn't felt like that since he'd left her to run off with Zelda Caprice.

It wasn't just sex, though that was part of it. It was emotional as well as physical, a combination of both. It was as though all this long while a piece of her had been missing, a piece she'd now found again.

She realised there were tears in her eyes, and her lips curved into a smile as they started trickling down her face. They were tears of joy.

'How do you feel?' Douglas asked.

'Terrified,' Norma replied.

Douglas grinned, it was the answer he'd expected. They were in a Dakota aircraft along with a number of Loyalist Spaniards whom Douglas had been training in the mechanics of parachuting. This was to be their first jump from a plane, as well as Norma's. At her request he'd been training her also.

The Dakota was flying at twelve hundred feet and would shortly be over an area just to the north of Massingham where the Spaniards, Norma and Douglas would be making the jump. They were going to be watched by a group of personnel from Massingham together with a guest of honour, the head of the British Political office at AFHQ (Allied Forces Headquarters-Mediterranean), Mr Harold Macmillan.

It was the beginning of June 1943, and the previous month

Tunisia had fallen to the Allies. And what a victory it had been! The axis capitulation had been the greatest massed surrender of fully equipped troops in modern history.

If it had been a memorable victory for the Allies it had also cost them dear. Nearly seventy thousand men had been lost - dead, wounded and missing. Thirty-five thousand British, eighteen thousand American and fifteen thousand French.

But for every man the Allies had lost, the enemy had lost five. In the end, fifteen full divisions had laid down their arms, two hundred and sixty-six thousand men, mostly German.

'Right then, hook up!' Douglas called out, for their parachutes would be activated by static line.

He went swiftly along the line of men, checking that everything was in order. Then he returned to Norma, checked her parachute, and hooked himself up behind her. She would be the second last person out, he the last.

Suddenly Norma had an overwhelming urge to go to the toilet to do a 'number one' as she'd used to call it. Well there was no chance of that of course, she could only hope she wouldn't disgrace herself.

The red warning light winked on, and they knew from their briefing on the ground that the drop was now only a minute off. There was no need to open the Dakota's side door, it had been left open at take off.

Douglas whispered in Norma's ear. 'Just remember to do everything I taught you and you'll be as right as Larry.'

Norma was wondering why she'd ever thought this would be a good thing to do. The training itself had been fun, but now she was actually airborne and about to leap into nothingness she considered it sheer madness on her part. She'd thought it a good idea at the time because it meant she'd have even more time with Douglas.

They'd been sleeping together regularly since Boxing Day. Douglas would stay the night at Casa Bon-Bon three or four times a week. Their feelings for each other had continued to grow, with a rolling snowball effect.

The red light winked out and the green went on. 'Go!' yelled Douglas unnecessarily as the leading Spaniard was already away.

'Oh mummy daddy,' Norma muttered as she shuffled

towards the door through which Spaniard after Spaniard was vanishing.

Half of them were gone now, each man following hard on the heels of the one in front. And then it was her turn.

Framed in the doorway, she hesitated. Below her the parachutes were billowing and drifting groundwards. The ground itself, even though she could see the watchers staring up, seemed a million miles away.

Lynsey hadn't frozen, she reminded herself. And anything a gel from the upper classes could do so too could a lassie from Bridgeton. Douglas was raising a hand to push her when she leapt from the aircraft.

There were several heart-stopping seconds during which she plummeted like a stone, and then thump! She was pulled upwards and backwards as her parachute fully unfolded. Her terror disappeared, replaced by elation. It was a sensation unlike any she'd ever experienced before. It was almost as if she'd suddenly learned how to fly.

Above her, Douglas was staring down at Norma in concern. Now that her parachute was safely open, the next point of danger was the landing. If she did that badly she could break an ankle or leg. She could even break her neck, he'd seen that happen before now.

He tore his gaze from her to focus on the Spaniards, many of whom were now down and gathering up their 'chutes. They were a fine bunch and quick learners. They would do well in whatever the powers that be had planned for them.

The ground was rushing at her now. Norma gathered her wits together, and forced herself to think coolly. She was determined not to make a hash of this., As she landed she pitched herself forward into the roll Douglas had taught her.

Douglas hit the ground several seconds later. He was up in a flash to punch his 'chute release. As the 'chute had already collapsed, and there was only a hint of wind, he left it where it was to run to Norma.

'How are you?' he demanded.

Her face was ablaze with excitement. 'Wow! Did I enjoy that! When can I do it again?'

He burst out laughing. He needn't have been anxious for her after all, everything had gone hunky dory for her.

'I've never been so exhilarated before. It was just amazing! When *can* I jump again?' she enthused.

She looked so gorgeous, so utterly delectable. And with that thought the laughter died on his lips, and a lump that seemed the size of an egg filled his throat. If the Spaniards and watchers hadn't been present he'd have swept her to him and kissed her there and then.

'When we're finished here I'll buy you a drink,' he said instead.

'Sounds marvellous.'

The lump was still in his throat when, a few minutes later, he met and shook hands with Mr Harold Macmillan.

'So what is this show you're taking me to see?' queried Norma. She and Douglas were in his Standard heading for Algiers. It was 15th June, her twenty-sixth birthday, and Douglas, having picked her up from Casa Bon-Bon, was taking her out for a celebratory evening.

'I told you in the villa, it's a surprise.'

She gave him a replica of one of his sideways looks. 'You're being very mysterious.'

'I mean to be.'

She had a sudden horrible thought. 'It's not something dirty is it?'

He grinned ambiguously back at her.

'Douglas! I don't like filth.'

'It's not dirty, I promise you.'

'Hmm!' She wasn't sure whether he was telling the truth or not, he could be such a damned clever actor when he wanted to be. It was one of the many reasons he'd made an excellent 'joe'. Well, if it was filth she'd walk out, she couldn't abide smut and dirt. As they said in Glasgow, it gave her a dry boak.

Then again, she reminded herself, Douglas was hardly the sort to take her to something dirty. At least he didn't seem to be the sort. On the other hand, you never really knew with men, did you?

'I don't care for surprises like this,' she stated.

He laughed, infuriating her. Leaning across, she took a tiny bit of khaki-covered thigh flesh between thumb and forefinger, and pinched hard. Something Lyn had used to do to her when they were young. She had the satisfaction of hearing and seeing him give a yelp of pain.

'That was sore,' he protested.

'It was meant to be,' parodying his earlier words.

'You're a sadist, Norma McKenzie.'

'So are you for keeping me dangling like this.'

'I told you, it's a surprise. It would hardly be a surprise if I let on what it was, now would it?'

She sniffed disdainfully.

'You'll enjoy it.' He paused, then added uncertainly. 'I think.'

She couldn't tell whether he meant that, or was acting again.

He patted his left hand side uniform pocket for the umpteenth time to reassure himself that 'it' was still there. 'It' was.

'Why do you keep touching that pocket?' Norma demanded.

'Do I?'

'Yes you do.'

'Bit of an itch. I'm not touching, I'm scratching.'

Well she certainly didn't believe *that!* 'Nonsense,' she retorted.

He treated her to another ambiguous grin, then started humming 'Lilli Marlene'. He was still humming it when they pulled up in front of the St George Hotel. 'We're here,' he announced.

She was disappointed. What sort of surprise was this? Not much of a surprise in her opinion. They'd been here any number of times before. It was quite old hat. Unless ... 'Have they got a new floor show, is that it?'

He shook his head.

'But there *is* a show here?'

He came round and opened the door for her. 'Shall we go in?' he smiled, evading her question.

They went through reception, and to the rear of that floor to a room close to the one where they'd entertained Brian. On entering the room Norma found it to be larger than the other, and a lance-corporal waiting for them with a film projector all set up ready to go. Norma was intrigued.

'Evening sir, evening madam,' said the Lance-Corporal, saluting them.

A brace of club chairs had been set at a reasonable distance from the mobile screen that dominated the far wall. 'Shall we?' Douglas said, indicating the nearest chair to Norma.

She sat. 'It's a film then?' she said to Douglas, who nodded. 'But when you said a show I thought you meant a live show?'

'These Americanisms will creep in. Impossible for them not to with so many of our Yankee cousins about the place.'

'You were misleading me deliberately.'

'Are you suggesting I'm *devious* Miss McKenzie?'

'Yes,' she stated bluntly.

'I'll take that as a compliment rather than an insult.'

'Take it as a matter of fact.'

'Shall I start sir?' the Lance-Corporal asked.

'What's the film?' Norma asked him.

The Lance-Corporal looked at Douglas for guidance. 'Wait and see,' Douglas said, and squirmed back in his chair. When he was comfy he gave the Lance-Corporal the nod.

The Lance-Corporal switched the lights out, returned to the film projector and set it in motion.

Norma couldn't think what the film was going to be. She gasped with pleasure when the title revealed all. *A Midsummer Night's Dream* by William Shakespeare.

'I know I said when the war was over, but do you mind?' Douglas whispered.

'I think it's a lovely birthday treat. Thank you.'

It was a cast of stars. Mickey Rooney played Puck, Jimmy Cagney playing Bottom, Dick Powell, Olivia de Havilland, Joe E. Brown . . .

A little later those so familiar words were spoken by Oberon.

> . . . I know a bank where the wild thyme blows,
> Where oxlips and the nodding violet grows . . .

She reached over, took Douglas by the hand, and squeezed it. As the Fairy King spoke that particular piece of verse so did she, mouthing it in unison with him.

> . . . More fond of her than she upon her love:
> And look thou meet me ere the first cock crow.

To which the mischievous Puck replied, 'Fear not, my lord, your servant shall do so.'

It was a glorious film; Norma adored every moment of it. Adored it for itself, and the association it had for her and Douglas. Far too soon it was over and the Lance-Corporal was switching the lights back on again.

She blinked after the darkness, and the flickering images on the silver screen. She stared at Douglas adoringly.

'There's more to come,' he announced, springing to his feet, and hauling her, for they were still holding hands, to hers. What now? she wondered, bubbling with anticipation.

He led her from that room to the one where they'd entertained Brian. While they'd been watching the film a painted wooden sign had been fastened temporarily above the door, which said, 'Savoy Grill'. Norma laughed with delight.

As they went into the room the *maître d'hôtel* bowed low and said, 'Welcome to the Savoy Grill, madam.'

The same table as before had been set, this time with a crisp, cream linen tablecloth, silver cutlery, white bone china, and Waterford wine glasses. The menus and winelists, which they were handed as soon as they sat down, were the ordinary hotel ones except with a false front saying 'Savoy Grill'.

'May I recommend a Maçon-Lugny to start with?' the *maître d'hôtel* suggested.

Norma looked at Douglas; he was the knowledgeable one about wine. 'A white Burgundy,' he explained. Then to the *maître d'hotel,* 'Yes, that'll do nicely thank you.'

The Maçon-Lugny, already chilled, was produced while they perused the food menu, and its cork deftly removed. With a flourish the *maître d'hôtel* poured a soupçon for Douglas's approval.

He made sure it hadn't been corked, held it up to the light to judge its clarity, then took it into his mouth to swish it from side to side, then finally chew it. While he was going through this rigamarole Norma could hardly hide her amusement. She thought it very funny.

'Most satisfactory,' Douglas pronounced solemnly. The smiling *maître d'hôtel* poured them both a glassful, then left them to further study the menu.

As soon as the man was out of the room Norma burst out

giggling. 'Honestly, I can't take all that wine malarkey seriously, it looks so pretentious!'

'For some it is, for others not,' Douglas replied slowly.

'And for you?'

'Well, let me put it this way. This is an excellent wine which the *maître d'hôtel* is justifiably proud in serving. If I was to treat it with less appreciation than it deserves then I'd be insulting the man. Which is the last thing I want to do when he has gone to such lengths on our behalf.'

She studied him shrewdly. 'You always have an answer, don't you?'

He smiled, and took another sip of wine. It was a *premier cru*, and as excellent as he'd just said. 'Now what are we going to eat?' he asked, side-stepping her question.

It was in the middle of the main course that Norma, thoroughly enjoying the fish she'd chosen, said, 'All this, *A Midsummer Night's Dream*, the Savoy Grill, is just perfect. You couldn't have given me a better birthday, it's one I'll never forget.'

'Oh!' he exclaimed, as though just remembering something. 'I haven't given you your present yet.' He fumbled in his left-hand uniform pocket to produce a small, blue box - the sort rings come in. Her mind shot back to another box, a black box containing an engagement ring.

She laid down her knife and fork, then opened up the box. There was a plain gold band inside.

'I'm asking you to marry me,' Douglas said as she stared at it.

She looked from the ring to him. Their eyes didn't just meet, they fused together. Electricity sparked and flowed between the two of them.

'I love you,' he stated quietly.

'And I love you. I've known for some time now that I do.'

'So will you marry me?'

'Yes, of course. When?'

'Just as soon as it can be arranged.'

He rose, came round to her, and brought her to her feet. Their eyes were still fused together. 'We'll have to ask permission of course.'

'Do you foresee any trouble there?'

'I don't think so.'

'We'll just have to keep our fingers crossed then.'

Simultaneously, as though on cue, they collapsed into one another's arms. They hugged, squeezed, cuddled and kissed, neither able to get enough of the other.

Norma woke, and stretched languorously. Douglas was lying sprawled asleep beside her, and outside the birds were singing.

She slipped from the bed, and walked to the spiral iron staircase that twisted to the main floor of the room some twelve feet below. Without bothering to put a dressing gown over her thin nightie, for it was already extremely hot, she went down the staircase and across the flagstoned floor to the heavy wooden and metalled door which led out to the verandah. She pulled the door open and sunlight streamed into the room.

She took a deep breath, then ran her hands through her hair. Over to the right, on the pebbled beach, some fishing boats had been drawn up. They were long and slim in design, similar to a Viking longship, only far, far smaller, and were gaily painted. Further along a group of fishermen were sitting mending nets. It was an idyllic setting for their honeymoon.

Their wedding had taken place the previous afternoon. They had been married by the SOE padre at Massingham. Every FANY not on duty had come, with several hundred other SOE personnel crowding in and round the purpose-built chapel that had been erected since the invasion. The chapel was part of the ever-widening sprawl that Massingham was rapidly becoming, the original Club des Pins now only a nucleus of the far greater whole.

When the ceremony itself was over, there had been a reception in the canteen with food and drink in ample supply. While the celebrations were taking place she and Douglas escaped in his Standard, heading west to the little village of Gouraya and the guest house where they were now lodged.

It was Douglas who'd known the village and guest house and said they should go there; as far as Norma was concerned it had been an inspired choice.

The building, a long and rambling one-storey affair, was Moorish in design – at least Norma thought it was Moorish – as was the interior.

The room was the most unusual Norma had ever been in, far

less slept in. The walls were open brick, one of which had been whitewashed. There were exotic rugs scattered over the floor, and several hanging on the walls. Also hanging on the walls were various knives, scimitars and intricately worked pieces of leather. At regular intervals around the walls were metal projections from which terracotta pots filled with sweet-smelling flowers and herbs dangled. The high ceiling was curved, and also open brick. Somehow it contrived to be both soaring and intimate at the same time.

For Norma the *pièce de résistance* was the sleeping platform bolted halfway up one of the side-walls to stick out over the area below. On the platform was a double bed covered with silk sheets and a light multi-coloured quilt. The platform was reached by the spiral iron staircase.

Norma placed her hands on her hips, letting them slide sensuously down the outside of her thighs. A puff of wind blew in off the sea, catching the bottom of her nightdress and making it billow.

'Absolutely gorgeous,' Douglas said behind her.

She turned to find him leaning on one elbow watching her. There was a soft smile on his face, and love in his eyes. Her feelings for him welled within her. 'How about some breakfast?' she asked.

He shook his head - breakfast wasn't at all what he had in mind. 'Not yet. Come back to bed Mrs Ross.'

A thrill of pleasure ran through her to hear that. It was the first time she'd been called *Mrs Ross!* That's who she was from now on, Mrs Ross. Douglas's wife, Gabriel's wife.

'Gladly, Mr Ross,' she replied.

She closed the door again and returned to bed where he was waiting for her with open arms, arms she sank into.

She wouldn't have thought it possible, but it was even better than the night before.

Norma was irritable as she completed her deskwork, it had been a particularly hard and trying day. The FANY contingent at Massingham had expanded during the past few months to reach its present two hundred and fifty. Apart from the work centred on the wireless station they were involved in everything from parachute packing to top-level staff duties, and Norma was in charge, and responsible, for every last one of them. There had been more than one occasion when she'd regretted having been promoted to captain.

She didn't work as a WT operator anymore as all her time was now given over to administration and management. Some of which she enjoyed doing, some of which she didn't.

There was a knock on her office door. 'Come in!' she called out without glancing up.

It was a grave-looking Douglas. 'Nearly finished?'

'I am now,' she replied, snapping the ledger in front of her shut.

'I thought we might go for a stroll?'

Her smile disappeared as she took in his expression and tone of voice. 'Is something wrong?'

'I'll tell you as we walk.'

She got up, put on her cap, and led the way through to the outer office, and from there into the street beyond.

'Let's go down to the beach,' he said.

They used her jeep, for it was a fair hike from there to the beach. She parked by a clump of dunes, and they got out.

'It's bad news, I can tell,' she said as they started over the sand.

'I'm afraid so.'

They walked a short way in silence, Douglas searching for words, Norma dreading asking the question that was whirling round in her mind. She knew from his demeanour that the news wasn't just bad but very serious indeed. 'Have you been posted somewhere else?' she asked at last, her voice thick with fear.

He gave her one of his sideways glances, and shook his head.

'Thank God for that!' she exclaimed in relief, thinking that was the worst news he could break to her. But she was wrong.

It was September, and they'd been married for three months. Accommodation had been found for them in one of the new, prefabricated buildings where they had a self-contained one-room apartment.

Douglas bent down, picked up a stone, and threw it out to sea. It made a dull plopping sound as it entered the water. 'I wish it were only a different posting,' he said.

'So what is it then?'

'I'm going back into the field.'

Aghast, she stopped dead in her tracks. 'But you can't! You're known to the Gestapo. It would be suicide '

'It's not France.'

'Then where?'

'Corsica. I'm going in with several others to link up with, and lead, partisan forces out there.'

She was stunned. Douglas going back into the field! She'd believed, as had he, that was all over for him, that he'd never again have to risk his life in such a way.

'We were only told an hour ago, the first inkling we had that this was on the cards.'

The inside of her head was spinning, and there was a faint taste of bile in her throat. Her stomach heaved, and heaved again. 'When?' she husked.

'Day after tomorrow.'

'So soon!' she exclaimed in dismay.

'I'm afraid so.'

'Can't you get out of it?' She knew as soon as she'd spoken it was a silly question. Even if he could have done, he wouldn't have. 'Sorry,' she added lamely.

He reached out and took her by the hand. 'Life during wartime certainly is full of surprises, isn't it?' He smiled, trying to lighten the situation.

'It certainly is.'

'Will you come and see me off?'

'Wild horses couldn't keep me away.'

He touched her on the cheek. 'You're the best thing that's ever happened to me. I want you to know that.'

She tried to answer, but couldn't. She was too choked with emotion. Hand in hand they resumed their walk.

The night before he left was the longest Norma had ever known, and also paradoxically the shortest. They made love again and again, far more times than they would have done, or been capable of, ordinarily, as though trying to cram into those few hours all the lovemaking that would have taken place during the period of parting that lay ahead.

Bodies slick with sweat, they clung to one another like two lost souls. At one point she cried, and he comforted her. Later, he too was overcome, and this time she comforted him.

Nor was it all hot passion and despondency, there was laughter as well. Norma literally cackled with mirth when, on reaching for the packet of cigarettes he'd laid on the floor, Douglas fell out of bed, cracking a shin which sent him hopping round the room clutching the offending foot and cursing volubly. They laughed, they cried, they made love, they even sang - a Harry Lauder number they both knew and liked.

And all the while they pretended they weren't hearing the clock tick tick ticking the seconds away. Till finally the alarm went off, and the precious seconds had run out.

Dusk was gathering as Douglas and the other agents bound for Corsica went aboard the waiting Lancaster. He paused to wave a final goodbye, then vanished inside. Norma's hand was still raised in farewell as the Lancaster's door slammed shut.

'Oh my love, come back safely to me, please come back safely to me,' she whispered as the Lancaster's propellers burst into life. Her eyes were bright with tears as the plane took off, its mighty engines thundering as it rapidly gained height.

The Lancaster grew smaller and smaller till finally it vanished from sight altogether. 'Please God,' she whispered. 'Please God.'

She dried her eyes before returning to her jeep, and the unmade bed that still smelled of Douglas, and their previous night's lovemaking.

# *Part III*

# LADY'S CHOICE
# 1945–48

## *Chapter Eleven*

It was a bitter cold November's day as the MV *Star of India* kissed the quayside at Southampton Docks. On board, Norma, one of the thousand-plus Forces personnel returning home to Blighty, stood at a passenger rail anxiously scanning the milling throng below. She was looking for Douglas, who'd promised to be there to meet her.

It was now six months since the end of the war in Europe, and two since victory over Japan. After the German defeat many of those at Massingham had been transferred to the SOE's Force 136 in the Far East which was working in conjunction with General Slim's Fourteenth Army. At the height of Massingham's activities there had been two hundred and fifty FANYs under Norma's command. This number was reduced to fifteen at the time of the Japanese surrender. Helen Rolfe had been amongst the first to leave for Force 136.

'There he is, over there!' exclaimed Violette, who was standing beside Norma, and pointed to their left. 'He's wearing a darkish coat and a trilby.'

Norma followed the direction of Violette's jabbing finger to spot Douglas waving frantically at her. She flailed an arm back at him while hot salt tears of pleasure ran down her face. It was twenty-six months since they'd last seen each other, since she'd seen him disappear into the Lancaster that was to take him over Corsica.

Corsica had been bad for him, very bad indeed. And after Corsica there had been one more field assignment for him which had been the worst of them all, before, finally, he'd been taken back to Britain and a desk job.

To begin with the desk job had been in Baker Street where he'd worked closely with M. Then Lieutenant-Colonel Roe,

DR for F, DF, RF, N and T Sections had been moved to pastures new, and Douglas had been made the new DR.

Norma's eyes locked onto Douglas's and, in that instant, it was as though they'd never been apart. Her heart swelled and her shoulders started to shake with emotion. 'Oh Gabriel, dear Gabriel,' she whispered to herself, and the tears became a flood.

'And there's Pam!' Violette screeched excitedly. And sure enough, fairly close to Douglas was Pam Parkinson waving like a mad thing.

The brass band went into, 'It's a Long Way to Tipperary', while folk on a higher deck began throwing toilet rolls, the long white ribbons of paper streaming through the air. Some were held at one end to connect ship and quayside.

'Come on, let's go,' Norma said as a brace of gangplanks were manoeuvred into place. They struggled back to the stateroom to pick up their hand-luggage – their heavier luggage had been put outside their stateroom earlier and had already been collected by the crew – and then made their way to the nearest exit point.

'How do you feel?' Violette asked.

Norma shook her head, words were beyond her. Only minutes now and she and Douglas, her husband, would be reunited. The sunburst of feeling she was experiencing was indescribable. At least for her anyway.

There was a great press to leave the *Star Of India*, but in an orderly fashion. The air was electric with excitement as row upon row of feet shuffled and struggled forward. Then Norma and Violette were on the gangplank itself, over a slash of dirty water, and onto the quayside. They were home. *At long last they were home!*

Norma saw Douglas carving his way towards her, and with a shock realised he'd shaved off his beard and moustache. That and the fact he was a great deal greyer than he'd been before to the point of being quite white in places. And then the sublime, magical moment when he swept her into his arms and pressed his lips to hers.

The tears Norma had managed to fight back now returned, hotter and saltier than before. When the kiss was over Douglas hugged her so hard she was certain he must surely break her ribs.

'Norma,' he husked. 'I can't believe it, I really can't. After all this while we're back together again.'

'I really can't believe it either. But it's true, it's true!' she whispered. This time it was she who kissed him.

After that kiss, she embraced Pam, and Violette, Douglas. 'We'll collect your luggage, the car's nearby,' Douglas said to Norma when that was over.

The four of them went into the quayside shed where the heavy luggage would be brought and there, Norma and Douglas hand in hand, they chatted about the sea voyage and Pam's journey down by train from London.

'As Douglas has a car with him can we offer you two girls a lift?' Norma asked as trolleys of cases and kitbags made an appearance.

'No, we can't!' Douglas exclaimed abruptly.

Norma turned to him for an explanation, and his expression became sheepish. 'It's not that we wouldn't be delighted to of course, but I . . .' He coughed. 'I've booked Norma and me into a little inn at Twyford just outside Winchester. I stayed there last night and arranged that Norma and I would return today.'

'He's gone all red,' Violette said, and laughed. It was true, Douglas was flushed with embarrassment.

Norma smiled; he'd done the right thing as far as she was concerned. It was very thoughtful, not to say romantic of him.

'Don't worry about us, we'll be absolutely fine,' Pam said.

All too soon they'd collected their luggage and it was time for Norma and Douglas to say goodbye to the other two. There was more hugging and kissing, and renewed promises to keep in touch. Norma was deeply saddened to be parted from Violette. They'd shared a great deal and become extremely close. Then she brightened again, remembering that she had Douglas once more.

Douglas led the way out of the mêlée into a car park, to stop beside a green 3-litre Lagonda tourer. 'This is it,' he said, running a hand lovingly over the bonnet.

'It's a beauty,' Norma breathed. And indeed it was a most handsome machine, long and low-slung, with a pair of large headlamps dominating its front.

'I couldn't resist it when I saw it in the Motor Market,' Douglas declared proudly.

The Motor Market! Norma thought with a thrill. A name from another time and place. To hear it again made her realise she really was going home to Glasgow. And then she reminded herself, home to Glasgow but not to Bridgeton and Cubie Street, but Burnside and Blairbeth Road, for she and Douglas would be living with his parents in their huge house with all the servants. A shiver of apprehension ran through her. A whole new life lay ahead of her as Douglas's wife, a life that would be, must be, as different to her days in Cubie Street as the proverbial chalk was from cheese.

'Do you want to drive? I've had you put on the insurance.'

'Can I?' she replied quickly.

He tossed her the keys. 'It's your car as well as mine, you know.'

She threw herself into his arms and kissed him again. 'I love you, Douglas Ross,' she whispered.

'And I love you.'

The Lagonda proved to be as delightful to drive as it was to look at.

The Hare and Hounds was a coaching inn several hundred years old. They were greeted by Mrs Hobbs, the landlord's wife, who told them their room was ready and waiting. Her son Henry, a lad in his early teens, took their luggage up for them.

The room was small but very cosy. A fire blazed in the grate, and there was a large scuttle of coal to refuel it with. There was also a bottle of champagne in an ice-bucket.

'Your idea?' she asked him with a smile, pointing to the bucket.

'Hmm! I thought tonight could be a sort of second honeymoon.'

'I like that idea too. In fact, I like it very much.'

He pulled the champagne from its bucket, and opened it, the cork going off with a bang and bounding across the room. Norma giggled with delight.

He filled two glasses and handed her one. 'To us, and the future,' he toasted quietly.

She sipped. 'Now can I make a toast?'

'Of course.'

'Here's to those who didn't make it. Marie Thérèse and the rest.'

His eyes clouded with pain, and he seemed to shrink a little in on himself. 'Yes, Marie Thérèse and the rest who didn't make it,' he repeated in a whisper. As he drank, face after face flicked through his mind, all of them people now dead.

Douglas roused himself from his reverie. 'I have some things for you,' he said, and crossed to get his suitcase standing by the side of the bed.

Some things for her? She couldn't think what they might be. She gasped when he produced an exquisite nightdress of snow-white satin, trimmed with lace. She'd never seen a nightdress so beautiful. It was simply gorgeous.

'It was made in Paris just before the war started. I thought you'd like it,' he said.

'Like it, I adore it!' she exclaimed, taking it from him and holding it up against herself.

'And there's a dressing-gown and underwear,' he added.

The dressing-gown was another stunner. It was a padded Chinese silk affair, black with crimson flowers. 'Mandarin-style,' Douglas explained.

There was masses of the underwear in white, pink, beige and French blue colours. It was the best quality underwear Norma had ever seen, far less owned.

Douglas laughed to see how pleased she was. 'You won't find anything like this lot in the shops, I can tell you.'

'So how did you come by them?'

'Contacts in France. I had them sent over especially.'

Douglas poured out more champagne. 'It's almost dinner-time, I've booked a table for two, and there's another bottle of this champagne on ice. We'll have to go down.'

She heard the undertones in his voice, and saw the same in his eyes. It was what she wanted also, but he was right, if the table was booked they should go down.

He tapped out on his glass: I love you.

I love you too. she tapped in return.

'Do you want to change?'

'Do you think I need to?'

He shook his head. 'It's hardly a formal place. Your uniform will be just fine.'

There was a jug and bowl of water in the room, which Norma used to wash her hands and face. She then applied some light make-up and powder.

'Oh, I almost forgot,' he said, and handed her a small bottle. It was a bottle of perfume, its smell was heavenly.

'You really are spoiling me,' she said.

'Why not? Today's a very special day after all.'

She dabbed a little of the perfume behind both ears, and in other strategic places. He watched her with a slitted gaze, thinking how much he felt for this woman, and how dreadfully he'd missed her while they'd been parted. There had been one particular night during his last field assignment when, certain he was about to die, he'd been convinced he'd never see her again. But here they both were.

Mr and Mrs Hobbs did them proud. Their table was in a secluded spot and had candles on it. The main course was venison, *poached*, Mrs Hobbs whispered, giving them a wink.

'In your final letter to me you mentioned briefly there was a job in the air?' Norma asked, tucking into the venison – the first time she'd ever eaten that meat, and finding it delicious, not at all too gamey for her taste.

'There's a job for a specialist in orthopaedics at the Victoria Infirmary where my father is,' Douglas explained. 'It's now certain that old McNulty, the present senior orthopaedic specialist will retire early in the new year.'

This was new to Norma. Douglas hadn't mentioned any of the details in his letter, only that there was the possibility of a job. 'Will it make any difference that your father's already at this hospital?' she asked.

Douglas pulled a face. 'He believes that's to my advantage, but I'm not so sure. I think it could just as easily be to my disadvantage.'

'What about the job itself, is it what you want?'

'Oh yes, very much so. However, I'm not convinced that the powers that be would consider me properly qualified for such a position. I'm afraid the war has played havoc with what you might call my going along the proper stepping stones for such an eminent post.'

'Could you do it?'

'No doubt in my mind that I could. The trouble is, will they think so?'

'Even if you don't get it there will always be other jobs, it's only a matter of time.'

'It would be nice to stay in Glasgow though. You see, once I accept a post as specialist it's more or less for life. I could easily end up in Cardiff, Belfast, Manchester or Inverness. At that level it's all the luck of the draw.'

Norma hadn't realised that. She didn't think she wanted to live permanently in any of the places he'd just mentioned, though of course she would if she had to. But, as he said, it *would* be nice to stay in Glasgow 'We'll just have to keep our fingers crossed then,' she said.

He tapped out a love message on the table, which made her smile. She tapped one back.

As they were waiting for the sweet to arrive she tapped out: I want a bath first.

Like me to scrub your back?

I can manage by myself thank you very much.

Spoilsport!

What if someone should see us coming out of the bathroom together?

So what? We're married.

You know what I mean.

I could scrub not only your back but other parts as well.

What other parts did you have in mind?

Tits.

Douglas!

And . . .

She interrupted him. If you're going to be disgusting I don't want to hear.

Why is that disgusting?

It just is.

I love you, have I ever told you that?

Once or twice, but never enough.

I love you. I love you. I love you. I want you.

And I love and want you too.

Do we have to eat the sweet?

Yes, it's on its way.

I'm not hungry anymore. Not for food anyway, only you.

Smoothie.

The difference between me and a smoothie is that I mean it.

I know that darling.

'Something wrong?'

Startled, they both glanced up to find Mrs Hobbs staring quizzically at them.

'No, nothing's wrong,' Douglas replied hastily.

'Then, excuse me for asking, but why were you both tapping the table as you were?'

Norma fought back a laugh, and stared at Douglas. Let him answer that.

'You mean like this?' he said, and tapped out: Help!

Norma dropped her gaze, and continued to fight back the laugh that was now bursting to get out. Her sides began to ache.

'That's right,' Mrs Hobbs nodded.

'It's eh ... eh ...' He cleared his throat. God, what to say! The last thing he wanted to do was launch into a lengthy explanation of the truth. 'It's a game actually.'

Mrs Hobbs frowned. 'A game?'

'We learned it in Algeria where we were both stationed for a while. The Arabs play it.'

Mrs Hobbs eyebrows shot up. 'The Arabs! Fancy that.'

Norma stuffed a balled fist into her mouth. Her chest was heaving, which she did her best to disguise by folding and hunching her arms over herself.

Douglas elaborated. 'Did you ever play that game as a child where paper wraps stone, scissors cuts paper, and stone breaks scissors?'

'I know the one. Yes, I did.'

'It's something similar to that.'

'Well, well, you live and learn don't you?'

'You certainly do,' Douglas beamed.

Mrs Hobbs placed Norma's prunes and custard in front of her. 'Are you all right, Mrs Ross?'

It hadn't really been that funny, but Norma had found it hysterically so. 'Something in my throat,' she spluttered.

'Can I get you a glass of water?'

'Please.'

Mrs Hobbs put Douglas's profiteroles in front of him, then hurried off.

'Game played by Arabs!' Norma whispered, choking with laughter.

'I thought it rather a good explanation.'

'And I thought it showed great ingenuity. Take a gold star and go to the top of the class.'

When Mrs Hobbs returned with the water Norma greeted her with a straight face. She drank some of the water just to be polite, and swore it had done the trick in clearing her throat.

Norma rose from the still steaming bath and reached for the fluffy towel she'd brought from their bedroom, one of the pair provided. Slowly, methodically, she began drying herself.

Douglas had been serious about coming into the bathroom with her, but she'd been adamant he didn't. It wouldn't have seemed right in a hotel somehow, though she certainly wouldn't have had any objections to it if they'd been in their own place.

Not that they were going to have their own place, she reminded herself. They'd be sharing the house in Blairbeth Road with Douglas's parents. She really would have preferred a place of their own, but he'd argued against it, saying it would be daft to spend money on another house when there was room and more for them in Blairbeth Road. She just hoped, and prayed, that everything was going to work out all right, that she'd hit it off with his parents. But then she was sure she would do, Solange sounded a gem of a woman, Forsyth – that silly name! – a bit like her own da.

At least she didn't have to worry about the way she spoke. She'd learned early on in the FANY that she had an excellent ear and had lost a fair amount of her Glasgow accent before meeting Douglas again. After he'd gone off to Corsica, anticipating the sort of people she'd have to rub shoulders with after the war if he survived – which thank God he had – she'd worked on her accent even further till now she spoke almost as well as Douglas himself. Solange and Forsyth would find no fault in that department.

When she was dried she doused herself with Johnson's baby powder and then dabbed on some more of the perfume Douglas had given her.

As she slipped into the nightdress she found that she was suddenly nervous about what lay ahead. It might be their second honeymoon but she felt as if it was their first, and this their first night together. She felt like a virgin going to her husband for the first time.

She combed her hair, considered applying a little make-up, and decided against it. She thought of Douglas lying in bed waiting for her, and butterflies fluttered in her stomach. Twenty-six months, she thought grimly. Such a long time for a husband and wife to be separated, such a long, long time. Putting on the Chinese dressing gown she gathered up her bits and pieces. She was ready.

He stared hungrily at her as she came through the bedroom door. She closed it quietly behind her. The key in the lock squeaked as she turned it.

'I stoked up the fire,' he said throatily.

'Good.' Since she'd gone for her bath he'd become as nervous as she was. That made her feel better. She was aware of his gaze rivetted to her as she tidied away the things she'd brought from the bathroom. When that was done she turned to him, and smiled.

'Come here,' he said.

She went slowly, taking her time. When she reached the bed she removed the Chinese dressing gown. 'How do you like the nightdress on?' she asked, and did a sort of twirl round the way she believed fashion models did.

'It's sensational. On you, that is.'

She sat on the bed beside him, and he reached out to place a hand on her thigh. Gently, and sensuously, he ran his hand backwards and forwards over her satin-covered flesh.

'It's sensational on, but I prefer you with it off,' he husked, the words thick in his throat.

She rose again to her feet, and the nightdress whispered to the floor. Naked, she stood before him.

He pulled back the covers to reveal that he too was completely naked, and ready for her. He drew her down till she was lying stretched alongside him. 'Oh Norma, how I've dreamed of this since leaving Massingham.'

'Me too.'

'I don't ever want to be separated from you again.'

'We won't be.'

He lightly kissed first one breast, then the other.

Her nervousness was gone, as was his. She could tell. A sense of peace descended on her. Peace intermingled with passion. 'Now,' she said.

He came over, and into her. She sighed with the sheer pleasure of their joining. 'Oh yes,' she murmured. 'Oh yes.'

Dracula's castle, that was her initial impression of the house in Blairbeth Road. Tall, gothic, and sinister. An impression that was further enhanced by the thunder and lightning storm raging outside.

'Won't be a mo',' Douglas said. He stepped out of the Lagonda, dashed to the large wrought-iron gates and swung them open.

They'd run into the beginnings of the storm at Crawford, and it had worsened steadily as they'd approached and come into Glasgow. Now the house in Blairbeth Road seemed to be at the centre of the storm. Flashes of lighning, again and again, split the coal-black sky directly overhead.

'My God, what a night!' Douglas said, climbing back into the car.

'Dreadful', she agreed, wincing as a particularly loud bang of thunder made the Lagonda's windows rattle.

Douglas drove in through the gates and parked in front of the main entrance. There was another car in front of them, a Daimler by the shape of it. In fact it was a Vanden Plas.

The door of the house opened and a man emerged carrying a large multi-coloured umbrella. 'Travers, the butler. Did his bit during the war as an ARP warden,' Douglas explained.

Travers came to Norma first, helping her out of the Lagonda and escorting her to the doorway where she went inside. He then returned for Douglas.

Norma found herself in a tiled vestibule. She stood there waiting for Douglas to join her.

'Thank you Travers,' Douglas said as he and the butler entered the hall. Travers closed the door behind himself and Douglas, let down the umbrella and placed it in a corner.

'This is my wife, Travers,' Douglas said.

Travers, a man of about fifty, Norma would have judged, gave her a small bow. 'Pleased to meet you, Mrs Ross.'

Her right hand had moved instinctively to shake his. She

turned this into a vague gesture of touching her coat lapels. 'And I'm pleased to meet you, Travers.'

'Welcome home, Master Douglas. And may I say on behalf of the entire staff how pleased we are to have you back again, and relieved that you came through the recent conflict unscathed.'

'Why thank you Travers, most kind.'

There was a tone in Douglas's voice that Norma had never heard before - she was soon to learn that it was the tone he employed when addressing servants. There was nothing patronising or condescending about it, but it stated clearly that a servant was a servant, and - no matter how highly thought-of or even treasured he was - a hired employee.

Travers assisted Norma out of her coat, then Douglas out of his. 'The master and mistress are in the large sitting-room taking sherry,' he said.

Douglas grasped Norma by the arm, giving her a warm smile as he did. 'Shall we?' She gave him a weak smile in return.

'I'll fetch your luggage from the car and take it up to your room,' Travers said.

'Which room is that?'

'Your old one, Master Douglas. The mistress instructed me to put you and Mrs Ross there.'

'Fine.'

Leaving the hall, they entered a circular reception area, the floor of which was green marble. There was old wood everywhere, mahogany and oak, and hanging from the wood-panelled walls were a number of pictures of highland scenes. Two complete suits of armour - one holding a sword, the other what looked like a pike - guarded a staircase sweeping upwards. Norma shivered.

'Cold? The house is always chilly in winter. Because of its size it would cost a fortune to heat properly,' Douglas said.

Although it was cold Norma didn't tell him it wasn't that which had made her shiver. The house, at least what she'd seen of it so far, was gloomy and forbidding, not at all as cheery and hospitable as she'd have wished it.

They went to a room that was exactly as Travers had called it, a large sitting-room. Some thirty to thirty-five feet long, Norma thought, and roughly half that in width.

The curtains on the windows were brocade, and gave the

impression of being extremely ancient. Everything in the room was old and the furniture positively antediluvian. The wallpaper was so faded it could well have been there since the turn of the century.

There was a wooden baronial-style fireplace in which a log fire was burning. Standing by the fireplace was Forsyth, while Solange was sitting smiling.

Norma took all this in as she and Douglas walked towards the fireplace, and his waiting parents. As they came closer Solange rose and surprised Norma by how tiny she was. Norma would later learn that Solange was only four feet ten inches tall.

Forsyth was fractionally taller than his son, broad shouldered, with a florid face. His thin, sandy-coloured hair was swept straight back from his forehead, and he had a distinct paunch.

Solange had the same sallow skin as Douglas, a pronounced aquiline nose – Douglas's was only slightly so – and dark, birdlike eyes. She couldn't have been anything else but French.

Solange said something very fast in her native tongue, which Douglas answered in the same language; then he had left Norma's side and enveloped his mother in his arms. Forsyth beamed on.

Finally Douglas disentangled himself. 'Mother, Father, I'd like you to meet Norma, my wife.'

Solange turned a penetrating gaze onto Norma. 'Welcome,' she said.

'Welcome,' Forsyth repeated.

Norma stared about her in dismay. She and Douglas were in their bedroom and it was simply ghastly. The carpet was threadbare; the wallpaper as faded as that in the large sitting-room; the curtains not only on their last legs but hideously patterned; the whitewashed ceiling now yellow with age. There was a huge oak wardrobe that was scarred and chipped all over, an oak chest-of-drawers in even worse condition, and an oak headboard – with inset mirror – over the bed. The bed itself was as hard as stone.

Norma laid out the two dresses she'd managed to acquire in London. They'd stopped off there so that she could personally hand in a report on the final days of Massingham to FANY HQ, and her letter of resignation from the Service. Being an officer, she'd felt it the proper thing to do to personally hand in the letter rather than merely sending it.

'Which one?' she asked Douglas.

They were dressing for dinner; he was in the process of knotting a black tie. It had shaken her that mealtimes were so formal, and that she was expected to dress for dinner every night. She was going to have to expand her stock of civvy clothes, and fast, if she was to do that. Which wasn't going to be easy as clothing was rationed.

'The blue I think,' he smiled.

There was a paraffin heater in the room which took the chill off the air. It would have been really cold, and damp, without it.

She hated the room! Well, things in *here* were certainly going to change, she was utterly determined about that. Even if she had to use her own money to bring it about. What amazed her was that Douglas seemed to find it quite acceptable – she would have thought he'd have considered it as awful as she did.

She was applying the final touches of her make-up when a gong sounded, announcing that dinner was served. She went downstairs on Douglas's arm, forcing herself to smile.

'And how exactly did you two meet? Douglas has told us hardly anything at all about you in his letters,' Forsyth queried.

Norma glanced at Douglas sitting facing her across the width of the long dining-table. Forsyth and Solange sat at its head and bottom, and so far apart they almost had to shout when speaking to one another. The dining-room was like all the other rooms she'd been in so far, horrendous in her view.

'We first met when I was at the Royal Free,' Douglas explained, taking a sip of claret.

'I was his patient,' Norma expanded. Then Douglas told the story of how she'd been blown up in Risinghill Street.

'Marvellous body of women, the FANY, I have tremendous respect for them,' Forsyth commented – a little pompously Norma thought – when Douglas had finished.

'You say you met at the hospital for the first time. When did you meet again?' Solange probed. She spoke perfect English, but with a pronounced French accent.

Douglas drank more wine, and wondered how to answer that.

He finally decided that as the war was now over there was no reason why his parents shouldn't know about the SOE, and his and Norma's involvement with it. 'She was my partner in England while I was in France, but because I was operating under a codename she didn't know it was me, the doctor who'd treated her at the Royal Free. Nor did I appreciate that the Norma I communicated with by wireless was my ex-patient. We met up later, in the flesh that is, in Algeria where we were both stationed with SOE. That was where and when we learned that we'd been partners.'

Solange and Forsyth had stopped eating to stare at their son. 'You were in France? You mean before the liberation?' Solange queried.

'Yes. I was an agent, a spy and saboteur if you like, for an organisation called Special Operations Executive. When I transmitted into homebase, F Section it was called, it was Norma on the other end.'

'A spy? But you're a doctor!' Forsyth exclaimed, flabbergasted.

'I can also speak French like a native and can easily pass as a born and bred Frenchman. SOE capitalised on that.'

Forsyth shook his head. 'I can hardly believe this. We had no idea. Not even an inkling.'

'Neither do my parents. Everything to do with SOE was a secret. My people all think I was a FANY driver and nothing else,' Norma said.

'Did you also go into France?' Solange asked with a frown.

'I have no French at all so that was out of the question. I had a good and close girlfriend who did go in however.'

'And didn't return,' Douglas added quietly.

Norma dropped her eyes. Remembering Lynsey and that last interrupted transmission always brought a lump to her throat.

'A spy and saboteur, it's incredible!' Forsyth muttered.

And assassin, Douglas thought darkly. But that was something not even Norma knew about. 'A lot of what SOE did was just that, incredible,' he answered.

'Your son is a very brave man,' Norma told the older Rosses.

Douglas made a gesture of dismissal. 'I was no more brave than thousands, if not millions of others.'

'There's brave and brave, and you were the latter,' Norma retorted.

He glowered at her.

'You *were*.'

'No more than any of the others who went into France as agents, or into Holland or Belgium or Yugoslavia or any of the other places that SOE sent "joes" into.'

'"Joes"?' Forsyth queried.

'SOE name for an agent,' explained Norma.

Douglas's glower intensified, he was acutely embarrassed.

'You were,' she repeated.

'Well, I don't agree, and that's an end of this conversation for now if you don't mind,' Douglas said, and turned to his plate.

Solange's birdlike eyes shone with fierce pride. Norma wouldn't have been at all surprised if her mother-in-law had suddenly burst into 'La Marseillaise'.

Douglas pointedly changed the subject and asked his father about a very tricky eye operation that Forsyth had listed for the following morning.

They retired into the larger sitting room for coffee and liqueurs. Once they were all settled round the log fire, and with rain lashing the windows, Solange said 'Douglas did mention in one of his infrequent letters that you were an officer. Is that correct, *chérie*?'

'Yes, I was a Captain.'

'With two hundred and fifty FANYs under her command when we were in Algeria,' Douglas said.

'An enormous amount of responsibility,' Forsyth acknowledged, nodding his approval.

'It was. I thoroughly enjoyed the experience, even if it was extremely difficult at times.'

'There were many French where we were, Mama. We both met de Gaulle.'

'You did!' Solange exclaimed.

'A great Frenchman,' Forsyth declared.

Norma couldn't help teasing. 'He was part Irish you know.'

Solange rounded on her. 'Never!'

'Oh yes. His mother's mother was a MacCartan, descendant

of one of the mercenaries who fought for Louis the Fourteenth against Marlborough.'

'You're storytelling,' Solange accused, shocked to think that such a famous French hero should in fact have foreign blood in him, and Irish blood at that.

'Not all that many people know about it, but it's true, nonetheless.'

'Well, I'll be jiggered!' muttered Forsyth. 'It's almost like hearing Montgomery was a Frenchman.'

'But he was,' Norma smiled.

'Eh? Now you are storytelling.'

Norma shook her head. 'Not so. The Montgomery family came to England from Normandy. I think, though I'm not a hundred percent certain, that they arrived with the Conqueror. What I am sure of is that Monty's ancestors were Norman-French.'

'How did you learn all this?' Douglas laughed.

'About de Gaulle, at Massingham where I had to read through various, non-secret, papers about him and his followers. It was Helen Rolfe who told me about Montgomery. Her family had the same history, and they *did* come over with the Conqueror.'

Forsyth put another log on the fire which had begun to die away. As he dusted off his hands there was a vivid flash of lightning outside, followed almost instantly by a loud crash of thunder.

'Speaking of families, we know absolutely nothing about yours, Norma *chérie*. Other than the fact they live in Glasgow, that is,' Solange said to Norma, smiling.

'You were very sparing with details in your letters,' Forsyth chided.

'Perhaps the outskirts of Glasgow? We couldn't think of any McKenzies with a daughter in Glasgow itself,' Solange went on.

'There is McKenzie the advocate, but he's got a son not a daughter,' Forsyth said.

Norma glanced at Douglas. She'd presumed he'd told his parents about her background, but apparently not. Nor was it something she'd thought to ask him during their journey up from Southampton. 'I come from Bridgeton,' she repied levelly.

Forsyth blinked. 'Bridgeton?'

'Before the war my father was a gardener with the Corporation Parks Department. During the war he was with the Pioneer Corps, and now the war's over he's returned to his old job at Glasgow Green. I had a letter from my mother just before I left Massingham telling me that.'

'I see,' Forsyth said slowly.

Solange's face had become set, giving nothing away. With a sinking feeling Norma realised they were bitterly disappointed in her. They'd presumed that Douglas had married someone of equal social standing.

'And you yourself, Norma *chérie*, what did you work at before the war? I take it you did work?'

Caustic undertones, Norma thought grimly. 'Yes, I was a professional ballroom-dancer.'

'Professional dancer!' Forsyth exclaimed, seeming to choke on the words.

'Professional *ballroom*-dancer,' Norma emphasised.

'She and her partner were the All Scotland Champions. Isn't that right Norma?' Douglas said.

She could have slaughtered him for putting her in this position. It was so humiliating. 'Yes.'

'How interesting,' Solange murmured, her face still set and closed.

Norma sipped her liqueur. It was Drambuie and should have tasted sweet. But it tasted sour to her. Why hadn't Douglas told them about her, prepared them for her! she raged inwardly. It was quite unlike his normal sensitive self. 'I have money of my own you know, a legacy,' she said. She knew fine well it was considered bad manners to talk about money amongst people like these, but she wanted them to appreciate she'd married Douglas for himself and not what he, or they, might have in the bank.

'Is that so?' Forsyth replied, raising an eyebrow as if to say, what are you talking about, twenty pounds, thirty?

'Enough to keep me in comfort, *considerable* comfort, for the rest of my days should that ever be necessary,' Norma spelled out.

'A relative who went abroad and made his fortune perhaps?' Solange inquired casually, thinking that money of that scale could never have come out of Bridgeton. Why, they were all peasants there!

'No, it was a man, a stranger, whose dead daughter I was the spitting image of. He died leaving me everything.'

'How extraordinary,' Forsyth said.

'It was rather. His name was Thomas Gallagher; his daughter's name was Morna. He used to come and watch me dance.' She paused, then added, 'Being financially independent was how I was able to join FANY.'

'I understand now,' Forsyth said slowly.

A pregnant silence descended on the room. Norma was acutely aware that her mother- and father-in-law were both staring at her. She took another sip of her drink and stared right back.

'Why didn't you tell them about me?' Norma demanded. She and Douglas were back in their bedroom, having just said goodnight to Solange and Forsyth, whose bedroom was further along the passageway.

Douglas lit a cigarette. 'I love you, that's enough for me. I don't care whether you come from Kelvinside, Bridgeton or bloody Mars.'

That mollified her somewhat. 'Nonetheless, you could see how disappointed they were. They quite clearly had higher hopes for you.'

He gave a light laugh. 'And her name is Catherine Stark. No doubt you'll meet her before long. She and Mama get along like the proverbial house on fire and visit each other regularly.'

This was new to Norma. 'And who is Catherine Stark?'

'Her father is Sir John Stark. He owns a number of companies and is on the boards of others. They figure prominently amongst what you might call the cream of Scottish society.'

'And what is Catherine to you?'

'A friend, a very old friend. But there was never anything more to it than that. At least not on my side.'

'And hers?'

'Oh definitely so, she made that plain to me years ago.'

'But you didn't fancy her?'

'Not in the least. As a friend, yes. Anything else, no.'

'But she's always held out hope?'

Douglas nodded. 'That's partially Mama's doing. It was her fondest wish that I marry Catherine. The family's wealthy and terribly well-connected. From Mama's point of view it would have been the ideal match.'

'No wonder she's so disappointed that you've married me instead.'

'She'll just have to get used to the idea – they both will in time, I promise you.' He took off his jacket and threw it across a chair. His tie quickly followed. Outside it was quiet as the grave, the storm having petered out and the rain having stopped. 'Will you do something for me, Norma?'

She was at the paraffin heater warming her hands. She noticed there were two bulges in the bed that told her hot water bottles had been put in. Thank God for that! 'If I can.'

'Please don't say to anyone else that I was brave.'

'But you were!'

'Think that if you will, but please don't say it to anyone else.'

'Your parents are hardly anyone else. It's only right that they should know such a thing about their son.'

'I've said to you before, I never felt brave. In fact, to put it crudely, I was shit-scared most of the time.'

'But it was because you felt like that and still went on to do all the things you did, that you are particularly brave.'

He shook his head. 'Well, I don't see it that way. So promise me, no more chat about me being brave? Please?'

Her anger with him had quite disappeared. She placed a now warm palm on his left cheek. 'If that's what you want.'

'It is.'

'Then you have my promise.'

He took her into his arms, loving the pressure of her body against his. He nibbled her neck, which made her giggle, then kissed her, which promptly stopped her giggling.

She squirmed as his tongue probed the recesses of her mouth. She felt him stir, felt his maleness nudging her thigh.

'Did you ever kiss Catherine Stark like that?' she asked when the kiss was over.

'I've only ever kissed Catherine on the cheek. Why, would you be jealous if I had?'

'Pea-green with it. If I met her, instead of saying hello, I'd scratch her eyes out.'

'Hardly the actions of a lady.'

'I'm no lady. I'm from Bridgeton.'

He laughed at that. 'I'll tell you this. You're more of a lady than many so called ladies I know.'

'Let's get into bed.'

'Are you propositioning me?'

'Unashamedly.'

He touched, then gently squeezed her right breast, which made her sigh. She caressed him in return, smiling to see the way his eyes narrowed.

'Oh Norma!'

'Oh Douglas!'

'Bed,' she repeated, and broke away from him to turn off the paraffin heater.

Despite the hot water bottles, the bed was freezing. They cuddled each other for warmth, and as they cuddled their fingers were busy feeling, kneading, caressing. Finally the bed was warm and both of them more than ready. She groaned with pleasure as he entered her.

'Bloody hell!' he swore, stopping in mid-action. The bed-springs were squeaking, making a tremendous racket. At least it seemed a tremendous racket to him.

'Didn't you know they squeaked?'

'How would I? I've never had a woman in here before. I was a virgin until I met you, remember?'

'Do you think they can hear?'

'It is frightfully loud.'

'That's the understatement of the year.'

He continued on, to stop again almost immediately. Norma began laughing at the ludicrousness of it, at the sheer, down-right silliness of it. And he began laughing as well.

'Do you know something?' she said, still laughing.

'What?'

'I don't care whether they hear or not.'

'Well I do. They're my parents.'

She had an idea then, which would stop the squeaking – a

new bed, a *non-squeaking* new bed, that was the first item on the agenda for their room, she decided.

Norma woke and stretched languorously. She felt absolutely marvellous, refreshed and very relaxed. She reached out for Douglas to discover she was alone in the bed. Opening her eyes she glanced around. She wasn't only alone in the bed, she was alone in the room.

Slipping out from underneath the covers she put on the Chinese dressing gown, and went over to the window to look at the view.

The window overlooked an extensive garden containing lots of flower beds, shrubs and trees, the latter mainly fruit trees. The garden disappeared round either side of the house.

After the night's storm it was a beautiful day. The light was extremely bright, while a touch of frost lent a sparkle to almost everything. A beautiful day, but a cold one. She'd have to wrap up well, she told herself.

She was about to turn away from the window when Douglas and Solange came into view. They were walking side by side, he with his head bent as he listened intently to what his mother was saying.

Now what was that all about? Norma wondered. From their physical attitudes, and expressions - which Norma could make out quite clearly - it appeared to be a very serious discussion. Now Douglas was speaking, waving his arms around in a most Gallic manner.

Norma frowned as a sudden thought struck her. Was she the subject of conversation? Was Solange complaining to Douglas about how bitterly disappointed she and Forsyth were that he'd married someone from Bridgeton, a social inferior?

Biting her lip she went over to the oak chest of drawers and started to get dressed. Her things had been unpacked and put away for her the previous evening, while she'd been at dinner.

She was running a comb through her hair, and speculating further about that conversation in the garden, when the gong sounded, announcing that breakfast was served.

Douglas and Forsyth rose to their feet as Norma entered the

dining room. 'You came down then, we thought you might want to sleep on,' Douglas smiled.

'No, I've had enough sleep thank you,' she replied, addressing all three of them, Solange also being present.

A long sideboard had been laid out with food. It was obviously a case of helping yourself, which Norma did now. There might be food rationing in force, but that didn't seem to affect the Rosses, she noted. There was a choice of boiled or fried eggs (not a sign of powdered scrambled which the *hoi polloi* had to endure), kedgeree, Loch Fyne kippers, toast, butter (she could tell it was butter and not marg by the colour), marmalade and jam. There was also tea or coffee. She opted for tea, toast, butter and jam.

'If you had lain in, Mama suggested I bring you a tray up after we'd finished here,' Douglas said as she sat down. Somehow Norma found this irritating. Perhaps it had something to do with having seen Douglas and Solange talking together, discussing her in the garden?

Forsyth glanced at them. 'Have to dash in a moment. Busy day ahead of me.'

'Any idea what time you'll be home?' Solange enquired.

He shook his head. 'I'll telephone late afternoon. Might know by then.'

Solange smiled at Norma, who smiled back. Had Solange been complaining to Douglas earlier on, she wondered again? If she had been, it certainly didn't show in her manner. Solange appeared pleasantness itself.

'And what about you two, what will you do today?' Solange asked, directing the question at Norma and Douglas.

Douglas looked apologetically at Norma. 'I have a pile of back *Lancets* and other papers I must plough through. An awful lot has happened in the field of orthopaedics during the war that I must catch up on, and be *au fait* with, if I'm to stand a chance of landing that job at the Victoria when it comes up.'

'Fine, you do that,' Norma answered. 'But I must go and visit my folks later on, round about teatime say. I was hoping you'd come with me - my mother and sisters are dying to meet you.'

'Of course I'll come with you.'

'Right, that's settled then. I'll give you a call when it's time to leave.'

Forsyth wiped his mouth with a napkin, and stood up. 'That's me,' he announced, and came round to kiss Solange on the cheek. Solange said something in French, which he responded to in the same language. Douglas laughed.

Norma found that irritating. She considered it rude for people to speak another language in front of her, which she didn't understand, when all the others did. Then again, she reminded herself, it was probably a long-standing habit of theirs to switch backwards and forwards between the two languages. They might not even realise they were doing it. She was just going to have to learn French so that she wouldn't be excluded. That seemed the answer to the problem.

When Forsyth was gone, Solange said to Norma, 'You mentioned sisters?'

'I have two, Lyn and Eileen. They're both younger than me.'

'And are they married?'

'Eileen was, but her husband was killed in a collision between the passenger train he was on and a goods train. She was twenty years old when it happened.'

Solange pulled a long face. 'How sad.'

'Lyn's been going out with someone for a while now, according to my mother. She expects them to get engaged soon.'

'Someone who was in the Armed Forces?'

'No, he was exempt.' Norma waited for Solange to ask what the chap did, but Solange didn't. Which was probably just as well, the chap was an engine fireman on the railways. She doubted Solange would have appreciated that.

'And your mother, what's her name?'

'Euphemia, but she's always been called Effie.'

'Euphemia, how pretty! I much prefer it to Effie. And your father?'

'Brian.'

'We must have the McKenzies over soon,' said Forsyth.

Solange dropped her gaze to stare at her plate. Picking up her side knife she buttered a small rectangle of toast. 'Yes, we must,' she answered vaguely.

Hell would freeze over first, before her folks were invited to Blairbeth Road, Norma thought grimly. For it was clearly evident that her mother-in-law, and perhaps her father-in-law as well, was a dyed-in-the-wool snob.

'After breakfast I'll show you round the house if you like,' Solange said, glancing up at Norma.

'That's kind of you. I'd like that.'

'Good.'

'You'll find me in the study when you get that far,' said Douglas.

Norma went over to the sideboard and poured herself another cup of tea.

'And this is the ninth, and final, bedroom,' Solange declared, opening a door. This bedroom was situated on a between floor in an out-of-the-way corner of the house. It was by far the smallest.

There was a musty smell inside the bedroom which suggested it hadn't been aired for quite some time. It had the same broad decor that all the others had, indeed that the entire house had – worn-out Victorian drear.

'I must say I'm surprised you haven't . . . well, done the house up before now,' Norma smiled.

'Oh no, we prefer it as it is,' Solange replied quickly. 'I don't think any of us would change a thing. Gives a sense of continuity, which is very important to us.'

Norma could see Solange was deadly serious, her mother-in-law genuinely did prefer the house the ways it was. There was bound to be conflict when she let it be known she wanted her and Douglas's bedroom redecorated and refurnished. What should she do, state her intentions here and now? Or should she speak to Douglas first and let him deal with the problem? The latter was the wisest course, she decided. The last thing she wanted was a row during her first day at Blairbeth Road. She was already regretting that she'd agreed to come and stay here – she should have insisted she and Douglas get a place of their own. But it had been so difficult to argue by letter, and his reasons for choosing Blairbeth Road had been so plausible.

'And now we'll go below stairs and I'll introduce you formally to the servants,' Solange announced.

Imperious, yes, that was the word to describe Solange, Norma thought to herself as they left the bedroom, imperious.

'What were you and your mother talking about in the garden

this morning?' Norma asked. She and Douglas were in the Lagonda, having just left Blairbeth Road for Bridgeton.

'You saw us then?'

'From our bedroom window. You appeared to be having a very serious conversation.'

'She wanted to know more about my work as a "joe", where exactly I went, what I did, that kind of thing. She was deeply shocked at some of the details I gave her.'

'I can imagine.'

'She said it was just as well she hadn't been aware of what I was up to, the worry would probably have given her a nervous breakdown. She's very highly strung, you know.'

'I hadn't realised.'

'Yes, very much so.'

'And was that all you talked about?'

He gave her one of his sideways looks. 'What do you mean?'

'Come on, you know fine well what I mean. They're obviously disappointed that you've married me. I thought perhaps she was taking the opportunity to register that disappointment with you.'

He changed gear, then drove for a few seconds in silence. 'Well?' Norma prompted.

'Your name did come up.'

'I was sure it had.'

'Of course she's not exactly thrilled that I've married a girl from the other side of the tracks, so to speak. But she thinks you're charming and intelligent and . . .' He suddenly exploded. 'And they're just bloody well going to have to get used to the idea. You're the woman I love, I've married you and that's all there is to it.'

'You said that to her?'

'I did.'

Norma smiled. 'When I was watching you, you became very Gallic, waving your arms about as if you were shooting off semaphore.'

He smiled too. 'When I'm with French people that half of me tends to be uppermost. Just as when I'm with the British the other side comes to the fore.'

'I want our bedroom redecorated and refurnished,' Norma stated bluntly.

His smile disappeared. 'What's wrong with it? I like it the way it is. It's how it's always been.'

'It's terrible, Douglas. I want to re-do it completely.' When he didn't reply she went on. 'I have to have some part of the house which is mine, which is *ours*. Otherwise I'm living completely in someone else's home, and that's hardly a good way to start our marriage.'

'Mama will be upset.'

'We can still get our own place, you know. I've never asked about your financial situation, but if you can't stretch to it, I most certainly can.'

'No, I much prefer to stay on in Blairbeth Road. It would be such a waste not to.'

'Then that room has to be gutted. I'll put up with the rest of the house if I have to, but not our bedroom.'

'You really find it that offensive?'

'Yes, I do. And I'm surprised you don't.'

'Perhaps . . . Well I don't know. I have such happy childhood memories of it. Maybe you see it differently to the way I do.'

He fumbled for a cigarette, put one in his mouth, and lit it. 'I'll ask Mama's permission when I get the chance.'

'Don't ask her, Douglas, *tell* her,' Norma replied softly.

He gave her another of his sideways looks. He found her very sexy when she was being determined. 'How about stopping outside the Victoria Infirmary so you can have a gander at it? After all, if I get that job it could be my place of employment for the next thirty odd years.'

'I'd love to see it. That's a terrific idea. And Douglas?'

'Yes?'

'About the bedroom, the first thing to go is that bed. Last night was all right, but I don't want to do it that way every night.'

'I'll see to it.'

'No darling, I will. Leave everything concerning the bedroom to me. And one other thing.'

'What's that?'

'I'm going to get myself a car.'

'But we've got this Lagonda!' he protested.

'When you start work you'll monopolise it all day long. Well, no thank you to that. I'm used to having my own transport, and want to continue to have it.'

'I'll buy you a car then.'

'Can you afford to?'

'I do have some money, but it's a tiny amount compared to what I'll inherit from my parents. Of course once I become a specialist I'll start to earn quite a bit, just as my father's been doing all these years.'

'I'll tell you what, in that case I'll buy this car myself. You can buy the next one for me.'

'Are you sure? I feel that being your husband I should pick up all the bills.'

'That's a very old-fashioned, and honourable, way of looking at marriage. I think the war has changed a lot of those old notions though, don't you? An awful lot of women have got used to being more independent than we were, and we're not about to toss that independence out the window just because the war's over.'

He regarded her quizzically. 'I'm not altogether certain I know what you're talking about?'

'It means I'll pay for the car, and you're not to worry about it. At least, for the time being that's what it means anyway.'

He was still thinking about that, and the best way to approach his mother about their bedroom when the Victoria Infirmary - the Vicky to those who worked there and lived round about - hove into view.

The Victoria Infirmary was an imposing grey edifice situated in the district of Battlefield, the latter named after the Battle of Langside which Mary Queen of Scots fought, and lost. 'It's a big hospital,' Norma commented as they parked opposite. And indeed it was. There was the urgent clang of an ambulance which went charging past them, and into an entranceway that would take it to Casualty.

'Big, busy and a fine hospital to work in,' Douglas said as the rear of the ambulance disappeared.

They had a good look at the Vicky, and were about to drive on when Norma spotted what seemed a familiar face. She frowned, trying to place the man. And then she had it. 'Mr Creighton!' she exclaimed, pointing at Creighton, who'd stopped to talk to another man.

Douglas turned to her in surprise. 'You know him? Creighton's the top neurologist in Glasgow. He's as big in his field as my father is in his. He's also, incidentally, a great friend of my father.'

Creighton was wearing the same black Homburg hat that she remembered so well – if it wasn't the same it was an identical twin. 'We called him to Cubie Street when my ma had encephalitis,' she exclaimed.

'And he cured your mother.'

She could remember it all as if it was only yesterday. Coming home on leave after Lynsey's death to find her mother alone, and suffering from a horrendous headache; asking Alice Henderson from downstairs to ring Doctor Dickie who'd told her Effie needed Creighton. The M&B Creighton had given Effie which it had turned out Effie was allergic to, and everyone thinking Effie was a goner. Then Lynsey appearing to her – she still didn't know whether that had been a dream or not – and the tingling sensation in her hands. Lynsey instructing her to lay her hands on Effie, and Effie's subsequent recovery. A miracle? She still thought of it as such.

Norma roused herself from her reverie. 'No, Creighton didn't cure Ma, I did.'

Douglas's eyebrows shot up his forehead. '*You* did?'

She recounted to him exactly what had happened, while he listened to her tale in obvious astonishment.

'Healing hands?' he said, and shook his head in disbelief.

'It's true, I assure you.'

'And have you had occasion to use this healing ability since?'

'No. That was the one and only time. Then again, I haven't tried to use it.'

'It's eh ...' He coughed. 'Excuse me for saying so but the whole thing sounds a bit far-fetched.'

'Mr Creighton didn't think so. My mother was in a coma and dying; neither he nor the rest of the medical profession could do anything to save her. And yet, within the space of a few seconds, her condition completely changed. She came out of the coma and lived.'

'And Creighton had no rational, medical explanation for what occurred? This turnaround in her condition?'

'None at all. He said my healing ability is probably latent and that Lynsey was a device, or catalyst, used by my subconscious, to bring the ability to the surface.'

Douglas looked over at Rodney Creighton, whom he held in great respect. He was amazed that the dour and humourless Creighton of all people should believe in something as airy fairy as healing hands. Why, that sort of thing was complete stuff and nonsense. There were certain psychosomatic instances where a bit of hocus pocus might do some good, but hardly in the situation that Norma had just described. There had to be a rational explanation for Mrs McKenzie's recovery. Even if Creighton hadn't come up with one there just had to be. As for healing hands and miracles, they belonged strictly to the Bible.

'I can see you're sceptical to say the least,' Norma smiled.

'I'm a man of science. I'd have to actually witness such an event before I believed it. I'm sorry.'

She dismissed the subject as not worth wrangling over. Effie was alive and well, that was all that mattered. 'Let's get on to Cubie Street. I can't wait to see them all again.'

Smiling cynically, Douglas put the car into gear and they continued their journey to Bridgeton.

Lyn opened the door. 'Return of the prodigal, with husband,' Norma said.

Lyn squealed with delight, and threw herself at Norma. The sisters embraced, the pair of them squeezing one another like mad. 'You're back! We've been expecting you at any time, but didn't know exactly when. Oh, let me have a dekko at you!' Lyn said, and thrust her older sister to arms' length. 'You look just terrific.'

'You too Lyn. By the way, this is Douglas.'

'You look terrific as well,' Lyn said, and roared with laughter while Douglas blushed bright red. 'Ma! Da! Eileen! It's Norma!' Lyn yelled into the house.

There was a terrific commotion. Effie was the first to appear, with Brian right behind her and Eileen behind him. They all rushed out onto the landing where Effie fell upon Norma. 'Oh lassie,' she cried, tears streaming down her face.

Norma hugged her ma, then Eileen joined in. Brian stood slightly apart, his expression one of deep love and fierce pride.

Douglas might have been there, but for the moment he only had eyes for Norma, his firstborn.

'Da!'

'Girl,' Brian whispered. She put her arms round him, and her head on his shoulder. 'Welcome home, girl. Welcome home,' he said, a choke in his voice.

Norma dashed away a tear, for she was crying too. 'Ma, Eileen, I'd like you to meet Douglas,' she said, standing up straight again.

'Hello Mrs McKenzie,' Douglas smiled, feeling somewhat selfconscious.

'Och away with you, call me Ma.'

'Then, hello *Ma*.'

Effie beamed. 'That's more like it.' She and Douglas shook. On a sudden impulse he kissed her on the cheek, which pleased her hugely.

'Eileen.' They shook. 'Pleased to meet you, Douglas.'

'Now let's away ben,' Effie said, and shooed eveyone through the door. She went into the kitchen to make some fresh tea, while the rest of them went into the living-room.

Norma was shocked by Eileen's appearance. She was thin as a stick, pasty-faced, her hair dull, lifeless, and scraped back into an untidy bun. This was as different to the vibrant, vital, ever-bubbling wee sister she'd watched grow up as could be. Charlie's death had put Eileen through the mill, and apparently was continuing to do so, right enough.

'So when did you get into Glasgow?' Lyn demanded of Norma. Brian and Douglas were renewing their acquaintance, as Brian ushered Douglas to what was normally his chair, the best chair in the house.

'Last night.'

'Wasn't that a humdinger of a storm? Fair gave me the willies listening to it,' Eileen said.

'It was pretty bad.'

'And the pair of you are staying with your parents, is that right?' Brian asked Douglas.

'In Burnside. It's a big house so there's plenty of space.'

'That's handy.' He reached for his pipe and tobacco tin which were sitting on the mantelpiece. 'And the army sent you back to Blighty some time ago, I understand?'

Douglas glanced over at Norma to see if she wanted him to spill the beans about the SOE, something they'd failed to discuss during their drive there. Her reply was a slight shake of the head; she wasn't sure yet whether she'd tell her family about SOE, but if she did it certainly wasn't going to be here and now.

'I got posted to London for a while. And then I was shunted round the place after that,' Douglas confirmed.

'He came down to Southampton in the car and met me off the ship,' Norma said.

'Am I right in assuming you've been discharged early like me then?' Brian asked Douglas.

'Yes, I was lucky. It's going to take quite some time before everyone's back in civvy street.'

'Da's got some news!' Eileen exclaimed suddenly.

Brian began packing his pipe. 'I was only told on Friday. I'm to be made foreman of Bellahouston Park. It means more money of course.'

'Oh Da, I am pleased!' Norma enthused.

'So's your ma. Me home and promoted into the bargain. She's thrilled to bits.'

'How many men under you?' asked Norma.

'Fifteen, when we have a full complement again.'

'Twelve more than Kilmichael House, and you were head gardener there.'

'Aye, that's a fact,' Brian acknowledged. It filled him with quiet satisfaction to think that was so.

'Now I want to hear about your time in Algeria. Da says Algiers where you were stationed was a marvellous place,' Lyn chipped in.

'We were stationed a little outside Algiers, fifteen miles to the west to be exact. I originally shared a villa at Club des Pins overlooking the beach.'

'Club des Pins! Sounds dead romantic,' Lyn sighed.

'It was, for some,' Norma smiled, glancing at Douglas. He smiled back.

'Did you drive many big wigs?' Eileen queried.

'Lots and lots.'

Effie came bustling in with tea and home-made scones, and for the next half hour Norma and Douglas talked about Algiers, the surrounding countryside, Club des Pins, the field hospital where he'd worked after the Allied landings, but never mentioning the names of Massingham, SOE, or any business connected with either.

'Now enough about us, tell me about this new boyfriend of yours?' Norma demanded of Lyn.

Lyn went all coy. 'His name is Iain and he's an engine fireman with LMS. He and I are like that,' she replied, and held out two crossed fingers.

'So is it really a walk down the aisle job?'

'I'm just waiting for him to pop the question, which I'm hoping he'll be doing any week now.'

'That's tremendous, Lyn. I'm happy as Larry for you.'

'I met him at a party and it was a click right away. I knew the first time he got me up to dance that he was going to be my fate. He lives in the Calton, so we get to see quite a bit of one another.'

'Does that mean he doesn't do all that many long distance runs?'

'He's mainly on the Cathcart Circle, but occasionally does part of the London run, sleeping the night at Crewe and coming up again the following day. But he doesn't do that all that often.'

The women gassed on, till finally Brian, fed up with all the female blether, said to Douglas, 'Do you fancy escaping down the road for a pint?'

Douglas was instantly on his feet. 'That sounds a smashing idea. I'm your man.' A few minutes later the pair of them were going out the front door together, with Effie shouting after them to make sure it was only the one pint mind!

'He's a dish, I'm fair impressed,' Lyn said to Norma the moment the outside door had banged shut. For now Douglas was gone they could talk about him.

'He suits me all right.'

'And he's half French?' But before Norma could reply she said to Eileen, giving Eileen a lecherous wink, 'And you know what they say about Frenchmen?' She shook her right hand as though it was burning hot.

'Don't be crude lass,' Effie admonished.

Norma couldn't help herself. She waved her right hand just as Lyn had done. 'He is! He is!' Which caused them all to burst out laughing, even Effie. Norma went on, 'The mother, Solange, is French, the father, Forsyth, Scots.'

'And what are they like?' Effie queried.

'She's toaty wee with kind of birdlike eyes, and *very very* French. He's pleasant enough, if a bit pompous at times.'

'You don't care for them,' Effie commented shrewdly.

'It's early days to be that definite. Let's just say I'm not as taken with them as I'd hoped,' Norma prevaricated.

Eileen started putting more coal on the fire from the scuttle standing beside it. 'And what about the house? What do you think of that?'

Norma screwed up her face. 'Dracula's castle, that was my first impression. If there had been bats flying round the chimney stacks I wouldn't have been at all surprised.'

'Sounds spooky,' Lyn commented.

'Well, it certainly was from the outside in last night's storm, I can tell you.'

'And inside?' Effie probed.

'Very gloomy. As for our bedroom, I took a complete scunner to it the instant I saw it. It's hateful, though amazingly, Douglas likes it. But he admits that his opinion is probably clouded by happy childhood memories of the place. It's the bedroom he's been in since he was old enough to have a bedroom of his own.' She went on to describe in detail every room in the house.

'Sounds very creepy,' Eileen commented.

'It is a bit. But I'm going to have our bedroom gutted and totally re-done, I'm determined about that. There will be nothing spooky, creepy or antediluvian about it when I'm finished.'

'That's it,' Effie said, nodding her approval, 'you start as you mean to go on.'

'Are the Rosses snobby? Noses in the air?' Lyn queried.

'Very much so, the parents that is. Not Douglas, he isn't in the least.'

Effie sat back in her chair, her lips thinning, her eyes becoming partially hooded. 'So how does this . . . Solange did you cry her?' Norma nodded. 'How do this Solange and Forsyth feel about you then?'

'To be frank Ma, I'm a big disappointment to them. But Douglas is certain they'll get over that before long.'

'Let's just hope they do. Otherwise it may be you've done the wrong thing in agreeing to live in Blairbeth Road.'

Norma sighed. 'That could be the case. But I'll give it a go anyway, if nothing else to show willing.'

'And they've got proper servants?' Eileen asked, fascinated by that idea.

'Oh aye, the full works. A butler called Travers...' Lyn sniggered, imagining herself ordering a fancy butler by the name of Travers around, 'a cook called Mrs Knight who's married to the gardener, and three maids,' Norma replied.

'*Only* three?' mocked Lyn. 'And does one of them wipe your arse for you after you've been to the bog?'

'Lyn!' Effie exclaimed, shocked. Honestly, what was the girl going to come out with next!

While Norma was smiling, thinking her sister's remark quite funny, Eileen stared into space, seeing another time and place. 'I can vaguely remember the servants at Kilmichael House, but only vaguely,' she muttered.

'A fine lot of people they were, I mind them all well,' Effie said, remembering faces and personalities.

'So tell us more about Blairbeth Road?' urged Lyn.

'I'm expected to dress for dinner every night.'

Tongue in cheek, Lyn replied. 'You always dressed for meals here. I've never seen anybody at our table in his or her bare scuddy. Have you Eileen?'

'Oh ha ha!' Norma retorted sarcastically. 'But that brings me to something else. I only have a couple of suitable frocks that I managed to pick up in London when Douglas and I stopped off there.'

'Coupons,' Effie cut in, catching on right away.

'You've hit the nail on the head Ma. I've spent all my coupons and need more, quite a few more actually. Can any of you help?'

'Extra coupons are no bother, if you've got the cash to pay for them that is,' Effie replied.

Eileen said. 'There are several black marketeers round here who'd sell you anything, including their granny, for the right price.'

'Good. I can't give you money right now as I haven't had the chance to go to the bank yet, but I will go tomorrow. When I've been I'll call back here and give you what you think you'll need, then you can send me the coupons on in the post. Would that be all right?'

'You'll have as many coupons as you want,' promised Effie.

'And there's something else. We desperately, and I mean desperately, need a new bed. So I'll need additional coupons for that.'

'Why a new bed?' Eileen queried with a frown.

'It's a bit embarrassing but... eh... the one we're in at the minute squeaks like Billy-O.'

Lyn guffawed, a rich fruity sound that reverberated round the room. 'And you can be overheard "at it". Is that what you're saying?'

Norma, blushing slightly, nodded. 'You'd hardly credit the racket the present bed makes, quite unbelievable. And the thing is that Douglas's parents are just along the passageway from us.'

'Dear me,' muttered Effie. She knew she'd have been mortified to find herself in that situation. She would hardly have dared move all night long, far less anything else. She could only sympathise with Norma and Douglas, and them having been separated for so long too.

'A new bed is a must, and as soon as possible,' Norma went on.

Eileen was gazing into the fire, remembering those four glorious, ecstatic nights she and Charlie had spent in the Adelphi Hotel, and thinking there would never be such nights, and pleasures, for her ever again.

'Right then, additional coupons for a new bed it is pet,' said Effie.

'So if the bed squeaked as badly as you say what did you do?' Lyn asked eagerly, dying to know the answer. Before Effie could tell Lyn off Norma changed the subject, nor would she return to it despite all Lyn's repeated attempts.

'Can I ask you something please Ma'am?' Phyl Casden asked. Phyl was the maid who, in addition to her many other duties, cleaned and tidied Norma and Douglas's bedroom. She was a horsey-faced woman with a drainpipe build of about Norma's age. Norma later found out that Phyl was a year younger than her, which is to say that Phyl was twenty-seven.

'Certainly. What is it?'

'You are the Norma McKenzie who used to give exhibitions at Barrowland aren't you?'

Norma smiled. 'Yes, I am.'

Phyl clapped her hands together. 'I knew it was you, I recognised you right off. A Mr Henderson used to be your partner.'

'That's correct. Michael Henderson, though he was always known to his friends as Midge.'

'You were a terrific couple, a real pair of bobby dazzlers. When the two of you took the floor it was like magic happening. Me and my china of that time used to go whenever we could to watch you.'

'You did?'

'We did indeed Ma'am. We were devoted fans. It broke our hearts when you and Mr Henderson stopped dancing.'

Norma turned away so that Phyl couldn't see her expression. 'Mr Henderson decided to go to America. He believed there to be more opportunities for him there.'

'And were there?'

'So I understand. We never kept in touch.'

Phyl tucked a stray wisp of hair behind an ear. 'You and he were in a class of your own. For my money, and a lot like me, there was no one else in Glasgow could touch you.'

'We won the All Scotland Dance Championship just before we... we retired.'

'I wanted to go and spectate at that, but couldn't because of the flu. I knew you'd win mind, it was a foregone conclusion as far as I was concerned.'

Norma laughed. 'We didn't see it at all like that. There was some very stiff competition. I didn't normally get the jitters when competing, but I did that night. I can remember that quite clearly.'

Phyl's eyes were shining with heroine worship when she said, 'I hope you don't mind me speaking out like this, but I've been dying to ever since you arrived and I recognised who you were.'

'Who I *used* to be,' corrected Norma.

'Well... you know what I mean Ma'am. Now I'd better get on with my work or I'll be in trouble with Mr Travers.' She went to move, then stopped again. 'And Ma'am, whether I'm on duty or not, if there's ever anything you want, or need, anything whatever, you've only got to say. It's my great honour to look after you Ma'am. Great honour.'

'Why thank you Phyl. I appreciate that.'

Norma left Phyl and joined Douglas in the study where he was poring over medical papers and back copies of the Lancet. The conversation with Phyl Casden had cheered her enormously. She felt she had a friend in the house - apart from Douglas that is - which made a big difference. A very big difference. She was humming gaily when she entered the study.

Norma couldn't wait to show Douglas the canary yellow MG she'd bought. It was a real cracker, and a snip at the price. She halted the MG, nipped out of the car and opened the large wrought-iron gates, then drove the MG to the main entrance where she parked it behind the Lagonda. She caressed the wooden rim of the steering wheel. The MG was a beauty, a proper stotter as they would have said in Cubie Street.

She was walking through the reception area, heading for the study where she presumed Douglas would be, when Solange appeared and beckoned to her. She stopped, waiting impatiently as Solange came over, for she was dying to drag Douglas outside and show him the car.

Solange came up and smiled. 'Don't bother Douglas just now *chérie.* He has one of Forsyth's colleagues from the Southern General with him. Mr Riach has kindly agreed to help Douglas catch up on the recent advances in orthopaedics.' The Southern General was another major Glasgow hospital situated in Govan.

'Oh!'

Solange hooked an arm round one of Norma's. 'Best he's left undisturbed for the moment. Don't you think?'

'I eh... yes, I suppose so.'

Solange's smile widened. 'Good.' And with that she drew Norma away from the study towards the small sitting-room which was only a quarter the size of the large sitting-room, and ideal for cosy chit-chats. 'In the meantime you and I can have a little talk together, no?'

'If you like.'

Once in the small sitting room Solange closed the door behind them. 'Mr Riach is an extremely clever man, so Forsyth says, and he knows about such things. However, that aside, Douglas tells me you wish to make changes in your bedroom?'

Norma felt herself tense. She hadn't expected Solange to approach her directly about the bedroom.

'Yes,' she replied.

Solange made a very Gallic gesture. 'I understand perfectly, of course I do. The room is your nest and you wish to feather it according to your own taste.'

'That's it exactly,' Norma replied. Was this going to be easy after all?

'You wish a new carpet perhaps? And curtains?'

'I want the room *completely* re-done,' Norma answered.

'I see.'

'Wallpaper, paint, carpet, curtains, furniture, the lot – top to bottom. And a new bed, the one we have now is . . . well, past its best, and most uncomfortable.'

Solange averted her gaze, she knew precisely what Norma was getting at about the latter. She had heard the squeaking, and very disturbing she'd found it too. 'I'm sure you'll do marvels with the room, a total transformation eh?'

'I hope so.'

Both women were now seated, staring at one another from either side of the fireplace. Solange nodded her head several times, then said slowly, 'All this will be expensive *chérie*.'

'I'll pay myself if need be,' Norma interjected.

Solange held up a hand. 'No need for that. But it strikes me it would be a waste of money should you and Douglas not end up using that room on a permanent basis.' She paused to let that sink in, then went on softly. 'We have to remember we have no guarantee he *will* get the job at the Victoria. I know Forsyth is positive he will, but what is it you British say? Many a slip twixt cup and lip?' Norma experienced a sinking feeling when Solange said that. She knew what was coming next. Solange continued. 'So I would suggest we leave the redecoration until, hopefully, it is confirmed that Douglas has landed that job, or if not that, another in Glasgow. Otherwise it would be a great deal of expense for nothing. Or very little anyway. Don't you agree?'

Reluctantly Norma replied. 'I suppose I do.' It did make perfect sense after all. Her own mother would probably have said the same thing.

'I know it's a myth that you Scots are mean, but why throw money away? That would be silly, eh *chérie*?'

Again reluctantly. 'Waste not want not, my father used to say when we were wee.'

'A man with his head screwed on the right way obviously. So we will leave all further discussion about your bedroom until after we know where we are.'

Norma had been looking forward so much to ripping that damned dreary wallpaper off and getting stuck in, for she planned to do the redecoration herself. 'With the exception of the bed,' she said emphatically. 'Even if we are only here for a short while I still want the new bed. We can always take it with us if we have to go anyway.'

That suited Solange who didn't want to hear any more of that squeaking, subdued though it was. She bowed her head, conceding the point. 'Do you want me to...'

'I already have everything in hand thank you,' Norma cut in.

'Then shall I ring for tea? And you can tell me all about this new car you've bought,' Solange suggested, reaching for the bell-pull that would summon Travers.

It wasn't till later that it dawned on Norma that Solange must have been watching her drive up to the house and must have known that she had been *en route* to tell Douglas about it. Which set her wondering again.

## *Chapter Twelve*

She found Douglas sitting on a bench in the garden staring at the falling snow. His shoulders were hunched, his expression morose and vacant. 'Hello,' she said. Then, louder, when she got no reply. 'Hello husband mine.'

He blinked, came back from wherever he'd been, and gave her a wan smile. 'Hello Norma.'

'You looked as though you were away with the fairies – ?'

'Something like that.'

She sat beside him. 'It's a lovely garden. It must be quite beautiful in the summer.'

'Knight has always done a good job on it. And yes, it is beautiful. I found myself often thinking about it when...' He trailed off, groped for his cigarettes, and lit up. 'I'm glad it's snowing for Christmas. It should always snow for then, though it rarely does.'

'When you were in France, were you going to say?'

He gave her one of his sideways looks. 'Don't you find it odd now that the war's over?'

'You mean anti-climactic?'

'That's it exactly.'

'In a way.'

He wiped snow from his face, leaving wet marks which made it seem as though he'd been crying. His liquid brown eyes were even more liquid than usual. They might have been endless brown pools into which you could sink forever. 'I feel like a bow that had been kept taut for a long, long time and then released. It's a very strange sensation.'

'Are you saying you wish the war was still going on?'

'Good Heavens no! God forbid! I can't tell you how many times I prayed for it to end, with us, the Allies, as victors of course. But now that it is over, and after all that training, and what I went through in the field, and the life and death responsibility that was mine as DR, it now all seems —'

'Anti-climactic,' she interjected.

He drew deeply on his cigarette, then blew smoke at the swirling gusts of snow.

'It's a huge transition for you, and others like you, to make. There's no denying that,' Norma said.

'Time, I suppose that's the answer.'

'I'm sure it is.'

'To readjust, to become... normal again I suppose.'

'Douglas?' He turned to face her. 'You've never told me anything about that very last field assignment you were on. Is that part of all this?' She watched his sallow complexion change to a distinct greenish colour.

'I don't want to talk about that. I can't,' he replied, his voice tight and raw.

'But is that to do with these moods you've been getting? For today's isn't the first you know, although it's the first time I've tried to speak to you while you were in one.'

'I didn't realise they were so obvious.'

'They are to me darling.'

'I'm sorry.'

She placed a hand on his thigh. 'There's no need to apologise, I understand.' She then tapped out.

I understand Gabriel. And I'm here whenever you need me.

'I know.'

He flicked his half-finished cigarette away. It hissed where it hit the snow. 'Speaking about this garden, I always wanted a pond in it when I was a lad.'

'A pond?'

'I adored frogs you see, and toads. I wanted a pond with lilies in it, and frogspawn and toadspawn. And newts, I rather fancied newts as well. They get gorgeous bellies on them you know. I remember seeing one that was salmon-pink underneath, quite spectacular.'

Norma wrinkled her nose. 'I don't like slimies, never have.'

'They're not slimy.'

'Of course they are!'

'People just *think* they are. Same with snakes, people think they're slimy also, whereas in fact it can be like touching parchment.'

'I wouldn't touch a snake for all the tea in China. Yuuch!' she said, the last an exclamation, and shuddered all over.

He laughed. 'They really aren't that bad. Honestly!'

'I have no intention of finding out one way or the other. The moment I see a snake I'm off. You won't see me for dust.'

'What about frogs and toads?'

'Loathsome creatures.'

'And newts?'

She shuddered again.

'You're just like Mama, she hates those animals as well. That's why I never had a pond as a lad, she wouldn't allow it.'

'Well that's one thing your mother and I are in agreement about. Anyway, I'm glad to see I've managed to cheer you up. You actually laughed a second or two ago.'

He put a hand on top of the one of hers that was still on his thigh.

Hello Norma.

She tapped on his thigh.

Hello Gabriel.

Thanks.

I don't like it when you're all mizzy. Makes me depressed for you.

Sorry.

Once you get this job the war will begin to fade into the past.

If I get this particular one.

I have every confidence you will.

His eyes flicked over her shoulder.

Mama's signalling from the conservatory.

Norma glanced round at the rear of the house, and sure enough there was Solange in the conservatory waving at them.

Who's that with her?

You mean the scrumptious redhead with the enormous...

Douglas! You have a fixation about enormous whatsits.

He waved back at Solange, acknowledging that they'd seen her, and were coming in.

You mean tits?

Breasts is the proper word.

Breasts, tits, knockers, bazooms, what's wrong with a bit of honest vulgarity? The redhead is Catherine Stark.

She stopped sending. 'Is it really?'

'I'm only surprised she hasn't been before now.'

Norma put a hand to her hair, and wished now she hadn't come out in the snow. Even though she was wearing a scarf her hair would be bedraggled as the snow had soaked through. And she didn't have any make-up on. Blast! Well she was damned if she was going to meet this Stark female looking like something the cat had dragged in. She'd pay her bedroom a lightning visit to sort herself out before saying hello.

As they rose from where they'd been sitting she told Douglas what she had in mind. 'I'll only be a jiffy and then I'll join you,' she said as they made for a rear door.

In her bedroom she launched into feverish activity. Less than five minutes after leaving Douglas she was entering the small sitting room, where she'd heard voices coming from, to discover Solange, Douglas and Catherine Stark standing round the fireplace holding drinks.

'Darling, I'd like you to meet Catherine, an old friend of mine and the family. Catherine, this is Norma,' Douglas introduced.

She wasn't a redhead, but ginger, Norma thought to herself. Ginger, the colour of marmalade, and cats. The nervousness that had been fluttering in her stomach vanished abruptly when she saw that, rather than Catherine having enormous breasts as Douglas had said, Catherine was flat as a board. That cheered her enormously.

'How do you do, Norma,' Catherine smiled, holding out a limp hand.

She's a bitch, Norma thought. A bitch through and through. And hard with it. 'I'm pleased to meet you at long last. Douglas has told me so much about you,' Norma smiled back.

The hint of a frown clouded Catherine's forehead, and her gaze flicked to Douglas as she and Norma shook hands, Norma making her grip as limp and unenthusiastic as Catherine's.

'We're having gin and tonics, what about you love?' Douglas asked Norma.

'Sounds absolutely marvellous,' she replied. Flat as a board! She felt so good she could have burst out laughing.

* * *

Norma was in her bedroom chatting to Phyl Casden while Phyl dusted, when she heard the commotion. Leaving the bedroom she hurried along the passageway to the top of the main staircase, when Douglas and Solange appeared from the large sitting room, Douglas with an arm round his mother.

'It came just now in the afternoon post,' he cried to Norma, waggling a sheet of paper. 'I've got the job at the Victoria. I'm to be their new junior orthopaedic specialist.' He'd had several interviews, the last of which had been the previous week.

Elation leapt in Norma. This was wonderful news. It was what she and Douglas had both been praying for.

'I start the first of April, April Fool's Day!' he said, and laughed.

Norma was about to run down the stairs and throw herself at him when Solange said, and was it her imagination or was there a hint of triumph in her mother-in-law's voice? 'He came directly to me so that I should be the first to know. Didn't you *mon ange*?'

Norma went very cold inside to hear that. And then annoyance flared. Why had he gone straight to his mother? It was *she*, his wife, whom he should have told first.

'Well, aren't you going to say anything?' Douglas asked.

'Congratulations.'

'We have decided to hold a party to celebrate Douglas's appointment,' Solange announced.

*We!* Norma thought. Solange and Douglas. *Not* Solange, Douglas and Norma, but Solange and Douglas, as if she didn't even exist. Her annoyance deepened.

'Don't you think that's a terrific idea?' Douglas said.

'Terrific,' she echoed, and started down the stairs.

'Forsyth insisted you'd get the post, and of course he was right, as usual. We are both very proud of you my son. Very proud.' Solange disentangled herself from Douglas. 'We will have the party this Saturday, so there is lots to do. I will ring for Travers in the study, and give him his orders. You join me there in half an hour Douglas and we will make up the invitation list together.'

Norma was seething now. There it was again, her being excluded. Why couldn't she have been asked to join in making up the invitation list? Even if she wasn't expected to make any suggestions Solange could have at least, for common courtesy if nothing else, made a pretence of allowing her to be part and parcel of the business.

'We will have music, and wine, and it will be a night to remember!' Solange enthused, her birdlike eyes shining with anticipation. 'Now kiss me again.' He did, on the cheek. 'Half an hour Douglas, half an hour!' And with that Solange swept away to the study.

Douglas went over to where Norma was standing at the foot of the stairs. 'You don't seem all that ecstatic. I was expecting more of a reaction from you.'

Should she say something? Or not? What amazed her was that someone normally so sensitive could also be so bloody insensitive. 'I am ecstatic I assure you. Perhaps I'll have more of a reaction later when the news has had time to sink in.' She gave him a sudden smile. 'Now I can get started on our bedroom.'

'You do approve of the party idea don't you?'

'Of course.'

'You'll enjoy yourself. I'll make sure of that.'

'I just wish...' That you'd come and given me your news first, she wanted to say. But didn't.

'Wish what Norma?'

'Nothing. And don't forget, half an hour in the study. It wouldn't do to keep your mama waiting.'

She left him to go back up the stairs. When she reached the top she glanced down again, and there he was, a puzzled expression on his face, still standing where she'd left him. She gave him a little wave before moving on out of sight.

She'd known the moment she'd clapped eyes on the dress that it was made for her. It was black, plain, and a knockout when on. It had cost her a small fortune, not to mention a number of the coupons that Effie and her sisters had been able to supply her with. But the money had been worth it. The dress was pure quality, and in excellent taste. She couldn't have asked for anything better to wear to Douglas's party.

A glance at the bedside clock told her that the party had been underway for just over twenty minutes now. She'd give it another fifteen before going down. As she hadn't been involved in any of the details of the thing she didn't see why she should be there to greet people, or help get the ball rolling. She would take her own sweet time, and go down when she was ready, and not before.

There was a tap on the door. 'Come in!'

It was Phyl Casden with a flushed face. 'Master Douglas has sent me up to see what's keeping you?'

Norma continued buffing a nail she'd discovered to have a slightly jagged edge. 'Do you think you could get me a dram?'

'Oh aye. And bring it here you mean?'

Norma nodded. 'What's it like below?'

'Murder polis. We told Travers he should lay on extra staff, but he wouldn't have it. Now we're all running around like chickens with their heads cut off.'

'Has Miss Stark arrived yet?'

'She was talking to Master Douglas when I left him.'

'What's she wearing?'

Norma listened to a description of Catherine's dress. It didn't sound a patch on hers. 'See if you can get me that drink then. But forget it if it's too much trouble.'

'I'll do my best.'

'A little bit of Dutch courage. It'll be the first time I've faced the family friends,' Norma explained.

Phyl was no fool. Aware that Norma was working-class by birth, she knew fine well what Norma was referring to. 'I'll make sure you get that dram, a big one too. And Master Douglas?'

'Tell him I'll be there directly.'

When Phyl was gone Norma listened to the music wafting up from downstairs. She wasn't sure whether it was classical or not, but whatever, it was stodgy as old porage. She thought of some of the bands she'd danced to in her time, and smiled at the memory. Now that was her kind of music, the sort to make your feet twitch and the blood race.

When another fifteen minutes were up, and with a large malt whisky under her belt, she rose and hoisted a smile onto her face. Then she went downstairs.

She spied Douglas right off deep in conversation with a most distinguished looking elderly gentleman and a woman whom she took, correctly, to be the gentleman's wife. She saw Solange glance over and give her what Effie would have called a sinker.

Pretending not to have taken the look on board, she made for Douglas.

She sipped at her fourth wine of the evening and told herself this glass was her final one. The last thing she wanted was to get tipsy. She was listening to a Sir Ranulf Fordyce wittle on about farming – apparently he owned a great deal of acreage in Perthshire, and deadly dull he was being about it too. All the man seemed to know about were crop yields, drainage and fertilisers. 'How interesting,' she murmured. Then, a few seconds later. 'How *very* interesting.'

'Why Norma, I've been trying to get to you all evening to compliment you. You look absolutely ravishing.'

Norma turned to Catherine Stark who'd come over with two other women, cronies of Catherine's she supposed. 'Thank you. How kind.'

'I'd like you to meet Henrietta Lockhart.' Norma shook hands with Henrietta. 'And Elsie Buchan.' Norma shook with Elsie.

Henrietta and Elsie were smiling as Norma was, but behind their smiles they were staring at her as if she was something nasty that had crawled out from underneath a stone.

'Do you know Sir Ranulf?' Norma queried.

Catherine gave a tinkling laugh. 'I hope so, he's my Godfather.'

The other two women and Sir Ranulf also laughed, thinking that a fine joke. Norma's smile never wavered.

Catherine and Sir Ranulf chatted briefly, then he excused himself and moved on.

'We were wondering...' Catherine started to say to Norma, and as she did a glance passed between Henrietta and Elsie that set the alarm bells ringing for Norma. Hello, she thought. They're up to something, 'if you'd care to join us this Wednesday for a ride? Pater owns stables at Eaglesham and the three of us meet up there every Wednesday morning at about ten and go for a canter. Would that appeal?'

Norma had another sip of wine while she considered the invitation. 'You *can* ride I take it?' Elsie asked, a sneer in her voice.

So that was it. They presume that because I'm working-class

I've never been on a horse, Norma thought. This was a little ploy to make her feel inferior, to underline that she was an outsider and not 'one of the chaps'. She'd been dead right in placing Catherine as a bitch. The other two clearly were as well. 'Sounds a jolly good suggestion. I'd love to come along,' she replied.

Three faces fell fractionally. 'Oh marvellous!' Catherine answered with difficulty.

'Ten o'clock on Wednesday? I'll be there. Douglas can give me the precise directions.'

'We'll look forward to that then,' Catherine said.

'So will I.'

At which point Douglas joined them with a Mrs Hills-Carmichael whom he wanted Norma to meet, and the three harpies moved off. One up for the home team! Norma congratulated herself.

'I thought it went very well. Didn't you?' Douglas said as he struggled into the bottom of his striped flannelette pyjamas.

Norma looked at him from their bed where she was already tucked up. 'I felt like a goldfish in a bowl. All eyes on me.'

'Well, people were bound to be curious. You were completely new to them after all.'

'I got the distinct impression they were waiting for me to hawk on the floor and pick my nose.'

He laughed. 'You're exaggerating.'

'Like hell I am!'

He slowly tied his waist cord. 'You were a success. They liked you.'

'Who said?'

'No one had to. I could tell.' He came over to sit beside her. 'I was proud of you tonight Mrs Ross.'

'Were you really?'

'Very much so.'

'No regrets?'

He frowned. 'About what?'

'Marrying me.'

'Not in a million years. Nor will I ever have any.'

She sighed. 'My da warned me that night at the St George

Hotel that I'd have to fit in at your and your friends' level. Tonight was my first big test.'

'And you passed with flying colours. I promise you.' He pulled the bedclothes back a bit and began stroking her. A gorgeous sensation that made her feel all warm and watery inside. 'I hear Catherine asked you out riding.'

'On Wednesday, yes.'

'Well there you are then. Even she's accepted you.'

He'd missed the whole point of Catherine's invitation, she thought to herself. He didn't realise it had been made out of malice to put her in her place, and to give Catherine and the other two a giggle at her expense. Which made her wonder about his judgement where the other guests were concerned. She squirmed as a hand came under the clothes to seek out, and find, her softest part. 'Switch the light off,' she whispered.

What they did next made her forget all about the party and watching eyes. For the time being, that was.

The hunter went over the dry stane dyke to land with a pile-driving crunch that sent an instant wave of nausea shooting through Norma. As the hunter galloped on, cold sweat broke on her forehead, and wave after wave of even more intense nausea followed the original.

Norma gritted her teeth, and clung on tightly. The sensible thing to do of course was rein in till she was feeling better again, but she was damned if she was going to do that.

Henrietta Lockhart came alongside on a grey. 'Smashing ride eh?' Norma grinned. Her reply was a curt nod, and then Henrietta's mount spurted ahead.

There were five of them. Herself, Catherine, Henrietta, Elsie and a female called Vivienne Gregory who seemed, on their short acquaintance anyway, to be a far nicer person than Catherine and co.

A hedge loomed ahead, this one taller than the dry stane dyke. A taste of bile came into her mouth as the hunter left the ground, a taste that became reality when the animal landed on the other side.

Norma groaned, and forced herself to swallow the foulness. What was the matter with her? She'd jumped on horses many times before and it had never previously had this effect. Then the world started to spin.

She wouldn't come off, *she wouldn't!* She refused to give the harpies that satisfaction. It would have made their day to see her go sprawling, and no doubt their month should she be unfortunate enough to break a bone or two. Grimly she hung on, and prayed that the ride would soon be over and they'd be back at the stables.

It began to rain, which was a godsend. The rain splashed against her face, helping to steady her and even banish the nausea somewhat.

The onset of flu? Norma wondered. For the moment she couldn't think of any other reason for her feeling as she did. But how extraordinary for it to hit her the way it had. Right out of the blue in the middle of a ride.

They were trotting back into the stables when the full force of the nausea returned with a vengeance. And once more the world started to spin.

Gratefully, and with her stomach heaving, Norma slid from the saddle. She patted the neck of the hunter before it was led away by a stablelad.

'You're not a bad rider,' Catherine admitted reluctantly to Norma.

Norma desperately wanted away from there as quickly as possible. 'I thoroughly enjoyed myself,' she lied. 'I hope you'll ask me again sometime.'

'We usually have a noggin of sherry before calling it a day,' Catherine said.

'It wouldn't be the first time we've all ended up legless after a ride out,' Vivienne Gregory smiled.

'Not today thanks.' Norma glanced at her wristwatch. 'I have an important appointment in town which I really must fly to keep.'

Henrietta and Elsie brightened on hearing that, something Norma, despite her condition, didn't fail to notice. She'd disliked those two before, but she disliked them even more now.

Norma took her leave of them all. How she managed to keep up the bright and cheerful presence she didn't know. 'Must dash, and thanks again!' she said, and sprinted for the MG parked close by.

She got in the car, slammed the door, and fumbled for the key. As the engine roared into life she gagged. She had to get out of here, and fast! Her rear wheels spun, and then the MG was tearing towards the main road leading back to Glasgow.

As soon as she was out of sight of the stables she wheeled the MG onto the grass verge, and shot from the car. Opening her mouth she let it all come out, a fountain of hideous vomit that spattered in all directions when it landed. Again and again, till finally her stomach was empty. But it wasn't finished yet, she had to endure several convulsive dry retches before at long last it was over, and the world stopped spinning. Using a clean handkerchief she wiped the sheen of perspiration from her face and throat.

'Christ!' she croaked, what a nightmare. At least she hadn't been ill in front of the others. She would have hated that. Nor had she come off the hunter, the humiliation of which would have been absolutely awful.

The beginnings of flu she told herself as she climbed back into the MG. Then she had another thought, perhaps she'd eaten something that had disagreed with her? It could be either.

Halfway home she felt top notch again, quite her usual self. Which made her think it must have been something 'off' she had eaten rather than flu.

And then she had a sudden idea. Why not? For old times' sake? When she came to the turn-off for Burnside she passed on, continuing towards the town itself.

She parked across the road from Barrowland and stared at it. The outside was in a fairly rundown state, but that was only to be expected. With materials and labour in such short supply during the war there were very few buildings that hadn't suffered as a result.

It was a long shot that she'd find Joe Dunlop there, for although middle-aged he was bound to have been conscripted at some point in the war, but it was just possible that he might now be back at his old job again. He wasn't. There was a manageress in charge of the dancehall who knew nothing of Joe's present situation, all she could do was confirm that Joe had indeed gone into the Forces, though which branch she couldn't say.

Before leaving Barrowland, with the manageress's permission, Norma went onto the dancefloor and gazed about.

How long ago it all seemed. With a jolt she realised it was nine years since Midge had walked out on her. Nine years! A lifetime. An eternity. Nine years during which there had been a world war, and she'd got married.

She recalled burning the wedding dress the night Don Caprice had come to break the news to her in Greenvale Street that Midge and Zelda had run off together. And burning the red shoes she'd been wearing the first ever time she and Midge had danced together.

There were tears in her eyes, which she wiped away with the side of a hand. Old times, good times, never-to-be-forgotten times. Who would ever have thought she'd end up in Burnside married to a junior orthopaedic specialist who was half French and an ex-spy? Life was strange right enough. Who could foresee the quarter of it? Certainly not her.

On leaving Barrowland she pointed the MG in the direction of the Gorbals, probably Glasgow's best-known, and certainly its most notorious, district. It was also where Silver's was located. As she'd gone to Barrowland with the vague hope of finding Joe Dunlop there, so too would she go to Silver's in the hope of finding Finlay Rankine.

On entering the studios she was confronted by a smiling woman at a reception desk. 'Can I help you?' the woman asked.

Norma was about to open her mouth to reply when a well-kent male voice exclaimed. 'I don't believe it! Is it really you Norma?'

She whirled to discover Finlay staring at her, out of one eye. The other had a black patch across it, the patch part of, and held in place by, a black band that circled his head. With a squeal she ran to him, and he wrapped her in his arms. 'Oh Finlay, it's so good to see you again!' she husked.

'You look tremendous Norma. Obviously being a FANY agreed with you.'

'It did. But you... the...?'

'Eye?' he finished for her.

She nodded.

'Flak over Germany. But listen, I'm expecting a client at any moment for a half hour's lesson. Can you wait, or come back?'

'I'll wait.'

'Do you remember the "greasy spoon" round the corner? I'll meet you there as soon as I can.'

She minded the café he was referring to well. She'd gone there often when working at Silver's after leaving Barrowland. 'I'll be there,' she replied.

A fat woman bustled into the studios, Finlay's client. 'Half an hour,' he whispered releasing Norma. Then, with a beaming smile. 'Why hello Mrs Clark, prompt as usual.'

Thirty-two minutes later by Norma's watch Finlay came striding into the café. He ordered a tea for himself, and another for Norma, then joined her at a wooden table. He took her right hand in his, and squeezed it.

'You look like a buccaneer with that patch on,' she said.

He treated her to one of his crocodile smiles. 'Does that mean at long last you fancy me?'

She held up her left hand and waggled her wedding ring at him. 'Too late for that Finlay. I'm a married woman.'

He exclaimed in delight. 'That's smashing. Who is the lucky blighter?'

She didn't tell him anything about SOE, completely missing out that part of the story, but explained about being blown up in Risinghill Street, and then meeting up again with the doctor who'd treated her at the Royal Free Hospital in Algiers where they'd fallen in love and wed.

'And you're happy?'

She nodded. 'Yes.'

'Then I'm happy for *you*.'

'When did you get back to Glasgow?' she queried.

'Early February. I'd managed to keep my flat on all the while, so there was no problem there. I reported in to Silver's who said I could start right away, which I did. It seems the ladies had been missing me.' He and Norma both laughed at the latter.

'And what's this about flak over Germany?'

'Shortly after you went down south to join the FANY I decided, what the hell! it was only a matter of time anyway, so why not volunteer rather than wait to be conscripted. So I went into the RAF where they, in their wisdom, made me a navigator. I flew Wellingtons for a while, then Lancasters. I lost the eye over Hamburg when the Lanc I was in took a direct flak hit. We were very lucky to get the Lanc home again, but we did. And that was the end of my flying war. It was hospital for a few months, a spot of leave, and then a desk.' He took a deep breath. 'And that's it.'

'You're still not married I take it?'

'No, there have been lots of ladies since I last saw you of course...' 'Of course,' she interjected, which made him smile before continuing. 'But nothing that was even remotely serious.'

He's changed, she thought. He wasn't the same Finlay Rankine she remembered. There was a sadness in him there hadn't been before. And... she groped for it. Yes, despite the old bravado, a sense of humility that was new. But then the war had changed an awful lot of people. Herself too no doubt.

They chatted at length about the pre-war days. The first time she'd come to Silver's inquiring about lessons, his propositioning her – they had a good giggle over that – all the way through to when she'd worked at Silver's before going south to join the FANY. It was a great chin-wag which they both thoroughly enjoyed.

Finally Finlay reluctantly said. 'I hate to break this reunion up but I have to get back for another booking.'

'We must keep in touch. See each other regularly?' she suggested.

'There's nothing I'd like better.'

She took a small notepad from her handbag and wrote out her address and telephone number, which she handed to Finlay. He wrote down his details for her.

'And I'd like you to meet my husband.'

He stared into those marvellous grey-green eyes, wondering about Midge. She hadn't mentioned Midge during their chat, so neither had he. 'Does your husband dance?'

'When it comes to that his middle name's Stiffie the goalkeeper.'

Finlay laughed. 'And do you still?'

'If you mean properly, how can I with a husband like that?'

'First chance we get, a turn round the floor eh?'

'First chance we get,' she promised.

Outside the café she kissed him lightly, and affectionately, on the cheek. 'Goodbye for now buccaneer.'

'Goodbye for now Norma.'

It pleased her that she'd made contact with Finlay Rankine again. It pleased her enormously. He was a true friend.

'Douglas?'

He mumbled something indistinct in reply, and pulled his share of the bedclothes up higher.

'Douglas, I'm going to be sick.' She'd woken a moment or two before to find herself in the same state she'd been in the previous Wednesday when she'd gone riding at Eaglesham. It was now the very early hours of the following Monday. 'Douglas please ...' She clamped a hand over her mouth.

'What is it?' he asked groggily, having finally come awake.

'Sick... I'm going to be sick,' she said, her words muffled from behind her hand.

He snapped on the bedside light, to blink at her. On registering the sheen of perspiration covering her face and neck he came wide awake. 'Can you make it to the toilet if I help you?' he queried.

She wasn't sure, but nodded anyway. He swiftly got out of bed, came round to her side, and assisted her to her feet. There was no time for the niceties of slippers and dressing-gowns – he just hurried her from the room, supporting her all the way to the toilet. There she sank to her knees before the WC, and spewed into it.

When she was finished he wiped her face and neck with a towel, gave her a glass of water to rinse out her mouth with, flushed the WC and took her back to bed. She explained how this was the second time it had happened to her.

He took her temperature and pulse, and made some checks. Well it certainly wasn't flu, nor was it food poisoning. He was positive about the former, fairly certain about the latter. 'Pull up your nightie,' he instructed her.

'How far?'

'To your breasts.'

'But it's cold in here,' she protested.

He rubbed his hands to warm them. 'I'll be as quick as I can.'

'Yes *doctor*,' she replied, taking the mickey.

He felt her tummy. 'Aren't you putting on weight?'

'Just a little,' she conceded. 'Well, I'm not working anymore, that's bound to make a difference. And your parents do keep an excellent table.'

His hands moved upwards. 'Is that tender?'

'Yes,' she answered, surprised. Wondering why she hadn't noted that herself.

'When was your last period?'

'You should know. You're my husband after all,' she teased.

He smiled at her. 'I suppose like most men I only notice when it happens. I don't put a date on it, or even know what time of the month it comes.'

'I'm due one shortly. Next few days or so.'

'You had a last period then?'

'Yes,' she said, again surprised. And then the penny dropped. 'Do you think I'm pregnant?'

'Was your last period normal?'

'No it wasn't,' she replied slowly, thinking back. 'It was a lot lighter than usual. A great deal lighter actually, only traces.'

'And the period before that?'

She frowned. 'You know that too was a bit odd. Not as light as the last one, but definitely on the light side.'

He tugged her nightgown back into place, then covered her with the bedclothes. 'I'd say you're in the pudding club!' he announced, and took a deep breath.

That rocked her. 'You're not a hundred percent sure though?'

'All the signs point that way. If you'd like we can go into the Vicky tomorrow and have some tests done?'

'I . . . Yes, let's have the tests done. Oh Douglas, if it's true are you pleased?'

'Pleased! If it's true I'll be walking on air. And how do you feel about it?'

'A baby, a ba-ba,' she whispered, her face lighting up in a huge grin. 'That would be marvellous. Absolutely marvellous.'

'Absolutely,' he agreed.

Flu and food poisoning! she thought. How dense could she be. The real reason should have been obvious to her.

He got back into bed. 'We'll drive to the Vicky first thing after breakfast.'

'Right.' Then, almost coyly. 'What would you prefer, a boy or a girl?'

'I honestly don't care. Just as long as it's healthy.'

'That's how I feel too. Oh Douglas, I'm so excited.'

'That's fine. But let's just not count our chickens until it's confirmed eh?'

Norma sniggered. 'It's not a chicken I'll be expecting to produce.'

'Idiot.'

It took them ages to get to sleep again, but when they finally did so they did holding hands. And with both of them smiling.

'A baby!' Solange cried, clapping her hands together in glee. She and Forsyth were in the small sitting-room at Douglas and Norma's request. Douglas had just broken the news – tests conducted at the Victoria Infirmary during the day had confirmed that Norma was indeed pregnant.

Forsyth was pleased as Punch, this was tremendous news. 'We must have champagne, nothing less, to celebrate,' he said, and crossed to the bell pull to summon Travers.

Solange took Douglas in her arms, and hugged him. She said something in French to him which he replied to in the same language.

Still embracing Douglas, Solange looked over at Norma. 'Congratulations *chérie*.'

'Thank you.' There wasn't going to be a hug for her, Norma thought. And she was right. She did get a peck on the cheek from Forsyth however, who'd gone quite puce from a combination of excitement and elation.

When Douglas told his parents about Norma being sick after riding with Catherine they both immediately showed concern. 'Nothing strenuous from here on in. Mustn't take risks,' Forsyth counselled.

'I wouldn't have gone riding if I'd *known* I was pregnant,' Norma replied.

'Of course not. Your head's screwed on the right way.'

'And she was sick early this morning. I was surprised you didn't hear us up,' Douglas said.

'I suffered a great deal of sickness with you Douglas,' Solange told him, and pulled a face. 'It was awful.' To Norma she added. 'You have my sympathy, *chérie*.'

Travers appeared, and Forsyth instructed him to go to the

cellar and pick out the best bottle of champagne. When he explained why they were celebrating, the butler was effusive in his congratulations to Douglas and Norma.

'It'll be a boy, I feel sure of it,' Solange said directly. Travers had left the room.

'You can't possibly know that!' Douglas laughed.

'I feel it here, in my water.'

Nonsense, Norma wanted to say. But restrained herself.

'Do you have a name in mind?' Solange inquired of Douglas.

'Give us a chance Mama.'

'Then we shall have to start thinking of a suitable one right away.' She really was convinced it was going to be a boy.

*We*! Norma thought. If Solange believed she was going to choose the baby's name she was wrong.

Solange turned to Norma. 'What a pity about your bedroom though.'

Norma frowned. 'I'm not following you?'

'You can't redecorate it now, not when you're pregnant. That would be dangerous. Don't you agree Forsyth?'

'Quite out of the question.'

'We could get decorators in,' Douglas suggested.

'But Norma has insisted she does your bedroom herself, to give it her personal touch. Such a good idea I think. So decorators are totally unacceptable to her. It just means she'll have to wait a while longer, have a little more patience, before setting to work and doing what she wants. Till after the baby is born,' Solange said silkily.

Norma was flabbergasted by this turn of events. She was, as the saying went, hoisted by her own petard. For she had, it was quite true, made a song and dance about doing the bedroom herself. Something she'd been so looking forward to, and for which, since Douglas had landed the job at Victoria, she'd begun gathering materials.

'I'm sure I'd be all right,' she said slowly.

'No no! You mustn't.' Solange paused, then added dramatically, 'What if you lost the baby *chérie*? How would you live with yourself?'

Norma felt the colour drain from her face. Such a thing would be... Well, it was just unthinkable.

'It's not for long really. Then, when the baby is here, you can roll up your sleeves and get down to it,' Solange smiled.

You cow! Norma thought, looking straight into those birdlike eyes. And when the baby was born it would be something else, another excuse for postponement. And another excuse after that, and another, till in the end hopefully, from Solange's point of view, the whole matter would just fade away and be forgotten. And then it dawned on Norma that there was more to it than that. What this was really all about was a battle of wills, Solange's against hers, as to who was going to be the dominant female in the house. And further still, yet another dimension, could it be that Solange was also trying to drive a wedge between her and Douglas? 'Even if I can't redecorate I can refurnish in the meantime.'

'A mistake. A bad mistake,' Solange said emphatically.

'How so?'

'To get it absolutely right these things must be done in sequence. First the decorating, then the carpet and curtains, then the furnishings. That way you can be certain everything fits as a piece, an ensemble. Do it any other way and you risk catastrophe. In fact you are courting it.'

What Solange said made sense, that was the damnable thing! Norma raged inwardly.

'I agree,' Forsyth nodded.

Norma forced a smile, and by God it was an effort, onto her face. 'What do you think Douglas?'

'What Mama says is logical.'

He rarely ever disagreed with his mother, Norma thought. He may have done all manner of fantastically brave deeds in France and Corsica, but at home he was a mummy's boy. Well Solange might have dominated Douglas long since, but she wasn't going to dominate her. Pigs would fly first! 'I've changed my mind,' she declared softly, and watched triumph creep over Solange's face.

'Good,' Forsyth agreed.

'You're all quite right. I mustn't try and decorate myself. It would be foolhardy.'

'Utterly,' Forsyth agreed.

'Nor will I call the professionals in. As I've said emphatically all along when the room is done I want it to have that personal touch.'

'After the baby is born,' Solange repeated.
'No, *before*.'
Solange's face froze. 'I thought you just said...'
'That I wouldn't do it myself? That's so. Nor would I think to ask Douglas when he's just about to start a new job. My father will do it in the evenings and at weekends, and I will supervise every single brushstroke he makes.'
'How clever of you love,' Douglas said to her, his expression one of admiration.
'But — '
'No buts Solange,' Norma interjected. 'That's how it's going to be.'
'Are you sure your father will agree?' Forysyth queried.
'He will. No doubt about it. Once he understands how important this is to me he'll be here like a shot. Wild horses wouldn't keep him away.'
There was a tap on the door, and Travers re-entered the room carrying the champagne and glasses. 'Would you care to pop the cork Master Douglas?' he asked.
Douglas laughed. 'Precisely what I should do. Thank you for suggesting it Travers.'
'Not at all sir.'
As Douglas was squeezing the cork with his thumbs Norma and Solange were staring at one another. Both of them were very still, both faces now completely expressionless.
The cork gave a most satisfactory bang and went shooting off across the room. She'd drive over and speak to Brian that night Norma decided. She'd have him start work on the bedroom just as soon as it was possible.
When the glasses were filled they all toasted the baby.

Norma's eyes fluttered, then opened as she came out of a deep sleep. She'd been having an afternoon nap, as she had every afternoon at Douglas's insistence. It was now May and she was six months gone. It wasn't proving to be a particularly easy pregnancy. She was suffering terribly from recurring bouts of sickness, swollen legs and chronic indigestion, and was never sure which distressed her the most. They were all bad, but in different ways.
She glanced about the bedroom, and smiled. Her da had

done a wonderful job on it. A better job than she would have done herself. Everything in the room was just perfect, exactly as she had envisioned it.

The walls, ceiling and woodwork were cream. There was a new fitted cornflower blue carpet and rust-coloured curtains that complemented the carpet. She'd been extremely lucky about the wardrobe, tallboy and dressing table - Brian knew someone who worked on the Docks and the furniture had come through him. It was Canadian-made, and very modern in design. Norma loved it the moment she'd seen it. And the lovely thing was she hadn't had to pay all that much over the odds for it either.

She glanced at the bedside clock. She'd be up in a minute or two and start getting ready to go to Cubie Street. As Douglas was working late - when wasn't he? - she'd agreed to have tea there and discuss the preparations for Lyn's forthcoming wedding.

Iain McElheney had proposed to Lyn in March, and told her he didn't fancy a long engagement. And so they were to be married next month, in June. Lyn had particularly chosen June because she thought being a June bride sounded ever so romantic.

Norma had a sudden idea which made her smile. The last time she'd been over to talk about the preparations Lyn had been worried about a lack of single men going to the reception. Nearly all Iain's pals worked on the railway with him, and were already married, the latter a result of being in a reserved occupation during the war - and they'd all been available when other men were away in the Armed Forces. Iain hadn't fallen till he'd met Lyn, and then, according to Lyn anyway, he'd fallen head over heels. Something Norma could well understand considering how gorgeous 'podge' was. If there was still a shortage of single chaps she'd suggest Finlay Rankine. An old smoothie like him was bound to be a huge success with the lassies going on their tod. Of which there were quite a number. Lyn's workmates from the SCWS in Morrison Street where Lyn was back working.

Norma got up, dressed, and freshened her make-up. On leaving the bedroom she ran into one of the maids and asked where Solange was. She wanted to say goodbye as she always did when going out for a while. She was informed that Solange was in the nearest bedroom to the stairs on the floor above.

Norma went upstairs wondering what her mother-in-law was up to. None of the bedrooms on the next floor were in use. She found Solange with Knight the gardener, who also doubled as handyman, Knight in the process of reassembling a baby's cot, the cot evidently having been dismantled in the past. 'What on earth's going on?' she queried.

Solange's face was glistening from exertion. 'I'm having Knight bring a lot of the stuff down from the loft where it's been stored these past years. What do you think of this crib, isn't it beautiful?'

The crib was wicker, and if not exactly beautiful certainly very pretty. At least it would be when washed down – it was covered in dust and even had a spider's web in it – and made up. 'Yes it is,' she replied diplomatically.

'I had it sent over from Paris you know.'

That tickled Norma's fancy. 'You mean it was Douglas's?'

'Everything Knight is bringing down was his. I kept it all.'

Besides the cot and crib there was a multitude of toys, baby clothes – including a christening gown – games, rattles and other noisemakers, and the *pièce de résistance*, an ancient pram.

'This room gets plenty of sun. It will make an excellent nursery,' Solange smiled.

Norma took a deep breath, Solange was at it again. The damned woman would never let up. 'For whom?' she asked coldly.

'The baby.'

'You mean my baby?'

'Yours and Douglas's, *oui*.'

Norma glanced again at the crib and partially reassembled cot. 'Are you suggesting our baby sleep here?'

'Of course.'

'But I don't want the baby to sleep in a bedroom other than ours, at least not for quite some time. To begin with I intend the baby to sleep in our bedroom where I can hear and see it.'

Solange shook her head. 'I can assure you that is entirely the wrong thing to do. Once the baby is used to sleeping in your room you will have the devil's own job breaking him of the habit.'

Norma was really irritated now. 'He, as you insist on calling the baby, might be a she. And he or she will sleep in our room for the first six to nine months of his or her life. I am quite determined about that.'

Knight continued reassembling the cot, pretending to be totally engrossed in what he was doing. His face might have been impassive, but inwardly he was laughing, enjoying every moment of this, and couldn't wait to tell Mrs Knight. It was time someone stood up to Her High and Mightiness as he and Mrs Knight called Solange. Good for the young one.

'You'll spoil the child,' Solange said, an edge to her voice.

'I disagree with you.'

'I'll speak to Douglas about this.'

Norma's eyes slitted factionally. Her stomach was afire with indigestion that this contretemps had brought on. 'You may be Douglas's mother, but I'm his wife.'

'He'll listen to reason.'

'He'll listen to *me*.'

Solange glared at Norma. 'The baby should have a nursery. We con . . . con . . .' She snapped her fingers in annoyance as for once her usually excellent English failed her.

'Converted?' Norma offered.

'We converted a bedroom to one for Douglas when he was a baby.'

'What you did then was your affair. What I do now is mine. When I consider the time to be right, between six and nine months as I have already said, I will put the baby in a bedroom of its own. But *not* one on another floor. I don't just consider that dangerous, I consider it downright cruel.'

Solange muttered something in French which of course Norma didn't understand. And probably just as well too, Norma thought.

'You don't wish a nursery then?' Solange said, reverting to English.

'A room for the baby to play in would be nice. If this is to be the nursery then that's all the baby will be doing in it. There is however the third bedroom in our passageway, the one separating yours and ours. That would be better still don't you think? And certainly I would be happy for the baby to sleep there when the time comes.'

Solange fumed silently.

Norma went on slowly, her voice now not only cold but filled with steel. 'And you're not hoisting that pram on me either. It's so old and decrepit Methuselah might have used it.'

Knight had to fight to keep his face impassive. Oh he was fair loving this. It was a proper treat.

'What about the crib and cot?'

Norma looked over at them again, considering them. 'The crib will be fine after a good scrub, the cot also providing it has a new coat of paint. Can you attend to those things Knight?'

'Yes Ma'am.'

It was on the tip of Solange's tongue to say she gave the orders in this house, but she bit back the rebuke. 'And the rest of the stuff?'

'I'm going out now and won't be back in till later. I'll go through it tomorrow and see what I can use.' She and Solange stared at one another, and you could have cut the atmosphere between them.

'Let me know what you decide about the bedroom downstairs, the one between yours and ours,' Norma said, and left the room.

She was just starting down the stairs when she heard a crash, which brought a wicked smile to her lips. Unless she was very much mistaken Solange had just thrown something in fury. She liked the idea of that, she liked it very much indeed.

She turned the MG into Cubie Street to come to a halt before her parents' close. She was struggling out of the car, her damned bump made manoeuvres like this one so difficult! when a well-dressed man appeared in the close mouth. She had a quick look at him, registering that his face was vaguely familiar, then continued with her struggle. At last puffing and peching, she made it to her feet. She slammed the car door and locked it.

The man was still in the closemouth, and staring at her. With an actual physical jolt, as if she'd been punched hard right between the breasts, she realised who he was.

'Hi!' said Midge.

He'd aged, but that was only to be expected. It was nine years after all. His face was thinner, and there were lines where none had been previously. His hair was blonder than she remembered, but his eyes were the same. Gorgeous blue peepers, Lyn had once called them, with a brightness to them that could dazzle and bewitch a girl where she stood. As indeed they'd once dazzled and bewitched her. Staring back at him she noted, amongst other things, that his neck was stained with embarrassment. Should she speak to him, or ignore him? Just walk on past. 'Hi yourself,' she replied after a good dozen seconds had ticked by. The Yankee form of address wasn't totally alien to her, she'd used it before – and been addressed by it countless times – at Massingham where, particularly towards the end of the war, there had been many Americans.

'I expected, hoped, I'd run into you. But hardly thought it would happen so soon.'

'Why, when did you arrive back?'

He attempted a smile that came out all sort of twisted and lopsided. 'I got into the house just two hours ago, would you believe.'

She didn't reply to that, just continued staring at him. As she did the stain on his neck began creeping upwards into his face. Her own face was devoid of expression, but at the same time hard.

'I'm away for a walk about. A stroll down memory lane you could say.'

'Oh aye?'

'You're looking good.'

'Am I? I don't feel it.

He coughed nervously. 'I heard from my folks that you were married, but not that you were . . .' He trailed off.

'Pregnant?' she finished for him as he seemed reluctant, or unable, to say the word.

'Congratulations. When are you due?'

'End of August.'

He nodded.

Her legs were murdering her, and her indigestion had started up again. Suddenly she felt fat and ugly and . . . just plain bloody awful. 'See you then,' she said, and made to brush by him, only to be stopped when he grasped her by the upper arm.

'We have to talk Norma.'

'I thought that's what we've just been doing?'

'You know what I mean.'

'You mean about you jilting me the day before our wedding to go hightailing off with someone else?'

The stain shot right up to the roots of his scalp. 'About everything,' he mumbled.

Some of the rage and anguish she'd felt that night in Greenvale Street when she'd burned her wedding dress and the red shoes surged again within her. What she did next she did without thinking. Her right hand flashed through the air to crack against his cheek. With an exclamation of surprise and pain Midge went reeling backwards and went crashing into the closemouth wall.

He shook his head, for he was literally seeing stars. That had been some smack, powerful enough to have come from a man. 'I can't deny I deserved that.'

She fought down her emotions, bringing them under control. 'And more.'

The stars faded into oblivion. When he looked again at Norma there were two of her. But already the double vision was readjusting, her twin images coming together. 'We should still talk.'

She was about to tell him to stick his talk up his bahookie, then abruptly changed her mind. Why not? He might think she was carrying a torch for him if she avoided a proper, arranged meeting, and that was the last thing she wanted. What she did want was him to know how happy and fulfilled she was. 'How long are you home for?'

'A fortnight.'

She needed a breathing space to prepare herself, physically as well as mentally. 'I'll meet you the day after tomorrow if that's suitable?'

'Where?'

She frowned as she thought about that. 'There's a City Bakeries tearoom this end of Sauchiehall Street. I'll see you there at four in the afternoon?'

'Four it is,' he agreed.

Leaving him still clutching his face she went further into the close, and up the stairs.

Norma was in the small living-room enjoying the whisky and water that Phyl Casden had fetched for her when Douglas came in. A glance at her wristwatch told her it was almost 10 pm.

'I'm bushed,' he said. He came over and kissed her lightly on the lips. 'May I?' he asked, indicating her drink.

'Help yourself.'

He reminded her of the first time she'd met him in the Royal Free Hospital, done in, almost out on his feet. She watched him drain her glass, then give a deep sigh of satisfaction.

'I was needing that. I'll ring for two more.'

'You're working far too hard Douglas, you really must ease off a little,' she said as he tugged the bell pull.

He ran a weary hand across his face. 'I've explained to you, I have to make my name, a reputation. I've got to get *established.*'

'Are you certain that's what it is?'

He glanced at her, his expression one of puzzlement. 'What do you mean?'

She opened her mouth to tell him, then decided not to. 'If you're not careful you'll end up as one of the patients in the Victoria rather than one of the doctors.'

He made a dismissive gesture, which annoyed her. 'Don't exaggerate.'

'I'm not.'

He crossed to the fireplace, gazed moodily into the fire burning there, and drummed his fingers on the mantelpiece. 'I met Mama on the way in. She mentioned about the pair of you having a real old ding-dong.'

She would have bet money that hadn't been an accidental meeting. Solange would have been waiting in ambush. 'It wasn't my fault.'

He gave her one of his sideways glances. 'Mama was only trying to help. I wish the pair of you would get along better.'

There was a tap on the door, and Travers came in. Norma stared grimly at Douglas as he ordered their drinks. She had no doubt that if she and he had met in Glasgow they would never have got married, Solange would have made sure of that. Solange had him wrapped round her little finger, as she had Forsyth.

'The baby is going to sleep in our room until I decide otherwise,' she stated firmly after Travers had gone again.

'I'm sorry, but I can't help thinking Mama's right about this.

That you're creating a rod for your own back. For both our backs.'

'Well of course I expect you to side with her,' Norma snapped.

'It's not a case of taking sides, it's a case of saying what I believe to be right.'

'You mean what your mother believes to be right.'

He picked up the poker and jabbed crossly at the fire. 'This is all I need after a day like I've had.'

She went to him, took the poker and replaced it in its stand, then put her hands on his arms. 'I've asked before, and I'll ask again. Can't we move house, get one of our own?'

His lips thinned into a stubborn line. 'Even if I wanted to, which I don't, now is hardly the time with me working all hours and you shortly about to produce.'

'After the baby's born then?' she pleaded.

'But you don't seem to understand, I like it here.'

'And you don't seem to understand *I* don't.'

'Why? That's what I fail to understand, why?'

She spelt it out for him. 'Your mother and I are incompatible. She wants to rule the roost and I'm just not having that.'

He gave a soft, and to Norma infuriating, laugh. 'You're exaggerating again. She's only trying to be helpful and kind.'

He was blind as far as Solange was concerned, but then she'd known that for some while now. He just couldn't imagine that his mother may be other than the angel he perceived her to be.

He went on. 'You're being over-emotional because you're pregnant, it affects many women that way. Everything will settle down after the baby arrives, you wait and see if it doesn't.'

She broke away from him when the door opened and Travers came in with their drinks. Douglas changed the subject, and refused point blank to have any further discussion about a change of house.

She reached out in the darkness to place a hand on his left shoulder. He was lying on his right, facing away from her. 'Douglas? Are you still awake?' He grunted in reply, but made no move to turn to her.

She removed the hand from his shoulder, squirmed as close to him as she was able and, using the other hand which was under the bedclothes, sent it snaking over the hill of his hip to plunge into the fly of his pyjama bottoms. Finding the mole in its hole she called it.

'Norma I'm absolutely whacked. It would take me all my time to raise a smile far less anything else.'

Slowly she withdrew her hand, and stared at his back. A back that seemed like a wall between them. This was the fifth night running they hadn't made love, which in the past would have been unheard of for him.

Was he really working all these long hours because he was trying to get established? Or was there more to it than that? Was he working as he was to keep out of *her* way? Could it be that he'd gone right off her because she'd put on so much weight she now resembled Two Ton Tessie? When she needed his love and reassurance most, he was denying her, in this particular instance literally giving her the cold shoulder.

It wasn't just lovemaking she wanted, the actual sex that is, but for him to put his arms round her, to cuddle her close and tell her he didn't mind in the least that she was the size of a barrage balloon, or that her legs were so swollen they resembled a couple of ginormous white puddings, with veins.

Tears bloomed in her eyes, to go rolling down her cheeks. She was still crying silently when he began to snore.

She was damned if she was going to be there first, so she arrived at the City Bakeries fifteen minutes late. Midge rose as she approached.

'I was beginning to think you'd given me a dissy,' he said, using the old Glasgow expression, meaning to be stood up.

She gave him an icy smile. 'When *I* make an appointment I keep it. I don't let the other person down.'

He winced, and went to help her into her chair. 'Let's order first,' he said, beckoning a waitress over. He asked for a pot of tea. She chose a cookie to go with the tea; he a scone.

When the waitress had gone Midge closed his eyes, massaged his forehead, then reached into a jacket pocket to produce a small brown bottle. He took two pills from the bottle, poured himself a glass of water from the jug on the table, and swallowed the pills with the help of the water.

'What are those for?' she queried, curious.

'Aspirins. I've had a blinder of a headache ever since I got up this morning.'

'You're looking pale,' she acknowledged, something she'd already noticed and put down to apprehension of their meeting.

He shivered. 'I think I've got a cold coming on. Not surprising really, the weather here is a bit of a shock to the system after California.'

She watched him shiver again. 'If I was you I'd take myself home to bed directly you leave here.'

'I'll see how I go, but I might well just do that.'

Silence fell between them during which he scraped a thumbnail with the nail of his other thumb. 'You said we had to talk?' she prompted.

'It's where to begin, what words to use.' He paused, then went on in a small, tight voice. 'In the letter I wrote to you at the time I said I was sorry for what had happened. I meant that, very much so.'

'You weren't sorry enough to stop you going through with it though, were you?' she replied tartly, which made him flinch.

'I did a right dirty on you Norma, I want you to know it's been heavy on my conscience ever since.'

'Good,' she said, giving him a thin smile.

'I'm not asking for forgiveness —'

'That's just as well,' she cut in, 'for you certainly wouldn't get any.'

There was another silence between them, during which he gazed at, as though mesmerised by, the tablecloth. 'God, I really hurt you didn't I?'

She just stared glacially at him.

'It was the lure of seeing the world Norma. I couldn't resist it. Not even for you. When Zelda dangled that carrot in front of me the temptation was just too great.'

She relented a little. 'I know,' she said softly. 'The wanderlust was always strong in you. One of the first things you ever told me was that your greatest desire in life was to travel and see the world.'

An inner glow came into his eyes. 'I've been to so many places I'd dreamed of and never thought I ever actually would see. LA, 'Frisco, Houston, Tampa, Baton Rouge, Kalamazoo, Kansas City, Chicago, Milwaukee, St Louis, Atlanta, New York – and that's in the States alone. I've also been to Canada, Hawaii, Alaska, Mexico, Panama, Bermuda, Puerto Rico, Jamaica, Haiti, and when I leave here I'm going to Cuba to meet up with Zelda. We're vacationing there, then when we return to Hollywood we're going to make a movie with the great man himself, Astaire. The movie is to be called *The Ziegfield Follies.*'

'Astaire? That is something.' She couldn't help showing enthusiasm at the name of Astaire. He was the best after all.

'Do you remember we saw him in *Dancing Lady* at Green's Playhouse? I said that dancing alongside him would be the ultimate, and you said —'

She remembered as though it was yesterday. 'That to be as *good* as him would be the ultimate,' she interjected.

Midge barked out a laugh. 'You do remember!'

'How could I forget? We were both dancing daft, and he was a dancing god.'

'And now I'm not only going to be dancing alongside him, but Zelda and I will have second billing.'

Second billing to Astaire, she was impressed. 'The pair of you have become that big then?'

He nodded. 'In the States. Not so much overseas, but in the States yes.'

She relented even more. His dreams had come true, even if they were at her expense. 'I'm pleased for you... Mike isn't it nowadays?'

'That doesn't sound right coming from you somehow. I'd prefer if you continued to call me Midge.'

The waitress arrived with their tea and a plate on which were their cookie and scone. 'I'll pour,' Norma told the waitress. Norma filled his cup, and handed it to him. 'And how is Zelda?'

Midge dropped his gaze. 'Fine, never better.'

'Didn't she want to come here with you?'

'When I decided to go home for a visit she decided to do the same. She's gone to Corvallis, Oregon, where she was born, and where her family still live.'

Norma filled her cup. 'Have you had children?'

'No, children don't fit into our plans. It's career first and foremost with us.' He reached up and massaged his temples. 'I swear this headache is getting worse.'

'Do you want to leave?'

'Not yet,' he answered quickly. He continued massaging his forehead. 'I suppose I've said what I wanted to, about the carrot being too big a temptation. I felt it was important, for both of us if that's not too presumptuous, that I face you like this. As I should have faced you that day I ran off, but didn't have the guts to do so. I wish I'd never taken the coward's way out and sent a letter instead.'

Norma took a bite of cookie, and slowly chewed on it. She may have suffered when he absconded with Zelda, but he had also. She derived a great deal of satisfaction from the confirmation of that. 'Are you happy? With Zelda I mean?'

'We have a good marriage, I can't complain,' he replied in a neutral voice. 'But what about you? You've married a doctor, I'm told.'

It hadn't been in her mind to do so, but all this talk of Hollywood, films, Fred Astaire and exotic places made everything seem very one-sided in Midge's favour. She thought she'd redress the balance. 'I married a spy who also happened to be doctor.'

Midge gaped at her in astonishment. 'A spy! You're having me one?'

'Not in the least.' She then went on to tell him about FANY, Douglas, SOE and Massingham.

'Well I'll be jiggered!' he exclaimed softly when she eventually came to the end of her tale. He regarded her with new eyes, who would have believed his Norma would have done all that! Then he corrected himself, she wasn't *his* Norma anymore. She was this chap called Douglas's Norma.

The article was on page two of the Express which Norma read every morning over breakfast. She was raising a cup of coffee to her mouth when the name leapt out at her. *Mike Henderson*, underneath that it proclaimed, *Stricken in Sauchiehall Street.* Slowly she replaced the cup on its saucer, and read the article through.

Midge had collapsed in Sauchiehall Street and been rushed by taxi to the Western Infirmary. From there he'd been almost immediately transferred to Ruchill Hospital. A diagnosis was yet to be made, but whatever the illness, Mr Henderson's condition was serious. This was followed by a potted history of

Midge's career, including the information he was shortly to star in a picture with Fred Astaire to be called *The Ziegfield Follies.*

Ruchill Hospital, Norma thought grimly. That was a fever hospital. She recalled how pale he'd been in the tea-room where they'd talked, and the headache he'd complained of. A headache that had come on, he'd said, just that morning. Whatever was wrong with him that must have been the start of it.

She read the article through again.

It had been a lovely wedding, Lyn in white and looking so beautiful that Norma had shaken her head in wonderment to remember 'podge' as she'd once been. The reception, where they now all were, was being held in the local Cooperative Hall, and was well under way.

Norma was sitting beside Eileen, Douglas standing beside her. The band, a three-piece affair, were giving it big licks, and Brian and Effie were up on the floor doing their stuff. As the dancers swirled by, Finlay Rankine gave Norma a wink, he being up with one of the single lassies from the SCWS. The lassie was giggling, her expression coy. Finlay was clearly a hit with her. But then wasn't Finlay nearly always with the women?

Norma glanced across to where Jim Fullarton was standing with his wife, the pair of them chaffing to the Reids. Jacky Fullarton had been one of those not to come back from the war. He'd joined the Merchant Navy and gone down with his ship during the Battle of the Atlantic. Jacky had left a widow, Sylvia, and a wean.

She turned to Eileen. 'I hope you're going to get up tonight and not just sit there like a right misery puss.'

'No one's asked me,' Eileen replied. 'And yes, I probably will sit here like a misery puss as you put it. My dancing days are over.'

'Don't talk rot!'

'Would you ladies care for another drink?' Douglas asked them. He was gasping for another beer himself; it was very hot inside the hall.

'A shandy would be nice,' Norma answered. 'And you Eileen?'

'Ach, why the hell not! I'll have a dram. But with lemmy loo mind.'

Norma saw Douglas's mystifield expression. 'Lemonade,' she interpreted for him.

'Lyn's got herself a good chap. They make a fine couple,' Eileen said after Douglas had left them.

Norma glanced over at Lyn and Iain, the pair of them having momentarily paused in their dancing to chat to the best man and his girlfriend who were also on the floor. She had to agree, they were a fine couple together. She and Eileen clapped as the music ended.

'You could grow bananas in here so you could,' Eileen complained.

Norma laughed, that was true enough. She watched Finlay escort the lassie he'd been up with off the floor, have a quick word with her, then, to her obvious disappointment, leave her to walk over to the band. On reaching the band he fell into conversation with their leader.

Two children went racing by playing cops and robbers, they belonged to someone on Iain McElheney's side. A cousin of his Norma thought. She smiled to herself. If she had a boy how long till he was running about just like that? She patted her tummy – the end of August wasn't far away. She wondered if Douglas was enjoying himself? The people here were hardly his sort after all, he was far more at home with the Catherine Starks, and that ilk, of this world. Still, if he wasn't enjoying himself it wasn't apparent.

Somebody let out a great wheech which caused a group of folk to burst out laughing. The Laidlaws and Mathers from Cubie Street were among them Norma noted.

The band leader tapped his microphone for attention. 'Ladies and gentlemen, some of you will know, others not, that we have amongst us here tonight a former winner of the All Scotland Dance Championship...' Whistling and cheering broke out. Norma glared at Finlay, he'd put the bandleader up to this. 'Norma McKenzie, now Mrs Ross. Can you give her a big hand please.'

It wasn't a big hand Norma got, it was an enormous one. The McElheney contingent, not to be outdone, clapping as hard and loud as the McKenzie one.

'You'll have to stand up and acknowledge it,' Eileen whispered.

She would too, Norma thought. It was only polite. Sod that Finlay Rankine! She stood and gave an inclination of the head to first one end of the hall, then the other.

Eventually the bandleader was able to go on. 'And not only was Norma a former winner of the All Scotland Dance Championship, she was also a professional at Barrowland where I myself remember seeing her before the war. You used to give exhibitions at Barrowland Norma, will you give us one now?'

Norma pulled a face, and pointed to her tummy which got a huge laugh. Finlay Rankine came striding up. 'You're not getting out of it that easily Norma. Will you partner me for the anniversary waltz? That shouldn't do you any harm.'

She hesitated, not sure. She hadn't intended dancing for obvious reasons, but then again, the anniversary waltz was so slow she would hardly have to exert herself at all. That was the reason Finlay had chosen it of course.

He treated her to one of his crocodile smiles. 'You did promise me a turn round the floor first chance we got,' he reminded her. 'And this is the first chance there's been.'

She looked for Douglas, wanting him to give her a nod of approval, but couldn't see him. 'Go on Norma!' someone shouted. 'Aye, go on,' Eileen urged.

She made up her mind, she'd do it. Another cheer rang out when she extended a hand for Finlay to take. 'You're a conniving bugger,' she whispered.

'I am, I am,' he agreed as he led her onto the floor.

When they reached the centre of the floor they stopped and Finlay took her into his arms. The band struck up, and they were away.

As they danced, gliding and seemingly floating round the floor, a thousand memories were tumbling through Norma's mind, all of them of her and Midge. Poor Midge, he'd transpired to have infantile paralysis, which the Americans call polio, and was still in Ruchill where he was fighting for his life. Zelda had come over to be with him and was staying in a hotel.

Norma had been shocked to the core to learn what was wrong with Midge. Infantile paralysis! That was a nightmare right enough. The terrible thing was that if he did survive, and please God that he did, it was almost a certainty that he'd be left with a physical disability of some sort.

What was really awful was that there were times in the past, many many times if she was truthful, when she'd wished all manner of horrible revenges on him for what he'd done to her. But now this had befallen him she wished with all her heart that it hadn't. There was no sweetness in the knowledge he could end up a cripple. No sweetness whatever. Somehow, and this was a source of wonder to her, his tragedy only added to what remained of her own hurt.

'You're as good as you ever were,' Finlay said.

Heartsore, she came out of her reverie. 'Flattery will get you everywhere.'

'Promise?' he teased, giving her a salacious leer.

She didn't reply to that. But he had succeeded in making her smile.

Douglas stood watching Norma and Finlay Rankine. What a marvellous and talented dancer she was, he thought, appreciating that fact for the first time. How she must hate to dance with him considering how he clumped round the floor. So graceful, even with that bump of hers, and the swollen legs she was forever grumbling about.

The band stopped, and Douglas led the applause. And thunderous applause it was too. Holding hands, Norma and Finlay took several bows, very small bows on her part, then he walked her back to her seat.

'You were terrific,' Eileen enthused to Norma as Norma sat down again. 'You too Mr Rankine.'

Brian and Effie came over to enthuse as Eileen had just done. As also did Douglas when he rejoined them with the drinks he'd gone to get.

'May I have the pleasure?' Finlay asked Eileen.

She blushed. 'No, I'm not getting up Mr Rankine. Thank you very much though.'

'You told me to go on, go on yourself,' Norma cajoled.

'Aye, a wee birl will do you the world of good,' Brian told his youngest daughter.

'No, but thanks all the same,' Eileen said to Finlay.

His face dropped in a comical fashion. 'I take your refusal personally Miss McKenzie.' Then, with the most disarming of smiles. 'And please call me Finlay.'

Her blush had become a full-blown reddie. 'It isn't personal I assure you.'
'How else can I interpret it?' he replied haughtily. Abruptly he changed his tone once more to become the beseeching plaintiff. 'And may I call you Eileen?'
She was totally thrown by this play acting. 'Yes, I eh...'
'I'll cry if you refuse me,' he said seriously.
'Ach away and don't be daft!'
'I will. I'm a most sensitive plant. Isn't that so Norma?'
'Oh *most*,' she replied sarcastically.
Brian and Effie were both grinning, enjoying this. They thought Finlay a right old hoot.
'So will you do me the great honour, please missus?' Finlay pleaded.
Eileen just had to laugh at that, missus indeed! She capitulated. 'Well the one dance then. I'd hate to see a grown man cry after all.'
Quick as a wink Finlay had Eileen by the arm, and was helping her to her feet. As he was doing so the bandleader announced another waltz. 'Will you lead or shall I?' Finlay asked Eileen, which got him a sharp punch in the chest from her, and a guffaw from Brian.
'Lord help us from comic singers, chantie wraslers and dance instructors,' Eileen muttered as they took the floor.
'Don't you like my patter?' Finlay asked in broad Glasgow.
'Your patter's like watter,' Eileen riposted in an accent as broad.
'Oh see you!' said Finlay.
'And see you *too*!' They were both laughing as the band struck up.
'Awfy man,' Brian commented to Effie, shaking his head.
Finlay Rankine was surprised, though now he came to think of it he should have foreseen the possibility. Eileen was Norma's sister. 'You've got it,' he said.
Eileen frowned, what was he havering on about now? 'Got what?'
'You're a natural mover, like Norma. I recognised it in her the first time I danced with her, just as I've recognised it in you.'
She wasn't sure whether he was pulling her leg or not. 'Is that more patter?'

'No, I'm serious.'

She was chuffed, pleased indeed to have been told that by a dancer of his calibre. She knew all about Finlay Rankine from Norma who'd often talked about him in the past before the war. 'Well thank you very much.'

'There's nothing to thank me for, I'm only stating what's fact. Some people are born with music inside them; others with the talent to paint, or act. Then there are those like myself, and Norma, and you with movement inside them. I think I can safely say you'd have been a first-class dancer if you'd ever seriously taken it up.'

'My husband...' she started to say, then trailed off.

'I met your husband at the All Scotland Dance Championship which Norma and Midge won, you'll recall we all went back to Joe Dunlop's to celebrate after, and Charlie and I had a bit of a blether there. We talked about the books he'd arranged from the library which had helped Norma and Midge so much earlier on. Norma told me what happened to him. I was very sorry to hear it, I thought him a nice man.'

Eileen glanced sideways at Finlay. There was no play acting about him now, his voice rang with sincerity. 'Nearly everyone liked Charlie, he was that sort of person.' She paused, then went on softly, 'What I was going to say was that Charlie always maintained I was a good dancer, but I just put it down to a little verbal syrup from a loving husband.'

'Verbal syrup or not, he was right.'

They danced on in silence, and then it was the end of the waltz. After the clapping had subsided Eileen was about to start from the floor when Finlay said, 'I know you only promised one, but how about another?'

She bit her lip, uncertain. She *had* enjoyed that mind you. In fact she'd enjoyed it a lot.

Norma took another sip of her shandy, it really was boiling inside the hall and she swore it was getting hotter. Not that the heat and discomfort were stopping people from having a rare old tear, it wasn't in the least. Nonetheless, maybe there were some windows somewhere that could be opened. She was about to mention it to Douglas when it suddenly caught her attention that Eileen had stayed up with Finlay Rankine. That pleased her, trust Finlay to take Eileen out of herself. He could charm the birds off the trees that man. Or, as someone had once crudely put it, a nun out of her knickers.

Norma was in the same 'greasy spoon' round the corner from Silver's where she'd previously rendezvoused with Finlay Rankine, and now she was back having arranged to do the same again. Masked by the table she rubbed the lower part of her tummy. The baby was moving, and she had chronic indigestion. There was only a fortnight to go till the big event, scheduled to take place at the Victoria Infirmary where Mr Wright, the senior obstetrician, would be delivering her.

Finlay came bustling in through the café door, gave her a cheery wave and asked, by means of mime, if she wanted another cup of tea. She nodded that she did.

'So what's this all about Norma? You sounded quite mysterious on the telephone,' he demanded when he joined her.

Norma put sugar in her fresh cup of tea, and slowly stirred it. This was going to be awkward, and the chances were high she was going to lose a pal. 'You're my friend Finlay, but Eileen is my sister.' She paused, then added softly. 'I'm worried.'

'Because we've been going out together?'

'Charlie's death gutted her. She suffered dreadfully because of it, and has continued to suffer. I'll do anything to stop her being hurt further.'

'Which you think I'll do?'

Norma raised an eyebrow. 'Look at your track record Finlay. You're strictly a love-them-and-leave-them chap, and that's the last thing Eileen needs.' Several seconds ticked by before she went on. 'I must admit I was surprised to say the least when she told me that not only had you asked her out, surprise number one, but that she'd accepted, surprise number two.'

'We are an odd couple, there's no denying that,' Finlay replied. 'I suppose you might call it an attraction of opposites. And perhaps that's why we get on so well together, which we really do.'

'But for how long? Eileen doesn't need a fly-by-night as I said.'

Finlay drank some tea, and thought about Eileen. 'I find your sister different to my women in the past – we actually talk to one another. We're relaxed in each other's company, I certainly am in hers and she says she is in mine. And if we talk there are other occasions when we say nothing, nothing at all, and neither of us minds. Just being together is a pleasure in itself.' He shook his head. 'No one is more amazed than me that this has happened, but it has.'

'Are you telling me the pair of you are in love?' Norma asked incredulously.

'Love is a word that has many shades of meaning. Eileen desperately loved Charlie, that's undeniable. As it's also undeniable that she's still in love with his memory. But she's come to care for me, which in itself is surely a form of love?'

'And how do you feel about her?'

'As you know only too well I had my flings before the war, but they were based on lust rather than love. Maybe I'm getting old, maybe the war changed me, but now I'd much rather sit and talk to Eileen than be in bed with one of those sexpots I knew previously.' He gazed at his cup, shifting it round in its saucer. 'I swear this to you though Norma, whatever happens I'll never knowingly hurt Eileen. As you've pointed out she's had more than her fair share of that already.' He glanced up to stare Norma straight in the eyes. 'You have my solemn oath on that.'

She believed him, and it made her happy for him, and enormously happy for Eileen. It also gave her a huge sense of relief for she'd been worried sick for Eileen.

'Incongruous, but there you are,' Finlay added, giving Norma one of his crocodile smiles which had become even more crocodiley since he'd acquired an eye patch.

'Eileen tells me you take her dancing quite a bit?'

'I'm gradually teaching her steps and techniques, which she enjoys learning. Who knows? He paused, and added eagerly, 'And she's started looking after herself better, hasn't she? I put my foot down about that. Insisted she have her hair done, wear make-up and generally spruce herself up. Nor did I get any argument on the subject. She just said right Finlay, and began doing it.

There had been a noticeable difference in Eileen of late. The entire family had commented on it, and were delighted by it. It wasn't an overnight transformation, but gradually Eileen was getting back to looking like her old self. 'I hope it works out for the pair of you,' Norma said, and patted him affectionately on the hand.

They chatted a while longer, then left the café. Norma's indigestion had been bad before, but it was positively raging now. She shouldn't have drunk that second cup of tea she chided herself. That had only made matters even worse.

'I'll walk you to your car,' Finlay volunteered.

'It's over there,' she replied, pointing to where the Lagonda was parked. She and Douglas had done a swap for the duration the previous week because she'd grown so large it had become too difficult for her to get in and out of the MG.

They had just reached the Lagonda when it hit her. Gasping in agony, and clutching her stomach, she sagged against the side of the vehicle.

'What is it Norma? What's wrong?' Finlay asked in alarm.

She tried to speak, but couldn't. The pain was too intense. She gritted her teeth instead, and waited for it to pass, which it soon did. 'It would seem the baby is coming early,' she said at last.

'What!' Finlay's face was a picture.

'Must get to the Victoria Infirmary.'

'Leave everything to me, I'll . . .' He broke off when, with a moan, she doubled over.

'Shit!' he swore.

Douglas paced up and down outside the delivery theatre. A glance at his watch told him it was now forty minutes since Norma had come in as an emergency admittance, and thirty minutes since he'd been informed.

He stopped abruptly in his pacing when Norma shrieked, a shriek that brought memories of the field hospital he'd been working in when Norma arrived at Massingham. He fumbled for his cigarettes and lighter, taking in the fact as he lit up that his hands were shaking like Billy-O.

He'd just resumed pacing when Norma shrieked again, this time even more loudly.

There was the sound of a smack, hand against bottom, followed by a lusty, protesting wail. 'What is it?' she croaked.

Mr Wright's face swam into vision, and he was smiling.

'Congratulations Mrs Ross, you have a lovely baby boy.'

A boy! So Solange had been right after all. 'Is he... Is everything there, as it should be?'

'He's absolutely perfect.'

'Ah!' she sighed. That had been her secret fear, as it probably was of most expectant mothers. That something would be found to be wrong with the baby when it was born.

Shortly after that the baby, wrapped in a length of white cotton, was placed in her arms. And then a beaming Douglas was by her side, bending over to kiss her on the cheek.

'It's a boy and he's perfect,' she croaked.

'I know.'

Douglas reached down and very gently placed a hand over the baby's front. 'Hello Lindsay.'

There had been quite a to do over what they called the child when it arrived. Solange had wanted a boy to be called Forsyth, but Norma, hating the silly name, had been vehemently against that. In the end the question of names had been resolved when Norma had come up with the perfect solution. If it was a girl she would be called Lynsey after Lynsey Dereham, if a boy Lindsay, a male version of the name. When she and Douglas explained who Lynsey had been, and that Lynsey had died working for the SOE in France, and by implication also for France and therefore a French heroine, Solange, being the patriot she was, had been forced to accept this compromise.

'How do you feel?' Douglas asked Norma.

Her eyelids were leaden, and she was physically drained. She was also extremely sore. 'Very tired,' she mumbled in reply.

'You've given me a fine son and heir. Thank you,' Douglas said, and kissed her again, this time lightly on the lips.

Norma smiled at him, then turned her head to smile at the baby.

When Douglas spoke to her again he got no reply. Still smiling, she'd fallen asleep.

## *Chapter Thirteen*

Norma glanced up from her soup plate, and over at Douglas who was sitting opposite her across the width of the dining table. He looked ghastly she thought, like a limp dishrag Effie would have said. There were coal black bags under his eyes.

It was April the following year, 1947, and Lindsay was now eight months old. And what a wee darling he was. It was rare for Norma to pick him up but her heart didn't turn over inside her.

He was in his cot now, with Phyl Casden keeping an eye on him. He still slept in their bedroom, but would shortly be moving into his own nursery, next door to theirs which she herself had redecorated from top to bottom.

Shortly after she'd returned from hospital with the baby, Solange had suggested she and Douglas employ a nanny. Initially she'd resisted the idea, not at all happy at the thought of a stranger looking after her child. And then one day, while Phyl was helping her bathe the baby, the answer had come to her. Phyl adored Lindsay and Lindsay adored Phyl. She'd put it to Phyl who'd agreed there and then. The following week Phyl had officially become Lyndsay's nanny, and a new girl had started, taking over Phyl's duties as maid.

Forsyth had been speaking down the length of the table to Solange, and now stopped to get on with his soup. Douglas finished his, leaned back in his chair, closed his eyes and gave a deep sigh.

'You look shattered,' Norma said quietly.

His eyes flickered open again. 'I feel it.'

'You really are working far too hard, Douglas. Do you realise it has been eight days since you last sat down to dinner with us. You were even absent on Saturday and Sunday night.'

'I have to get established, make a name for myself. I've explained that to you countless times,' he replied, a trace of annoyance in his voice.

'And I've told you countless times that you'll end up as one of the patients if you're not careful. You must stop driving yourself the way you are.' She appealed to Forsyth. 'What do you say? Don't you agree?'

Forsyth paused in his eating. His eyes flicked to Douglas, then to Norma. 'Douglas is making a big impression at the hospital, I can tell you that. People are coming to speak very highly of him.'

Douglas shot Norma a look that said, see!

'What he's doing is rapidly becoming detrimental to his health, and I don't need to be a doctor to diagnose that,' Norma stated bluntly.

Solange said something to Douglas in French, which he replied to in the same language. God how it irritated Norma when the other members of the family did that! She was trying to learn the language, but not getting on very well at all. It was rapidly becoming more and more obvious that learning foreign languages just wasn't her forte. Nonetheless she would persevere, she was determined about that.

'I beg your pardon?' Norma said after there had been another interchange between mother and son, making the point that she didn't understand.

'Mama says there is nothing wrong in being ambitious, that it is an excellent quality to have.' Norma had to stop herself from glaring at Solange. 'But that perhaps I have been overdoing it a bit.'

'More than a bit,' Norma said quietly, surprised that Solange had even partially agreed with her.

'What you should have is a hobby, I find mine most relaxing and recuperative,' Forsyth chipped in, having now finished his soup. He collected matchboxes and books of matches, of which he had thousands from all over the world. Seeing they were now all finished, he rang the handbell for Travers.

'I don't have time for a hobby,' Douglas muttered dismissively.

'Then perhaps you should make time,' Norma snapped.

They fell silent when Travers entered the room to remove

their plates and stack them on a trolley. Before leaving the room again to fetch the next course he refilled their wineglasses.

Douglas lit a cigarette between courses in the French manner, and looked thoughtful. As soon as Travers was gone he said, 'There is one hobby that appeals. In fact it appeals a great deal.'

'What's that?' Norma inquired.

He gave her a sideways glance. 'I'd love to build and maintain that pond I once told you about. You know, frogs, toads, newts . . .'

'Eech!' Norma burst out, which caused him to laugh. 'Horrible, slimy things!' she added.

'He always wanted a pond as a boy,' Solange said.

'And you forbade it.'

Solange shrugged her shoulders. 'I don't exactly appreciate those animals either.' Her eyes darted to Norma, then quickly away again. 'But maybe not so much now as I once did.'

Douglas seized on this. 'Does that mean you wouldn't now object to me building a pond?'

Solange lifted her wineglass, sipped its contents, and didn't reply.

'I'm against it,' Norma said levelly to Douglas.

He puffed on his cigarette, and studied her through the smoke. 'I can appreciate you don't like frogs, toads, etc, but think how educational they will be for Lindsay when he's old enough to appreciate such things.'

'A pond could be dangerous with a young child about,' she riposted.

Douglas chuckled, infuriating her. 'There will be no danger I promise you. And a pond would give me a great deal of enjoyment. A great deal.'

'I loathe slimies, they give me the creeps. I can just imagine me staying out of the garden altogether because it's crawling with them.'

'Aren't you being just a little selfish *chérie*?' Solange smiled. 'As Douglas has pointed out, a pond would be most educational for Lindsay when he's older.'

Norma stared hard at her mother-in-law. The cow was doing this just to spite and annoy her. She didn't believe for one instant that Solange had changed her mind about slimies. As for Solange accusing her of being selfish – how hypocritical of

Solange who, ignoring the educational benefits at the time, had forbidden the young Douglas to have a pond.

Solange turned her attention to Douglas. 'Where will you build this pond?'

Norma knew then that she'd been outflanked by her mother-in-law, and her lips thinned in anger. If she'd been in favour of this pond that damned woman wouldn't have entertained the idea.

Travers and the new maid came in with the next course.

The young woman's face filled with stark, and total, terror when he pointed his pistol at it. 'No please . . . please . . . there's been a mistake,' she pleaded, sinking to her knees, her hands outspread in a gesture of entreaty.

But there had been no mistake, his orders were clear. His finger tightened on the trigger.

'No,' she whispered, her last word on earth.

The pistol fired, and everything seemed to happen in slow motion. He imagined he saw the bullet fly from the pistol's muzzle to home in on that spot where the bridge of her nose emerged from the bottom of her forehead.

Slowly, oh so slowly, her face exploded into a million gory, bloody bits. Blood sprayed, while pieces of bone, brain, skin, hair and other tissue flew, everywhere. The most gruesome, awful sight he had ever seen. And he had made it happen.

Douglas came awake with a start to find his body had gone rigid as it always did when he had *the* nightmare. He was lathed in sweat, his mouth desert-dry, his throat constricted. He was breathing very quickly, his chest pumping out and in like some hard-worked bellows.

He turned in the darkness to look at the outline that was Norma. He hadn't woken her, she was still sleeping soundly.

He took a deep breath, then another, forcing his breathing to normalise, which it did after a few seconds.

Of all the things he'd done in the war that was the one that had affected him most. It haunted him, and he knew it was going to keep on haunting him till his own dying day.

Slowly, oh so slowly, her face exploding into . . . Making a small animal-like sound he jammed a fist into his mouth. It would be hours before he got back to sleep, if indeed he did at all. Hours of torment, remembering, reliving . . .

Norma plucked the teat of the now empty bottle from Lindsay's mouth and handed it to Phyl Casden. She then put Lindsay over her left shoulder and gently patted his back. She was rewarded by a long burp, followed by another. When she judged he was properly winded she gave him to Phyl who would now change him.

She gazed lovingly at her wee son as Phyl laid him out and began stripping off his nappy. It had been a great disappointment to her that she hadn't been able to feed him herself, but in the event that had proved impossible. And so a bottle it had had to be. At eight months old he was now on a combination of milk and solids.

'I thought I'd put him in his pram and take him for a walk in the King's Park,' Phyl said.

'Fine. Just make sure he's well wrapped up as there's still a nip in the air.'

'Phyl will make sure of that. We don't want you catching a chill, do we bonnie baby?' Phyl said, and chucked Lindsay under the chin, which made him smile and blow bubbles at her.

Norma kissed him on the forehead, then took her leave of the pair of them as she was off out. She'd say goodbye to Douglas before she went, and knew where to find him.

She put on her coat and scarf, then made her way to the rear garden. And there he was, just as he'd said he'd be, digging the hole that would become the pond.

It was the morning following his decision to build the pond, and the first Saturday he'd stayed at home since starting at the Victoria Infirmary. If building the pond meant she was going to see more of him at weekends then that at least was something in its favour.

He spied her at last, stopped what he was doing, and waved. She continued on over to him.

'You're off then,' he said.

She viewed the already sizeable hole with distaste. 'I'm still worried that a pond will be dangerous.'

He sighed. 'It'll be safe as houses once I've put some netting over it, which I will personally fix in place just as soon as Lindsay becomes mobile. All right?'

'Hmm,' she answered reluctantly. 'How deep is it going to be?'

'Two feet. Twelve long, eight wide and two deep. Any other questions?'

His tone was sarcastic. And not only sarcastic, but patronising also. 'No.'

'Then I'll see you later. Give my regards to your family.'

'I will.' She was off to Cubie Street to have lunch. He was impatient to return to his digging, nor was he doing anything to disguise his impatience. 'Cheerio for now then,' she said, and gave him a quick kiss on the lips.

She hadn't even completed turning away from him when his spade thunked back into the earth.

'And where is it tonight?' Norma asked Eileen, whose relationship with Finlay Rankine was continuing from strength to strength. And what a change for the better that relationship had wrought in her sister Norma thought. For quite some time now Eileen had been back to her old self, as she'd been before Charlie's death.

'We're going jigging, though I don't know where.'

Lyn wasn't present, having moved into her own house when she married Iain McElheney. The two of them now lived in a single end in Parkhead. Nor was Brian there. He'd gone in to do some work, and was going straight from there to a football match.

'Speaking of jigging,' Effie said as she laid a plate of margarined slices of cut pan loaf on the table, 'Midge Henderson is home. An ambulance brought him back from Ruchill Hospital earlier on in the week.'

Norma thought of the last time she'd seen Midge Henderson, that day in the City Bakeries when he'd told her he was going to make a film with Fred Astaire. Well he'd be making no more films, or not as a dancer anyway. He'd survived the infantile paralysis, but what an horrendous price he'd had to pay for that survival. He was now paralysed from the waist down. 'Have you spoken to him?' she asked her mother.

'No, but I have to Alice. She says he's very depressed. But that's only to be expected, I suppose.'

'Who would have thought it, Midge Henderson ending up in a wheelchair,' Eileen said, shaking her head in disbelief.

'Aye,' Norma mused, who would have thought it. What agony and sheer torture his new state must be for him. Midge, who used to dance like a dream, now unable to walk, not even put one foot in front of the other. And that's how he was going to be for the rest of his life.

When the meal was over Norma said, 'I think I'll away down and say hello to Midge. I feel I should.'

'You owe that man nothing after what he did to you. Not even the time of day,' Effie said bitterly, beginning to gather up the dirty dishes. She'd never forgiven Midge for what he'd done to Norma.

'I wouldn't wish what's happened to him on my worst enemy,' Norma stated quietly.

Effie shot her daughter a dark look. 'I know I shouldn't say this, that it's not right. But maybe he's only, at long last, got what was coming to him.'

'Ma!'

'I know, lass, but that's how I feel.'

Norma left the house as Effie and Eileen were starting on the washing up, to chap on the Hendersons' door. It was Leslie, Midge's Da, who answered.

'Well hello!' he exclaimed, pleased to see her. For he'd aye been fond of Norma. Midge might be his only son, and a son he dearly loved, but he too had never forgiven Midge for what he'd done to Norma. He'd understood *why* Midge had acted as he had, but had never forgiven Midge for the manner in which it had been done. As far as he was concerned, and he'd told Midge by letter, Midge had brought shame on the entire Henderson household.

'Ma mentioned Midge was back. I thought I'd pay him a visit.'

'Come away in Norma, you'll find him in his old bedroom.' Leslie closed the front door behind the pair of them, then called out. 'Midge, there's someone here to see you!'

She didn't have to be shown where his old bedroom was, she knew. She found him sitting by the window in his wheelchair with a tartan travelling rug draped over his now useless legs. He didn't appear at all pleased that she'd come.

Her heart went out to him. How pale and frail he looked, a shadow of his former self. He'd lost a great deal of weight, and his shoulders were bowed in a combination of resignation and defeat. A lump that felt the size of an egg came into Norma's throat. How the once mighty were fallen indeed. 'Hello,' she said, not smiling in case he misinterpreted that.

He scowled at her. 'Come to gloat have you?'

'Don't talk stupid,' she snapped back.

He seemed to relax a little on hearing that. 'I saw you arrive from the window. That's my chief occupation nowadays, staring out the window like some nosey wifey with nothing better to do.'

He was bitter all right, that stood out a mile. 'I am sorry for what's happened to you Midge. And I mean that.'

His mouth twisted cynically. 'Are you?'

'Yes, I am.'

Their eyes locked, and he read in hers that she was telling the truth. He also read pity there, which made him writhe inside. 'Did you hear that Zelda left me? Once she knew it was definite my dancing days were over she hopped it back to the States.'

'Yes, I had heard that.'

'What you won't have heard is that she's divorced me. One of those Mexican jobs. I got notification of it the day before I left Ruchill.

Had he expected any different? Norma wondered. Zelda had shown her colours all those years ago when she'd dumped the dying Don to run off with him. 'Has she found another partner?'

He barked out a laugh that was more self-mocking than anything else, and answered her wondering if he'd expected anything different. 'Oh I would imagine so. And if she hasn't already, I'm sure she soon will have.'

Norma was tempted to say what she thought of Zelda, how she both despised and detested the woman. But decided, thinking that might turn the knife in Midge, not to. 'So what are your plans now? Will you return to America?'

He glanced away from her, and on out the window. She couldn't be certain, but she imagined she could see a glint of tears in his eyes. 'No, I won't return to America,' he replied in a voice so soft it was almost a whisper.

'You'll stay here then, in Cubie Street?'

'That's it. I've no alternative, other than go into a home that is. And I certainly don't want to do that.'

'No,' she agreed.

He ran a hand through hair that was lank and lifeless, then brought his attention back onto her. 'And what about you? How are things with you?'

'Can't complain. I'm pregnant again.'

'So soon!' he exclaimed.

Norma was surprised too, but not because of the relative shortness of time involved. Douglas so rarely approached her nowadays it had frankly amazed her that she'd been able to get pregnant. Weeks could pass, sometimes a month or more, without him showing any interest in that direction. Nor was there any point in her making the advances – when she tried that all she got was how tired he was after a long and arduous day at the hospital. And yet, one of the very few occasions they had made love since Lindsay's birth had resulted in her becoming pregnant again. 'Douglas says I must be just naturally fecund.'

Midge frowned, he didn't know the word. 'Fecund?'

'Easily put in the club,' she laughed, thinking to herself Midge wouldn't, couldn't, appreciate the irony of that statement. Just how true it actually was.

Midge was about to laugh with Norma when he chillingly recalled that he would never make a female pregnant now, nor ever again have one. The ability to do that, like his legs, was forever lost to him. 'I'm happy for you,' he said in a strangled voice. 'Very happy, Norma.'

With a flash of insight she realised what his tone, and his anguished expression, really meant. He glanced away from her, and on out the window again, and this time there was no doubt whatever, there was a glint of tears in his eyes.

'I'd better be going,' she mumbled.

'Aye. Well it was thoughtful of you to drop by,' he replied, continuing to look on out the window.

'Goodbye for now then Midge.'

'Goodbye for now Norma.'

Alice was waiting for her in the hall to show her out. The two of them spoke briefly at the front door, then Norma left Alice to away upstairs again. Before going in she stopped and had a weep, knowing that in his bedroom Midge was doing the same.

When she left the closemouth half an hour later she glanced up at Midge's bedroom window before getting into the MG, and there he was, a pale face partially hidden by net curtain, staring down at her.

She swithered whether to wave, and decided not to. Climbing into the MG she drove off.

Midge watched the MG till it turned into Gallowgate, and was lost to view. Then he went back to just watching the street.

Sir John and Lady Stark, Catherine's parents, were throwing a Summer Ball in the St Enoch Hotel, and naturally enough the Rosses had all been invited. It was a glittering affair with the *crème de la crème* of lowland Scottish society there. All the titled, nobs, and high heid bummers was how Norma thought of it to herself.

Catherine had an escort for the evening, a young chap – far younger than Catherine – who'd come over to Norma as a right pain in the backside. With his poppy eyes, thinning hair, and receding chin, Archibald Paterson certainly wasn't a looker.

Catherine's two cronies were also in attendance, Henrietta Lockhart with an Irish fellow – now he was a dish – and Elsie Buchan on her lonesome. Vivienne Gregory too was there, though Norma hadn't spoken to her yet. Vivienne had been part of the party that had gone riding out at Eaglesham the day Norma had been invited, and the one member of the party that Norma had quite liked. A little earlier Norma had been told by Douglas that Vivienne was married to the tall, bearded man she was with.

'And how are you getting along with this pregnancy? Solange tells me you had a great deal of trouble with the last one,' Catherine inquired of Norma, her voice loud and sharp, and with no sympathy whatever in it.

'This one isn't nearly so bad,' Norma replied.

'No indigestion? Solange said you had an awful time with that.'

'Some, but nothing like so severe as it was with Lindsay.'

'And what about . . .' Catherine's gaze slowly dropped to the lower part of Norma's gown, then just as slowly was raised again till she was once more staring straight into Norma's eyes. 'What about your legs? They got all horribly swollen before I believe.'

Oh she was a bitch Norma thought, smiling. If she ever got pregnant Norma hoped she went through all the agonies of hell with it. 'A little puffiness round the ankles, that's all on this occasion.'

'Oh good!' Catherine exclaimed mildly, matching Norma's smile.

'I think we're having a girl as Norma's symptoms are so different from when she was expecting Lindsay,' Douglas said.

Archibald Paterson stopped a passing waiter and they all exchanged their empty champagne glasses for full ones. 'Jolly tiptop ball, thoroughly enjoying,' Archibald said to Catherine.

'I think we're all enjoying ourselves,' Douglas said, making smalltalk.

'I don't suppose you know many people here,' Elsie Buchan smiled at Norma, her tone silky on the outside.

Norma sipped her champagne. 'No. Not many.'

Solange and Forsyth joined them. 'We were just commenting that poor Norma doesn't know many people here,' Catherine said to Solange, the faintest tinge of malice in her voice. 'I simply must take her round and introduce her.'

Solange, registering the tinge of malice, caught on right away. Her gaze flicked to Norma, then back again to Catherine. 'What an excellent idea,' she enthused.

Oh God! Norma thought. Here it was again, another device to try and show her up. She glanced at Douglas, was he blind as well as deaf? Didn't he realise the claws were out and doing their best to rake? Oblivious, that's what he was, quite oblivious to what was really going on. Not for the first time since returning to Glasgow she wondered what had happened to the sensitivity she'd once credited him with having.

She could just imagine what Catherine's introductions would be like. The sneer in the voice, the smirk. The combined condescending and patronising tone. Nothing would be said outright of course, but it would be all there nonetheless. She'd be made to feel like Cinderella of the fairystory, somebody masquerading as what she was not. 'Douglas can introduce me to who he thinks I should meet.'

'And I shall help. I insist!' Catherine said emphatically.

'Yes, you must,' Henrietta Lockhart told Catherine, her eyes flashing with amusement.

Norma looked at Forsyth for help, but he didn't appreciate what was going on either.

'Catherine?'

They all turned to Sir John Stark who'd approached them unseen. With him was a man Norma, with a sudden jolt, her mind flying back over the years, recognised right away. He was a lot older looking of course, but unmistakable nevertheless. 'Catherine, I'd like you to meet a longstanding, and very dear, friend of mine whom I don't see nearly enough of nowadays. Catherine, this is the Earl of Arran and Clydesdale.'

The Earl took Catherine's proffered hand and kissed the back of it. 'Delighted,' he murmured.

'Father has often talked of you. I'm just surprised we haven't met before now.'

'The Earl has become something of a recluse, haven't you Biffie?'

The Earl nodded. 'I used to be far more gregarious...' He shrugged his shoulders. 'There we are.'

'Now let me introduce you to everyone here,' Catherine said, and proceeded to do just that. When she came to Norma, whom she'd purposely left to last, the Earl frowned.

'Mrs Ross? Mrs Ross?' he muttered, and shook his head. Norma's face struck a terribly familiar chord in his memory, but he was unable to place her. Should she remind him, should she not? Norma wondered. And then he had it. 'Norma McKenzie! Of course!' he exclaimed. 'By all that's wonderful!'

Norma was on tenterhooks. Was this going to be embarrassing or what?

'You *know* Norma?' Catherine frowned.

'Of course I know her. How could I forget her! Many's the time I dangled her on my knee when she was a child.'

Which was true enough, Norma thought. She could recall him doing so.

'Good gracious!' said Forsyth, that was the last thing he'd expected the Earl to say.

'And how are your dear parents and sisters?' the Earl demanded eagerly of Norma.

'Fine Earl.'

'Dearie me, what memories you bring back Norma. What marvellous memories. I lost touch with your father you know. One thing and another, the war.'

'Yes,' she nodded.

'And this is your husband.'

'I have that pleasure,' Douglas answered, totally mystified, as were the others, as to how Norma knew the Earl of Arran and Clydesdale, and the Earl her.

'You must let me steal Norma from you for a short while. I have so much I'd love to talk over with her.'

'Please do.'

The Earl turned to Sir John whom Norma had met on arrival at the Ball, the host and hostess having personally welcomed every guest as they entered the Grand Hall where the ball was taking place. 'Will you excuse us?'

'Of course Biffie.'

The Earl extended an arm to Norma. 'Shall we find a seat my dear? Or we could dance if you prefer?'

Norma gestured to her bump which, in the past few weeks, had started to become quite noticeable. 'I'd prefer to sit.'

'Then sit we shall!' the Earl said. And, with Norma's arm crooked in his, he led her away.

Catherine, Solange, Henrietta and Elsie Buchan stared after Norma in astonishment. Then Catherine swung on Douglas to ask how Norma knew the Earl.

'I really have no idea,' he replied. It wasn't till a little later that he recalled Norma mentioning the Earl's name to him shortly after he'd revealed to her that he was Gabriel. Then the jigsaw fell into place, Norma's father had been employed by the Earl when the Earl had owned a house in Kirn. And it was the Earl who'd originally found Brian a job with the Glasgow Parks Department.

As Norma walked away with the Earl she was filled with a huge sense of relief. Thank God the Earl had appeared to save her from a potentially extremely embarrassing situation. And what a smack in the eye for Catherine and co. The incident quite made her night.

It was about an hour later that Norma went to the toilet where she ran into Vivienne Gregory. 'Oh hello. I was hoping to have a word with you,' Vivienne said.

Norma couldn't think about what. 'Oh?'

'I only learned recently that you were in the FANY during the war. Is that correct?'

'Yes.'

'Then perhaps you'd care to meet two of my chums who are coming to tea on Tuesday afternoon. They were also in FANY.'

'Really!' exclaimed Norma, immediately interested. 'What are their names?'

'Heather Innes and Madeleine Pallin. They both ran canteens, Heather for the Polish Forces that were stationed in Scotland.'

'Did they join through the Scottish Headquarters?' Norma queried. A Scottish HQ having been established some while after she had joined FANY.

'In Perth, yes.'

'As they were purely on the Scottish side I wouldn't know them, but I'd be delighted to meet them. We probably know some folk in common, FANY wasn't that vast an organisation after all.'

'So you'll come Tuesday?'

'I'd like to very much.'

Vivienne opened a tiny clutchbag to produce a card which she handed to Norma. 'Shall we say three?'

'Eh . . .' Norma hesitated. She could be on dicey ground here, but did want to find out just what was what. 'How well do you know Catherine Stark and her friends?'

'I know them, but we're not exactly close. My husband Jim is a business associate of Sir John's, and I keep my horse at the stables in Eaglesham. We have a town house ourselves, so it's convenient for me to keep my horse there. Why do you ask?'

'Just curiosity,' Norma lied.

But Vivienne was no fool. Catherine had been sweet on Douglas Ross for years, everyone knew that. And Douglas had married this girl Norma whom Catherine had hinted to her that day in Eaglesham wasn't exactly out of the top drawer. Furthermore, Catherine could be a proper bitch when she wanted to be. Vivienne put two and two together. She took Norma by the hand, and squeezed it warmly. 'Till Tuesday then. I'll look forward to it.'

There was that in Vivienne's eyes and expression which told Norma she'd be most welcome in Vivienne's home, and that this was no trap to have another dig at her and her background. 'And so shall I,' she answered with enthusiasm.

Vivienne's invitation made Norma feel chuffed in the extreme. She felt she was on the verge of making a friend amongst this new circle she now moved in.

It was a glorious July day with the sun cracking a clear blue sky that was devoid of even a wisp of cloud. Norma hummed happily to herself as she drove in the direction of Blairbeth Road. She'd just had a smashing afternoon with Vivienne Gregory, the pair of them having gone to an art exhibition and then taking coffee afterwards. She'd thought the night of the Summer Ball when Vivienne had invited her to tea that Vivienne might turn into a friend, and so it was proving to be. She and Vivienne got on like the proverbial house on fire.

Norma was still humming as she drove in through the wrought-iron gates and parked behind Douglas's Lagonda. He was at home, as he was to be at home all that week, though not on holiday. He was writing a paper, which he was very excited about, and which he'd told her was something of an honour to have been asked to do.

It was a struggle getting out of the MG and she made a mental note to tell Douglas they were going to have to swop cars again soon as they'd done before Lindsay arrived.

Once inside she went straight to the study expecting to find Douglas there beavering away, but the study was empty. Wondering where he was she went upstairs to Lindsay's nursery, only to discover that too was empty.

She met Nettie Simpson, one of the maids, in the passageway. 'Do you know where Miss Casden and Lindsay are?' she asked.

'While you were out Miss Casden took a sudden raging toothache, and your husband packed her off to see a dentist. He said he would look after Master Lindsay until she got back.'

Well that explained that, Norma thought. Phyl had mentioned having several tooth twinges of late, though had done nothing about it. 'And where is my husband and Master Lindsay?'

'I believe they're in the garden Ma'am.'

'And my mother-in-law?'

'She's having a nap Ma'am.'

Good, Norma thought, she'd have Douglas and Lindsay to herself. Forsyth was at the hospital of course.

Norma resumed humming as she tripped down the staircase. It really was a beautiful day, so beautiful and sunny in fact it had even contrived to do the impossible, namely make the inside of Castle Dracula appear almost a pleasant place to be.

There was a letter for Norma on the silver tray in the reception area which she had missed on the way in. She exclaimed with delight to recognise Helen Rolfe's handwriting. She popped the letter into one of her two pockets, she would read it later when she could take her time over it.

She was thinking about Helen as she went out into the garden, stopping to smile when Douglas and the pram came into view. He was slumped in a deckchair with a straw hat pulled over his eyes. There was an open folder on his lap which he'd either been reading or writing in before dozing off. The pram was beside him, at the edge of the pond.

He'd made an excellent job of his pond, she had to give him that. There were various lilies in it and all manner of weeds, the latter which, he'd explained to her, oxygenated the water. As of yet there were no slimies as he'd completed the pond well past spawning time, but there would be the following year when Douglas would stock it with spawn from some marshy land he knew over at Muirend. The pond wasn't empty though, he had put half a dozen goldfish in.

Norma took a deep breath, and closed her eyes. What a fabulous day it was! She listened to the steady drone of bees, a sophorific sound that would soon have sent her off had she allowed it to. Opening her eyes again she watched a red admiral flit by. And then a pair of cabbage whites caught her attention, one of them seemingly chasing the other as though they were having a game together.

She continued on to Douglas and the pram, and as she neared

them she noticed something on the netting which covered the pond at water level. Lindsay's big teddy that Eileen had given him she thought. Phyl was forever dressing it up for him as though it was a doll and the wee monkey must have thrown it out of his pram.

She glanced up as a plane passed overhead. An RAF plane she saw. It was most unusual for either a military or commercial aircraft to fly over Burnside. She could only remember it happening once before since she'd come to live in Blairbeth Road.

'Douglas?' she called out. 'Douglas, I'm back.' He mumbled something but didn't waken. She turned to the pram, and the instant she looked into it an icy-cold hand gripped her heart. The pram was empty.

With a whimper she whirled to stare with horror at what she'd thought from a distance was Lindsay's big teddy. But it wasn't the teddy at all, it was Lindsay, face down, arms and legs enmeshed in the netting. He was quite still.

She galvanised into action. Throwing herself forward she went down onto her knees by the verge of the pond, grabbed hold of Lindsay, and pulled him to her, at the same time grasping hold of the netting with her other hand. The netting ripped away with the frenzied force of her action.

Lindsay's face was tinged blue, his eyes open and staring. There were bits of weed clinging to his cheeks and in his mouth. He wasn't breathing.

'Oh my God! Oh my God!' she whispered, her hands all thumbs as she tried to free him from the netting entangling his arms and legs. Swearing loudly she took hold of the netting and hauled on it so that what had still been secured to its fixings now broke away.

Douglas came out of his sound sleep. What was going on? What was happening? He blinked, still disorientated, trying to focus. What was Norma doing with Lindsay? And why was the pond netting all . . . The sight of Lindsay's blue-tinged face went through him like an electric shock. He erupted from his deck-chair to swiftly kneel beside Norma and the boy.

'Do something! Do something!' Norma urged him as she tried to massage Lindsay's front. She'd learned how to do this in FANY, but her mind had gone blank, she couldn't remember the details of what she'd been taught.

'What happened?' Douglas demanded.

'Pond, he was face down in the pond.' Sick bubbled into her throat and out over her lips. It was something she was only dimly aware of.

Douglas fought to control the panic that was threatening to engulf him. He thrust Norma aside and started to massage the child's heart. 'Get the weed out of his mouth,' he ordered Norma, who did so. Feeling as far back as she could with a finger to find out if there was any lodged at the rear of the throat, which there wasn't.

She began crying, hot scalding tears that flowed down to mix with the streaks of sick on her chin. She began to shake violently all over.

She didn't know how long Douglas massaged. A few minutes? Ten? It seemed like all eternity. Finally, he stopped, and bowed his head. 'It's no use, the wee fella's gone,' he said, then he too started to weep.

She stared at the body of her bonnie boy whose arms and legs were still enmeshed in the netting. He'd come out the pram, fallen onto the netting face down, become entangled, and because his face was downwards hadn't been able to cry out. And like that, a fish in a net, he'd drowned. Throwing back her head she screamed out her agony. She screamed and screamed and screamed, and as she did it was as though something snapped inside her.

Travers emerged from the house at a run, and behind him two of the maids. Solange appeared in an upstairs window.

'Norma! Norma!' Douglas shouted, trying to take hold of her to shake her, but she pushed him away.

The pain brought Norma out of her hysteria, an explosion of it that caused her to gasp and bend over. Then, in rapid succession, the pain hit again and again. 'No! Please God no!' she pleaded, realising what was occurring.

Douglas and Travers both caught her when she lapsed into unconsciousness.

She came to, to find her eyes were gummy and that there was a terrible metallic taste in her mouth. The unmistakable smell of a hospital filled her nostrils.

'Mrs Ross? I'm Mr Imlach who's looking after you.'

And then she remembered. 'Oh my wee boy . . .' she whispered, and fresh tears started to flow. Mr Imlach looked grimly on. There were times he considered being a doctor the most awful job in the world. This was one of them. 'And . . .?'

'I'm sorry Mrs Ross. It was a stillborn birth. There was absolutely nothing we or anyone else could have done.'

She turned her head away from Imlach to stare at a blank wall. Her mind, her body – her oh so empty body – were numb. She might have been dead, as dead as the baby she'd lost, as dead as the wee son she'd dragged from the pond.

She pictured Lindsay as she'd last seen him. The bluish tinge to his face, his eyes open and staring, his body limp. Bits of weed still clinging to his cheeks, though gone from his mouth. But Imlach was speaking again. She tried to concentrate, to make sense of his words.

'I said your husband is outside. Shall I send him in to you?'

'No, I don't want to see him.' There was a long pause, then she added. 'Not yet. No, not yet.'

'I'll tell him that then.'

Her tears were blinding her, but she didn't care. She felt she'd never care about anything ever again.

She saw Douglas the following day. He came into her room carrying a bunch of flowers and a small case containing some clean nighties and other things from Blairbeth Road. She ignored the flowers when he laid them on her bedside table. There was a wooden chair which he placed beside the bed, and sat on. She waited for him to speak. It was ages before he did.

'I thought . . . I honestly believed I'd reined Lindsay properly in,' he mumbled eventually.

'Are you saying you hadn't?' She kept her voice neutral, though it was an effort to do so.

He swallowed hard. 'It's not clear. There's the possibility that I only half did the buckle up. If so either the strap worked its way loose, or else Lindsay somehow managed to open it himself.'

'They can't tell?'

Douglas shook his head. 'I have to say that I might not have buckled him in at all, that I forgot about it. I just . . . well I can't believe that of myself, that I'd be so careless.'

'You mean you don't want to believe it?'

He was unable to hold her gaze and looked away. 'My mind was full of the paper, and I was so damned tired. I had a dreadful night the night before. I was awake for hours before we got up.'

'You never said.'

'I'm often troubled with insomnia, far more than you've realised. I've never let on not wanting to bother or distress you.' He paused, then continued. 'I've wracked my memory trying to recall exactly what I did do, and I can't.' There was another silence between them. 'Aren't you going to say "I told you so" about the pond?'

'No,' she answered in a whisper.

'Thank you. I — ' He broke down, dissolving into tears.

Norma watched him impassively.

She took a deep breath, and closed her eyes. What a fabulous day it was! She listened to the steady drone of bees, a sophorific sound that would soon have sent her off if she'd allowed it. Opening her eyes again she watched a red admiral flit by. And then a pair of cabbage whites caught her attention, one of them seemingly chasing the other as though they were having a game together.

She looked back to Douglas and the pram, and there was Lindsay, standing up in the pram, staring down into the pond. He began to topple, ever so slowly, like some tiny tree that had just been felled.

She screamed a warning to Douglas, but he didn't hear. Hair streaming out behind her she raced for the pond, only for some reason she was moving as slowly as Lindsay was falling. He hit the netting to send a great splash of water drops arching high into the air. Face down he struggled, but the more he did the more enmeshed he became. She could see it all quite clearly even though she was yet some distance away.

Finally, at long last she reached the pondside where she dropped to her knees. He was still alive, she could tell from the bubbles streaming to the surface. She reached down to grab hold of him, to pull him free. *And her hands went straight through him.*

Frantically, again and again she tried, but her hands

wouldn't connect. They criss-crossed through his body as if she was a ghost, unreal. Screaming again, she came back to her feet – everything continuing in that strange slow motion – to go to Douglas asleep in his deckchair.

Once more it happened. When she tried to grasp hold of Douglas her hands went straight through him, just as they'd done with Lindsay.

Her screaming turned to a shouted plea. 'Douglas! Douglas wake up! *Wake up!*' He continued asleep, unhearing.

She returned to the spot she'd just come from to find that the bubbles had stopped. And with that she resumed screaming. Why couldn't she get hold of Lindsay? Why couldn't she save him? Why couldn't Douglas hear her? Why couldn't...

'There, there Mrs Ross, it's all right. You're only having a nightmare,' a soothing female voice whispered from afar.

'My boy, my little boy...' Norma mumbled.

'Yes, I know. I understand.'

'Can't... can't seem to...' There was a sharp prick in her right arm. 'I can't seem to... Oh Lindsay, Lindsay, mummy's here, but I can't seem to... can't seem to...'

Blackness, as though she was in some deep dark cellar whose only door had just been clanged shut, closed in on her. And she knew no more.

Norma stared at herself in the mirror above the washbasin. Her cheeks were sunken and she was hollow-eyed. Her complexion was muddy, unhealthy looking. She placed the black hat on her head, and pinned it so that it would stay in position. She carefully tucked several stray wisps of hair out of sight, then dropped the veil down over her face.

She was dressed entirely in black, in clothes she'd had Effie buy and bring into the hospital.

It was the day of the funeral, and the day Norma was to leave the hospital. She'd insisted that the latter coincide with the former, and had a reason for that insistence which she hadn't confided to anyone.

The Procurator Fiscal, as was his duty in such cases, had held an inquiry into Lindsay's death, his judgement being that death had been by misadventure. The PF had called personally, along with a WPC, at the hospital to take her statement.

Douglas came into the room. His hair had gone snow-white since Lindsay's death. 'Are you ready?' he asked in a quiet voice.

'Yes,' she replied, her tone firm and unemotional. He picked up her case and they went out into the corridor where Sister McLeish was waiting to say goodbye.

'Can I have the case,' Norma said to Douglas, which took him by surprise. He gave it to her, she in turn passing it on to Sister McLeish. 'If you can use any of the contents on the ward, please do. Otherwise I'd be obliged if you'd get rid of them for me.'

'Right Mrs Ross.' Sister McLeish held out a hand which Norma shook. 'Goodbye, good luck.' Only three words, but they had a wealth of meaning and understanding in them. Norma nodded her appreciation.

'Let's go,' Norma said to Douglas, and strode off down the corridor. There was only one item she'd kept from those Douglas had brought into the hospital for her, that was the ivory comb with overlaid silver grip Finlay Rankine had given her when she'd left Glasgow to join the FANY. She wouldn't have parted with that for all the tea in China.

Outside the Victoria, Douglas led the way to where their car was parked. 'The Vanden Plas, I didn't think either the Lagonda or MG was suitable. I was going to hire but Father and Mama thought we should use the Daimler. They're hiring instead.'

Norma remained silent, just waiting by the front passenger door until Douglas unlocked it for her. She slid inside, her first ever time in the Vanden Plas.

Douglas got into the driver's seat, and glanced at his watch. They were on schedule. Engaging the gears he started off for Rutherglen where the funeral parlour they were using was, and where the funeral would be departing from. He'd wanted it to leave from Blairbeth Road, but Norma had vetoed that, saying *she* wanted it to leave from the funeral parlour. He hadn't argued, but had capitulated instantly.

They drove some way in silence. 'I don't understand, why did you leave those bits and pieces with Sister McLeish?' Douglas asked eventually. Norma continued staring out the window and didn't reply.

'Norma?' He got no answer to that either. Holding the wheel

with one hand he groped for his cigarettes, and lit up. 'I'm going to have to live with this for the rest of my life you know,' he said in a strained, tight, voice.

She glanced at him, her eyes cold and hard as diamonds. 'So am I.'

Outside the funeral parlour the hearse and three cars were parked waiting for them. Forsyth and Solange were in the leading car; Effie and Brian in the second; Lyn, Iain, Eileen and Finlay in the third. Norma had insisted that only the immediate family attend the funeral. With the exception of Brian it was the first time the two families had met.

Douglas drew up beside Forsyth and Solange, and the hearse slowly moved off. He followed on behind, the other three behind him.

When they arrived at Rutherglen Cemetery Douglas came round to help Norma from the Vanden Plas and she told him curtly she could manage. Douglas and Brian carried Lindsay's small coffin down to the graveside; Forsyth and Finlay the coffin of the stillborn female baby.

The minister, Bible in hand, was already by the graveside. He had a few brief words with Norma and Douglas, then the service got under way.

Most of it was a jumble of words as far as Norma was concerned. When everyone else sang, she didn't. When the two coffins, under the guidance of the cemetery people, were lowered into the grave, she was the only female present not weeping. She was cried out; she had no more tears to shed.

Finally it was all over, and they began drifting back to where the cars were. Solange had offered to lay on a meal for the mourners, Norma had said no.

When they reached the cars Norma called out quietly to Brian. 'Da, could you come here please.' When Brian had joined her and Douglas she turned to her husband, stared him straight in the face, and said, 'I'm not going back to that house in Blairbeth Road. I'll never step inside it again. I'm leaving you.'

That pole-axed Douglas. He was completely lost for words.

'There is one thing, and one thing only, that I want from Blairbeth Road, the rest you can do with as you please. And that's the photograph of Lindsay in the brass frame.'

Douglas, still unable to speak, nodded. He was shocked, bewildered, his mind frozen like a block of ice.

'Take me home to Cubie Street Da.' Brian grasped her by the elbow and led her to his hired car where Effie was waiting.

Forsyth, sensing something was wrong, crossed over to Douglas. Brian assisted Norma into the car, then gestured to the rest of the family not to query anything for the moment, but to get into their cars and follow on.

A stricken Douglas watched Norma drive away. She didn't even glance once in his direction.

Brian answered the knock on the outside door. 'I brought the photograph Norma asked for,' Douglas said, looking even more awful and wretched than he had at the funeral three days previously.

Brian held out a hand. 'Thank you.'

'Can I...' Douglas nervously licked his lips. 'Can I see her? Please?'

Brian wasn't at all sure he agreed with what Norma had done in leaving Douglas. But she'd made her decision and, right or wrong, he'd stand by her, and it. 'I'm sorry, but she doesn't want to see you.'

'If only I could —'

'She was adamant about that,' Brian interjected.

Douglas realised there was no point in arguing. He gave Brian the photograph in its brass frame, a frame Norma had herself chosen. 'Wait!' he exclaimed when Brian went to close the door on him. Brian hesitated.

'I know she said she didn't want anything else from Blairbeth Road, but I brought her MG over anyway. It's outside the close mouth.' He handed the car keys to Brian. 'Tell her...' He took a deep breath. 'Tell her ...' He changed his mind, and shook his head. Turning away from the door and, with head bowed, shoulders slumped, made his way back down the stairs again.

Brian shut the door, leaned against it, and closed his eyes. 'Shit!' he swore softly. Then he went through to the bedroom where Norma was.

She was sitting in the rocking chair they'd brought from Kirn, and which had aye been a great favourite of his. He told her who had been at the front door, and what had been said. He gave her the photograph and car keys.

'Thank you Da.'

'There's a fresh pot of tea just making, do you want to come ben?'

'No.'

'Will I bring you a cup in here?'

'No thanks.'

'Is there anything you want?'

'Only to be left alone Da.'

When Brian was gone from the bedroom she held the photograph out in front of her and gazed at it. After a while she clasped the photo to her bosom, and slowly began to rock back and forth.

## *Chapter Fourteen*

'Come away in,' Eileen said to Alice Henderson who'd just chapped.

'It's yourself I want a wee word with, Eileen.'

'Well you're not standing on the landing while you do so, it's perishing,' Eileen replied. It was mid October and freezing outside. The weather forecast was that there might be snow.

Entering the living room Alice discovered Brian sitting smoking his pipe on one side of a blazing fire, Effie knitting on the other. Norma was at the table polishing the brasses, a job she enjoyed doing, and found relaxing.

Brian rose out of politeness. 'No no, sit where you are,' Alice said. Brian sank back into his comfy chair, and Alice sat on a wooden chair that Eileen brought over from the table.

'I've come to thank you for your invitation, it was most kind of you to ask us,' Alice said to Eileen. The invitation referred to was to Eileen and Finlay's wedding reception which was to take place in a fortnight's time. 'Leslie and myself will be delighted to attend.'

'Good,' Eileen nodded.

Alice coughed, and looked uncomfortable. 'I hope you won't be offended, but Midge won't be going.'

Eileen glanced at Effie. Effie hadn't wanted Midge to be included in the invitation, but she had said it wouldn't be right if he wasn't. They could hardly leave out Midge and invite his parents who, despite the fact their son had jilted Norma, had been the best of neighbours down through the years. And it would have been a terrible insult to the Hendersons not to ask them when the rest of the close was being invited.

'I'm sorry to hear that,' Eileen replied.

'And why can't he go?' Effie asked bluntly, but politely.

Alice started to rub her hands together as if she was washing them. 'It's not a case of can't, but won't,' she answered truthfully. Then, seeing Effie's expression. 'Oh it's nothing personal, I can assure you, which is why I came up to explain the situation to Eileen. It's just that, well I don't know if you've realised it or not, but Midge hasn't been over the door since he came back from Ruchill, not once. Leslie and I have argued with him and badgered him till we were both blue in the face, to no avail. He refuses to leave the house.'

'But why?'

'He doesn't want folk to see him in his wheelchair. He feels . . .' She groped for the words, 'just so much less than he was I suppose.'

Norma laid aside the soft cloth she'd been using to shine up a candlestick. Now that she came to think of it, she hadn't seen Midge out and about since she'd returned to live in Cubie Street. She'd been caught up so much in her own grief the fact hadn't registered. Nor had it registered with anyone else in the family as no one had commented.

Alice, becoming more distressed with every passing second, went on. 'He just sits in that room of his staring out the window and brooding. He doesn't even read, we get books from the library for him, but they lie there untouched. It's a real worry.'

'He can't go on like that,' Norma said.

'You try telling him that.'

'It must have been particularly hard for him having been a professional dancer, his legs and feet being the tools of his trade so to speak,' Brian commiserated.

Alice nodded.

'You can tell him that Finlay and I understand, and that no offence has been taken,' Eileen said softly.

'That's why I wanted to explain it myself.'

'Here, I'm not being sociable. I'll put the kettle on,' Effie said, rising.

'Och don't bother for me. And I'd better get back, I've left Midge alone in the house. Leslie has gone to visit a crony of his who's down with the bronchitis.'

'You bide and chaff a wee while,' Norma said to Alice. 'If you don't mind I'll go and have a talk with Midge. Maybe I can persuade him to go.'

'Oh if only you could! It would do him the world of good to get out.'

'Then you put that kettle on Ma,' Norma said, getting up. She went with Effie through to the kitchen where she washed her hands, after which she returned to the living room for Alice's front door key, intending to let herself into the Henderson house. When she had the key, she went away downstairs.

Midge glanced over from where he was sitting by the window, his face creasing with surprise to see it was her framed in his doorway. 'Hello,' she said.

'Hello,'

'Do you always sit in the dark?' For although the hallway light was on, his bedroom was in darkness.

'There's nothing wrong with being in the dark. I like it,' he replied aggressively. Then he remembered he hadn't spoken to her since she'd come back to Cubie Street. In a far softer voice he said, 'I was shocked to hear what happened. That must have been dreadful for you.'

'Aye, it was.'

'Words are so inadequate at times. So all I'll say is I'm sorry, and have you know I mean that from the very bottom of my heart.'

She appreciated his simplicity, it was the way all condolences should be given. She went over to him and kissed him on the forehead, which seemed the right thing to do. 'Thank you.'

The wheels of his chair whispered away from her. There was a click, and light from a tablelamp flooded the room. 'I can't have you here in the darkness with me, what would folk think?' he said, and laughed, a laugh that was sharp-edged and bitter.

'I've come to talk to you Midge.'

He gestured to a chair. 'Park your bum and tell me what about.'

He didn't speak like an American anymore, she noted. That had disappeared. 'Your ma says you won't go to Eileen and Finlay's wedding reception?'

He dropped his gaze and began picking imaginary bits of fluff from the tartan travelling rug draped over his legs. 'No.'

'Can we talk frankly? I am an old friend after all.' When he didn't answer she went on. 'You can't stay cooped up in this room and this house for the rest of your days. That's absurd.'

'Not to me it's not,' he replied defensively.

'What are you scared of?'

'I don't wish to go on with this...'

'I asked you what you're scared of Midge?' she interrupted.

He coloured slightly. 'Thanks for coming in Norma. I did want to see you, and would have come up before now except I have this little trouble getting up and down stairs.'

'You could have come up if you'd really wanted to. Your da would have helped you.'

He put his left thumb in his mouth, and started to chew its nail.

Norma decided to change tack, and tone. Very gently she said, 'You're going to have to start learning to come to terms with things, as I'm having to learn. God knows it isn't easy, but it has to be done.'

He stopped chewing his nail, his expression now a combination of anguish and despair. Slowly, reluctantly, as if he was divulging some awful secret, he replied. 'It's the pity I can't stand. The pity in people's eyes when they look at me and see what I've become, what I've been reduced to.'

'That's natural, for you and them. But no reason for you to hide yourself away like a hermit.' She paused, then added, 'If you don't want people to feel pity for you then you've got to stop feeling pity for yourself. That's the key.'

'And how can I *not* feel pity for myself? I've lost the use of my legs for fucksake!' he erupted.

'Yes you have, and that's something you're going to have to accept. Just as I'm having to accept that my little son is drowned, and that my baby daughter will never now be born.'

'Jesus!' he breathed, and ran a hand though his lank and listless hair.

She went over to him, and knelt beside his chair. 'So will you go to Eileen and Finlay's reception after all? It's as good a time and place as any to break out of this self-imposed isolation. To get out once more to face the world.'

A shudder ran through his upper torso. 'It's not really as good a time and place Norma. You're wrong about that.'

She frowned, failing to understand what he was getting at. 'I'm not with you?'

'I couldn't... I couldn't bear to sit in a wheelchair and watch you dance with someone else. That would just tear me apart inside,' he admitted in a choked whisper.

She nodded. She should have realised that would be sheer torture for him. But she had a solution. 'If I promise you that I won't dance with anyone, anyone at all, will you promise me to go?'

He went back to chewing the same nail as before.

'Do you want to be stuck away in this room for the rest of your natural? Is that what you really want?'

'No, of course not.'

'Then I ask you again. If I promise not to dance with anyone will you promise me to go?'

There was a long pause during which it was clear that a mental tussle was going on. Finally, he made his decision. 'I promise,' he said quietly.

'That's settled then,' she said, and rose to her feet. She stared at him, and he stared back. 'If I don't see you before I'll see you there. We'll sit together, all right?'

He gave her a weak smile. 'All right.'

As the front door clicked shut behind Norma, Midge was reaching out to switch off the table lamp so that he'd once more be in darkness. He hesitated, thought about it for a few moments, and then withdrew his hand. He'd leave the light on.

Norma turned away from the makeshift bar in the big rear room of Dow's pub where Eileen and Finlay's wedding reception was being held. She'd been to the bar to get drinks for her and Midge, and was now about to take them back to where she'd left him.

'Norma, wait up!'

Norma looked round to see Eileen making towards her. The wedding ceremony itself had been in a registry office a little over an hour and a half previously, and had gone just dandy. Eileen had been positively radiant as Finlay had slipped the ring onto her finger. A Finlay, it must be said, who was self-conscious for once in his life, which had amused Norma no end.

'How are you doing? Enjoying yourself?' Eileen asked as she joined her oldest sister.

'I am. It's a great reception.'

'Everyone appears to be having a fine old time.' She paused, then added. 'I never said at home but I was doubtful about coming back here to Dow's rear room, it being a bit of a barn. But in my heart of hearts it really was where I wanted the reception to take place, and so we settled on it.'

'I never asked, not wanting to appear nosy, but I take it Finlay knows this is where you and Charlie had your reception?'

'Oh aye.'

'And it doesn't bother him?'

'Not in the least. There's no jealousy on his part about me and Charlie, none at all. In fact, we often talk together about him. At times it's almost as if... I hope this doesn't sound perverted, but it's almost as if Charlie was still here in a way and that we were a threesome, Charlie, Finlay and me.' She laughed. 'It does sound perverted doesn't it? But it isn't at all.'

'Well I certainly don't have to ask if you're happy. You're fair bursting with it.'

'That's true Norma. I thought it was all finished for me when Charlie died. And then Finlay came along and I got a second chance.'

'I'm so pleased, for the pair of you.'

'We're an odd couple, as Finlay puts it. Like two strangely shaped pieces of carving that don't look like they'd fit together to form a whole, but surprisingly do.'

Norma pecked Eileen on the cheek. 'If I don't get a chance in the hubbub of your going away, have a smashing honeymoon. Any idea where you're off to?'

Eileen shook her head. 'Finlay's keeping that to himself. But wherever I'll tell you where it won't be, and that's the Adelphi Hotel. Dow's pub is one thing, the Adelphi Hotel quite another. That would have been quite wrong, in bad taste even.'

One of the neighbours from Cubie Street shouted Eileen's name and she waved she'd be right over. 'I'll away back to Midge then,' Norma said.

'Before you do.' Eileen placed a hand on the top of her sister's right arm, and drew Norma fractionally closer to her. 'After Charlie died I thought that was the end of it for me, as you know. But it wasn't. I want you to remember that.' And having said what she'd waylaid Norma to say, Eileen moved off, crossing to the neighbour who'd shouted to her. Norma stared after Eileen for four or five seconds, then began weaving a path through tables and chairs back to where Midge was waiting.

'Here you are,' she said, handing him the dram he'd asked for.

'I'd better not have too many of these,' he replied, waggling the glass at her. 'I don't want to be drunk in charge of a wheelchair.'

Norma laughed, and he laughed too.

'It's good you can make jokes about yourself,' she told him when they'd stopped laughing.

'You know something?'

'What?'

'That's the first time I have since,' he tapped his legs, 'this happened.'

'Then tonight's a breakthrough.'

'So it would seem.' He paused, then added softly, 'Thank you for persuading me to come.'

A few minutes later Finlay joined them, and gave Norma an exaggerated bow. 'May I have the pleasure Miss McKenzie?' he asked, using her maiden name.

'I'm not dancing tonight Finlay. But thanks for asking.'

'Och come on, you wouldn't refuse me on my wedding night surely?'

Midge started to look uncomfortable, thinking Norma was going to have to break her promise to him. And with Finlay too, by far and away the best male dancer in the hall.

But Norma was adamant she wasn't going to break her promise. 'Finlay, I'm not dancing this evening, not with you or anybody. Now please, as we are friends, don't press me.'

Finlay treated her to one of his crocodile smiles, thinking she was just having him on. He was about to do precisely what she'd asked him not to, when she reached over and took Midge by the hand. There was that in the gesture made him realise, as Norma had wished it to convey, why she didn't want to dance. And a quick glance into Midge's face told him he was right.

Norma saw that Finlay had got the message, that he understood. 'Why don't you get Mrs Rankine up?' Norma suggested. 'She's the one you should be tripping the light fantastic with.'

'Mrs Rankine?' Finlay repeated, and barked out a laugh. 'That's the first time I've heard her called that. And yes, I'll do just that.' He gave Norma another exaggerated bow, and

Midge a wink. Then left them to go off and seek out Eileen.

Norma raised her glass to Midge. 'Slainthe!' she toasted.

'Slainthe!' Midge repeated, his eyes shining with gratitude.

Norma, Midge, Alice and Leslie Henderson left the reception together. Effie and Brian were staying on for a wee while longer to continue chaffing with an aunt and uncle of Finlay's who they'd hit it off with.

'I'll push,' Norma said when they were outside Dow's pub. Then to Midge. 'If you don't mind that is?'

'I don't mind at all.'

Their glances held, and she read in his that he meant what he said. He *didn't* mind, which pleased her. In fact it pleased her a great deal.

They started off for Cubie Street, Alice and Leslie, arm in arm, in the lead with Norma and Midge following directly behind.

'So you enjoyed yourself after all?' Norma teased Midge.

'You know I did.'

'And I enjoyed myself too.'

'You didn't feel you'd missed out by not dancing?'

She shrugged. 'I get nowhere near the kick out of dancing as I used to, so not doing so wasn't that much of an imposition. Do you know "Lily of Laguna"?'

Her so abruptly changing the subject momentarily threw him. 'Eh?'

'I said do you know "Lily of Laguna"?'

'Aye, of course I do.'

'Right then. One two three go!'

From there they sang all the way back to the closemouth, Alice and Leslie readily joining in. They sang 'Lily of Laguna', 'Pedro the Fisherman', 'Red Sails in the Sunset', 'She'll be Coming Round the Mountains When She Comes' – as many of the old favourites as they could cram in in the distance.

It was rare.

A week that Sunday Midge was in the middle of reading the *Sunday Post*. He might not read anything else but he never missed The Broons and Oor Wullie, when the door to his bedroom opened and his father came striding in.

'Right lad, you're for out,' Leslie announced.
'No I'm not.'
'Yes, you are! Those are orders,' Alice said from the doorway where she'd appeared holding one of Midge's warm winter coats. She marched over to Midge and, with the help of Leslie, started getting Midge into it.
'What is all this?' Midge protested.
'We told you, you're going out.'
'But I don't want to go out. I want to stay here.'
'Hard cheese!' Alice answered, struggling to get an arm into a sleeve.
'You're going and that's an end of it,' Leslie informed him. 'And you should be so lucky to have a young woman, no I should say young lady, offer to take you out for the day.'
'What young lady?'
'The pair of you are having a picnic. Spam and jam sannies with a flask of good strong tea to wash it down with,' Alice added.
'What bloody young lady!'
'Language!' Alice admonished, waving a right forefinger under her son's nose.
'*What* young lady?' Midge pleaded as Alice did up his front coat buttons.
'Norma. She's taking you for a run in her car,' Leslie replied.
Norma! That cheered him, and a small smile curled the corners of his mouth upwards. He'd only seen her from the window to wave to since the reception.
'She says you need a breath of fresh air, and I can only say I heartily agree with her. Why just look at you, you're as peely wally as anything,' Alice said vehemently.
Midge rubbed a hand over his face. He couldn't argue there, he was peely wally. Suddenly he was excited at the prospect of going somewhere, anywhere. Particularly as it was with Norma. *Because* it was with Norma, he corrected himself.
When Midge was ready – well wrapped up, for despite the sun shining outside it was still very cold – Leslie pushed his chair out of the house, and bumped it down the stairs. Outside on the street they found Norma and Brian waiting.
Brian opened the MG's passenger door, then turned to Midge who'd been brought alongside. 'Right,' he said. He and Leslie

bodily lifted Midge out of the wheelchair and manoeuvred Midge into the car seat. When they'd done this Norma got into the other side. 'Ready?' she asked.

'Aye.'

'Then let's be off.'

Brian and Leslie waved to them from the pavement; Alice and Effie from respective windows as they drove down Cubie Street and into Gallowgate.

'I feel like I've been kidnapped,' Midge said.

'Is that a complaint?'

'Would it make any difference if it was?'

She laughed. 'Not in the least.'

'Then it isn't. It's an observation.'

How easy it was between them again, she thought. Just as it had been in the old days when they'd been together. Before he'd . . . She put that memory forcibly from her mind.

'Where are we going then?'

'Where do you fancy?'

He gestured at her. 'It's your car. You choose.'

'What would you think of a trip down the coast to the Cloch Lighthouse?'

'I'd think it was a good idea, just the ticket.'

She grinned. 'The Cloch Lighthouse it is then.'

He watched her drive, noting how expertly she handled the car. The machine transformed into an extension of herself. 'You drive well.'

'Thank you. I did a lot of it earlier on in the war with FANY, fourteen and sixteen hours a day sometimes.'

'Did they teach you?'

'No, I eh . . . learned in Glasgow before the war and FANY.' She wasn't going to tell him she'd taken up driving shortly after he'd run off with Zelda as a device to stop herself thinking and brooding.

'Ma mentioned in one of her letters that you'd come into money.'

'From old man Gallagher who used to come into Barrowland to watch me because I was the spit of his dead daughter Morna. Remember?'

'How could I forget!' Midge laughed. 'And he popped off leaving you a pile?'

'I don't know if I'd call it a pile exactly, but certainly enough to keep me comfortably off for the rest of my days.'

'Well, good for you Norma. I suppose that means you didn't have to worry about money when you walked out on your husband.'

Norma shifted uneasily in her seat. She wasn't too keen on Midge talking about Douglas. 'Yes,' she replied quietly.

'Can I ask you something about him? Something I've been wondering about. I mentioned it to my father but he didn't know the answer, and he said it wouldn't be polite to ask your folks about it.'

God, what on earth was he going to come out with? She dreaded to think. 'What do you want to know?'

'It's a real Glasgow question. His mother is French, right?'

'Yes.'

'So is she a Catholic?'

Now Norma knew what he was driving at. And he was right, it was a real Glasgow question, Glaswegians being almost paranoic where religion is concerned. Or to be more specific, where Catholicism and Protestantism were concerned. 'She is.'

'Does that make him one then? And if it does did you turn when the two of you married?'

Norma smiled. 'I thought you were broad-minded? I thought you'd travelled?'

'I am broad-minded, and I certainly have travelled. But I'm still curious.'

'Once Glasgow always Glasgow,' she riposted.

'Particularly when other Glaswegians are involved,' he acknowledged, and they both laughed.

'Douglas is a Protestant so I didn't have to turn,' she explained. 'It was my father-in-law's wish that as Douglas was to be brought up in Scotland and as he himself was a Protestant, then Douglas was to be one too. I doubt my mother-in-law was very happy about that, but she agreed, and so Douglas was baptised into the Church of Scotland. Curiosity satisfied?'

He nodded.

'Good.'

They swung into the Great Western Road which would quickly take them out of Glasgow. 'I can smell the sea already,' Midge said, closing his eyes and letting his head drop back.

'You can smell the sea in Sauchiehall Street sometimes. You don't have to leave the city for that,' she jibed.

'You know what I mean!'

She glanced at him. 'You're looking better already. You're beginning to get some roses in your cheeks.'

'And I feel better already. As if I were undergoing a spring-clean.'

'And not before time. How long is it since you came out of Ruchill?'

'Nearly seven months.'

'Well now I've winkled you from the house a second time I'm going to make sure you get out more often. And there's no use saying you won't want to go, I'll drag you down the stairs screaming if I have to.'

'Why Norma?' he asked, suddenly very serious.

'Why what?'

'Why are you doing this for me?'

She considered that for a few seconds, then replied softly. 'Because I hate to see what you're doing to yourself. And alsc ...' She hesitated, then added in an even softer voice. 'Also maybe it's good for me to be concerned about somebody else's problems rather than just my own.'

He nodded. 'I understand.'

They went via Port Glasgow, Greenock and then Gourock. When they reached Cloch Point, Norma drew the car off the road and onto the grass verge from where they had a splendid view of the Firth of Clyde.

'I could murder a cup of that tea I was promised,' Midge said.

Norma got the picnic things out and soon they were delving into the sandwiches and being thawed out by the steaming tea.

'If you look just over there, to the right, that's Dunoon,' Norma said, pointing. 'Kirn, where I was born and where we lived before coming to Cubie Street, is to the right of that.'

'I'd forgotten about Kirn. You left there, when?'

She had to think, work it out. 'Let me see, I was fourteen, no fifteen at the time. And I'm thirty now. So it was fifteen years ago.'

He shook his head in amazement. 'As long as that!'

'Fifteen years we've known one another,' she mused.

'Murray Muir's engagement to Jenny Elder, it was during

their party in the street that I first clapped eyes on you.'

'No, that was when we first spoke and you asked me to dance. The first time we saw each other was in Gilmour's shop when I went in with my sister Lyn to get a few messages. You were in front of the counter chaffing to Chic Gilmour who was serving.'

'Oh aye, you're right,' Midge said, remembering.

'That was the day we arrived in Glasgow.' She screwed up her forehead in memory. 'It's coming back to me now. I was still fourteen when we came to Glasgow, and we saw each other in Gilmour's shop, and I was fifteen on the day of the engagement party when we danced together for the first time. And you annoyed me by calling me a bairn!'

'Well I was very ancient myself – I would have been seventeen then.'

'Most venerable,' Norma agreed, and they both laughed.

They reminisced right through the picnic, and most of the way back to Glasgow, Norma taking them the alternative route which was through Largs and Johnstone. She had a reason for this other than just a change of scenery to their outward journey.

When they reached Paisley she said. 'I brought us back this way because it takes us into the south side, and not all that far from Rutherglen. I'd like to stop off at the cemetery and pay a visit, which I do every Sunday. do you mind?'

'Not at all,' he replied, sobering up.

She parked outside the cemetery. 'I won't be long.'

'You take as long as you want. I only wish I could go in with you.'

She nodded, then got out the car and went through the gates into the cemetery. When she finally returned her face was stony, and there was a cold look about her that had nothing whatever to do with the weather.

'Okay?' he queried gently.

'Yes.' She started the engine, engaged the gears and drove slowly away.

Going down Mill Street he placed a hand on her thigh nearest him. There was nothing sexual about the gesture. Rather it was one of understanding, comfort and sympathy. He kept his hand there for quite some time before removing it again.

* * *

'Not fair!' Midge exclaimed as Norma threw yet another six to win her third successive game of Snakes and Ladders. 'I think you're cheating.'

'I am not!'

'No one can be that lucky without some kind of humphery mumphery going on.'

'Humphery mumphery yourself. You're just a bad loser, that's all.'

'I'm nothing of the sort.'

She stuck her tongue out at him. 'You are sought.'

His reply to that was to cross his eyes at her, and blow a loud raspberry.

'Disgusting,' she said. 'Want a cup of coffee?'

'Please.'

She left him to gather up the bits and pieces and put them away in their box while she went through to the kitchen. When she'd put the kettle on, she returned to the living room where she stoked up the fire. It was a Wednesday night in December and she'd come down to keep Midge company while his parents were out at the pictures. His sister Katy wasn't at home anymore, having married an Irishman towards the end of the war and moved to a place called Portadown. Since their run down the coast the previous month Norma had been seeing quite a bit of Midge, taking him out in the car when she could get the petrol and staying in with him, sometimes when his folks were there, other times when they weren't, to talk and play various card and board games which she'd discovered they both enjoyed.

When the kettle started to sing she went back again to the kitchen and made the coffee. While she was doing this she swithered whether to bring the subject up or not. The last thing she wanted to do was raise false hopes.

'There's a terrific heat off that fire. Best coal we've had in ages,' Midge commented when Norma rejoined him, and handed him his coffee.

'Midge, I want to talk to you.'

'Oh aye?'

'The truth is I don't really know whether I should do this or not. However, for better or worse, I've decided I'm going to.'

He was both mystified and intrigued. 'Do what?'

'Tell you a story.'

He gave a short laugh. 'Is that all?'

She sat in one of the armchairs by the fire, from where she regarded him steadily. 'It's a story about my mother and me, and what happened in '41.' She began to tell him of the time when she'd come home on leave to find Effie seriously ill, and what had occurred after that. As she spoke Midge's expression grew more and more intent and he became more and more entranced by what she was telling him.

Finally the story was over. She sipped at her coffee to find it had gone completely cold.

'Healing hands? Is such a thing really possible?'

'According to Mr Creighton it is. He says it's a well-documented fact that some people have this ability to cure by merely placing their hands on an inflicted or diseased person. Mr Creighton told me he was a sceptic until he witnessed a holy man in India cure by this method, after which he became a firm believer in the phenomenon.'

'And you have it, this ability?'

She gave him a rueful smile. 'I did that time with Ma. There was no other explanation for what took place. She was dying through a combination of encephalitis and her allergy to M & B, and then suddenly she wasn't dying anymore, but had recovered.' Norma paused, then went on hesitantly. 'But I must emphasise that this is the only time this miracle, what else could you call it? has worked for me.'

'Have you *tried* to make it work? Have you tried it on anyone else?'

'No.'

Midge couldn't help the excitement from creeping into his voice. 'So you don't really know if you could make it work again or not?'

In a tremulous whisper she replied. 'No, I don't.'

He licked lips that had suddenly gone dry. It was ridiculous, too far-fetched. And yet. And yet it had worked on Mrs McKenzie. Norma said it had. 'Do you think it might –'

'I don't want to raise false hopes Midge, that's the last thing I want to do,' she interrupted. 'But on the other hand it seems to me to be worth a try. After all, what have you got to lose?'

He glanced down at his useless legs. 'Nothing at all,' he replied quietly.

'And there is something else. Remember when I wanted to improve our dancing I went to the library and Eileen's Charlie got me books on the subject? Well, thinking about this, and your infantile paralysis, I decided I'd do the same again, that I'd read up on what was wrong with you. And that's where I learned of the coincidence.'

'What coincidence?' he demanded harshly.

'I discovered that infantile paralysis is caused by a virus infection which specifically attacks the anterior, motor, horn cells in the spinal cord. It may also, however, affect the brain, especially the mid-brain, producing encephalitis.'

'You mean what your mother had?'

'Her encephalitis was probably caused by a different virus. But nonetheless you see the tie-in?'

'And you think that if you can cure your mother you can cure me?'

'No no, I'm saying I'm willing to try if you are.'

Midge took a deep breath. The excitement that had come into his voice was now hammering inside him. 'You're damn right I am!'

'You sure?'

'Of course I'm sure!' he exploded. 'As you said, what have I got to lose?'

'Right then.' She rose from the chair, took Midge's cup and saucer from him and laid those with her own on the table. Then she returned to stand in front of him.

She looked thoughtful for a few moments. 'The lights I think,' she muttered. She went and switched off the overhead light, then the standard lamp that was in a corner. After which she returned to Midge.

He was covered in gooseflesh, and had prickles all over the tops of his shoulders. His stomach had tightened into a knot.

Norma stood in the darkness, the only illumination coming from the fire, and wondered what to do next. She decided to go down on her knees in front of Midge.

When she was so positioned she removed the tartan travelling rug covering his legs, dropped it aside, and placed her palms and outspread fingers on his thighs.

Midge swallowed hard as he watched Norma close her eyes, then bow her head in concentration. Oh to be able to walk again, to leave this bloody chair behind forever, to ... A cold sheen of perspiration burst on his forehead.

In her mind Norma conjured up a picture of Lynsey as Lynsey had appeared to her in her mother's bedroom. Lynsey stared sorrowfully at her.

Please Lynsey, help Midge as you did my mother, she pleaded silently.

Norma made Lynsey come closer. As before, there was a faint luminous glow surrounding Lynsey. And every so often she sort of shimmered as if it was an act of supreme willpower that was keeping her there.

Please Lynsey, help Midge as you did my mother, Norma pleaded a second time.

Lynsey's sorrowful stare transferred itself to Midge. Then she glanced back at Norma, and the hint of a smile touched the corner of her mouth. Your hands, she said.

Norma, with her hands still on Midge's thighs, visualised herself holding them out to Lynsey, and waited for Lynsey to make them tingle as they had done with Effie.

Lynsey's smile widened a fraction, and as it did ... Norma waited expectantly for the strange tingling to invade her hands. She waited in vain.

She tried again, starting at the beginning where Lynsey appeared to her. And again nothing happened, no tingling, no sense of energy flowing into Midge.

She opened her eyes and looked up at Midge. 'I'm sorry,' she said, removing her hands.

'What do you mean?'

She sat back on her heels. 'Nothing, nothing at all.'

'Maybe ...'

'No maybes Midge, there was nothing. Nothing happened. I did my best but it just didn't happen.'

He bit back bitter disappointment. He felt like cursing, but didn't.

She shook her head. 'Perhaps the power was only given to me as a one-off thing.'

'Do you think that?'

'I honestly don't know, Midge. I'm just as in the dark,' she smiled thinly, thinking at the moment that was literally true, 'about this as you are. Mr Creighton said that my healing ability could be latent and that Lynsey Dereham was a device, or catalyst, used by my subconscious to bring that ability to the surface. That's why I've been thinking of Lynsey, recreating events as they occurred in Ma's bedroom, trying to get that device or catalyst activated again.' She pulled a long face. 'But as I just said, I failed to do so.'

This time he did swear. 'Fuck!'

She knew she'd done precisely what she hadn't wanted to, raise his hopes only to dash them again. 'I'm sorry,' she repeated.

'Just because it didn't work this time doesn't mean it won't, he said doggedly. 'Let's have another attempt?'

'I don't . . .'

'Please Norma?' Then, throwing her own words back at her. 'After all, what have we got to lose?'

How could she refuse? She couldn't. 'All right then.' She decided that on this occasion she would keep her hands free so she could physically extend them when entreating Lynsey.

Coming back to her knees, she closed her eyes and bowed her head.

'What you're talking about isn't medicine as I know it,' Rodney Creighton said. Norma had made an appointment to see him, and was now facing him across his desk. She'd just finished telling him about her sessions with Midge, and how each of them had ended in total failure. 'I can't even begin to advise you how to turn on this talent of yours which was so successful with your mother.'

'I thought . . . Well it seemed the natural thing to consult you for advice. You do believe in healing hands after all, and you are a doctor.'

Creighton frowned. 'How many times did you say you'd tried with Mr Henderson?'

'Half a dozen occasions in all.'

'Hmmh!' Creighton mused, and leaned back in his chair. This was a real poser.

'If you can't suggest anything then I'll give up. I've already told Mr Henderson that.'

'And what did he say?'

'What could he say. I just feel rotten about the whole business now and wish I'd never brought it up with him.'

'It was a gamble that didn't come off Miss McKenzie. You mustn't reproach yourself.' He paused to turn something over in his mind. When he spoke again it was in the same neutral tone that he normally employed. 'May I ask, Miss McKenzie, are you a religious woman?'

That surprised her. 'I don't exactly go to church every Sunday. But yes, I am.'

'Then why don't you try the power of prayer to unlock the door to your gift. That might possibly be the answer.'

She stared at the specialist. 'What an odd recommendation for a doctor to make,' she said slowly.

'Is it really? Love and prayer, Miss McKenzie, aren't they the two strongest forces in the universe?'

'But I don't love Mr Henderson,' she blurted out.

'Excuse me for presuming, but you spoke about him as though you did.'

'Well I used to, but that was a long time ago.'

'Oh, I see!'

Of course she didn't still love Midge. Or did she? Had she ever fallen out of love with him? One thing was certain, she had been in love with Douglas when she'd married him. But at that time Midge had been out of her life, and unlikely ever to return into it. Could you love two men simultaneously? Of course you could, an old love and a new. Certainly she hadn't thought of herself still to be in love with Midge. Or to put that another way, she hadn't thought about it at all. Was she?

She brought her attention back to Creighton.

'What do you think?' Norma asked having just pulled the MG into the kerb and parked.

'About what?' Midge queried, mystified.

She pointed over to their right. 'That house.'

Whatever was she on about? Was it some sort of game? 'It's a very nice house. Why?'

'It's a bungalow actually, which means there are no stairs to go up and down. It has a lovely garden out at the back, and a small one in the front as you can see.' She sucked in a breath.

'And savour that air, country fresh! A far cry from the pong you get in Bridgeton eh?'

'A far cry,' he agreed. 'Norma, what is this all about?'

'Have you ever been to Nitshill before? I hadn't until a couple of days ago. It not only smells like the country round here, it is the country. The village is surrounded by fields which at other times of the year,' it was mid-February, 'are filled with cows, sheep, horses and, I don't know! all sorts of animals. And there are several woods. One over there,' she said, indicating. 'And a smaller one down that way.' She indicated in a different direction.

'The area is new to me,' he confessed. 'And yes it is very countrified.'

'You like it here then?'

He wished she would get to the point, this was becoming aggravating. 'Indeed, it's most pleasant.'

'And the bungalow?'

He glanced again at the bungalow in question. 'Looks very solidly built.'

'How would you care to live in it? With me.'

He turned to stare at her. 'Say that again?'

'I'm not joking Midge, I mean it. How would you like to live in that bungalow with me? It's up for sale and I could easily afford the price.'

He was dumbstruck. This was completely out of the blue.

'Staying up flights of stairs in a tenement is a terrible drawback when you're in a wheelchair. You're utterly reliant on others, which in your case means your father as you're too heavy for either your Ma or I to get up and down. It would be totally different in a bungalow, we can put in a couple of small ramps at the front and rear and you can come and go as you please. Think of the freedom that would give you?'

It would indeed. He couldn't argue with that.

'And here there would be the gardens for you to sit out in during good weather, and then there's the pub just along the road if you fancied a pint. It would be a whole new way of life for you.'

He swallowed hard. 'You and I, *together*?'

'That's right.'

He glanced away, and an expression of anguish came over his

face. 'I thought you understood. It's not only my legs that don't function, it's everything down there. I'm not a man anymore, not in that sense of the word.'

'That won't matter, Midge,' she told him softly.

He shot her a look which clearly said *liar*!

'It won't, I assure you. Lindsay's death and losing the baby has left me . . . Well, let's say I'll be content to settle for a cuddle.'

'You would?'

She nodded.

He wasn't the only cripple, he thought. But the damage inflicted on Norma was in her mind, not her body. 'I know a shop where we can buy those ramps,' he said.

'We'll go there now.' And they did.

Norma was walking up Sauchiehall Street. She'd come into the town for a rendezvous, had arrived early, and so was doing a wee bit of window shopping to pass the time.

The typewriter was in a pawnbroker's window, and the moment she set eyes on it, it gave her an idea. She and Midge had been living in the bungalow for four months now, and were both well settled in. Locally they were known as Mr and Mrs Henderson, something that had been assumed, and which they'd agreed not to deny.

Midge had changed for the better. Gone was the moroseness and listlessness of Cubie Street, replaced by a restless energy that was forever sending him prowling round the house and village in his wheelchair. Quite simply he needed something to occupy his mind and for a while now Norma had been trying to think of an activity or project to fill the bill. The typewriter she was staring at just could be the solution.

Going into the pawnbroker's she bought the machine, then had the man load it into the boot of her Austin 12 which she brought round to the front of the shop. The Austin 12 had swiftly replaced the MG after they'd moved to Nitshill because it was far easier, being a larger vehicle and a saloon, to get Midge in and out of.

Norma reparked the Austin 12 where it had been before, then hurried into Treron's tearoom where she found Vivienne Gregory waiting for her. It was the first time she'd seen Vivienne since that nightmarish day the previous July when she'd left

Vivienne to return to Blairbeth Road, and find Lindsay dead in the pond.

Vivienne rose as Norma approached the table at which she'd already been sitting. 'Hello,' she said, not quite sure whether a handshake or kiss was in order.

'Hello Vivienne,' Norma replied somewhat shyly. She made to kiss Vivienne on the cheek, just as Vivienne stuck out a hand. That caused them to laugh, and broke the ice. She kissed Vivienne on the cheek, and Vivienne did the same to her.

'It's good to see you again.'

'And you,' Vivienne smiled.

They sat. 'You've been on my conscience,' Norma said. 'You were the only friend I had amongst the circle I moved in when at Blairbeth Road. There was no need for me to stop seeing you because I'd walked out on Douglas.' She hesitated. 'Or don't you agree?'

'If I didn't I wouldn't be here.'

A waitress came over, and they ordered tea and crumpets. When the waitress had left Vivienne said, 'On a number of occasions I nearly asked Douglas for your address so I could look you up. In the event I never did. After what happened I wasn't sure you'd want to see anyone who might remind you.' She paused, then asked tenderly, 'So how has it been for you?'

'To begin with it didn't bother me whether I lived or died. Let's just say I now prefer to live.'

Vivienne reached across and squeezed Norma's hand. 'Good.'

'You've seen Douglas then?'

'Jim and I had him to dinner a fortnight ago.'

'I suppose I should ask how he is?'

'A man demented is how I'd describe him. He's going through absolute hell. I heard on the grapevine that if it wasn't for his father he'd have lost his job at the hospital. Apparently the standard of his work has fallen right away.'

Norma stared grimly at Vivienne. 'I can't say I feel any sympathy for him. I don't.'

'When he was at dinner he spoke about you. He misses you dreadfully. He blames himself totally for what happened.' Norma didn't reply to that, and silence fell between them. Eventually Vivienne said, 'Did you know he's left home?'

'What! I don't believe it!' That really rocked her.

'It's true.'

'I couldn't get him out of that mausoleum, and away from his damned mother. I pleaded with him but he wouldn't budge.'

'Well he's left now, shortly before Christmas. I'm not clear on the details, he was vague about those, but there was an unholy row that involved Catherine Stark.'

'Catherine Stark?'

'I think, reading between the lines, that his mother must have been trying to do a bit of stage-managing to which he strongly objected.'

Norma nodded, that made sense. 'Trying to replace me with her I'd imagine. A liaison Solange has long favoured.'

'But not Douglas?'

'No. He likes Catherine as a friend, but that's as far as it goes. Something Solange has always refused to accept, as has Catherine herself.'

'And so Douglas decamped. He's renting a flat in University Avenue. A one-bedroom affair which he says is liveable in, if only just.'

'Well, well, well,' mused Norma. Douglas had moved out of Blairbeth Road! That really was a turn up for the book.

Their tea and crumpets arrived, and Vivienne played mother. 'Do you mind if I make an observation concerning your marriage – you might not appreciate it?' Vivienne asked slowly.

'Go ahead.'

'I know you lost Lindsay, and the child you were carrying. But because it was Douglas's fault doesn't mean he feels it any less than you do. In fact, with the guilt he's riven by, surely it's fair to say he feels it even more? And on top of losing Lindsay and the baby you were carrying he also lost you.' She paused for emphasis. 'You got rid of him – he lost you.'

'Are you suggesting I forgive him?'

Vivienne shook her head. 'It's not my place or business to suggest any such thing. But I would like you to consider that your children had two parents, and it's not only you that's grieving for them. And that, no matter how you might feel towards him, Douglas is still in love with you.'

'He said that?'

'When he came to dinner, yes.'

'You don't think I should have left him?' Norma accused.

'I can tell you this, I've thought about it and if I had been in your position, and Jim had been in Douglas's, I wouldn't have left Jim. Mistakes were made that had tragic results, but I wouldn't have left Jim because of those results. But then again, what's right for me isn't necessarily right for you.'

Norma stared into her cup as she stirred her tea. It wasn't tea she was seeing, but a pond with Lindsay lying face down in the netting covering the pond. Then the vision changed to Massingham and happier times. How good it had been between her and Douglas then. She came out of her reverie as Vivienne asked her a question.

'How are you getting on staying again with your parents? Everything going smoothly there?'

Norma lifted her cup, and sipped its contents. While she was doing this she regarded Vivienne over the cup's rim. Should she tell Vivienne about Midge and their bungalow, or not? It was something she'd been debating with herself since telephoning Vivienne to arrange this meeting. 'Can you keep something to yourself? Not that it's a secret, I would just prefer it didn't go any further for the time being.'

'My lips are sealed,' Vivienne promised.

Norma believed her. Vivienne was the type who kept her word. She started at that day sixteen years previously when she and Lyn had walked into Gilmour's shop.

Norma kneaded Midge's left calf as she'd learned to do. She began at the buttocks, worked her way down the left leg, and then the right. It was a ritual she performed every day, as had Alice Henderson before her. The people at Ruchill had said it was necessary to maintain proper circulation, and keep the flesh and muscles as healthy as was possible in the circumstances.

Midge grunted. 'Ouch! That was sore,' he complained.

'Sorry,' she smiled in reply. A smile that froze on her face as the import of what he'd just said sunk home. His back suddenly stiffened as it sunk home on him also.

'Oh my God!' he breathed, and twisted round to stare at her in wonderment.

Heart thumping, she took a small piece of flesh between thumb and forefinger, and nipped.

He grimaced.

'You felt that?'

He swallowed hard, and nodded. At the back of his mind he was noting that there was a feeling of unreality about the moment, as if he'd somehow slipped into a dream situation.

Norma was feeling exactly the same way. 'You're certain? You're not just imagining it?'

Had he imagined it? Was it just wishful thinking? 'Pinch me again.' She did, and this time he laughed, a laugh that died and choked in his throat. A hint of tears gleamed in his eyes. 'That was quite, gloriously painful.'

She lightly tickled the same spot. 'How about that?'

'Yes.' Nodding vigorously. 'Yes, yes!'

She moved further down his left calf. 'And there?'

'Yes . . . no . . . I'm not sure.'

The nip she now gave him was the most vicious yet, it left an angry red weal on his skin.

'Definitely. But nowhere near as much sensation as further up.'

She quickly went over his entire lower torso, but there was only one small section that registered feeling. The section was roughly circular, and about four to five inches in diameter.

Midge reached behind him and touched the area for himself. 'Do you think this might be the start . . .?' He trailed off.

'I honestly don't know. What I do know is that when I rubbed you there yesterday you felt nothing.'

He tickled himself, and what had been a gleam of wet became actual tears which welled in his eyes, spilling over to trickle down his cheeks. 'I must go back to Ruchill right away and report this to the doctors there,' he husked.

'Yes, right away,' she agreed.

'Oh Norma!'

She took the hand he held out to her, and clasped it tightly to her bosom. Bending over she kissed a tear-stained cheek.

Half an hour later, Midge bubbling over with excitement, they pulled up in front of the hospital's main entrance.

Norma let herself in through the cemetery gates as she did every Sunday, and started down the path that would lead, via a side path, to the grave. She was several rows behind the one the grave was located on when she spotted him. She hadn't seen the

Lagonda out on the street so he must have parked it round a corner. Or perhaps he'd changed his car as she herself had.

She stopped, and stared at him. He was standing sort of hunched up with his hair, longish and unkempt, flapping in the stiff breeze. His shoulders were shaking.

She walked a little closer and saw that he'd brought a bunch of flowers which he'd laid on the grave. Then she got a good look at his face and understood what Vivienne had meant by him being a man demented.

A man demented and riven with guilt, Vivienne had said, both plainly obvious to Norma. His contorted, agonised expression showed only too clearly the depth and agony of his emotions. Douglas Ross, her husband, was living in hell.

She had the urge to go to him, to speak. But couldn't bring herself to do so. Turning, she walked silently back up the path. She'd drive round for a bit, then return later.

The party was Norma's idea, and had come to her during one of the daily visits to Ruchill that had followed the localised return of sensation to Midge's left calf. Sensation that had swiftly begun to spread out from the original area, and then appeared also in the right leg.

When it was eventually confirmed that he would be able to walk again - and what a joyous never-to-be-forgotten day that had been! - Midge had declared to Norma that he was going to continue to keep his new progress secret from his parents until such time as he was able to give them the surprise of their lives by going to Cubie Street and walking in on them.

Norma's idea was, rather than surprise the Hendersons, then surprise all their friends and relatives piecemeal, why not surprise the entire kit and caboodle at once? Midge had thought that a terrific suggestion and so, with his legs technically fully operational again, Norma had gone ahead and arranged the party they were now at. And the venue? Where else but the big rear room of Dow's pub.

Norma smiled to herself. *Was* it her healing hands that had brought life back to Midge's lower torso? Or was that something which would have happened anyway? Only God had the answer to that and, as the saying went, he wasn't telling. Her smile widened a fraction. As far as she was concerned the whys and wherefores were irrelevant, the important thing was that Midge was back on his pins again.

Norma brought herself out of her reverie to gaze about her. Alice and Leslie Henderson were chaffing with their daughter Katy who'd come over with her husband from Northern Ireland for the occasion. And beside them Beryl and Bob Gillespie who'd helped her and Midge with their dancing all those years ago when she and Midge were first starting out.

And there were the Fullartons and Reids. While across on the far side talking to Granda McNaughton from number 22 was Rodney Creighton. She had rung Creighton personally to invite him to the party, and had hinted heavily that, in the light of the last conversation they'd had, he might find it more than interesting. He was the only person at the party who had any inkling what the celebration was all about.

Eileen and Finlay, looking radiantly happy, went gliding by, dancing to a foxtrot the small band was playing. If an odd match, it was certainly proving a successful one Norma thought. And now there was talk of Finlay opening his own dance studio with Eileen as a partner. She might invest some money in that, she contemplated. And decided there and then she would.

She glanced at her watch. The party had been going for an hour and forty minutes, long enough for it to get warmed up and for those who drank to have something of a bucket. She judged the time was ripe.

'Now?' she asked Midge who was beside her in his wheelchair.

He looked round the hall, came back to her and nodded. 'Now,' he agreed.

She went up to the band, and had a word with them when they'd finished the foxtrot. She then returned to Midge and pushed his wheelchair out into the centre of the room. 'Ladies and gentleman can I have your attention please!' Norma called out. As the chatter and general hubbub died away she noted that Creighton was staring at her very expectantly indeed.

When she had silence she went on. 'Many of you are wondering why Midge and I are holding this party. We told you when we invited you that the reason for it was an extremely important one, but didn't say what that reason was. Friends, relatives, neighbours, we'd now like to show you that reason.'

Whispering broke out, folk speculating amongst themselves.

Norma again appealed for silence, which she got. 'As most of you will know Midge and I were professional dancers in the thirties, the last occasion we danced together being the night we won the All Scotland Dance Championship.' She paused for effect. 'Until tonight that is.'

She signalled the band who struck up, as she'd instructed them, an old-fashioned waltz. She then held out a hand to Midge who accepted it, and rose from his wheelchair.

Somebody screamed. For the most part people just stood and sat there, goggling at what was taking place, looking stunned.

'It's been a long time, Midge.'

'A long long time,' he agreed, taking her into his arms. And with that they moved off round the floor.

As they danced Norma began to cry. The first time she'd done so since Lindsay's death, and losing the baby.

Midge was driving them home; since getting the power of his legs back he drove at every opportunity. Like walking, it was something he'd come to believe he'd never do again.

'Creighton was right, we were lucky we never gave anyone a heart attack,' he said.

'I should have thought of that you know. Wouldn't it have been awful if that had happened? Thank God it didn't.'

'Thank God for more than that,' he stated quietly.

'Yes,' she agreed in the same hushed, almost reverential, tone of voice.

Midge took a deep breath. 'I want to return to the States, Norma, that's the place for me. My legs are getting stronger all the time, and their movement improving. If they go on as they are there's every hope that I can dance professionally again. But if it turns out I can't I can always develop my writing and earn a living from that. In fact I wouldn't mind being a screenwriter at all. A screenwriter of musicals say.' He glanced at her in the darkness. Since she'd given him the typewriter he'd written and sold a number of stories to various magazines. The response from the magazines and public alike was that there was no doubt he had a career ahead of him as a writer if he so chose. 'You're going to enjoy it in California, I know you will. And just as soon as you're divorced we'll get married.'

She'd known he was going to ask her this, but until she'd got to dance with him in the big rear room of Dow's pub hadn't known what her answer would be. When she'd started to cry it was as though a purging was taking place, a purging that had sorted all manner of things out for her, and left her seeing clearly, aware of where her path lay. 'I won't be coming with you, Midge, nor will I be getting divorced. I'm returning to Douglas.'

Midge was shocked to hear that. He'd thought it was all finished between Norma and Douglas. 'But I love you,' he protested, 'and always have done. And although you haven't said, I'd come to believe you still loved me.'

'I do love you Midge, and always have done just as you have me. But now you're better I know our futures aren't together. Mine is with Douglas, my husband, whom I also love.' She paused, then added, 'You and I came together a second time because we both needed each other. Now you can walk again and I... well I'm healed as well. What I must do now is go to Douglas and help him, give him all the understanding, support and forgiveness that I'm able.'

'Will he want you back?' Midge asked desperately.

'Oh yes, I'm certain of that.'

'Perhaps if you and I were to talk further. There's also the possibility of us resuming our partnership. I haven't even touched on that yet.'

'No Midge. You have your way to go, and I mine,' she said firmly, and with finality.

They drove for about a mile during which neither of them spoke. Then Midge said, his voice crackling at the edges, 'I want you to remember this. If ever you need anything, if there's anything you ever want me to do, you only have to write or phone.'

'Thank you.'

'If only bloody Zelda had never come to Glasgow!' he suddenly exploded vehemently.

With tenderness and affection she replied. 'Thinking about it, maybe what happened with Zelda was for the best. You longed to travel, see the world, whereas at the time that didn't appeal to me at all. If we had married then the odds are that you would have come to resent me after a while, resent me for tying you down. We may have loved one another, but with hindsight, I doubt very much the marriage would have lasted.' She smiled softly, and in a voice that matched her smile added, 'Let's face it Midge, you and I just weren't to be. Not then, not now.'

Douglas must have been standing behind the door for she'd no sooner knocked it than it swung open. 'Hello Norma,' he said.

'Hello.'

'Come in, come in. It's not much I'm afraid, but it suits me for the time being.' She glimpsed a tiny kitchen, then she was in the living-room.

'Students usually live in these flats so they're fairly plainly done out,' he explained.

It wasn't that bad actually, she thought, gazing about. A woman's hand would soon work wonders.

'I must admit I was surprised when you telephoned me at the hospital.'

She took off her coat and hat, and gave them to him. He looked absolutely appalling, quite ghastly. 'If you want me, I'd like to come back to you.'

His body jerked all over, as if he'd been given a jolt of electricity. 'Eh?'

'I said, if you wish I'll come back to you. We'll be man and wife again.'

He stared at her, hardly daring to believe his ears. 'Yes,' he answered simply.

'Are you sure? Things weren't all that good between us before the . . . before the accident. They'd deteriorated considerably.'

He sat facing her, and ran a hand through his snow-white hair. 'That was all my fault. Working too hard, finding it difficult to fit back into civvy street. And then there were the nightmares you see, I never really spoke to you about those. Nightmares, or the same nightmare over and over again that has haunted me ever since the last field assignment I went on. That day in the garden with Lindsay I fell asleep because I was so tired, so terribly tired. I'd had the nightmare the night before and been awake for hours before getting up.' He stopped and sighed. A lost, lonely sound that seemed to come from the very depths of his being.

'I've asked you to tell me about that last field assignment in the past, but you never have. Do you want to now?'

He lit a cigarette with trembling hands. Took a deep drag, and blew the smoke savagely away. 'After Corsica, and even though I was known to the Gestapo, I agreed to return to France. It was something directly connected with Oberon Circuit, and my responsibility.' He recounted the story, quietly, but clearly, reliving it all yet again. Finally he finished.

'That, then Lindsay and the miscarriage to live with. Poor Gabriel,' she whispered.

He looked at her through tortured eyes. 'I've wanted you back more than anything Norma. You coming here today and saying what you have has been a dream come true.'

'There's something you must know though, something I have to tell you.' Now he listened while she recounted about her and Midge.

'And Midge has gone?' Douglas asked after he'd digested her story.

'He flew out of Prestwick this morning. I saw him off.' She gazed deep into those tortured eyes. 'Do you still want us to get back together?'

'Yes,' he repeated.

'A new start Douglas. As from this moment, a new start.'

'Do you wish me to come and stay in this house of yours?'

She shook her head. 'That wouldn't be right. I'll sell it. You and I will stay here in your flat until I can find,' she corrected, 'until *we* can find a house of our own. Just one condition though, I would prefer it to be on the north side, in a completely opposite direction to Burnside and Blairbeth Road.'

'In the opposite direction,' he agreed. 'We'll go as far out on the north side as you like.'

There was a little pause, then she said softly. 'That's it then.'

'That's that.'

They both rose. 'I brought a case with me. It's in the boot of the Austin 12 that's parked outside. Would you care to go and get it for me?'

He crossed to her, reached up and tapped on her jawline.

I love you Norma.

'And I love you too.'

'Give me your keys and I'll get that case.'

She kissed him, a shy tentative kiss as though they were kissing for the first time. 'Have you eaten?' she asked suddenly.

Then, when he shook his head, 'Would you like me to make us some supper?'
'I've only got eggs in.'
'Milk?'
'There are two full pints.'
'So how about an omelette?'
He grinned. 'Sounds marvellous. And I have a bottle of wine. A rather special St Emilion.'
'Omelette and St Emilion it is.'
Now he kissed her, a darting peck on the lips. 'Do you want me to show you where things are?'
'You get my case. I'll find what I need.'
When he was gone from the flat she went into the kitchen, which was so tiny you couldn't have swung the proverbial cat in it, and sure enough quickly found what she was after.
She cracked a couple of eggs into a bowl, added milk and salt, and as she beat the mixture began to sing. A happy song.